THE
DARK
ROOT

THE DARK ROOT

ARCHER MAYOR

THE MYSTERIOUS PRESS

Published by Warner Books

A Time Warner Company

HIGHLAND PARK PUBLIC LIBRARY

Copyright © 1995 by Archer Mayor
All rights reserved.

 Mysterious Press books are published by
Warner Books, Inc., 1271 Avenue of the
Americas, New York, NY 10020.

 A Time Warner Company

The Mysterious Press name and logo are registered trademarks of Warner Books, Inc.

Printed in the United States of America

First printing: December 1995

10 9 8 7 6 5 4 3 2 1

Library of Congress Cataloging-in-Publication Data

Mayor, Archer.
    The dark root / Archer Mayor.
        p.   cm.
    ISBN 0-89296-558-4 (hardcover)
    I. Title.
PS3563.A965D37   1995
813'.54—dc20

                                                95-21304
                                                    CIP

*To the men and women of the Brattleboro Police Department,
with many thanks for your support, hard work, good humor, and dedication.
This book, and all its siblings, would be lesser creatures without you.*

*To Joe, Gene, Peggy, Dan, Bonnie, "Pete," Dave, John, Terry, Cathy,
Bob, Tammy, Phyllis, Russ, Lynn, both Sherwoods, Peter, Randy, Ricky,
Mike, Steve, Renae, Matt, Carol, Marshall, Fred, Richard, Bob, Rich,
Steve, Sheila, Brian, Jackie, Bruce, Liz, John, Anita,
Gary, Mari, and Chuck.*

Acknowledgments

This book, more than any of its predecessors, draws upon the knowledge, experience, and helpfulness of a wide variety of law enforcement personnel, a few of whom were retired and working from recent memory when we spoke, but most of whom took a calculated risk in trusting me to reflect some of their methods of operation. The translation from fact to fiction was mine alone, of course, as are any errors that may have been committed in the process. Without singling out individual names, therefore, I would like to thank the organizations listed below for so willingly lending me a hand. I hope I did them—and their officers—justice.

The Brattleboro Police Department
The Vermont State Police
The US Border Patrol
The US Immigration & Naturalization Service
The Federal Bureau of Investigation
US Customs
The Royal Canadian Mounted Police
The Montreal Urban Community Police
The State's Attorney's Office for Windham County, Vermont
The US Attorney's Office, Burlington, Vermont
The Hartford Police Department, Hartford, Vermont

THE DARK ROOT

Chapter One

"M-80, 0-45."

It was late, cold, and the streets had been quiet for hours, giving the tension in the caller's voice a chilling element of dread. I paused on my way to the wall-mounted mail slots as the night dispatcher leaned forward and depressed the *transmit* button with his thumb.

"80." Charley Davis kept his voice flat, only his narrowed eyes betraying his concentration. Every call was a potential crisis, and the police dispatcher was the crucial linchpin.

"I'm on a vehicle stop—for speeding—above mile-marker nine, northbound. Three adult males. Dark-blue Chevy Nova, Pennsylvania plates." 0-45—Marshall Smith—recited the registration slowly, so Charley could enter it into the terminal before him.

Waiting for the computer to respond, Charley keyed the mike again. "45 from 80. You want some company?"

The response was instantaneous. "10-4 on that."

Immediately, the other two patrol units spoke up from where they'd been eavesdropping out in the cold winter darkness, eager after a long, slow day.

"M-80, 0-32. I'm on Vernon near Cotton Mill."

"M-80, 0-60. It'll take me about eight minutes from West B."

I silently pointed to myself before Charley could answer either one.

Mile-marker 9 was on Interstate 91, a few hundred feet above Exit Two—only two minutes away from where we were standing. He nodded and let everyone know simultaneously. "45 from M-80. 0-3's on his way. Two-minute ETA."

It was cold enough to make the snow creak underfoot in the parking lot. The patrol car's engine moaned before kicking over and the seat was hard as stone beneath me. As I swung onto Grove Street, heading quickly for the interstate, I fiddled with the small, cranky video camera mounted to the dash, slapping it once to make the image on the tiny screen settle down.

It was nearly midnight on a Wednesday in the middle of January. A few hours earlier, a snowstorm had been cleared from Brattleboro's major roads. All of which made a speed stop of three males on the interstate more than a mere anomaly. It was sharply out of place— enough to put any cop's suspicious nature on alert.

I didn't play the lights or siren. For one thing, there was nobody around to warn off the streets; but I also knew what tactical mode Smith would be adopting. Blinding the occupants of the car ahead with both his "take-down" lights and spotlights, he would slam his door twice—making them think there were two of him—and he would circle around to the back of his cruiser, approaching the car from its right rear, away from his own lights and from an angle the occupants wouldn't be expecting. While they were craning their necks to see him coming up on the left—and possibly hiding weapons or contraband out of his sight to their right—he would be watching them unobserved, in the dark, before finally knocking on the passenger window with his flashlight and lighting them up. It was a safer approach than the standard one, but it also could make everyone involved as jumpy as hell.

My role was to be discreet—available if needed, invisible if not— so that no overly sensitive motorist could later claim we'd been ganging up. I therefore cut my lights once I got on the interstate and coasted to a silent stop behind Smith's cruiser a hundred yards farther up. As expected, he was crouching shy of the Nova's right-rear window, talking to the passenger in the back, his eyes on all three occupants.

"0-3 is 10-23," I muttered into the radio, letting everyone, including Smith, know I'd arrived. I adjusted the video camera's lens to cover the whole scene, hit the *record* button, and got out of the car, being careful not to slam the door. I positioned myself between the guardrail and the cruiser, just shy of where the dazzling take-down lights blistered out ahead. All around us, the snow-smothered banks and trees and the wide, empty road shimmered in the phosphorescent blue-and-white flashes of the electronic strobes.

Marshall Smith, his head wreathed in the vapor from his breath, backed away from the stopped car and came toward me, a driver's license in his gloved hand. "Thanks for coming, Lieutenant. You're up late."

I kept my eyes on the dark outlines of three heads furtively conferring. "Catching up on paperwork. What've you got?"

He stepped around me and opened his own passenger door, reaching in for the radio mike. "Nothing too bad yet—I clocked them going eighty-five—but they give me the creeps." He paused to read the license to Dispatch.

"How so?" I asked.

"The rear passenger fits the profile to a T—talks too much, lots of body language, nervous as hell. They're all pretty tense, and it's not because of the ticket . . . They're Asians," he added as an afterthought, although I knew that detail had been at the top of his list.

Charley's voice came over the radio, "Dark-blue Chevy Nova, 1990, registered to Diep, Edward." He gave an address in Philadelphia that matched the one on the license in Smith's hand. "Pennsylvania says it's valid."

Marshall frowned and lapsed from his usually strict radio protocol. "Thanks, Charley." His eyes strayed uncertainly to the source of his concern.

"You want them out of the car?" I prompted.

He nodded and reached in for a clipboard. "Yeah—let's see if they'll play."

He returned to the car and tapped on the rear window to make them roll it back down. I could hear him reciting the particulars of a "consent search"—that the registrant was being asked to agree to a search of the vehicle of his own free will, and that he had the right to refuse such a request, either now or at any time during said search.

I couldn't hear the response, but the front passenger door opened.

It amazes me how many people go along with this procedure, knowing full well what they're carrying in a car. Dozens of successful busts for drugs, guns, illegal aliens, or alcohol have sprung from consent searches, all of which would have been impossible except for the intimidating power of the uniform—an influence defense attorneys invariably strive to drive home in court later.

The cause of Smith's uneasiness became obvious as the first man unfolded from the passenger side of the car. In the arrhythmic strobe lights, his face—smooth, emotionless, almost pretty—lacked any show of humanity. His features, though clearly Asian, paled against an aura of pure menace.

Maybe my shock was greater because of Marshall's description of the chatty, high-strung rear passenger. The thin, mocking smile of the man before me, his look of utter contempt, reminded me of a spoiled child coolly torturing a small pet. His eyes, seemingly unaffected by the lights, took me in as if I were the one on center stage, and he the observer from the shadows.

Smith asked him with immaculate politeness if he'd mind being frisked for weapons.

Without removing his eyes from mine, the man unbuttoned his overcoat and disdainfully lifted his arms to the sides in what was obviously a practiced gesture. Instinctively, I made sure I wasn't standing between him and the hidden camera behind me. Smith checked him quickly but thoroughly and sent him back to stand with me.

"How are you tonight?" I asked without introduction or apology.

The smile widened slightly and he nodded silently.

"What's your name?"

"Truong Van Loc." The voice was soft and smooth, like the face, and equally devoid of feeling.

"You have any identification, Mr. Loc?"

I expected the usual fumbling for a wallet, but this man knew he was under no such obligation, not legally. His hands stayed still by his sides. "No. And my last name is Truong. Loc is my first name. We do it the other way around."

"Where you from?"

"California."

"Whereabouts?"

"Oakland."

"Where in Oakland?"

He didn't answer, but turned slightly to look back at Smith frisking the second man to emerge—shorter, older, with a pockmarked face and a worried expression—the driver, Edward Diep. Even in the cold, I could see the sweat on his forehead. His eyes shifted from spot to spot, looking for cover, for solace.

"Your friend doesn't look very happy."

Truong Van Loc shrugged. "Bad horoscope this morning."

"What's his name?"

For the first time, Truong hesitated slightly. "We call him Jimmy—it's a nickname," he finally answered.

I seriously doubted that, but before I could challenge him, Smith finished with the driver and sent him back to join us. I suddenly wished I had one of the other patrol units here as well, so that all three men could be interviewed separately. I stopped the driver with my hand and turned to Truong, trying to keep my voice low enough that Diep—or Jimmy—couldn't hear it over the engine next to us. "Where were you all headed?" I resumed.

"North."

"Canada?"

"Montreal." Truong retreated to the cruiser's trunk, forcing me to either speak louder or turn my back entirely on the newcomer.

Frustrated, I reversed myself instead, abruptly facing Diep. "Your buddy tells me you have a nickname."

Diep's eyes widened and flitted between the two of us. His mouth opened.

"Tell him, Jimmy." Truong's voice floated over my shoulder, easy and cold, suddenly closer, making the name a threat.

Diep looked like he'd prefer to have a coronary. "Me good guy," he finally blurted, his voice rapid and heavily accented.

"How long you lived in Philadelphia, Mr. Diep?"

He nodded. "Yes, yes."

Smith glanced over to me. I pointed at his last customer, now emerging from the back seat of the Nova, and made it clear Smith should talk to him privately. I didn't want Truong pulling the rug out from under me twice.

"So what's the attraction in Montreal?"

"Friends." Truong's smile was becoming strained. Diep merely nodded in agreement.

"How many days are you planning to be there?"

"Three or four."

"You go up there a lot?"

"Some."

We stood in silence for a moment, watching Smith talk to the third man, whom he'd intuitively turned around so he couldn't see his companions. It was a dicey moment—a small gap where the grantor of a consent search could reverse his approval, given enough time to think—and I worried that Truong Van Loc would shortly put it to Edward Diep to do exactly that.

"Where you from originally, Mr. Truong?" I asked, hoping to steer his mind to other matters.

"Vietnam." His eyes didn't shift from Smith.

I moved slightly to block his view, putting my back to both Smith and Diep—not the safest position, but worth the risk. Despite the apparent inanity of the conversation, I felt I'd embarked on a mental chess game that deserved my full attention. "That must've been tough, leaving your own country."

Refocusing on me, the sardonic smile returned. But I got him to react, which gave me a momentary advantage. "It wasn't my country anymore," he murmured.

"Was it hard getting out?"

The cold, blank eyes widened, and he further opened up. "They can make magazine stories and movies, but none of you will know." It was the longest sentence I'd gotten out of him so far, and it betrayed a passion—and a hesitancy with the language—that he'd been keeping to himself.

"Did you leave your family behind?"

Smith finished with the last passenger and sent him back toward us—I could hear him muttering excitedly to Diep—but I had Truong on a small roll now, and I didn't want to give him up.

"My brother come with me."

"The others didn't make it?"

He shook his head, his eyes straying off into the distance. "They stayed."

"Is your brother in California?"

Again, I'd caught him off guard. His face hardened. "He is dead."

"How?"

But I'd taken him further than he wanted to go. He blinked once, scowled at me, and growled something incomprehensible over my shoulder at his companions, who instantly ceased their chatter. I stepped away so I could see all three of them. The last one was the youngest—in his teens or early twenties—more excited and nervous than Diep, but with Truong's shark-dead eyes. The backs of his hands had tattoos peeking out from under the cuffs of his coat—a frequent, if unreliable, sign of gang membership.

I spoke louder to include the other two. "You're lucky you didn't come through here a few hours ago—we had a pretty good storm."

The young man gave me a dismissive look, his hands flitting about his waist, as if looking for someplace to rest. "You don't know shit, man. We get worse snow than you all the time. This shit is nothing."

Truong hissed a single word. The young man shook his head like a startled, angry horse, and clammed up.

"What's your name?" I asked him.

"I already told the other guy." His accent, unlike those of the other two, came straight from American television.

"Now you can tell me."

"Henry Lam. And I don't have no ID."

"Lieutenant?"

I glanced over at Smith, who was backing out of the car. "Wait here," I told the three men. "One of us will be right back."

Keeping my eyes on them, I met Smith halfway to the Nova. "What's up?"

"When I was looking around the back seat, a panel fell open under the bench. There's nothing behind it, but it's pretty obvious what it's for."

I borrowed his flashlight and traded places with him. Squatting down, I could clearly see what Smith had discovered. A hinged panel lay flat on the floorboards, revealing a cavity about two feet deep, running the entire length of the seat. I lay on my stomach and slid forward until my head was almost inside the compartment, but, moving the flashlight around, I couldn't find a trace of anything suspicious.

I finished Smith's search of the interior for him, removed the keys from the ignition, and walked to the car's trunk, pointedly not asking permission for this expansion of the search, as was standard. But the trunk, aside from the spare tire, was blatantly empty—no rags, no soda cans, no excess tools, none of the usual debris we all end up carrying around for no discernible reason. There was also no luggage. In fact, for a five-year-old private vehicle, this car was about as aseptic as a rental unit. Even the glove box had been meticulously emptied.

I closed the trunk, checked the engine compartment purely for the sake of thoroughness, and then returned to the now-shivering, sullen, and silent little group under Smith's watchful eye.

I dropped the keys into Edward Diep's hand. "If you'd return to your car and wait just a few minutes more, we'll process your paperwork. Feel free to restart the engine and crank up the heater. Thanks for your cooperation."

All three of them shuffled by. Truong Van Loc paused a moment to look me in the eye—the mocking, superior expression back in place. "No luck?"

I resisted the bait. "Have a nice evening."

I turned off the video camera in my cruiser and sat next to Smith as he filled out the speeding ticket and sent the Nova on its way north. Finally, he slid back in behind the wheel, stored his clipboard, cleared with Dispatch, and let out a sigh.

"What did you get out of the kid?" I asked.

"Mostly a lot of 'shit this' and 'shit that.' But for a guy who talked like a bad movie, I had the feeling he'd cut my guts out for the thrill of it. Still, compared to the one you were talking to, he was a charmer. They gave me the creeps. Sorry I bothered you for nothing."

"Don't apologize. After you stopped them, did you talk much with the driver?"

"Diep? Yeah. I gave him the usual lines, and he fed me the usual 'who, me?'"

"In fluent English?"

He raised his eyebrows quizzically. "Fluent enough."

I nodded, half to myself. "Figures. Where did Henry Lam say he was from?"

"Boston."

"One from Boston, one from Philly, one from Oakland, California. Did Lam say they were headed for Montreal?"

"Yeah—for the day."

"My guy said three or four days—with no luggage. Visiting friends?"

Smith shook his head. "Business."

"So much for getting their stories straight. The nasty-looking one didn't even know Diep's name."

We stared in silence at the blank road ahead of us. Smith had killed his lights, so now only the moon played off the tapering snowbanks, pointing the way north like an arrow for three men with a mission.

"So what were they up to?"

"I don't know. At least we got three names and a few details we can feed into the system. Maybe that'll give us something."

The brief pause that followed emphasized the slimness of such a chance.

"I'll tell you one thing," I finally added, "I bet somebody in Montreal's going to be real sorry those three get there."

Chapter Two

Three months later, with the snow nestled only into those nooks and crannies where the sun couldn't reach it, I got a call at home—*our* home, I was becoming used to saying, which Gail Zigman and I had recently bought on Orchard Street in the quasi-rural no-man's-land between Brattleboro and smaller "West B," as the locals call it.

The caller was Sergeant George Capullo, an experienced patrol veteran of many years. "Sorry to bother you, Joe."

It was after midnight. I blinked at the jet-black skylight above the bed, trying to clear my brain. "What's up, George?" Gail rolled over beside me, her eyes still shut, and slid a naked thigh across my legs.

"We got a call for a disturbance on Wantastiquet Drive about forty minutes ago. A neighbor reported a big commotion and people screaming next door. By the time we got there, everything was quiet and the homeowners wouldn't let us in."

"Who're we talking about?"

"Thomas Lee and family. Owns the Blue Willow. He's got a split lip and a bad cut on his forehead, but he won't cooperate—doesn't want an ambulance, won't let us in, and claims he fell downstairs. If both he and the neighbor are telling the truth, I'm guessing he took a good half hour to hit the floor."

"The neighbor see anything?"

"That's why I'm calling. She saw a dark-green sporty number with out-of-state plates peeling out right before we showed up. She didn't get the registration, but she thought she saw several heads through the car's back window. Normally, I would've forced the issue and demanded entry, to see if everybody was okay, but I really don't smell a domestic here. I think something else is going on, and I thought you might like an early crack at it."

I reluctantly slid free from Gail, still speaking softly on the phone. "Okay, George. I'm on my way."

Wantastiquet Drive is not a neighborhood the police are called to visit much. A gentle, peaceful street, trailing off of the heavily traveled Putney Road, its postwar, middle-class homes are the sort one typically associates with suburban New Jersey. The lawns are littered with swing sets and bicycles, and basketball backboards hang like recreational targets over cluttered two-car garages.

The address George had given me was on the Connecticut River side of the street, although the implication was misleading—any potential view of the river was blocked by several rows of tall, sound-absorbing trees, planted to block the noise from the train tracks at the foot of the steep embankment.

I parked my car behind George's, a few houses down from the Lee residence. He was sitting alone with his lights out, the gentle country music from his radio occasionally drowned out by some terse murmuring on the scanner. I squatted down by his open window. From what I could see, every single light was on at the Lee's, in contrast to the tomb-like darkness of its neighbors. The effect told less of a nest of night owls, and more of a forlorn desire to ward off evil with artificial brightness.

"Any movement?"

George shifted the chew of tobacco he had stuck in his cheek. "Nope."

"You said a neighbor heard people screaming. She understand any of it?"

"Not a word. And the car could've been from anywhere. She only knew it wasn't Vermont because the numbers were dark on light, instead of the other way around."

"Didn't get the make of the car?"

He laughed softly. "It was dark-green, low-slung, and had four wheels. She'd probably swear to that much on a Bible."

I straightened back up. "Well, let's give it another shot."

We cut across the lawn to the house's front door, taking advantage of the angle to peer through the windows as we went. But translucent curtains, while they let the light out, didn't show much of what was going on inside. I paused for a moment before ringing the doorbell. All was quiet.

It took several attempts at the bell and my pounding on the door to finally rouse a response from the other side.

"Who is it?" The voice was male, slightly high-pitched, and hesitant.

"This is Lieutenant Joe Gunther, of the Brattleboro Police. Could I have a few words with you, Mr. Lee?"

"We already spoke to your men."

"I realize that, sir, but you have to understand that this is an unusual situation. We need to talk."

I guessed it was no more than the man's innate sense of politeness that got him to reluctantly open the door, if only a crack. His injuries, to my unfortunately practiced eye, had all the earmarks of a classic beating.

"I fell down the stairs," he said in careful English. "I am sorry I disturbed others, but I am all right—in perfect health."

"Is the rest of your family here?"

"Yes. We are all here. Everyone is okay."

"May I come in, Mr. Lee?"

There was a cry of pain from somewhere behind him. Lee whirled around, obviously near panic, and called out something in Chinese. A woman's voice answered. Through the gap in the door, I caught a glimpse of a house in turmoil—two crooked pictures on the one wall I could see, a side table leaning drunkenly on a shattered leg, the hallway rug wadded up and shoved against the baseboard.

Apparently appeased by the unseen voice, Thomas Lee swung back to block my view again. "I have nothing more to say, Lieutenant. Thank you for your concern." The door moved slightly.

I blocked it with my foot. "Mr. Lee, please. Your closing that door won't make this situation go away. We know you didn't fall down any stairs, unless you were pushed. We know several people in a car with out-of-state license plates were here before our first unit arrived.

I can plainly see that your house has been ransacked and that someone inside is in pain. Based on all that, we cannot walk away from this."

The stress on Lee's face tightened into anger. "We have broken the laws?"

I adopted my most diplomatic tone of voice, hoping to avoid a show of force. "Mr. Lee, look at this from our side. You are a prominent and respected citizen of our town. You have a wife and daughter. It's our job to protect all of you, if necessary from one another."

His eyes widened in horror at the implication. "I didn't do anything to my family. What are you meaning?"

I spread my hands. "How can I answer that? You won't talk to me. Either your wife or child is hurt in there, it's the middle of the night, and there was enough noise here to wake up the neighbors. Normally, that adds up to a domestic dispute. Considering the way you look, and the fact that you're the strongest member of the family, I hate to think what shape the others might be in."

"This is wrong. You are wrong," he shouted.

"Then prove it. Let us in. Let me talk to them."

His face jammed up with frustration. Thomas Lee was no stranger to us. The Blue Willow was a popular, highly profitable restaurant, and almost everyone I knew had at one time or another enjoyed at least one meal there. It also employed a huge and faceless staff of Asian workers, some of whom we suspected had bogus papers. One of the INS's two Vermont-based investigators had dropped by the restaurant recently, but what he'd found—beside a suddenly diminished crew that day—hadn't been enough to warrant any action. Nevertheless, it was a common law-enforcement assumption that the Blue Willow was one of dozens of way stations along the Montreal–Boston–New York illegal-alien pipeline.

Lee, of course, knew of our suspicions, and no doubt guessed that our present interest fell a little shy of the altruism I'd just spouted. But he also knew we had him over a barrel. Slowly, as if yielding to a great weight, the door finally swung back.

Without a word, he stiffly led us back to the kitchen. Throughout the house, furniture was broken, pictures smashed, closets emptied and their contents ripped and torn, and spray paint had been used on the walls. If this attack had taken a half hour, it seemed a short time for such utter destruction. The people responsible had obviously been experienced.

The kitchen was in similar turmoil, its cabinets empty, the floor covered with a gritty, slippery mixture of food. The refrigerator stood wide open, there being nothing left inside to protect from room temperature.

At the counter separating the breakfast nook from the rest of the room, an exhausted and anguished middle-aged woman was daubing the face of a teenage girl with a wad of alcohol-dampened cotton. The girl, whom I guessed to be about sixteen, was strikingly pretty, despite the livid bruise on one cheek and the cut on her chin that her mother was trying to tend. The girl's expression, however, was unmistakable. It was the same blank-eyed look of desolation and loss I'd seen haunting too many victims of sexual assault.

Thomas Lee wordlessly introduced his family with a vague wave of one hand. I nodded formally to both women and introduced myself. The mother didn't answer; the girl didn't seem to know I was there.

I stepped closer to them, gently putting my hand on Mrs. Lee's to interrupt her ministrations. "I need to ask you some questions."

She shook her head. "No question."

"Mrs. Lee," I continued, intending my words more for her husband and daughter than for her, since I remembered hearing she understood little English. "I think I know what happened here. Your home was invaded and you were attacked. Your daughter may have been hurt in ways you don't want to think about. Is that right?"

"No question."

I stood in front of the daughter, forcing her to look at me. I kept my voice to just above a whisper. "I'm Joe Gunther. What's your name?"

She took a long time answering, as if trying to separate me from a crowd of other pictures all shoved together in front of her. "Amy."

"Amy, would you like to see a doctor?"

Her eyes flickered over to her father, who didn't move a muscle. Nevertheless, I gestured to George, who immediately escorted Thomas Lee docilely into the other room. Before the door shut behind them, I could hear George starting a conversation, trying to get Lee to open up. I hoped one of us would get lucky, but I wasn't counting on it.

"What do you say, Amy?"

She shook her head ever so slightly. "No," she whispered.

"What happened here is wrong, but we can only help you if you help us."

"No."

"You realize this won't just go away?"

Her eyes seemed to regain their focus slightly. She looked at me with more care.

Instead of answering my own question, I tried a tangent. "These people aren't like vandals on a joy ride. You saw how fast they worked, how thorough they were. They're professionals. Do you think there's anything you can do against them on your own?"

Her voice was barely audible. "No."

Reluctantly, I played on her fears. "What do you think will happen when they come back?"

Her mother was looking from one of us to the other, at least getting the gist of what I was saying. She put her hand flat on my chest. "No question."

Her daughter said something conciliatory to her, but Mrs. Lee's action seemed to have stiffened Amy's resolve, I hoped to my advantage. I was immediately disappointed.

"My mother's right. We have nothing to say."

Knowing what she'd just gone through, I couldn't keep the frustration from my voice. "Amy, please. I understand your parents' reluctance. I've been to Asia. I know the distrust they have for most cops. But you've lived here most of your life. You know what we stand for. We're the ones that can stop this from happening again, to you or someone else."

But she shook her head. "Talk to my dad. I won't go against him."

"That's what my partner's doing right now. You wouldn't be going against him, anyhow. Do you want these characters to kill your father next time? Or to assault your mother the way they did you?"

She winced at the image, and I was angry at having to use it, but the knowledge that I was about to leave here empty-handed was beginning to burn inside me.

As if in confirmation, she shook her head one last time. "I'm sorry. I cannot speak with you."

I looked at both of them—their faces haggard, bruised, fearful, but set—and let out a sigh. "All right. I won't add to your problems." I pulled out my wallet and removed a business card. "If you want to talk to me for any reason at all, even if it's unrelated to what happened tonight, please call. I really am here to help." I took out a different card and wrote Gail's name on it. "You know about Women for Women? The women's crisis organization? Gail Zigman is on their board. She's also a rape survivor. You can call her or them and ask for help, too. They know what you've been through. They're caring and supportive and they have nothing to do with us. Everything you tell them will be confidential. They will only be interested in your recovery. If you won't talk to us, at least promise me you'll give them a call."

She gave me a small smile and nodded at last, taking both cards.

I reached out and gently touched her shoulder. "Good luck. Think about what I said. Get your folks to let us help."

I left them to go into the other room—the remnants of a dining room—and found George and Thomas Lee standing against opposite walls, looking like they'd been the cause of the shambles between them. Lee's expression was a sterner, darker version of his daughter's determination; George merely rolled his eyes in frustration when I looked at him.

I crossed over to the restaurant owner. "My guess is these people told you to fall into line or be targeted again. Am I right?"

Predictably, he didn't answer.

I pulled out another business card—one of my own. "You can reach me here, day or night. I'll give the dispatcher your name and instructions to locate me, no matter when. Okay?"

He took the card and nodded.

There was an awkward silence. I rubbed the back of my neck and turned toward the front hallway. "Good luck. I hope all this is worth risking your family."

Outside, I paused on the lawn to take in a deep breath of cold air.

George Capullo shook his head wonderingly—a lifetime small-town cop, whose experience ran deep but narrow, and didn't include Asians. "I'm not real clear on what happened in there."

"I'd say a home invasion—standard Chinatown extortion. Three or more creeps kick down a door, trash the place, rape and/or beat the occupants, rob them blind, and if there's a business involved, apply a little pressure for future regular payments. Kind of like how Al Capone made gin joints subscribe to his 'protection' service during Prohibition. I'll order some surveillance of the restaurant to see what comes up, but I doubt they'll be that obvious."

"I thought home invasions only happened in Boston and places like that. What's to be gained here? We don't have a Chinatown. You think one of the other Chinese restaurant owners worked him over— a little hard-nosed competition?"

Startled by the suggestion's compelling simplicity, I turned and looked back at the house, as silent now as its occupants, and found my memory returning to the speed stop on the interstate back in January, and to three closemouthed Asians whose presence had reeked of violence. In the weeks that followed, I'd discovered that Truong Van Loc, while never convicted, was suspected of having organized-crime connections in California, and that another man with the same family name—presumably the brother he'd mentioned—had been killed in a gang-related shooting years ago. Two days following that conversation by the roadside, the Montreal Police had reported finding one of their own Asian gang members killed execution style, with a bullet in the back of his head.

I glanced at George and began walking back to the cars. "I don't know, but my gut tells me we're in for a lot worse than that."

Chapter Three

Several weeks later the snow vanished completely, replaced by the first crocuses poking up through the remnants of winter's drab coat. The days became longer, and warmer in fits and starts. The town of Brattleboro, sprinkled across a crazy quilt of hills, ravines, and twisting streams in Vermont's southeastern corner, turned gradually leaf-green, hiding its two-century-old industrial grit under a brand-new flourish of spring-fresh foliage. Its residents, shut inside for months, began trickling out into the streets and playgrounds and parks, to look around at the world like newly awakened bears—a small segment of which were eager for a first square meal.

In response to them, our business began its seasonal adjustment.

Petty vandalisms, car break-ins, graffiti rampages, parking-lot parties, back-street drag races—all the warm-weather crimes endemic to a large quasi-rural town of thirteen thousand people made their annual reappearances. The self-styled teenage homies came out feeling restless, and got busy venting the cabin fever they'd been storing up over the winter. All according to established routine.

And all of which made the phoned-in report of an explosive car fire in the middle of Route 30 enough to empty the office of almost everyone who didn't have to stay there.

Especially since the driver was reportedly still in the car.

Route 30 is the main artery from town heading northwest into Vermont's interior. It is a favorite route of skiers in winter, leaf-peepers in the fall, and kayakers and canoeists in the spring, the last of which are attracted by the broad, shallow, rock-strewn West River, which hugs the road along the valley floor for over twenty-five scenic miles, north of Brattleboro.

But this time, negotiating the breakdown lane alongside a growing line of stalled drivers, my attention wasn't drawn to the rushing water. Violent deaths in this area were still rare enough to get the adrenaline pumping, and regardless of what had caused it, I knew this fire was going to be front-page news, and a number-one concern of the town manager, the selectmen, and the press, until we put it to rest.

About two miles out of town, pinched between a fifty-foot-high cliff to the west and the river to the east, I found a flattened, still-flaming, blackened hulk of a car, seemingly pinned in place by a tall, thick, tapering column of black, oily smoke.

Parked around it, looking paradoxically festive, stood a shiny collection of fire trucks, rescue vehicles, and police cars, all festooned with variously colored flashing lights. A few firefighters dressed in turn-out gear and breathing apparatus were casually hosing down the wreck from a safe distance. It was clear neither the car nor its driver would benefit from any more heroic effort.

The initial excitement over, the other responders were killing time, clustered together near one of the trucks, waiting until things could be cleared away and the road reopened. A maintenance crew and a flatbed truck had already been requested, and traffic was being rerouted along the Upper Dummerston Road, which luckily paralleled Route 30 along this one stretch, above the cliff to my left.

I found an unobtrusive place to park and approached the group. Patrolman Sol Stennis, an enthusiastic one-year veteran of our force, was among them.

"Some mess," he commented quietly.

I glanced over at the smoking car. In the few gaps the breeze created in the acrid cloud surrounding it, I could clearly see the charred skeletal remains of the driver, slumped over the blackened steel hoop of the steering wheel.

"You find out anything?" I asked him.

He removed his hat and rubbed his forehead. "I asked around when

I first got here, but I couldn't find any witnesses to the actual explosion. I talked to the people who called it in on their car phone—a couple from Williamsville—but they came up on it after it was already burning."

"There was no other car?"

"Not that anyone knows of, and there's no impact debris that I could find. I tried looking at the blacktop for skid marks, but by the time I got here, it looked pretty much like this."

We were standing on a thin film of foul-colored water extending in all directions, obliterating anything that might have been underneath. The road was straight and flat along this section, well paved and wide-shouldered. It was the middle of the afternoon, the weather was clear, and there were no trees, telephone poles, or boulders nearby that the car might have struck. And yet, it looked like it had lost a fight with a freight train. Beyond the damage the flames had done, it was twisted and bent beyond all reason.

Stennis followed my gaze. "Think it might have been a car bomb?"

I shook my head. "It looks more pushed in than blown apart. I wish we could get close enough to read the plates."

I looked up at the nearby cliff. It was a mix of beige rock and clinging vegetation, the latter of which thickened near the top, becoming a row of spindly trees that peered down at us like quiet, elderly onlookers.

Except for one of them.

I crossed the road toward the river, glancing over my shoulder until I had a flatter angle.

Stennis tagged along. "What is it?"

I pointed to the cliff's distant edge. "See how that tree's been torn up? Lower limbs ripped away on one side, bark stripped near the bottom? And a little below it, caught on that bush about halfway down. See that branch?"

"Damn," Stennis muttered next to me. "The son-of-a-bitch must've come off the Upper Dummerston Road." He studied the otherwise unblemished cliff, visualizing the arc the car must have taken to end up where it was now. "Jesus. He must've been flying."

I ignored the unintended pun. "Where're you parked?"

He pointed to a patrol unit just north of the logjam of emergency vehicles.

"Good. We'll take your car and circle around from the north."

We were threading our way between trucks when I looked over my shoulder for one last glance at the scene. The *Brattleboro Reformer's* Alice Sims, just leaving her own car, caught sight of me and came running, waving her note pad.

"Shit," I muttered. "Hang on, Sol. I better make a no-comment."

"Joe," Sims called out as she caught up to us, "what happened?"

Alice Sims was the local newspaper's "courts-and-cops" reporter, a job she'd inherited from Stanley Katz, who'd since been bumped upstairs to editor-in-chief. Like Katz, who in his prime had defined the word *shark*, Alice could be fiercely tenacious. Unlike him, she didn't find it necessary to be personally offensive in the process. Dealing with her—especially with memories of him—was a comparative pleasure.

"Don't know yet. I just got here."

"Was it a bomb?"

I raised my eyebrows, feigning surprise at the very subject that had come up not two minutes earlier. "Whoa, Alice, this isn't Detroit. We're starting with the premise of a car accident. There is absolutely nothing to indicate a bomb at this point."

She turned to face the still-crackling fire, her voice incredulous. "You saying that was a fender-bender?"

I shrugged and pointed to the fire chief standing by the largest of the trucks. "Ask him. He was here first. We're just beginning our homework. I'll let you know what we find out."

She followed my advice, and Sol and I resumed our way, but I could already hear the clock ticking. Whatever this was, we already knew Alice was at least partially correct—this had been no simple accident, even if it hadn't featured a bomb.

By now, the southbound traffic had been turned around and detoured back to the road we were headed for, which fed into Route 30 about a half mile north of the crash site. The upper road differs from its more-traveled neighbor in almost all respects. Tree-shaded, narrow, twisting, and hilly, it is the pastoral introvert to Route 30's high-speed extrovert. Along most of its length, the road keeps far from the edge of the bluff overlooking Route 30, allowing for properties to be developed on both sides of it.

Not far below the northern intersection, however, geography dictates a single exception. Here, the river to the east and the hills to the west squeeze the two roads to within seventy-five feet of one another, and they become separated only by a narrow grassy shoulder, a ragged row of trees, and fifty feet of altitude. At this confluence, we found two fresh, clear furrows of a car's wheels slashing diagonally across the threadbare grass to the edge of the drop-off. No guardrail had ever been planted here, either because of a shortage of funds or the lack of any apparent need.

"Damn," Stennis murmured as we slowly rolled by and parked in the short driveway of a house several hundred feet farther on.

Due to the roadblock below, traffic was unusually heavy, which didn't help me in collecting additional evidence. I risked becoming road kill several times to check the asphalt for telltale signs. Stennis nervously accompanied me, occasionally waving at passing cars in an ineffectual effort to slow them down. We continued in this fashion for over a half mile, while I slowly filled my pocket with odd pieces of vehicular scrap, most of it plastic.

Stennis was visibly relieved when I finally moved to the shoulder for the walk back. "What've we got?"

I pointed at a couple of angry, fresh skid marks in the middle of the road, as yet unaffected by the passing stream of cars. "Those come in a series almost—at regular intervals—and they're from two cars, like they might've been punching it out at high speed. At the best, it means some high jinks run amuck, but in any case it's a homicide."

Sol picked up on my growing sense of dread. "Alice'll love that."

"Let's hope she doesn't find out right away."

He stared at me, slightly startled. "It won't take her long after we cordon this area off." He pointed ahead to where the car had left the road.

"I want to use a low-profile approach, at least for starters. There's not much here anyhow. You take the necessary pictures and measurements now, and I'll have J.P. do the rest later. I'll order a canvass of everyone on the street—find out if they saw or heard anything. And maybe we can plant some innocuous citizen-complaint story in the paper about hot-rodders along here—it might stimulate a witness who saw something when they were driving through. It's hard to believe two cars could have duked it out in broad daylight without *somebody* noticing it."

"Why not just tell the paper what we found? Alice'll probably put

two and two together anyhow, and get pissed off that we played cute,"
Sol said.

"Could be, but right now you and I are the only ones who know
how that car ended up down there—except for whoever helped launch
it. That could be an advantage. And if nothing else, it'll spare us
fending off a lot of questions we can't answer yet."

"What about the canvass? That's not too subtle," he persisted.

"We can still use the hot-rodder ploy—tell people we're trying to
corroborate the complaint." I patted my pocket. "In the meantime,
I'll give this stuff to J.P. See if he can't match it to some make and
model. And I'll have a statewide be-on-the-lookout issued for any cars
with fresh front-end damage. The local body shops can be checked
out, too."

I stopped suddenly. "Did you notice anyone unusual or out of place
down below, watching the fire—maybe making sure their handiwork
was terminal?"

He mulled it over for a few seconds. "There were some kids."

I began to shake my head, but he interrupted me. "No. I mean
kids from Brattleboro, not this neighborhood. Sally Javits and the
Beaupré brothers. They must've heard about this pretty quick to get
all the way out here this fast."

"Who do we have down below?" I asked, pointing toward the lip
of the tree-shrouded cliff.

"I heard Smith checking in."

"Have him find out if Javits and the Beauprés are still there."

Stennis keyed the radio mike he had clipped to the epaulette of his
uniform jacket and relayed the inquiry. Several minutes later, I heard
Smith report back empty-handed. Stennis just raised his eyebrows at
me.

We'd reached the edge of the torn-up strip of grass. "Find them.
But again, make it discreet. I don't want them knowing we're looking
for them, and I don't want anyone else thinking they're snitches."

I left Stennis by the side of the road and walked alongside the deep
furrows in the earth.

The ruts showed the wild tearing of a car out of control, fighting
momentum and energy in a desperate effort to avoid the plunge ahead.
But the end had been inevitable. Examining the damaged tree from
close up, I saw that the car had already been airborne at the time of

impact, launched into space by an inconspicuous shelf of rock some six feet shy of the edge. The car had obviously taken off into the void with such speed, the tree must have been the only reason it hadn't flown clear to the river.

I stepped as close to the cliff's rim as I dared, but aside from the smell of burning rubber and the column of smoke curling up from below, I could see nothing of what had brought us here. In less than a month, I thought, even the scant signs we'd found of a person's final moments of panic would be dulled by time, weather, and the onslaught of spring growth.

I hoped our case wouldn't suffer a similar fate.

*   *   *

Over the next day and a half, J. P. Tyler, our department's forensics specialist, could do little with the debris I'd collected from the Upper Dummerston Road, nor did he read much more from the skid marks than I had. He confirmed my hypothesis, however, that there'd been two cars, traveling at up to a hundred miles an hour, and that one had butted the other from behind.

The canvass didn't add much more. The two cars had been heard by some, seen by a few more, and been variously described as black, green, blue, brown, and "dark"; as hatchbacks, sports cars, sedans, coupes, and one "cabriolet"; and as having been occupied by anywhere from one person to four, none of whom had been identified. One of the witnesses said he'd heard shots. The newspaper story the next day about mysterious hot-rodders didn't produce a single phone call.

The wreck, as expected, yielded a bit more. A 1986 Dodge Duster, registered to Alfred John Hutchins—address Brattleboro—it had been stolen twenty-four hours earlier. The plates had been crudely altered, with a 3 changed to an 8, and a C to an O, and the car had been newly repainted, although not by Mr. Hutchins. These few details were presented by Tyler with morose apologies. Of our five-member detective squad, Tyler was only perfunctorily interested in day-to-day police work. Forensics was his joy, and he always felt doubly let down when he hit a blank wall—by his own dearth of training and equipment, and by the limitations of the science in which he placed such faith.

We shipped the charred skeleton off to the state's medical examiner,

Dr. Beverly Hillstrom, but I was pretty sure that unless we could find a dental chart to match it, it would remain a John Doe for some time.

Alice Sims had not yet done the deductive math Sol Stennis had worried about—connecting the crash site to our canvass of the Upper Dummerston Road. We'd diverted her with leaks about the stolen car and our search for the driver's identity. But I knew it wouldn't be long before she put it together, and let everyone know we were dealing with homicide.

It was therefore with considerable relief that I received a call from Sol at ten o'clock that night at the office.

"I think I found those three kids. You know the pond at the top of Rice Farm Road?"

I did. Located on a long, winding dirt road connecting Brattleboro's north end to the village of West Dummerston six miles farther up, the pond was an artificial water hole carved into the top of a hill overlooking the West River Valley. Because of its peculiar location, fishermen, canoeists, and hikers could enjoy the twin pleasures of being on a pond and a mountaintop simultaneously.

I told Stennis to pick me up. During his brief tenure on the force, he'd made an art of keeping tabs on the town's restless youth, and in a hub employment center like Brattleboro, with a daytime population of forty thousand people, a police force of twenty-eight quickly learned not to puff up its detectives at the expense of the patrol officers. Becoming a detective was still a reward, as in all departments, but we, more than most, encouraged our patrol to become independent investigators.

It was early spring yet, and while the leaves had come out, the nights were still cool and the bugs hadn't quite hatched. It was the peaceful hiatus between winter and summer, and never lasted long enough for my liking. I sat back in Stennis's passenger seat, enjoying the breeze through the window. The sepulchral blur of the woods raced close by us in the darkness, absorbing like a dark blotter the glimmer of our headlights.

The southern approach to the pond was as dramatic as the site itself, emerging as it did from the folds of the forest. At one moment, we were climbing in low gear, encased by trees on one side and a steep dirt embankment on the other, when abruptly the bank ceded to the pond's smooth, flat expanse, not five feet from the driver's window. It was like taking an escalator from the bottom of a lake and suddenly breaching its surface, without a ripple. A little farther on, the road leveled out so near the water's edge that the latter's black, glassy plane began mere inches from our tires. It perfectly mirrored the canopy of stars overhead, doubling its impact and making me feel I was floating in space.

"There they are," Stennis muttered, oblivious to the scenery.

Ahead, parked on a tiny peninsula, was a single small car, its lights out, looking more like a washed-up boulder from a distance, except that in its midst glowed three tiny orange eyes—cigarettes belonging to ghostly inhabitants.

Stennis pulled up alongside and switched on his brilliant, side take-down lights, wiping away the stars, the illusion of private spaciousness, and, quite on purpose, establishing our dominance. His voice, however, was just as conspicuously quiet and gentle. He spoke first to the girl in the back seat. "Hi, Sally. Been a while."

Large, broad-shouldered, her pale face almost perfectly round, Sally took a purposeful drag on her cigarette and blew the smoke out the window. She made a visible effort to ignore the blinding effects of the light.

"Hey, Stennis." Her voice was hard, flat, but not unfriendly, showing she was both used to this kind of approach by the police and always in control, in style if not in fact.

Sol picked up his flashlight and shined it into the shadows of the car that his rooftop lights couldn't reach, directly into the faces of the two young men sitting in the front. Both of us watched how their pupils reacted, how their expressions changed. They mimicked their more assertive companion, with less success, but boldly enough that we could tell they were clean—the cigarettes were just that, and those were only sodas balanced on the dash.

"Mike. Pete. How you doin'?" Stennis asked.

The one at the wheel was Mike Beaupré, the older brother by a year. "We're doin'."

"What're you up to way out here?"

"Staying out of trouble," Sally answered from the back.

Sol nodded and killed all his lights, acknowledging that he was taking them at their word. "Any trouble in particular?"

I saw her smile in the glow of her cigarette. "You should know."

"We don't do too bad."

Mike chuckled. Cadaverously thin, with his baseball cap perched back on his head and a sharply protruding Adam's apple, he looked like an animated scarecrow. "Only when you catch us."

"I haven't had to come after you in a long time."

"You just haven't caught him at nothin'," Peter called out from beyond his brother. He was the low man on the totem pole. The three had been inseparable friends since childhood and, despite their youth and unremarkable appearance, were tough in ways I'd never been at their age. While they all had records, none of their crimes had been more than petty in nature. But their experience had given them stature among their peers, and they were worthy of our grudging respect. Which was why Stennis was allowing the conversation to follow the etiquette of the street.

"Oh, I don't know," he now said, following up on Peter's quip. "You might've settled down a little in the past year."

Mike mulled that over, gently bobbing his head. "Gettin' older."

It was a comment an uninformed adult would have smiled at, but we knew the backgrounds of these kids—the neighborhoods and families that had shaped them. None of it compared to the ghetto of a big city, of course, but their lives had still been marked by neglect and violence and poverty.

Stennis returned to the point, now that the social amenities had been observed. "You're a long way from downtown tonight."

"Think you'd be happy 'bout that," Sally said guardedly.

"I'm not complaining. A little curious, maybe."

"We needed a break, man," Pete spoke up.

Mike nodded silently.

"The burned car?" I asked quietly.

Sally turned her head and stared at me. I didn't have the rapport Sol had with them, but they knew me as a straight player.

After a long pause, she said, "Yeah."

"Who was the driver?"

"Benny Travers."

Sol let out a low whistle. "No shit."

"What happened?" I asked.

Her face was hard to read in the gloom. Travers and she had been more rivals than friends, both street-level yielders of influence, but with significantly different management styles. While Sally was more of a consensus builder, albeit with a hard right hook, Travers had been a typical bully. Older by ten years and more traveled than Sally, he'd done hard time, had a rough reputation, and, being originally from out of state, hadn't had the local ties that we tried to work to our advantage.

"He got whacked," she finally answered.

"By who?"

"Don't you know shit?"

"We know you were at the scene before we were."

The implication hung in the air for a long, still moment.

"I got a call," Sally finally said.

"Who from?"

She looked around restlessly, as if suddenly constricted by the small car. "I don't know."

"We think Sonny did it," Mike said.

Stennis was incredulous. "Sonny Williams? You're shitting me."

Sally was contemptuous. "Not Williams. Jesus. Williams couldn't whack *himself*, for Christ's sake."

"A new player," I said quietly, as a point of fact, although it was the first I'd heard of him, too.

"No shit," Mike muttered angrily.

Sol remained undaunted. "Who the hell's Sonny?"

"Bad news." Sally's face was hard, shut down—scared, I suddenly realized.

"He in town tonight?" I asked.

"Could be. Some of his boys are."

"Do we know them?"

She shook her head. "You will. Benny was nothin'—a free advertisement."

"What does this Sonny want?" Sol asked, obviously frustrated at having completely missed a new development in his streets.

"Some of the action, of course," Sally said bitterly. "He's moving to get a gang going. . . . Fucking chink."

I sat forward and stared at her. "He's Chinese?"

"I'd be pretty stupid to miss that."

"Where's he from?"

Sally was suddenly angry. "Jesus, Gunther—fucking China. What d'you think?"

But Mike knew what I meant. "I don't know where he's from—maybe the West Coast. But some of his boys're from Montreal."

Chapter Four

Chief Tony Brandt stared into the bowl of his ever-present pipe. The conversation with Sally Javits and the Beauprés had triggered an intense investigation into the last days of Ben Travers, but forty-eight hours later, we still had little to go on.

"Does Sonny have a last name?"

"Not that we know of. Even the *Sonny* part might be bogus, as well as his actually being Chinese. That was Sally's opinion, but she's probably met all of three Asians in her life. Nobody else we've interviewed has set eyes on him, although the paranoia on the street's making him look like Fu Manchu. Everyone's keeping very quiet on this one."

Tony frowned and shoved the pipe back into his mouth. He'd recently had the flu and was looking run-down. He was not in the mood for a publicity-grabbing major case. "You quoted one of the boys saying, 'Maybe Sonny did it.' Do we have any evidence pointing one way or the other?"

"Supposedly Sonny made a move on Benny's drug business. A meet was arranged between principles and seconds. Everybody puffed out their chests and strutted around and Travers was dead within twenty-four hours. People drew whatever conclusion suited them."

"But Sonny hasn't swooped in to grab Benny's business?"

We were sitting in Tony's office, and he, as usual, had his long, thin frame draped along an old tilt-back office chair, his legs extending across a paper-strewn desk. The smoke from his pipe hovered like a fog bank a couple of feet above us.

"Not visibly," I answered. "But I don't think drugs are Sonny's only interest anyhow. Sally told us he'd made a move on Scott Fisher's burglary operation, and supposedly Alfie Brewster's worried Sonny's been hustling some of his girls. Maybe Benny overreacted to the same kind of overture and Sonny got rid of him. Or maybe he was killed because he was the toughest of the locals, and Sonny needed to set an example. There's talk of a real gang being formed, with guns, money, and fast cars—a lot more sophisticated than the bands of kids we have roaming around here now. It wouldn't take much to win a lot of them over."

"I'd love to chat with Sonny—just to introduce myself, if nothing else—but I was told he's out of town, and the people he's left behind aren't talking."

"They Asian, too?"

"His head lieutenant is—named Michael Vu—a graduate of the Dragon Boys gang in California. He has a rap sheet for sexual assault and extortion, but he's clean right now. He prides himself on being inscrutable, and he's got an ironclad alibi for when Travers went for his drive."

Tony let out a sigh. "Sounds like he may be a dead end, at least for now."

I rubbed the back of my neck. Tony and I had known each other for decades, and he'd been chief for much of that time. We were also close friends, so I empathized with his unhappiness. The ticking clock I'd worried about when Alice Sims approached me at the crash site had recently gotten louder. She had finally connected the hot-rodder ploy with Benny's death, and she'd even ferreted out his name by talking to some of the same kids we'd interviewed—although not Sally Javits—so the pressure on Tony to explain a few things had suddenly become greater.

I therefore tried to give him something hopeful. "There may actually be more to this. Remember that home invasion about a month ago—Thomas Lee? I went back to the neighbor who saw a car squealing away from there just before we showed up that night. At the time, she said she knew the car wasn't from Vermont because the plates had dark numbers on a light background. Last night, I parked opposite the Lee house and held up a variety of license plates against my own car—from New Hampshire, Massachusetts, Maine, Quebec—and had her stand in her window to see if any of them rang a bell. She pegged the one from Quebec."

He looked at me quizzically. "So?"

"So it was an Asian-style crime against an Asian family. That vehicle stop Marshall Smith did on the interstate in late January was a carful of Asians, all of them with contradictory stories, no luggage, an empty secret compartment on board, and heading for Montreal. And now this thing with Sonny . . . All Asian-related. All with ties to Montreal."

"The vehicle stop had nothing to do with us. It was dumb luck Smith was out there."

I conceded the point with a wave of my hand.

"I'll go along with the other two, though," he added. "You call Montreal?"

"They never heard of Michael Vu or any of the boys we've identified, and they said 'Sonny' is a common pseudonym. Of the hundred-and-some-thousand Asians they've got in their town, maybe two-dozen rap sheets have that name, and they didn't sound too interested in mailing me pictures of them."

"I wouldn't have either," Tony murmured. "How 'bout Thomas Lee. You speak with him after that night?"

"Yup. Still won't talk."

Tony removed the pipe and tapped its contents out into a large ashtray, shaking his head and looking doubly glum. "Well, until you prove otherwise, that's all beside the point anyhow. Concentrate on nailing whoever killed Ben Travers. I've been stalling the press on whether this car crash was youthful high jinks gone wrong or murder, but if they get a whiff of Montreal hit teams and the 'Heathen Chinee,' we'll be knee-deep in shit in no time. Who do you have working the case now?"

"Besides me, Ron Klesczewski and Sammie Martens. J.P.'s wrapping up the forensics, but that's mostly logging whatever comes back to him from the crime lab."

He looked slightly puzzled. "That enough people?"

"For what we've got to work with, yeah. Benny's inner circle was small, and they're all playing dumb. We haven't even been able to track what he did between getting out of bed that morning and getting himself burned to death seven hours later."

I got to my feet and moved toward the door.

Tony aired a possible alternative. "If I were one of Ben's more ambitious lieutenants, hungry to grab his turf and not get caught, Sonny and his Chinese tough talk would have seemed like the perfect combination of an opportunity and an alibi."

I paused at the door and looked back at him. "Good point."

"Put on more people and get clear on where you're headed. The answer to your problem may be less complicated than you think." He patted the pile on his desk. "And this is thick enough without any race-discrimination suits added to it."

*　　*　　*

I didn't have long to wait for the Benny Travers case to open up slightly. J.P. Tyler was waiting in my office, much happier than when I'd seen him last and holding a long, thin, shiny piece of twisted metal in his hand.

"Going in for dowsing?" I asked as I circled my desk and scanned the messages that had been left there.

J.P. twirled the piece between his fingers like a baton. "It came off the burned car. Just got it back from Waterbury."

I smiled at him and waited as he carefully placed it before me. Waterbury, Vermont, was the home of the state-police crime lab, where all the local police agencies sent their evidence for detailed forensic scrutiny. Most departments our size and larger had specialists like Tyler who had some scientific training, but none of us had the money for the schooling and equipment that would have made them real experts.

"It's a strip of aluminum molding from the A-post on the driver's side. See that hole?"

I looked at where he was pointing. The hole looked like it had been made with a heavy-duty paper punch, but with a small, dark smear on one side. "That stain is a copper-zinc mix left behind by a bullet. The hole would fit a nine millimeter, a thirty-eight, or a three-fifty-seven."

A small chill tickled my neck. There could be several explanations of why Benny's car had a bullet hole in it, but the obvious one was what Sally had already prophesied—which meant that both Tony's dour mood and the media's enthusiasm would soon be further stimulated. "This the only one you found?" I asked.

His eyebrows rose at my seeming lack of gratitude. "There might've been holes in the windows, but the heat and the crash took care of them."

"I'm not complaining," I said soothingly, pawing through the papers on my desk. I finally located the file I was after and flipped it open. "The one witness who reported hearing gunshots was walking his dog about a mile shy of where Travers went over the edge . . . Here it is: 'Three shots—sounded like firecrackers.' As usual."

I handed the file to him. "If the bullet's a nine millimeter, chances are it came from an automatic, which means there might be shell casings somewhere along that stretch of road."

He took the file, smiled happily, and headed out the door. "I'll rally the troops."

"Keep this as quiet as you can, okay?" I called after him.

He'd left the aluminum strip in my care while he made his phone calls. I picked it up and looked at it more closely. It was stained and scarred by the heat, but, unlike its owner, it must have broken free of the actual wreck.

Except that Ben Travers hadn't actually been the owner. I reflected on that for a moment, realizing that the car might be more informative on Travers's last day than his associates had been.

I picked up the phone and dialed Willy Kunkle's extension, taking advantage of Tony's advice to bring on more people.

"Yeah?" His voice, predictably, sounded both bored and surly.

"You want some action?"

"Probably not."

"Good. Don't move." I left my office for the squad room outside, dropping the metal strip off at Tyler's desk, and walked around the cluster of sound-absorbent panels that separated four work areas in the room's center. On the far side, I found one of the most effective— and least appealing—of my subordinates. Willy Kunkle was an unrepentantly sour, recalcitrant, difficult human being with whom nobody liked to work, but whom everybody respected for the results he brought in. He was a cop from the old school, who missed the rubber hoses and hot lamps, hated Miranda and all lawyers, and longed for a more liberal department policy on stun guns and night-sticks.

Just as Sol Stennis specialized in Brattleboro's troublesome kids, Willy had monopolized the town's hardcore underworld. He was inti-mately connected to the activities, it seemed, of every deadbeat druggie, child molester, wife beater, and thief in town. Asked to enter that arena and extract information, he was almost invariably successful where none of us could scratch the surface. Rumors had it his track record was directly related to some flagrantly illegal interrogation techniques, but no one I knew had ever actually witnessed him crossing that line, and no single complaint had ever surfaced from the social swamp he frequented.

Of course, he may not have needed such methods. God knows, we found him unpleasant enough to give him what he wanted just to get rid of him.

Which had nothing to do with the arm.

Disabled by a sniper's bullet years ago, Willy Kunkle's left arm hung shriveled and useless by his side, its hand usually stuffed into his pants pocket so it wouldn't flop around. He used it often to grim advantage, pulling it out on appropriate occasions like a veiled threat of the horrors he could deliver if provoked, or playing it for sympathy with women he was targeting. His was truly a twisted talent to behold, although my being his sole admirer was probably the only reason he was still employed as a cop.

"So what wonderful opportunity you dumpin' on me now?" he asked as I approached.

"It's right up your alley. Find out what happened to the car Benny was driving after it was stolen. J.P. says it had just been repainted, and Benny didn't do paint jobs. That suit your fancy?"

Kunkle gave a disgruntled half shrug. "I'll see what I can do."

Harriet Fritter, the squad secretary, poked her head around the corner. "There you are. Call on line two—Beverly Hillstrom."

Vermont's medical examiner and I had become old friends ever since we'd discovered a shared propensity for taking no situation at face value—a prejudice we'd often either separately or together stuck our necks out to satisfy. While we'd never met socially, and still referred to one another by our respective titles—largely because of her oddly formal style—we'd formed a trusting relationship I doubted she had with many others.

As a result, Beverly Hillstrom was often the first and most elucidating sage I consulted in a homicide investigation, as well as the one I could count on to keep digging until she'd found every nugget a corpse had to offer.

I therefore settled down with some anticipation to hear her cool, almost aloof assessment of the charred corpse I had sent her, hoping that I would at last learn a little more of how Benny Travers had met his fate.

"I must say, Lieutenant, you certainly redeemed yourself for not having sent me anything for quite a while. Thank you for the dental records, by the way. They were a definite necessity."

"So it's one-hundred percent that the body is Ben Travers?"

Even here, I noticed with a smile, her scientifically suspicious nature stirred uncomfortably. "My X rays of the teeth match the records."

I allowed her that, without comment. "And what did he die of, officially?"

There was a moment's hesitation, during which I subconsciously braced myself. Hillstrom was usually not one to equivocate on such matters. "Given the state of the body, I'm going to have to hedge my response a bit."

"You mean given the crash and the fire?" I asked hopefully.

This time the answer was familiarly quick in coming—and forever put to rest any chance that Benny might have just fallen asleep at the wheel. "No—given the beating, the bullet, the crash, and the fire, in that order."

"The beating?" I repeated inanely, having already been subliminally warned about the bullet by Tyler's discovery.

She laughed softly, obviously pleased. "Let me start backwards. With a body this badly charred, the natural assumption is that the fire was the lethal agent. That's what I first wanted to determine, therefore, and indeed it proved easy to do. Mr. Travers's air passages showed little soot or searing; his carboxyhemoglobin concentrations were only slightly elevated; he showed none of the subendocardial left-ventricular hemorrhaging that is common to death by fire; and while his skull was blown apart by intracranial steam pressure, most of the fractures were unaccompanied by cerebral contusions or signs of hemorrhaging, as would have been present with immediately lethal blunt violence to the head."

"I'm not sure what that all means."

"It means your Mr. Travers sustained significant trauma at several stages, any one of which might have done the trick all by itself—given enough time. The problem is that, since they all followed one another in rapid succession, it becomes difficult to name a single absolute cause of death."

"If this is going to get complicated, could you humor me by not going backwards? I'm getting nowhere on this case, and I'd appreciate at least one straight answer from someone."

She was immediately sympathetic. "Of course, Lieutenant, but let me preface my statement with a warning that some of it will be educated conjecture. When you have these many layers of successive dam. ge, it becomes like an archeological dig, and the margin for error increases."

"I understand."

"I think Mr. Travers was in a fight to begin with, one in which he used his fists and wherein he sustained his first severe trauma, to wit, a severely fractured left zygomatic—that's the bone around the eye socket—with resulting damage to the sphenoid—the bone lying behind the eyeball. He also had a left-temporal fracture which I believe could have eventually led to intracranial bleeding and death."

"He couldn't have gotten all that in the crash?"

"Technically, yes, but for reasons I'll explain later, I don't believe he did. I should add that he also sustained two broken teeth and a broken knuckle at this point, all of which indicate the beating I alluded to earlier.

"Next, we have the bullet, which entered the body from behind, just above the left scapula. It nicked the subclavian artery, ricocheted off the clavicle, fracturing it, and was thereby redirected downward into the left lung, where I found it."

"Was it a nine millimeter?"

"It could be. I sent it to Waterbury for analysis. I can tell you it was fairly intact. But the damage to that artery, which as you know is a major blood vessel, was severe enough that he would have bled to death eventually."

"How eventually?"

She hedged a little. "That's difficult to say, given the subsequent damage to the body, but if the subclavian is totally severed, life expectancy usually doesn't exceed a minute. Mr. Travers's wound wasn't quite that bad, so, in my estimation, it would have proved lethal within fifteen minutes."

"Doctor, we have witnesses saying the shooting occurred during a high-speed car chase. Assuming that's when Travers got hit, could he have kept driving, and for that matter, could he have been driving at all with his head smashed up?"

Here, there was no hesitation. "Absolutely. Some head injuries take hours to days before rendering the patient unconscious, and since this man was already driving at the time he was shot, I see no reason he couldn't have continued some distance before the blood loss took its toll."

"But still, basically, flying off that cliff was pure gravy."

"Yes and no. Remember when I said there was but a *little* soot in his airway, that his carboxyhemoglobin concentrations were only *slightly* elevated? Well, the fact that I found even those traces tells me he was still alive—if barely—when the car caught fire."

"Jesus," I muttered.

The sympathy in her voice matched my own for a moment. "Yes. He didn't have an easy time of it. Anyhow, his barely being alive at the end is why I suspect the specific cranial damage I highlighted earlier was inflicted well before the crash. If you break a man's bone and kill him immediately thereafter, there will be some evidence of bleeding at the site of the fracture, *but*—and here is the important point—that evidence will be scant, difficult to detect, and similar to if the bone had been broken *following* death. Do you follow me?"

I merely nodded at the phone.

"In fact," she continued, "that was the case with the explosive fractures resulting from the built-up steam inside the cranium, along with the heat-related fractures of many of the long bones of his arms and legs. By their very nature, all of those obviously occurred after death, and therefore showed no signs of contusions or bleeding. Similarly, the few fractures I have connected to the crash preceding the fire showed *slight* hemorrhaging, which is again consistent with the scenario we've established. Only those breaks to the left-temporal and zygomatic bones, and to the teeth and knuckles, show extensive post-traumatic bleeding. That's why I believe he got them in a fight."

There was a slight pause while we both contemplated all she'd told me. She was no doubt thinking of anything she might have left out. I was wondering if any of it would do me any good, including the recovered bullet.

I therefore fished for more. "Did he have any drugs in his bloodstream?"

"Not there, but there were residual traces of cocaine in his organs, dating back a day or more."

"Alcohol?"

"Some, but below the legal limit."

"How 'bout stomach contents?"

"Pepperoni pizza and chips, recently consumed."

That grabbed my interest. "Within an hour of death?"

"I'd say so."

I made a mental note to follow up on that. If we found who'd sold the pizza, we might also discover what Ben Travers had been up to shortly before his death, and perhaps with whom.

"Could you do me an enormous favor and hold off releasing the cause of death to the press for a bit?"

"Maybe a couple of days. Will that be enough?"

I certainly hoped it would, and that his death—even though a homicide—would be proven the result of an altercation with some long-standing local rivals. But I couldn't imitate Tony Brandt's trick of ignoring the larger implications before me.

Unlike him, I was conscious of something larger stirring in the background—a growing threat that was going to make Ben Travers's death look like a small, initial skirmish between two large opposing forces.

"It'll have to be."

Chapter Five

Gail's voice was clear enough on the phone to be coming from the room next door, which made it all the more disappointing that she was instead back at the Vermont Law School in South Royalton, where she was auditing a course on advanced criminal procedure. "You sound tired."

"A little frustrated maybe. I just found out today that the body has a bullet in it."

"I was wondering about that. Tony's comments in the paper today sounded a little cagey. Who was Ben Travers anyway? The article said he'd been the driver, but they didn't go into details."

I took my shoes off awkwardly, cradling the phone in the crook of my shoulder, and lay back on the bed, conscious of how empty the house seemed without her.

A half year ago, Gail had been a victim of sexual assault. That had put us both through an emotional wringer—and forced us to reexamine a long-standing but oddly tentative monogamous relationship. Now, having abandoned our separate homes and bought a house together—something both of us had resisted for over fifteen years—I for one was realizing the downside to the move. During the few months we'd lived together, before she'd gone back to school to brush up an old law degree in an effort to switch careers, I'd become used to having her as an intimate part of my everyday life. A widower of almost three decades, I'd been anticipating a reawakening of long-dormant sensations, and now found myself lonely and disappointed by her absence.

I kept all this to myself, addressing her question instead. "Benny was one of our regulars. Stole a car or two, knocked off a gas station, did a little pimping, fencing, vandalism, and general mayhem, and served about eight years total for it all. Lately, he'd been trying to corner the local drug market. He ran a small outfit—not really a gang—but they were tough and well-organized by our standards."

"And you don't have any leads?"

I smiled at that. After a double career as a successful realtor and an outspoken town selectman, Gail was returning to more conservative interests of yore, hoping to pass the bar and eventually clerk for a state prosecutor. I sensed some of her newfound enthusiasm in the question.

Unlike many of her liberal friends, most of whom had viewed our relationship skeptically, I hadn't been too surprised at her desire to pass the bar. Not only had her interest in my world been growing steadily over the years, but the rape had developed in her a strong desire for a hands-on role in law enforcement. I did wonder sometimes, however, how our life together might be affected in the long run, with one of us a cop and the other a state's attorney.

I answered her indirectly. "The natives are restless, worried about old alliances. Nobody wants to talk to us until they get a better sense of where the power's shifting."

"All because of Travers?"

"Somewhat—he did leave a small vacuum. Mostly I think they're afraid of some mysterious Asian named Sonny. He's the one who's really stirring up the pot, but he's very coy—working by remote control."

"And killing Travers was part of some grand strategy?"

"The locals see it that way. They smell an organized outsider trying to push his weight around—and they're wondering where they stand. In their eyes, Benny's fate was a demonstration of what happens to those who don't submit. 'Course, people like Travers don't tend to live forever in any case. Tony thinks one of his own people did him in, and that they're using the Asian angle as cover."

"You don't agree?"

"I don't have enough to agree or disagree. I've just got a feeling it's bigger than that. Hillstrom gave me an idea of what Travers went through before he died. You were right about that part—it wasn't just a joyride gone bad, like we implied to the paper. He was tortured, beaten, shot, and finally rear-ended off the Upper Dummerston Road at a hundred miles an hour. He must have been terrified—running for his life. Ben Travers was known to stand up to anyone, including us, so the question that keeps running around my brain is: Who was it that got him so scared? And the only answer I come up with dates back several months and shouldn't have anything to do with Ben Travers . . . although it may involve Sonny . . ."

I could visualize Gail shaking her head as my voice drifted off and my mind began outdistancing my words. "You want my imput," she broke in, "you better think out loud."

I shifted my position on the bed. "The last time I saw someone that frightened was after the home invasion I told you about. Do you know if Amy Lee ever contacted Women for Women? I called her about a week later to check up on her, and she told me she had, but I never checked with the center to confirm it. It never occurred to me she might be lying."

"I don't know," Gail answered. "I can find out for you. You think Sonny did that, too?"

My mind was off running again, filled with images not of Ben Travers or a traumatized Amy Lee, but of the malevolent Truong Van Loc—and the recently met, cocky Michael Vu. "Maybe it was someone Sonny hired."

We hung up so she could check with her contacts at Women for Women. I sat staring at the opposite wall, my loneliness supplanted by the hope that I'd finally shaken the right tree branch. Tony Brandt had cautioned me against pursuing the "Heathen Chinee," as he'd put it, but I was becoming convinced that therein was hidden what I was after.

Asian crime was a growth industry—rising with a bullet on every metropolitan police chart in this country and Canada, especially since one of its global strongholds—Hong Kong—was going back to the Communist Chinese in 1997. Asian criminals were well-organized, well-financed, ruthless, and highly mobile, and they favored urban centers with large Asian communities. Marshall Smith's discovery of a carful of young Asian men who didn't know each other, and were driving through the middle of the night for a vague and ominous-sounding rendezvous in Montreal, fit the traditional profile for an Asian hit squad. The fact that rural, thinly populated Vermont had so far been left on the sidelines of this latest criminal trend didn't mean that things couldn't change.

Policemen by their nature tend to be professional paranoids—that's what helps keep them alive, or at least relatively healthy. So it was no stretch for me to connect a suspected hit team we'd met by accident, to another we believed had visited the Lee family, to yet a third we were only hypothesizing had murdered Ben Travers. Coincidences were not something I trusted at face value, so three in a row struck me as too much to ignore. Despite Tony's advice that I concentrate on who killed Travers, I was starting to think I might have better luck broadening my horizon.

Gail called back ten minutes later. "If Amy Lee ever contacted Women for Women, they don't have a record of it. Sorry."

"Don't be. Now I can do something I should've done a while ago."

*　　*　　*

Amy Lee did not look good. She walked with her head down, her feet shuffling along the sidewalk. She was much thinner than the last time we'd met and her clothes hung on her awkwardly. Her hair was dirty and unkempt, and she had a habit—a virtual twitch—of looking furtively about her, as if something invisible and malevolent were stalking her, which I didn't doubt it was.

I swung out of my car and approached her gingerly, my expression open and friendly. She hesitated at the bottom of the path leading to the high school's front door, obviously considering flight as an option.

"Amy?" I called out softly. "Remember me?"

She looked at the ground as I stopped before her, and nodded silently.

"I was wondering if we could talk a bit."

"I don't want to be late for class." Her voice was a monotone.

"You won't be. This'll only take a couple of minutes." I gestured to a grassy area off the path, where the building's corner provided a little privacy. "How 'bout we go over there?"

Students were parking their cars in the lot across the street, shouting and laughing at one another as they headed for the building. No one gave us a glance as I gently steered her to the spot I'd indicated. Still, I made sure to position her with her back to the passing crowd.

"How have you been?" I asked.

"Okay." I could barely hear her.

"You didn't call that place I told you about, Women for Women."

She shook her head silently, her eyes still glued to the ground.

I crouched down, pretending to pluck absent-mindedly at the spring-fresh grass, but actually so I could look up into her face without challenging her. "Amy, what happened to you was a crime, and you were its victim. In that way, it was no different than if you'd been hit by a drunk driver. Both things come out of nowhere and leave you shattered. The difference is you haven't done anything to help yourself get back on your feet. You might as well be still out there, in the middle of the road."

Her lower lip was trembling. She wiped her nose with the back of her hand, like a child, and murmured, "It's hard."

I reached out and touched her other hand with the tips of my fingers. "You not getting much support at home?"

"They're angry that I can't let it go."

"But you need help to do that, don't you?"

She gave a small shrug. "I guess."

"Amy, if I drove you there, would you be willing to meet with the people at Women for Women?"

She looked at me for the first time. "My parents would kill me."

"They don't need to know—not at first. This would be just for you."

She rubbed her forehead and glanced at the entrance to the high school.

Interpreting the gesture, I said, "I can take care of them. I know the principal."

"Will you tell him?" she asked, suddenly alarmed.

I shook my head. "No. I'll make something up and make sure he doesn't contact your folks."

There was a long silence.

"What do you say?" I finally asked, almost in a whisper.

"Okay" was her equally quiet response.

I stood up and grasped her hand in mine. "I'll take you to my car first. You wait there while I set things up."

Like an abandoned wanderer, she took me on faith.

Ten minutes later, after a chat with the principal and a quick call to Women for Women, I rejoined Amy Lee in my car, where she was sitting wedged into the far corner of the front seat, her body pressed against the door, her eyes fixed to the ground outside her window.

Now, I thought, comes the hard part, where I hoped I wouldn't be seen as a manipulative and heartless hypocrite. I settled next to her and closed my door, adding to the sense of privacy, even though the human floodtide outside had dwindled to a few latecomers who were jogging across the school's broad lawn.

"Amy, before I take you to Women for Women, can I ask you a couple of questions about that night?"

As small as she was, her body made a spontaneous effort to shrink even further, hunching over. She finally brought her knees up to her chest until she was sitting in a tight ball.

"I don't want any details," I added quickly, "nothing you're not willing to tell me—just some general things. Would that be okay?"

"I don't know."

"Fair enough. Let me ask something to start, and you see if you want to answer. If you don't, that's fine."

I paused, not really expecting a response, and then asked, "How many of them were there?"

There was an extended silence. Finally, just as I was about to move on, she murmured, "Three."

"Good. Were they Asians?"

She nodded almost immediately.

"Did you or your parents know them?"

She shook her head vehemently. "No."

"Do you know why they chose your home?"

Slowly, she covered her face. A moment later, her whole body began shaking with her sobbing.

I remained quiet for a while, trying to convince myself that what I was doing was for the good of all. Having failed that, I reached into my pocket and pulled out three photographs I'd had J. P. Tyler extract from the video of the speeding stop on the interstate during the winter, plus an old mug shot of Michael Vu.

"Amy, I'm sorry. We'll go now. There is just one last thing. Will you look at these photographs and tell me if any of them look familiar?"

She took a deep breath and turned slightly toward me, her face flushed and streaked with tears. I held up a shot of Edward Diep, the driver of the Nova, using him to warm her up to the process and expecting to draw a blank.

She shook her head. "No."

"Okay. That's fine. Here's another one." I held up Henry Lam's picture, saving Truong and Vu's for last.

But my plan, and my hopeful expectations, were upended. Amy focused on Lam's sneering, insolent face, let out a scream, and began grappling wildly with the door handle, trying to escape from the car, her body thrashing hysterically.

I dropped the pictures and grabbed hold of her, wrestling her arms to her sides to spare us both possible injury, and then gave her as comforting a body hug as I could in that awkward confinement, issuing soothing noises into her ear as I did so. Had there been any witnesses to all this, I knew I would have made immediate dual appearances before a disciplinary board and on the front page of the newspaper. As it was, we just sat there for several minutes, until I felt confident enough to release her.

I then surreptitiously locked her door, started the engine, and began to drive as quickly as I safely could toward Women for Women, and whatever solace they could offer her. From what I had just witnessed, they had their work cut out for them.

During the drive, I kept up a steady patter, fueled partly by my own guilt, but also to keep her from doing anything drastic. Her reaction had made me wonder if this girl, traumatized and isolated and emotionally cast adrift, wasn't veering precariously close to self-destruction.

I never did show her the last two pictures, as badly as I wanted to. But putting Henry Lam at the scene had convinced me that the three Asian-related events were interconnected—parts of something bigger. The trick was going to be deciphering the common connection.

Susan Raffner, the director of Women for Women, and one of Gail's best friends, came out personally to greet us as I pulled into the center's driveway. I'd told her something about the situation over the phone, but I could tell from her expression that she hadn't been expecting the near basket case I delivered. And yielding to a cowardly instinct, I didn't confess how much I'd exacerbated the situation. Amy Lee would get the same supportive treatment in any case, and I wouldn't have to put up with the deservedly baleful comments I knew I'd get otherwise.

It was with some relief, therefore, that I heard Dispatch trying to locate me over the car's mobile radio just as I was wrapping up the introductions.

I leaned in through the driver's window and unhooked the microphone. "M-80, this is 0-3."

"Could you hook up with 0-10 at 234-B Canal?"

"10-4."

I made the appropriate noises to the two women, neither of whom was paying much attention to me, and took my leave.

"0-10" was Willy Kunkle's radio name, and the address I'd been given was one of a collection of more or less derelict buildings that were used as either storage units or auto-body shops, one of which I was hoping had painted the last car in Benny's life.

I pulled up to a place advertising wheel alignments, body work, and while-you-wait grease jobs, and saw Kunkle leaning against the doorjamb of one of the bays, either enjoying the promising but still-anemic spring sunshine or trying to escape the screaming sounds of power tools emanating from within. He had the contented look of a truant officer who'd just nailed one of his worst offenders.

"You find the painter?" I asked as I walked up to him.

"Moe Ellis—body man by day, artist by night." He jerked his thumb over his shoulder at the gloomy interior of the bay behind him. "He's inside."

"You talk to him yet?"

"Nope. Thought I'd leave the honors to you. You want me to hang around?"

I nodded. "You'll scare him a hell of a lot more than I will."

"I scare everybody more'n you do," he muttered as he abandoned his sunny spot to follow me inside.

The noise enveloped us like an ear-splitting fog, accompanied by the pungent odor of hot metal. One car occupied the center bay like a body stretched out on a morgue table, its paint either overcoated with red Bondo or ground away to bare steel, and completely covered with a layer of dark grit. One man, wearing ear protectors and a breathing mask, was leaning into a door panel with a sander, and another, partly obscured by the hood of the car, was sending up a shower of fiery sparks from a welding torch.

I glanced back at Kunkle, who pointed at the welder.

We stepped through the tangle of power cords and air hoses snaking across the floor and approached Moe Ellis from the front, struggling not to look at the mesmerizing, retina-burning chip of sun where the torch tip touched the metal. I stood patiently, waiting for him to finish his weld. Kunkle, true to form, killed the gas at the bottle. Behind us, the grinder suddenly died.

Ellis straightened, startled, and looked around, blinded by the dark lens of his helmet. "What the fu—" he began muttering as he lifted the visor, and then he froze, his eyes fixed on Kunkle, whose powerful right hand was still resting on the control knob of the acetylene bottle.

"Hey, Moe." Willy gestured with his chin to the other man, who was staring at us uncertainly. "Go get some coffee."

Ellis looked from one of us to the other. With a theatrical flourish, I pulled out my badge and wordlessly showed it to him, my expression as cold and still as Kunkle's. Ellis's companion quickly left the building.

"Been up to no good, Moe," Willy said flatly.

"What? I haven't done nothin'."

"How 'bout an eighty-six Duster, with a brand new coat of midnight blue?" I asked.

There was a telling hesitation. "You got the wrong guy. I haven't done a paint job in months, and that was an Olds—red."

Kunkle shifted his weight. It wasn't much of a gesture, but Ellis took a frightened step backward, bumping into a large tool chest on castors.

"Moe, there's nothing illegal about painting a car, unless you know something about it you shouldn't."

Ellis licked his lips. "What do you guys want?"

"Tell us you painted it," Willy said.

"Okay. I painted it."

"For who?" I asked.

"I don't know. It was delivered to my place when I wasn't there, and the deal was done on the phone."

This time, Kunkle stepped forward, took the welder's helmet off Ellis's head, and placed it on the tool chest behind him, bringing his face two inches from the other man's. "Careful, Moe."

"We're digging into a murder case, Moe. Not car theft," I added.

His eyes grew wider. "I don't know nothin' about murder."

"So tell us about a hot car instead."

There was a long, quiet moment while he considered his options. "I want a lawyer," he finally said.

"You don't need a lawyer, you stupid bastard," Kunkle said in a near whisper.

Ellis pulled at his ear nervously. "I don't?"

"Who delivered the car, Moe?" I asked.

"You're not looking to nail me?"

Neither one of us responded. He hesitated again, and finally said, "Benny Travers?" as if it were a question.

"What did he tell you?"

"What he usually . . . I mean, he said he was in a hurry."

Kunkle retreated to his previous position at the gas bottle. "So when did you do it?"

"The same night—the night before he died."

"And when did he pick the car up?"

"Right after. He never left."

Willy's eyes narrowed. "What bullshit is that? He took it wet?"

Ellis looked slightly alarmed again. "Not wet-wet, but before it should'a been moved."

"Why, Moe? Why the rush?" I asked again, searching for the panic that had dogged Benny's heels.

"I don't know."

Kunkle suddenly lunged forward and punched the helmet next to Ellis's head, sending it clattering across the floor. "Stop fucking with us, asshole. You let him drive away without asking? Not even you're that spaced out."

Ellis actually cringed, crouching down near the car's bumper, and raised his hand to shield his face. "Jesus Christ. What's with you guys? I really don't know. I asked, but he wouldn't tell me. I told him it would screw up the job—that he was just pissing his money away— but he wasn't interested. He told me to fuck off."

"He was nervous?" I asked.

"That's what I'm telling you. He hung around while I did the job— kept bugging me to hurry up . . . not to worry about the fine stuff. Drank every beer I had in the goddamn house. He was wired."

"Did he say where he was going?"

Ellis shook his head. "Nope. Just said he had to get movin'—not where, and not why."

"You know where he was living?"

"I heard he had a place on Elliot once, but I also heard he moved. He did that a lot."

That much we'd already found out. "And you never saw or heard from him again?"

He straightened up slowly, sensing the worst had passed. "Next I knew, a couple 'a days later, I was readin' he'd been the one that got fried in that crash. Was that the murder you talked about?"

Willy gave him a withering look. "Don't think out loud, Moe. It doesn't make you look good. We said *a* murder—not his."

Ellis gave a small shrug.

"And don't think," Kunkle added, "that you're still working part-time painting hot cars. That's over. You're on our shit list now, get it?"

He nodded silently.

"And don't forget that we just did you a big favor. Right?"

He began looking thoroughly depressed, realizing what this favor might cost him someday. "Okay."

We left him to contemplate life's odd twists of fate.

*   *   *

Sammie Martens was waiting in her car when we stepped outside the body shop. "I heard you guys were here. Didn't want to barge in and catch Willy torturing another witness."

To my regret, Willy smiled with pride.

"You got something?" I asked, slightly irritated.

Sammie was looking pleased herself. "I found out where Travers ordered his last pizza, and where it was delivered."

My mood thus brightened, I bowed theatrically and gestured to the street. "Lead on. We're right behind you."

We didn't have far to go. We returned down Canal to Birge, along which the old Estey Organ warehouses stood side by side, clad entirely in dark slate—the latest in fire prevention well over a hundred years ago—and descended Baker Street to the bottom of a steep dead end.

Where Sammie eventually pulled to a stop was typical of Brat-

tleboro's eccentric layout. From being in the middle of Vermont's
fourth-largest town at the top of the hill, we were now in the dooryard
of a rambling, sagging, decrepit old farmhouse, perched on the edge
of a large, weed-choked field. Blocked from our view by trees and
brush, our urban surroundings might as well have been a figment of
imagination. Even its sounds were muffled by the distant rushing of
nearby Whetstone Brook.

But the place held little charm. What some other town might have
exploited as the sylvan setting for a condo project, or a pocket municipal
park tucked away by the water's edge, the powers here had left to rot.
The building was deserving of an arsonist's care, and the field had
been scarred by a wide dirt road leading to a scattering of retired
appliances, rusting car bodies, and assorted trash.

We assembled in front of the silent, abandoned-looking building.

"This is it?" Kunkle asked quizzically.

Sammie merely crossed the hardscrabble front yard and hammered on
the door with her fist. The sound echoed dully throughout the house.

"When did the delivery take place?" I asked, joining her on the
rickety porch.

She was peering through one of the side windows. "A little over an
hour before we found him in flames. I talked to the delivery boy, and
showed him Benny's mug shot. No doubt about it."

I stood beside her, shading my eyes with my hands to see through
one of the dusty panes. "You know who owns this?"

"Gregory Rivière. He's behind on his town taxes, and he comes up
on our computer as a 'known associate,' but we've never actually nailed
him for anything. From what I could find out, he's originally from
Wisconsin and did some drug time in New York. He's supposed to
be out of town right now."

"Well," I said, straightening up and wiping the dust from my
hands, "I guess we better round up a search warrant."

For the second time in a quarter-hour, Sammie smiled with self-
satisfaction, retrieving the very document from her back pocket and
handing it to me. "Blessed by the Honorable Judge Harrowsmith
himself."

Kunkle laughed behind me, and turned the doorknob. The door
swung open without protest.

We crossed the threshold and paused. There is always a sense of

trespass that accompanies an uninvited search, unabated by the knowledge that we are there by legal sanction. I can always feel the absent
owner's spirit cringing as we poke about, examining details unknown
by even his or her most intimate friends. On the other hand, the
uneasiness is counterbalanced by an intense curiosity, suddenly
unleashed to run rampant to its heart's content. All the taboos of
closed doors and forbidden rooms, drummed into us from childhood,
are removed. Armed with a search warrant, especially one worded as
generally as what Sammie had secured, we were freer than thieves in
the night.

The initial pickings, however, didn't generate much excitement.
Befitting a house with no lock on the front door, the place at first
didn't offer any more than the junk-clotted field below it. Sparsely
furnished, evil-smelling, choked with dust and mildew, it appeared
totally deserted.

Until Sammie appeared from around the kitchen door, pale and
serious. "I think I got something."

I'd been combing the contents of a box-strewn dining room, finding
nothing but old clothes and unpacked household items. Willy appeared
from the neighboring living room, attracted by the tone of Sammie's
voice.

We both joined her at the kitchen entrance.

"I don't think we should go much beyond here without calling
Tyler," she advised.

Over her shoulder, we could see the remnants of a bag of chips and
the famous pizza, part of it still in its box, along with one half-eaten
piece, draped like a Salvador Dali imitation over the edge of the
counter, its red drippings hard and dry on the floor beneath it.

As in some perverse parody, however, the floor and counter weren't
only soiled by old tomato sauce. There were large quantities of dry
blood intermixed with it, extending far beyond the capabilities of a
single pizza. A ragged trail of it led across the floor to a chair, which
was daubed in enough dry blood to look sloppily painted with the
stuff.

"Far out," Kunkle murmured admiringly.

"What do you think?" Sammie asked. "Grabbed from behind as he
stood at the counter, his back to this door, cut or hit hard enough to
make him bleed, and then dragged to the chair?"

"By at least two men," Kunkle agreed. "Benny was a big boy."

Along the wall next to us there was a row of glass-doored cabinets over a second counter. Sammie pointed to shards of glass and more blood splayed across its surface, indicators of another wound. "He must've put up a fight."

But I was looking at the chair, less interested in how he'd been brought there than in what had happened to him once he'd been seated. Against Sammie's good advice, I carefully picked my way across the room, studying the floor as I went, making sure my feet disturbed nothing. The others stayed put.

The chair had been turned away from a small table shoved up against the far wall, to face the length of the room like a witness stand does a courtroom. From closer up, I could clearly see the chair's two front legs were strapped with broken bands of blood-smeared duct tape, another length of which I found stuck horizontally across the chair's back. There was a final, balled-up wad of tape lying under the table, presumably used to tie Travers's hands behind his back, and a pair of blue jeans, blackened by old blood, slashed to ribbons. Across the top of the table were the oblong smears of a knife which had been repeatedly placed there—and obviously repeatedly used.

I began to understand why Ben Travers had been in such a hurry when he'd flown off the Upper Dummerston Road.

Chapter Six

Jack Derby, the newly elected state's attorney for Windham County, was a startling contrast from his predecessor, James Dunn. Tall, slim, with bookish good looks set off by a pair of tortoiseshell bifocals, Derby was the kind of man Rotarians like to invite over for lunch. He favored sport jackets over suits, appeared easygoing and conversational, never hesitating to stop in a hallway or on the street to answer a question or respond to a comment, and generally came across as an approachable, regular kind of a guy—a man you could trust with your vote.

But however engaging, Derby could also be as tough, demanding, and ruthless as Dunn.

Sitting in Tony Brandt's office, Derby was slouched down, relaxed, a ready and interested smile on his face, but with eyes as cool and calculating as a pool shark's.

He held up a finger. "So you think Ben Travers, already hot to leave town, escaped in a stolen car after being tied to a chair and tortured by Sonny and his boys. But for all intents and purposes, there is no Sonny, the man you think is his lieutenant has an alibi, as do his goons, and you have no reliable witnesses to Travers's intentions, the torture, the car chase, or the final flight off the cliff."

He held up two fingers. "Then you've got these three supposedly

connected episodes—a suspicious traffic stop, a suspected home invasion and rape, which may or may not have involved one of the men
from the traffic stop, and Travers's death, which may or may not have
involved Asians. Speaking strictly legally here, that's about it, right?
The bottom line is that, aside from the Travers homicide, you really
don't have anything, and even that's looking iffy."

Neither Brandt nor I responded. Derby had, in fact, accurately
summarized what we had. On top of that, Alice Sims had made her
boss proud. She'd picked up that Benny might've been done in by a
"Chinese named Sonny," and had made it pointedly clear in that
morning's paper that the police were being less than straightforward
with the facts, despite Tony's reluctant admission that we were indeed
dealing with a homicide.

Derby made a gesture to alleviate our discomfort. "Okay. You asked
me to listen to what you've got, and you heard my opinion. Now tell
me what you're *going* to get. Maybe that'll sound better."

I looked out the window at the ebbing light. Most of the day had
been spent picking over every square inch of the Rivière house off
Baker Street—and locating Mr. Rivière himself, who was visiting a
brother at the federal pen in Rahway, New Jersey. We'd found lots
of junk to pick through, but none of it, I felt certain, would end up
having anything to do with Benny Travers.

So what did I have to tell Derby, or anyone else, for that matter?
That I felt a vague sense of foreboding—that this was somehow a
precursor for all hell breaking loose? I had no tangible evidence—a
pool of blood on a seat, a terrified look in a young woman's eyes, an
expression of malice on the face of a Vietnamese crook.

"What I hope to find out," I finally said in answer to his question,
"is why Ben Travers was in that house."

"You think he was there to meet with Sonny?" Derby asked.

I shook my head. "I doubt it. He was nervous as hell the night
before, hassling Moe Ellis to speed it up, hoping to hit the road in
an unknown car before the paint even dried. And yet, eight hours
later, he was still in town, eating pizza. But not at one of his usual
haunts, and not hanging out with his usual friends, at least according
to them. He was alone, his back to the door as he chowed down for
lunch, waiting for someone he trusted. For some reason, he felt the

heat had lessened a bit between the time he last saw Moe and when he was trussed up in that chair.''

Brandt's weary face looked slightly brighter as he heard echoes of his own advice from twenty-four hours earlier. "Waiting for one of his own people?"

"That's what I'd like to find out. I already have Stennis scouting around. And we do have one piece of hard evidence. Tyler came up with some shell casings from the Upper Dummerston Road. They're nine millimeter, and they have a rectangular firing-pin impression that's supposedly unique to a Glock. No fingerprints, though."

Derby was already shaking his head, looking doubtful. "Where exactly were these casings found?"

"Along the stretch of road where one of the witnesses said he heard shots."

The SA's eyes narrowed suspiciously. "Hold it. I thought you had a whole bagful of conflicting testimony on that. This sounds like a prime witness."

I pursed my lips. Brandt answered for me. "Not for your purposes. He's a notorious flake—confesses to crimes he didn't do, claims to know when the world is ending. It was dumb luck we got him on one of his lucid days."

"We do have a way to link the casing to the bullet they dug out of Travers, though, at least circumstantially," I added. "Tyler also got a call from the state crime lab. The bullet was ingrained with the white-powder residue of the car's rear window, and it was basically smooth, with no lands or grooves from standard rifling."

"Glocks have polygonal barrels," Brandt filled in.

Derby gave a half shrug. "I guess if you found the pistol, I could use it, but even then, I'd need more—like the person who pulled the trigger."

He suddenly launched himself out of his chair and leaned against the windowsill to stare out at the parking lot. "To be honest, I think you boys may be up a creek, unless somebody spills the beans, and from what I hear about Asian gangs, that's not what they do. They're worse than the Mob about informers." He turned to face us. "Hell, if that girl's family won't tell you about the rape, which one of Sonny's cohorts do you expect to suddenly open up? You've got a problem."

In the following silence, Derby checked his watch, gave us a dazzling smile, and concluded, "Well, gotta go. Thanks for filling me in. Good luck with the *Reformer*."

He closed the door behind him. We both watched him crossing the outer office through Brandt's interior window, waving at a few people and tossing a wisecrack at the dispatcher on the way out.

"Pretty cruel," I commented.

"He's got a point," Brandt muttered fatalistically.

I rose to my feet, my determination fueled. "About our having a problem? It's early yet."

He gave me a half smile. "Oh, yeah? What've you got that you didn't want to tell him?"

I crossed over to the door. "I'm hoping to educate myself a bit. But if what we've got is the start of some new Asian trend, then we'll see more of it soon, and if they keep doing things like high-speed chases in the middle of the day, then we'll nail 'em before long."

My optimism was obviously not catching. Brandt, looking older and more tired than I'd seen him in years, merely said, "I hope so."

                    *   *   *

Early the next morning, tucked into my small corner office in the detective squad room, I began the day by pulling a slim address book from my pocket and dialing an in-state, long-distance number.

"State-police criminal division."

"Dan Flynn, please."

There was a brief pause. "VCIN—Flynn."

VCIN stood for the Vermont Criminal Information Network, of which Lieutenant Daniel Flynn was director. The title sounded loftier than it was, since there were only two people in the office. Nevertheless, it was a grand experiment, and a credit to both Flynn, who'd thought it up in the first place, and to the Vermont State Police, who'd given him their blessing.

The principle of VCIN was childishly simple—establish a central clearinghouse for intelligence from every police agency in the state, using a process Flynn called the "pointer system." If I fell over a crook named Bubba, for example, I sent his particulars to Dan, who entered them into his files on a "pointer card," which he then tagged with my name. If any other cop, at any future date, came across Bubba and queried VCIN about him, Dan would know to put that other officer in touch with me. The beauty was that my file on Bubba never actually left my office—just his name and a few pertinent details. That one technicality guaranteed that no one could "steal" my case—a paranoid, and all-too-common concern of ambitious cops everywhere, and one around which Flynn had wisely constructed his system. As a result, from having no such operation three years ago, the Vermont State Police were now sharing information with—and acting as a conduit for—some thirty-five local law-enforcement agencies out of a possible statewide total of fifty-nine.

That, of course, was not the full extent of Flynn's resources. His office was also connected to all the standard federal networks, both here and in Canada—as were many of the rest of us—and to Interpol. It also fielded information from the hundreds of Vermont State Troopers out in the field, and communicated with state-police agencies throughout the United States.

All of which made Dan Flynn a good man to know. The fact that he was also pleasant and enthusiastic—if a little overly talkative— was a much-appreciated extra, something his greeting drove home now.

"Joe. I haven't heard from you in months. What you been up to?"

"Nothing much. Things've been pretty peaceful."

His rich laughter deafened my ear. "Don't bullshit a bullshitter, boy. I read the newspapers. Soon as I heard about it, I ran Travers through my system here, just to see what popped up—professional curiosity."

"What did you find?" I asked, curious myself. Travers's wasn't one of the names I would have thought to submit.

"He was a bad boy. You know he used to ply his talents in both Rutland and Bennington?"

"Yeah, I'd heard about some of that. Nothing to do with Asian gangs, was it?"

Dan Flynn laughed again, this time with a hint of conspiracy. "You know how it works, Joe. You want details, I give you the guy who handled the case. Period." He hesitated a moment, and then added, "But what about Asian gangs?"

"I think I may have something cooking down here. That's actually why I called."

"Got any names?" I could visualize him with his fingers poised over his computer keyboard.

"Yeah—four. Edward Diep, Truong Van Loc, Henry Lam, and Michael Vu." I spelled each one out for him.

There was a prolonged pause while I heard him typing feverishly away. When he spoke again, I knew I'd definitely hooked his interest. "I found Michael Vu."

I sat up, surprised that such a long shot had actually worked. "You're kidding. Where?"

"Hartford—Detective Heather Dahlin. Vu's been pegged to illegal aliens and possible extortion."

I quickly wrote down Dahlin's name, silently blessing VCIN and the foresight that had created it. "Anything else?"

"Not in-state. I take it you already tried the feds."

"Yeah—nothing except that Truong's brother was killed in a gang fight and that Vu has an old California rap sheet."

Flynn grunted sympathetically. "These people all Vietnamese?"

"I guess so. Truong said he was."

"Vietchin? Of Chinese ethnic origin?"

"I don't know. Why?"

" 'Cause if they are, they may still write their names using Chinese characters—being from the old country is a big source of pride to them, especially since they're discriminated against in Vietnam. If you can get their names in character form, then you can translate the characters using the so-called Standard Telegraphic Codes, kind of like Morse code—and then we can send them via teletype to Interpol, or the Hong Kong police, or whoever else you think might be useful."

"The names I've got won't work?"

"Not overseas. I've tried names that had 'Bob,' or 'Mike,' or whatever in them, and I've hit a dead end nearly every time. They pick those when they get here. 'Course, they might work with other US agencies, like Vu did with me."

"Okay. Thanks. Why did your ears perk up when I mentioned Asian gangs?"

"They're suddenly getting popular. Border Patrol's nabbing them in growing numbers, crossing over from Canada. INS says fully staffed Chinese restaurants are starting to open where there's little or no market for them, and then showing the IRS a booming business. Our troopers are reporting more sightings. Burlington PD thinks they might have a small gang in the making."

My mind went back to Thomas Lee, owner of the Blue Willow. "The restaurants are laundering money?"

"Some of 'em are. And covering a drug-distribution network and an illegal-alien pipeline and credit-card fraud, and who knows what else. Of course, I have to tell my own people that of the three thousand Asians we have in this state, probably ninety percent are clean as a whistle. But it's always the bad apples, you know? And Asian bad apples are worse than most—well-organized and super-insular. We've found that some of the more suspicious restaurants get supplies like napkins and straws and the rest exclusively from Chinese suppliers in New York, or Boston, or even Montreal, instead of buying them from local distributors. Everything they do keeps them isolated from the rest of society. Part of that's cultural, I know—but part of it's real clever, too. I mean, what do we care about a truck making weekly deliveries of tofu and shit like that up and down the state? We don't, and we're never going to know how much on board is tofu, and how much is dope or dirty money. These boys are sharp."

"You getting reports of home invasions and extortion?" I asked, thinking again of the Lees.

"Nope. Usually those kinds of crimes happen in a Chinatown, or at least a residential area where you have a whole lot of Asians lumped together. Vermont's still mostly just a road between two spots. And I hope it stays that way—none of us has the manpower to tackle it if it really got hot."

As if he'd been eavesdropping on his own torrent of words, Dan Flynn suddenly stopped and reflected back on what had started this whole lopsided conversation. "You said you thought you had something cooking. What did you mean?"

"I wish I knew. It may just be a small local disturbance, but it's gotten very violent very fast."

"Well," Flynn concluded after a small hesitation, "call again if you need any help. In the meantime, if you like, I'll run a query through the system about Asian crime in general—see if any towns besides Hartford and Burlington have been having any trouble. Maybe we can come up with a common thread."

That was an unexpected offer from a very busy man, and it gave me a sense of comfort that we weren't necessarily alone on this—whatever it turned out to be.

*   *   *

Sol Stennis hit his own pay dirt an hour later, calling me from an office at the back of the Hooker-Dunham Block annex on Main Street. "I think I found Vince Sharkey."

Sharkey was the elusive second-in-command of Ben Travers's small inner circle. As unpleasant as his late leader, but without the latter's native authority, Sharkey's compensating manipulativeness had made him a natural suspect as Ben's killer in Brandt's eyes. To me, that very same trait was why I thought him incapable of such boldness.

In any case, he'd become scarce following a brief preliminary interview with Ron, conducted right after Benny's body had been identified.

Downtown Main Street, with only a few exceptions, consists of a double row of nineteenth-century, red-brick buildings—squat, grimy, determinately permanent, and, for all that, distinctly statuesque. Having survived well over a century, these stolid, functional monuments to a long-past industrial era had finally acquired the kind of patina bestowed on certain elder statesmen.

But like a celebrity's fame, the impression disguised reality. The Hooker-Dunham Block, almost directly across from an incongruously dinky Dunkin Donuts shop, was a typical result of the renovator's art—it was an undistinguished, albeit practical, maze of apartments, offices, shops, hallways, and even a small theater. Its innards had been chopped up and changed so often since its glory days that it was anyone's guess how many rooms, complete with inhabitants, might have been accidentally sealed off forever.

The row of buildings lined the entire east side of the street, and cut off a potentially beautiful view of the Connecticut River and the New Hampshire hills lying just beyond. As a result, that abandoned strip of shoreline had been left to the railroad track, the garbage barrels, a few haphazardly parked cars, and a veritable jungle of tall, scraggly weeds—a prime hangout for the drunk, the dispossessed, and those just wanting to be left alone.

It all spoke richly of Brattleboro as a whole, and went far to explain why many people found the town appealingly unique. Neither left to decay in economic depression nor totally gutted and replaced by urban renewalists hell-bent on the latest architectural kick, Brattleboro had thrashed and battled its way up the food chain like a born survivor, making do with what it had, creating citizens of whoever was willing to stake a claim, and establishing itself as an outspoken, politicized, often contradictory place to live. Old and new, rich and poor, native and flatlander—and, most pointedly, right wing and left—all existed in a jostling, noisy harmony that baffled outsiders and embued residents with a begrudging sort of pride.

Stennis had told me to find him in some offices at the back of the building, on the Main Street level, which put them about three flights above the train tracks. He met me in the reception area and guided me down a rear corridor. "We're going to Mary Cappuce's office. She's got a front-row seat from her window," he explained, as if he was making sense.

Mary Cappuce seemed nonplussed to see us, giving us a small wave of the hand before returning to her computer. Stennis parked himself to one side of a large, open window that did have a commanding view of the grubby, cluttered scene below. Like crows from a rooftop, we could consider our pickings at leisure. Unfortunately, I was still a little vague on what those pickings were supposed to be.

"See that big bush down there, between the tracks and the riverbank, just to the far side of the utility pole?" Stennis asked, pointing.

"Yes."

"There's a narrow path to the far side of it—leads down to the water's edge. It's a favorite hangout for dope smokers."

Mary's voice floated up behind us. "When the wind's right, I feel like I'm having flashbacks."

I smiled and shook my head—small-town police procedure at work. "And that's where he's hanging out?" I asked Sol.

"Tracked him there not fifteen minutes ago."

"He alone?"

Stennis looked a little less confident. "That I don't know. There's no clear view of the actual river edge—part of its appeal. I thought you might want to go down and talk to him, while I guarded the rear." He pointed a little farther down the tracks, where even I could see a faint worn path cutting through the grass. "Just in case he's not in a chatty mood."

Battle plans drawn, I nodded my agreement, thanked Mary for her hospitality, and led the way back outside.

We descended a variety of cement, wooden, and metal stairs until we reached the bottom of the building's downhill side, and emerged from a service entrance among trash cans and debris. Across the double row of railroad tracks, the weeds and brush looked impenetrably dense, and much taller than they had from above.

We split up and approached the jungle from different angles; I headed for the far side of the huge bush Stennis had pointed out earlier. Just before I took the path behind it, I glanced up at the window we'd been using and saw five women clustered around Mary, eagerly watching the proceedings. I hoped they'd be in for a dull time.

While the day was not at all hot, it felt close and uncomfortably warm amid the dry, dusty, dense vegetation, a sensation no doubt enhanced by not knowing what lay even a few feet ahead of me. I moved slowly down the steep embankment, and as quietly as possible, so that by the time I emerged along a narrow strip of trampled grass lining the water and decorated with a few wooden boxes to sit on, I caught four young men sprawled out on the ground completely by surprise. The joint they'd been smoking flew into the water as they all made a mad scramble up the path Stennis was blocking.

They didn't even make it to the bushes. As the first of them was about to vanish, Stennis magically appeared, planting his hand against the first one's chest.

I pointed a finger at Sharkey, the last one in line. "You stay. The rest can go."

The first three sheepishly hurried past the cheerful-looking Stennis, who'd stepped aside to let them by. Vince Sharkey was left staring sullenly at the ground.

"I'll give you two a little privacy," Stennis said affably, and followed the others back to the railroad tracks.

"You gonna bust me?" Sharkey demanded, folding his arms across his chest in an effort to inflate his size. He was more fat than muscular, but big nevertheless, with the prominent brow and single-line thick eyebrows that caricaturists routinely place on dim-witted bullies.

Vince Sharkey was not the kind of kid I liked. The product of as poor a home as any of them, he'd shown no interest in taking any road other than the one he'd pursued from the time he could walk. A natural troublemaker, he'd forever made the people who'd tried to help him rue their efforts, and had made it a point to screw up every decent opportunity offered him. While by instinct no bleeding heart, I did understand why a good number of our younger customers had become the way they were, and, despite our being on opposite sides of the law, I'd even developed a grudging benevolence for some of them, like Sally and the Beauprés. But Vince was not one of those, and I knew for a certainty that he'd end up either killed or doing hard time before too many more years went by. He had long ago worn out his welcome with me.

I pointed to a box by his side. "Sit."

He hesitated, pondering whether to give me a hard time, but he, again unlike the lately departed Ben Travers, was no natural leader. He sat.

"Tell me how Benny died."

"There's nothin' to tell. I didn't know what happened to him till after. I hadn't seen Benny for days."

"Was that the way it was supposed to go down?"

He looked at me sharply, alarmed, which lent me confidence that I was on the right track. "What's that mean?" he asked, about a full count too late for believability.

I picked a time and date at random. "What were you doing around two o'clock the day before yesterday?"

His face registered total bafflement. "How the hell do I know?"

"You don't remember?"

He shook his head, his confusion deepening. "What's to remember?"

"What were you doing at two o'clock the day Benny died?"

"He didn't die the day before yesterday."

"Answer the question."

Vince shook his head, regaining confidence. "I was with a girlfriend and another guy."

"Give me times."

He pretended to think back. "Maybe from ten to four that afternoon."

"And the day before yesterday?" I repeated.

He gave me a glare and began to get up. I caught his shoulder and pushed him back. "What the fuck do I care about the day before yesterday?" he growled at me angrily.

"You don't know what you were doing at two in the afternoon? Who you were with? Where you were, even? Think hard."

"I was around, okay? I was on the street, maybe, or visiting friends."

I didn't speak for a long time, but turned to look out over the slightly rippled surface of the broad river beside us, enjoying the cool breeze. "It's funny how you know exactly what you were doing when Benny died almost a week ago, but have no idea about the day before yesterday. I guess that's because you didn't need an alibi."

"I don't know what you're talking about."

"Benny was pretty spooked the night before he died. What did you tell him the next morning to get him to stay in town?"

He opened his mouth to answer, but I interrupted him. "You say you hadn't seen Benny for days. How many days, Vince? And be careful. Don't make a mistake. The two of you were seen together."

He licked his lips.

I cut him off again as he started to speak. "Whoa, Vince. You look like you're getting nervous. Don't mess this one up. This could be important."

"I don't remember," he shouted at me, again trying to stand up.

I pushed him back a second time, toppling him from his seat. "Not good enough, Vince. The alibi's got to stick all the way. Hanging out with your girlfriend for a few hours won't cut it. Didn't Sonny tell you that? Shit, yes. If we find out you and Benny were together too close to the time he died, you're still in it up to your neck."

"What the fuck're you talking about?" he screamed.

I stepped forward and stood over him, staring down, gaining confidence from the fear in his eyes, knowing I was pinning him down. "I'm talking accessory to murder, Vince. Not actually being there doesn't matter. You set Benny up. You swallowed Sonny's line of bull, but Sonny fucked you over. He needed someone to hang this on in case things got hot, and who better than old Vince—the dumb number-two man?"

He shook his head, incredulous. "You *talked* to him?"

I crouched down, my face close to his. "Don't you know how it works, you dumb bastard? What does he give a shit about a zero like you? He didn't tell you what he was going to do to Benny, did he? And when Benny gave him the slip and had to be chased down, what was Sonny supposed to do? Cover his ass, that's what. Pull in Plan B. Guess who Plan B is, Vince?"

I pulled away suddenly, leaving him sprawled out on the ground, looking awkward and small. He gathered his legs under him and sat up, rubbing his head, trying to think.

"You're full of shit."

"Sonny told you to get hold of Benny before he split town, and tell him you had to talk—just the two of you, at the Rivière place. That's what the alibi was for, right? Give you some cover for when Sonny met up with Ben. And you actually believed the alibi was to protect you from being tied to an illegal *conversation*? Boy, oh boy, Vince, Sonny must've thought you were a gift from heaven, you're so stupid."

Vince sprang up from his crouch and threw himself at me. Anticipating it, I sidestepped, cupped the back of his neck with my hand as he went by, and gave him a helpful shove, letting his own momentum finish the job for me. He fell face-first into the shallow, muddy water by the bank.

Unfortunately, the gymnastics played against me. The cold water cleared his head, and while he grappled back onto shore, spitting and cursing, he also emerged holding the one flaw to my approach. Looking up at me with his hair plastered to his face, he demanded, "Are you going to bust me?"

But I, too, had a Plan B. I gave him a big smile. "Bust you? Vince, you're a nobody—Sonny's right on that one. Think of the paperwork, the time, the wasted money. Much easier to let Sonny finish chewing you to little pieces—that way I'll have more on him when I bust him. You're much more useful as bait."

I turned away then and quickly retraced my steps through the brush.

Sol Stennis was standing guard by the tracks. "Have fun? I heard a splash."

I thought about the gauntlet I'd just thrown at Sharkey's feet. "The first of several, I hope."

Chapter Seven

Geographically, Hartford Township is a hard item to pin down. Of the five villages that form it, three—Hartford, White River Junction, and Wilder—are so seamlessly joined as to be the same entity, while Quechee and West Hartford, economically and physically removed, are like far-distant satellites. Adding to the confusion is West Lebanon, New Hampshire, a stone's throw across the Connecticut River, whose high-pitched commercial bustling makes all the others look like suburbs.

But even the village of West Leb, as it's called, falls prey to competition. Its tax-free commercial advantage is in turn subverted by the most highly developed shopping strip within a forty-mile radius, stretched out along Route 12A about a half mile to the south.

The Hartford Township–West Leb hub, therefore, suffers a bit from second-class status. It's not quite where the bargain buyers flock, and with high-class Hanover just to the north, home of Dartmouth College, it's not where the elite shop for designer wear or hobnob over micro-brewery beer in expensive, tasteful, low-fat eateries.

It is, on the other hand, a major crossroads, marking the juncture of two interstates and Vermont's Route 4, which, according to Detective Heather Dahlin, was a distinctly mixed blessing.

"We're a transient stopover—a place to take a leak, grab a burger, sleep a few hours, and get back on the road. If you're an illegal alien heading south or a flatlander going skiing, chances are you've stopped here. We've got more motels, hotels, and fast-food joints than anywhere between Burlington and Concord. For the type of Asians you're talking about—the ones who go from place to place, work for peanuts, and live like hamsters, it's a custom fit. We might not have a hundred Asians in town at any one time, but whenever we check them out, it's always a new batch."

"They're all illegal?" I asked, surprised at the high number.

"Oh, no. Fewer than ten percent have no papers at all, and maybe ten to twenty percent more have counterfeit documents. But we don't have the expertise to tell the real stuff from the fake. And by treating them all the same, moving them constantly from one place to another, their handlers make it even harder for us to separate the ones who should be here from the ones who shouldn't."

"And most of them live there?" I asked, looking to where she was pointing. We were slowly driving by a large, neglected, empty-looking pile of a building on one of White River Junction's least affluent streets—White River already being the poorest of the township's five cousins.

"We've counted forty at a time in that one, stacked like cordwood, sometimes ten mattresses to a room. We've basically got three types of Asian in this whole area—year-round residents who just happen to be Oriental, transients who live in places like that—illegal and otherwise—and the dirt bags that control 'em. The first group's the majority, and they're no more trouble than anyone else."

"What do you do about the others?"

Dahlin shook her head. She was a tall, muscular, attractive woman, with short blond hair and a permanently determined expression. She was one of only three detectives on a force of twenty sworn officers, and I had no doubt she'd honed her personality meeting any and all opposition on its own ground.

"Not much. We come here a lot less than we do to places with one-tenth the occupants, and that's usually only because some outsider is raising Cain. They keep to themselves, take care of their own problems, and stay out of trouble. The interesting statistic is how rarely we *are* called. They're so quiet, it makes us suspicious."

She smiled and shook her head at the irony. "There're others reasons, of course, but they're all just as vague. Like, why it is that when most of them work in West Leb and Hanover, they sleep over here? It's not necessarily cheaper, and it's an inconvenient commute. All we've been able to figure is they're taking advantage of the two jurisdictions. Work in one state, live in another, it keeps the cops from getting to know them too well—same reason they're kept on the move. I can show you a couple of restaurants that have worn paths in the grass running from their back doors to the interstate."

She shifted in her seat restlessly. "But it's all smoke and no fire. The Border Patrol and INS come down here once in a while, wander around, set up a roadblock on I-91, catch a few illegals. For those few days, the population drops. And as soon as the feds are gone, they're all back. The seven Asian restaurants in the area do good business— like a ton of other people around here—but retail turnover is hot and heavy, especially in food. Rents go up, competition is fierce, and when the economy wobbles, even the best go under . . . except for those seven. They just keep plugging away, paying all their bills in cash. And it's not because they're great advertisers or community boosters. They do zero along those lines. It all sounds like money laundering at the very least, but we've never found a shred of evidence. We can't even say all the owners are in cahoots with the crooks, 'cause we're pretty sure most of them are as coerced as the illegals. They either have to play along, or they're shit out of luck. Basically, you could call us racist paranoids about all this stuff, and I wouldn't be able to prove you wrong."

I nudged her toward the topic at hand. "You must've had some problems, though. You filed a report on Michael Vu with Dan Flynn. What was that about?"

She pulled over into a side street and killed the engine in the shade of a large maple tree. A pleasant, flower-scented breeze drifted in through the open window.

"That creep," she murmured and turned to face me, her gray eyes narrow with anger. "He's in the third group—the bloodsuckers that keep the others in place. I look at these people, they come from the far side of the world, pledging thirty to forty thousand dollars to some shit to get them over here, and they end up like gerbils in a box, working for years so they can pay off their debts. The FBI says alien smuggling is the most profitable of all organized Asian crime activities. I can believe it."

She paused, took a breath, and then resumed. "We had a case a few years back. A small group was using a motel room as a warehouse for stolen goods—mostly clothing, bundles of it, stacked to the ceiling. They were going around to all the big retail outlets and robbing them blind. We nailed the actual thieves—never got the bosses—and found out they came from Fukien Province in China. They were illegals who hadn't been able to keep up on their debt payments to the smugglers by doing legitimate work, because every time they saved enough to make a deposit, they were robbed, sometimes six times in a row. Finally, the smugglers—the same ones who were ripping them off, of course—gave them a choice between being killed or tortured—or having their families take the rap back home—and becoming thieves. They were given a quota. The men we talked to had been doing this for years, and still they weren't even close to settling their debt.

"The kicker is we only talked to the men, because the women we caught with them were bailed out as soon as the paperwork cleared—never to be seen again. We found out it was so they could work as prostitutes in the city until their tab was settled. A vice cop I know in New York told me that. 'Oh, yeah,' he said, 'they keep 'em locked up.' One girl he knew had to turn four hundred tricks before they let her go." She paused and looked out at the quiet neighborhood around us. "The saddest thing is that when I asked the men we caught how they felt about it all, they had no anger for the people who'd abused them. They were just humiliated at having been caught and probably getting deported. It was the shame they'd brought on their families that really got to them."

"Are all the transients you see on their way south?" I asked after a few moments.

"It's a mix. The same New York cop told me they have employment agencies to place illegals and legals both, all over the country, so we probably get some of those. My guess is that most of them are in a pipeline, though. Not, as I said before, that we have proof of any of that.

"The handlers don't add up to much in numbers," she continued. "No more than twelve at most—and while they come and go, too, they tend to be more stable, which gives us a chance to get to know them. That doesn't mean they ever get busted, of course. We know they're crooked only because they act that way—they shepherd what I call the worker bees, they come and go from the restaurants without paying their tabs, they drive around in expensive cars, and they basically look like enforcer types.

"Michael Vu was one of them, although he didn't run with the others—he was flashier and a lot more arrogant, which I guess is why he drew my attention. I nailed him twice coming out of restaurants with a red envelope full of cash—red is a good-luck symbol, like a neon sign saying 'extortion'—but the owners wouldn't fess up. Everything was all smiles and politeness, and Vu went on his way both times, with the money. That's why I filed his name with Dan—it was the only way I could get even . . . pathetic."

"If he didn't run with the others," I asked, "what was he then? An independent? Part of a different gang?"

She didn't answer immediately, giving herself time to reflect. I became aware of a bird high above us in the tree, singing for all it was worth, lending an incongruously cheerful note to our conversation.

"First off," she said finally, "I don't think there are any independents among the crooks—not truly. Everybody's connected—through race, through religion, family, geographical origin, you name it. You kick one hood over here, and everybody knows it from San Francisco to Hong Kong. The confusion comes because various groups free-lance a lot. I hear the Vietnamese are bad that way, but they also contract out to the tongs, or to each other, or to anyone else who needs muscle, especially when cash is low. Makes it hard to pin them down, not knowing who and when, or even if, they're tied to somebody.

"Michael Vu came out of nowhere, and until you brought him up, he'd disappeared into nowhere, but I still think somebody ran him, and I'd bet that somebody ran the guy who ran him, too. I definitely got the sense Vu called a lot of his own shots—like when he extorted those restaurants. That was pure free-lance stuff. But I felt he wasn't his own boss either—that he kept within some limits that'd been set for him."

"Any idea why he left?"

"Nothing I could prove. Corporate shuffling, maybe. He was only here a few months, but we'd see him in phone booths and at the post office sometimes, and we followed him to a meet with some people in a motel room once—we never could get an angle on who they were. They used phony names, paid in cash, and drove a rental car. But he sure wasn't tied to the local boys. They hung out together some, but I always sensed some hostility. We even heard tell of a shoving match between him and one of the head guys here, not long before he left."

"You think he was in competition?"

She hedged her response. "Could be. There was no violence between him and the locals except that one time, as far as we know—but there was always that distance. Now that you mention it, given his style and the short time he was here, it's possible Vu was testing the market, putting the squeeze on people to get a reaction and a little spare change, and then reporting back to some boss . . . it would fit."

"You ever heard of someone named Sonny?" I asked.

She shook her head.

I tried out the other names I'd accumulated, with the same results. She finally said, "I'm sorry. I guess I haven't been much help."

"I wouldn't say that," I answered. "We're doing this brick by brick, and you've just given us quite a few."

*   *   *

Ideally, after my conversation with Heather Dahlin in Hartford, I would have assigned round-the-clock surveillance of Michael Vu, as well as the two buildings in Brattleboro that housed an ever-changing community of Asians, and the four Asian restaurants in town. But our operating budget being what it was—and considering that I'd already put a tail on Vince Sharkey—that was out of the question.

What I did was less dramatic, less effective, and more affordable. The following morning, I brought the entire detective squad up to date, sharing with them my suspicions that we were being market-tested for an Asian gang.

"I think you're getting paranoid," Willy said flatly, a toothpick in his mouth and one foot propped up on the edge of the conference table. "You said yourself that they feed off each other. What do you guess we have in this town? Maybe a hundred and fifty Asians, four hundred in the whole county? Nothing close to a Chinatown."

"What about Sally Javits?" countered Sammie.

"I think she's paranoid, too," Willy answered. "What do a bunch of kids know, for Christ's sake? They chuck a brick through a window now and then, spray paint a wall, do a little dope, scare a few merchants who're dumber than they are. The first slope who walks in with a gun and a sales pitch has 'em all standing around bawling."

"I know you're not going to like this," I interrupted, "but that's the last time I want to hear 'slope' or 'gook' or anything like it. It's wrong, it'll only cause problems we don't need, and it'll alienate the very people who might otherwise help us."

Kunkle rolled his eyes. "I seriously doubt you'll get any help from them."

"Look," I said, "I'll keep this short, but I want you all to hear me loud and clear. There are just over three thousand Asians living in Vermont—that's fifty percent more than all the state's blacks, making them our largest minority. Exactly two of them are in prison. Ninety percent of the others have a work ethic and morals that make the rest of us look degenerate. So while Asians may seem a whole lot different from us, they're to be treated like everyone else. Do I make my point?"

"If Sonny was only making a sales pitch by killing Benny," Sammie said quietly, getting us back on track, "he did a hell of a job, and his target sure shoots a hole in the they-only-feed-on-their-own theory."

I nodded to Tyler. It had been two days since we'd discovered where Travers had eaten his last meal, and I was behind on Tyler's progress. "What more do we have on Travers's death?"

His voice slid into its professorial mode. "We've been able to piece together what happened to him in the house, more or less, but the people who did it went out of their way to be neat and tidy." He pulled several sheets of paper from a folder before him. "This is my report—finished this morning. It doesn't include the blood and fiber samples we sent up to Waterbury. Those results won't be back for a while, but I don't expect much anyway. From what I could determine, most of the blood came from Travers, and even if the blood we found under the broken glass on the other counter came from someone else, there's probably not much we can do with it."

He sat back in his chair, getting comfortable. "The blood was a help in one way. There was so much of it that his attackers couldn't get near him without either stepping in it or touching it. Problem is, they all wore gloves—surgical latex gloves, from what I could tell—and those slip-on things surgeons wear over their shoes. We could still tell the general shoe size—which was small, by the way—and the fact that there were three men involved, but that's about it.

"I analyzed the cut pants. The knife used was razor sharp, and from the marks left on the tabletop, it was the size and shape of a fillet knife, with a thin, slightly curved blade. But they must've taken it with them, so I can't confirm any of that.

"We also found a blue plastic bag, ten-gallon size, which was used over the victim's head. It was under the table, wadded up behind the pants."

"How do you know it was used over his head?" asked Dennis DeFlorio. Dennis was our robbery/burglary/B & E specialist, just back from vacation. Neither my best nor my brightest, he was nevertheless my most consistent subordinate—not given to moods, or prone to office politics, and utterly dependable to do exactly what he was told, if little beyond that.

"Teeth marks on the inside," Tyler answered. "You could tell they'd used it to cut off his air supply and that he tried to chew his way out. Suffocation's not the point, of course. It's just a way to build up panic."

"The voice of personal experience?" Willy cracked.

J.P. gave him a rare but telling hostile stare. For all his seeming detachment, Tyler was not unaffected by the ghostly agonies left behind at many of the scenes he investigated. He covered his sensitivity well, but he took no pride in pretending he was unaffected. To his own rare credit, Willy dropped it, feigning a sudden interest in his coffee.

"The point is," J.P. concluded, "that this was neither spur of the moment nor the work of amateurs. It's difficult to extract oneself from such a scene without leaving something incriminating behind. But that's what these people did. And the use of gloves and booties implies prior experience."

"How 'bout the duct tape?" I asked. "Could you trace that?"

He shook his head. "It's cheaper-grade stuff—something you could get at any discount store anywhere. In fact, that's the reason Benny got away. At some point, they must've either taken a break or gone off to talk privately, because they all left the kitchen and went into the living room. I found small traces of blood from their feet in there, and I could tell from disturbances in the dust where they'd cleared three seats for themselves. Travers took advantage of the opportunity to tear his right hand free and get loose. He escaped through the kitchen door, which leads into a sort of garage-barn combination, where he'd hidden the repainted car."

A donut halfway to his mouth, DeFlorio asked, "Without his pants?"

Sammie gave him a scowl and pushed Tyler's report toward him. "They'd been torturing him, Dennis. They cut his pants off and used the knife on his balls. He didn't care how he looked."

It wasn't totally fair. This was the man's first day back on the job, and Tyler had been delicately circumspect in his description of Travers's ordeal. Dennis's hand froze. He looked around self-consciously, murmured, "Right," and replaced the donut in its colorful box.

I tried to cover the embarrassed silence. "Ron, what's Vince Sharkey been up to since we put that tail on him?"

Klesczewski pulled a note pad from his jacket pocket and flipped it open. "Not much. Hanging around the Flat Street address that houses some of the Asians, watching from his car, partway down the block."

"Is there any sense that he's up to something?"

Ron shook his head. "He's been meeting with his boys, but so far we haven't seen anything unusual."

I looked over at Willy. "Anything from your sources?"

"Word has it you threw Vince in the river. Right now, it sounds like he's more pissed at you than at any goo . . . Asian. Things have settled down a bit over the last two days. Vu and his people have been quiet, the old patterns are starting to pick up again, and nobody's seen hide nor tail of Sonny."

"But what about Benny's operations?" I pressed him. "What's the feeling out there? Is Vince going to inherit the business, or is he going to have to fight Vu for it?"

Kunkle wobbled his hand from side to side equivocally. "Vince doesn't get much respect without Benny around. If Vu or Sonny knocked off Benny to grab his business, there's not much Vince can do about it."

"So, was hassling Scott Fisher and Alfie Brewster and the others just his looking for a soft spot, or is Sonny out to dominate everything in town?" I asked.

Sol Stennis, who was in on this meeting because of his knowledge of juvenile crime, now spoke up for the first time. "Vu's been dropping by the local hangouts a lot, talking to the kids like a recruiter, using

Sonny's name. He's paid for a few parties and takes people for drives in a new Beemer he just picked up. Rumors are he's offering drugs and guns and cars to any converts. It's looking pretty serious. He's also been making regular visits to the Asian restaurants and businesses, probably to keep himself financed."

I turned to Billy Manierre, the rotund and avuncular chief of patrol, who commanded the uniformed troops. "We can't afford an around-the-clock tail on him, but I want Michael Vu to see us damn near every time he looks up. I want him pulled over for minor traffic violations, questioned for anything he or one of his people does that warrants a conversation, and I want everyone he deals with to feel the same heat. Keep in touch on the radio when you see him around town, and keep him company as much as you can. And take pictures—I want to build a photo album of everyone he contacts. Asians, whites . . . I don't care. And get names if you can. Don't be subtle. Word should get out fast that dealing with Michael Vu is like dealing with us."

Manierre nodded, and I addressed the others. "In the meantime, I want us digging into this clown's background, beyond just his rap sheet. I want calls made to California to find out where he came from, who he hung out with, where he's been. I want to know what he's been *suspected* of doing, as well as everything he's done. Dennis, once you've checked what's on your desk, maybe you could start on that.

"Also, none of us yet has even set eyes on Sonny. I want to find out how the two of them keep in touch. Find out if Vu makes a habit of using a particular pay phone. And ask around about Sonny, too—find out who, if anyone, has seen the guy, or had a conversation with him, and if they have, get a description, a psychological profile, anything you can. We need to know who Sonny is.

"And, J.P.," I asked Tyler, "don't give up on that crime scene yet. That routine with the tape, the chair, the knife, and the plastic bag sounds like a practiced MO. Circulate the details everywhere you think makes sense, especially cities with big Chinatowns, like San Francisco and New York. And don't forget Canada. Toronto not only has the oldest Chinatown on the continent, but it's considered the primary transshipment point for aliens coming into this country."

Tyler nodded silently.

I held up a cautioning finger and looked specifically at Kunkle.

"But, remember, leaning on Vu does not mean leaning on every Asian you come across. It's the innocent people who are the primary targets of gangsters like this, so we're working for them, not against them, all right?"

"What about the tail on Vince?" Ron asked. "You want that maintained?"

I thought for a moment. My just-completed speech to the contrary, I hadn't totally overruled Willy's dismissal of all this as paranoia. Twenty-four-hour-a-day surveillance was beginning to sound excessive, especially given what little it had produced. Besides, if we started watching Michael Vu with a magnifying glass, we'd pick up Vince Sharkey if he wandered within sight.

"No," I answered him, "I think we can call it off."

But a small doubt lingered—one I hoped I wouldn't come to regret.

Chapter Eight

"Joe, there's a call for you on line four. A Mr. Crocker," Harriet Fritter announced from the new phone console on my desk. "He says it's about the hot-rodders on Upper Dummerston Road."

"Thanks, Harriet," I answered to thin air, without touching the phone, a disengagement from the norm I found fundamentally rattling, despite having had this new phone system for over a month.

I picked up the light, flimsy-feeling receiver. "Mr. Crocker? Joe Gunther."

"Oh, hi." The voice was a light tenor, slightly breathless. "My name is John Crocker. I've been out of town on business all week, and I got back last night and was going through my mail when I saw the article in the paper about the hot-rodders you were looking for on the Upper Dummerston Road."

"What do you do for a living, Mr. Crocker?" I asked, to slow him down a little.

"What? . . . I design lenses."

"For glasses?"

He gave a small but pleased laugh. "Oh, no. Optical lenses for high-resolution equipment. I've had some of my designs sent into space. One of them flew on the shuttle."

"And you live in town?"

His voice had lost its nervous edge, and I instinctively began forming an opinion of him as a witness. "North of town—Hillwinds."

"Nice place." One of the most expensive in the area, in fact, and located off the Upper Dummerston Road.

His *yes* sounded vaguely embarrassed, so I got to the point. "You saw some of these hot-rodders?"

"Good Lord, yes. I was almost killed by one of them. It was the day I was heading out on this trip I mentioned. I was driving past the golf course, going south, when I saw two of them heading right toward me, across both lanes, at a terrific rate. I pulled over as far as I could and slammed on the brakes—put one wheel in the ditch."

"Did they hit you?"

"No, no. I don't know how they missed. It couldn't have been by more than an inch or two."

"Did you see them go by?" I asked, visualizing him with his hands over his eyes.

"I'd thrown myself across the seat, thinking that might give me a little more protection when we collided."

I nodded to myself and let out an inaudible sigh. "So you didn't get a good look at them."

"Actually, I did—at one of them."

I froze in my chair, suddenly alert. "Can you describe him?"

"Well, I don't know how good I'd be at that, but he was young, and Oriental."

"Mr. Crocker, where are you calling from?"

He sounded surprised. "My office. On Main Street. The Bank of Vermont Building."

"Would you mind if I dropped by and finished this conversation face to face? I have some pictures I'd like you to look at."

"Right now? Well . . . I guess that would be all right." He gave me the number of an office on the second floor.

The Bank of Vermont Building, named after the establishment on the ground floor, was a rare successful attempt at integrating a modern structure with its hundred-year-old neighbors. As squared off as they were, and with a complimentary touch of red brick around its foundation, the bank was nevertheless a light and airy addition to the block, slightly recessed from the sidewalk and adorned with a couple of small trees on each corner. It took me all of five minutes to walk to it from my own architectural tribute to Dickens.

Crocker's office was behind a plain door, marked only by the number he'd given me. A slight, short man, with glasses and a receding hairline, John Crocker matched his tentative tenor voice perfectly. "Mr. Gunther?" he asked as he opened the door himself. He gave me a moist, limp hand to shake. "I guess they don't call you 'Mister.' I am sorry. Is it 'Officer'?"

"'Joe' will do fine. Something occurred to me on the way over. Why didn't you report this near-accident?"

He cast his eyes to the floor and shuffled his feet slightly. For a man who must've been in his forties, he reminded me of a nerdy teenager caught in a lie. "I was running late. I had a plane to catch at Bradley, and once it was all over, and I found that my car was okay and that I could back it out of the ditch, I didn't see the point. I hadn't gotten the numbers off the license plate, and I didn't think there was much anyone could do in any case." He lifted his eyes slowly to meet mine. "Was that breaking the law or something?"

"No—not to worry. I appreciate your calling us now."

He smiled shyly. "You're welcome."

I looked around the large, bright office, dominated by several enormous drawing boards parked in a row. Opposite me was a bank of windows and an incongruously beautiful view of Mount Wantastiquet across the sun-dappled Connecticut River. "Can we sit somewhere, Mr. Crocker? I'd like you to look at a few photographs."

"Of course," he said, circling the drawing boards and pulling chairs out from under two of them. "Where would you like to do this?"

I joined him with my back to the windows and looked down at the designs attached to the boards. From the little I could decipher, they were simply huge circles, crosshatched with lines and covered with neat, incomprehensible, mathematical markings. I shook my head slightly and pointed vaguely at one of them. "Can we lay them across that?"

"Sure, no problem." He swept aside a couple of rulers and a pencil, and pulled one of the chairs over to join the one already there. They were tall, well-built, and surprisingly comfortable to sit in.

"You saw two cars abreast," I began, "heading your way at a high rate of speed?"

"That's correct." His knees were drawn up, his hands in his lap, like an attentive student.

"What color were they?"

"Dark green and dark blue," he answered without hesitation. "The green one was closer to the ground, like a sports model, and it was slightly behind the other one."

I was encouraged by that. Dark and low matched the description Thomas Lee's neighbor had given to the car we suspected had carried out the home invasion. "Which one was in your lane?"

"The green one. At the time, I thought it was trying to pass. While I was gone on this trip, after the conference came to a close every day, I was sort of on my own, not being a very social person. So I tended to go to bed early, like I do at home. That's when all this kept coming back, like a nightmare. The day it happened I was running late—I had something else to focus on—but at the conference, I guess I realized how close I'd come to getting killed, so I kept reliving it, and each time I saw things more clearly."

"You mentioned seeing one of the men."

"Yes. The driver of the green car. When you think of it, he and I came within just a few feet of one another, if only for a second," he added with a smile. "I was looking at him because I thought he was going to kill me, of course. But he was staring right through me— like he couldn't have cared less whether we hit each other or not. It was creepy. I've seen that face every night since it happened—totally empty of feeling, except a kind of cold rage."

I decided to put his recall to the test. I placed ten photographs across the board surface of the drawing board. All of them were Asian, including recent surveillance shots of Vu and some of his colleagues, and the stills I'd had Tyler extract from the video of Truong, Diep, and Lam.

John Crocker didn't hesitate. As soon as the picture of Truong Van Loc hit the table, he said, "That's him."

"Let me put the others down," I cautioned, "just so you can be absolutely positive. Some of these photos look alike."

In fact, they did. I'd made it a point to find at least one near-match for every player I knew personally, and as luck would have it, two of them had the same general features and long hair as Truong.

But Crocker didn't budge. "That's him," he repeated. "Without a doubt."

I collected the pictures and put them back in my pocket. "You said one of the reasons you didn't call this in was because you hadn't gotten the license numbers. Does that mean you got a glimpse at the plates themselves?"

"Oh yes, they were heading right at me. The blue car was from Vermont, and the green one from Quebec."

"How can you be so sure?" I asked, a little startled.

"I was born in a small town. I look at every car that comes at me that way. First the plate, to see if it's from in-state, then the face, to see if the driver's somebody I know."

I smiled at his answer, at the familiar chord it struck. I waved to half the drivers on the road when I was out driving around, as they did to me. It was just something you did, living in Vermont.

*   *   *

The satisfaction—in fact, the vindication—of finally putting Truong Van Loc's face and name to one of Benny's killers was only offset by the little I could do with the information at this point. Issuing an arrest warrant was hopelessly premature, since I still needed more evidence. We hadn't found the car, or the famous Glock, or Truong's reputed companions, and it could have been argued in court that at the time Crocker saw Truong, the latter was merely in the midst of recklessly passing another car.

The best I could do, therefore, was issue a New England and Canada-wide BOL—be-on-the-lookout—bulletin, featuring Truong's picture and vital statistics.

I was in the middle of doing the paperwork for just that when Harriet's disembodied voice came over the phone speaker, advising me that Heather Dahlin was on the line.

"What's up?" I asked her when I picked up the phone.

"We got a call from the hospital an hour ago about an Asian woman in her thirties who came into the ER complaining of abdominal pains. According to her, she fell late last night. She didn't do anything about it at the time because she thought the pain would go away, but this morning it got worse than she could bear, so her husband drove her in. The docs looked her over, diagnosed internal injuries, got her into the operating room. She died of internal bleeding."

"She say she fell downstairs?" I asked, sensing a familiar scenario.

"Better than that. The hospital called the PD because they didn't buy her story. Based on their experience, she had all the signs of someone who'd been beaten to death. A unit went over, checked out the body, and discovered she was Asian *and* the wife of one of the restaurant owners I was telling you about. That's when they called me. We all went over to the husband's house, and found out he wasn't looking too good either. Nor was his house."

"Home invasion?"

"That's what we think, but we hit the same wall you did. He said she fell downstairs, that he tried to grab her and fell with her. We could see the house was trashed, of course, but he won't talk about it."

"How're you going to deal with it?" I asked.

"We'll play it by the numbers—it is a homicide, after all—but we'll probably get nowhere," she said dismissively. "The interesting thing is, I checked out the Asian hot spots to see what I could pick up, and guess what I found?"

Now I understood where she was headed, and the reason for her excitement. "New players."

"Bingo. Those tough guys I told you about who gave Michael Vu the cold shoulder? Can't find a single one of 'em. They've all been replaced by new people."

"Vietnamese?"

"No, no. It's a mixed bag, like before. I haven't found out who's who yet. But I thought you'd like to know."

"Thanks, Heather. I'll update Dan Flynn. Maybe he'll have heard something from his end."

*   *   *

"You know," Flynn said minutes later, "you've got an amazing sense of timing. I've been calling around, and you and Dahlin aren't the only ones seeing changes among the Asians. I've had feedback now from Burlington, Rutland, Springfield, and a few odd spots like Newport and St. Albans. It's nothing much, and most of the people I talked to said they hadn't even filed reports within their own departments, much less been tempted to let me know, but there's been movement."

"What kind?"

"Power shifting, mostly. Old faces being replaced by new ones. The point is, it's happening all over the state, all at the same time."

"Any more mention of Michael Vu or Sonny?"

"I asked. With Vu, I got nothing, but Sonny cropped up with the Burlington PD and with INS."

The mention of INS sharpened my interest. "What did Immigration say?"

"They were a long shot, since Dahlin's pointer card said Michael Vu was into illegal aliens. But they said they'd heard Sonny's name just recently. A couple of illegals the Border Patrol handed over to them said that Sonny had made the arrangements. I called a friend at the Border Patrol. He couldn't help me with Sonny or Vu or any of the other names I had, but he did say the number of Asian crossers had gone up, and it looked like the regular channels were either being changed or challenged."

"By a competitor?"

"Who knows? Asian illegals are the tightest-lipped of all of them. Sonny could've been operating for years, and we just tumbled to it now. And habits in border crossings change all the time, for all sorts of reasons. That's the problem with all this information—you can mold it to fit whatever theory you want."

That last comment made me stop and think a moment. "Dan," I finally asked, "what's your own gut reaction? Am I way off base here?"

He laughed. "Hell, Joe, you're talking to somebody who's paid to see conspiracies under every rug. I'm a believer."

I hung up the phone and contemplated where we stood. In conventional terms, I was in trouble, having a rape with no complainant and a murder with skimpy evidence. Only Truong Van Loc was good news, since I was convinced his reappearance could have far-reaching consequences.

But even there, I was in a jam. Assuming I was heading in the right direction, it was starting to look as though Truong and Sonny and the others might be involved in federal-level violations. Which meant that if some government agency suddenly took an interest in this case, and the state's attorney was willing to wash his hands of it, our sole reward would be a pat on the head for some preliminary ground work, and the hope that somebody might end up doing federal time.

Which gave me scant comfort. The old bloodhound in me was reluctant to give up the scent of a good case, and I had a habit of following things to the end.

Chapter Nine

It was near five o'clock in the afternoon when Ron Klesczew-ski yelled through my office door, his face flushed with excitement: "Something hot's going down."

I caught up to him halfway across the parking lot. "What the hell's happening?"

"A source at the bank called," he said, unlocking his car. "She just paid out fifty thousand dollars cash to the owner of the Century Cinema, Peter Leung. He was nervous as a cat. She said she thought he might have a heart attack right on the spot. He even dropped some of the money he was stuffing into a briefcase. She knows she could get fired for giving us the tip, so I figured we better give it a look."

"Where's Leung now?" I asked, swinging into the passenger seat.

"Heading home, I think. A patrol unit picked him up on the qt about four minutes ago heading west on Route Nine. He lives out on Green Meadows." He suddenly gave me an apologetic look as we sped out of the parking lot. "I know this may be nothing—that he has the flu and a mortgage payment due at the same time or something—but I thought we better play it safe. Ever since you tumbled to this Asian thing, I've been reading up, and home invasions where one family member is sent out for the cash while the rest are held captive are supposed to be pretty common."

"No problem," I said, privately wondering if Ron would ever over-come the insecurity that would probably forever keep him halfway up the corporate ladder. His actions just now had been flawless—fast, decisive, and intelligent—but I sensed that had I raised one finger in opposition, however wrongheaded, he would have folded his tent. Still, I comforted myself, he had come a long way—he never would have stuck his neck out this far in the old days.

We pulled onto Route 9 and picked up speed heading west.

"What've you got lined up?" I asked him.

"In addition to the patrol unit and us, I had Harriet rally what she could get of the special-reaction team. They're to stand ready at the West B fire station. I hope that's okay."

"Fine with me." I didn't know where Peter Leung lived specifically, but I was familiar with Green Meadows. A short horseshoe attached to the side of Greenleaf Street, it was an archetypal slice of suburban America, with ranch-style homes, lawns with swing sets, a swimming pool or two, and graceful young trees coming into bloom. It was as far from the town's meaner streets as it could get, both physically and psychologically. If this did turn ugly, though, and Ron's worst fears were realized, Green Meadows could well become a combat zone.

Not knowing which scenario might play out—or even if Leung was heading home—was going to severely cramp our style. The safest approach—sealing off his street, evacuating the neighbors, waiting for the transaction to go down, and then picking up the pieces—was almost ludicrously out of the question. Instead, we would have to be discreet, leaving the patrol unit and the SRT people nearby but out of sight, and making the approach to Leung's house ourselves, without visible backup, without body armor, and with only our concealed sidearms for protection.

The radio crackled beneath the dash. "0-8 from 0-20. Subject car has pulled into Green Meadows."

Ron unhooked the microphone. "10-4, 20. Find a spot where you can see both ends of the street. 0-3 and I are going to make a direct approach." He looked over at me questioningly. I nodded without comment.

We pulled off Route 9 onto Greenleaf Street and drove up a short distance to Green Meadows's first entrance. Ron paused a moment and looked around. Almost completely hidden by a large, leafy tree farther up and across the road, a fender and part of the windshield from 0-20's patrol unit looked like any other parked car.

"Where's he live?" I asked as we entered the horseshoe.

"Right in the middle. East side."

I glanced over at him. His eyes were straight ahead, scanning the street before us, his tension completely at odds with the smells of spring wafting in through the open windows, the sounds of a dog barking in the distance, of a mother somewhere calling for her child. I took a deep breath to relax.

"There," he said, "gray house, red roof."

It was all but indistinguishable from its neighbors in mood and tidiness, but it had a strange stillness about it, emphasized by shut windows and drawn curtains. One car was parked outside the closed garage, another—sportier, more pretentious, built for speed, and with Massachusetts plates—was by the curb. Both were empty.

Ron pulled over beyond the house, on the opposite side of the street. He cleared with Dispatch on the radio, killed the engine, and wrestled a portable radio from his pocket. "0-8 to all units and Dispatch. 0-3 and I are approaching the front entrance. The SRT can stand by out of sight on Greenleaf beyond Green Meadows."

A small chorus of muttered "10-4s" followed us as we left the car and walked slowly across the street, keeping several feet apart from each other. Ron held the radio in his hand, hidden behind his leg as he went.

I watched the windows for any movement, hearing the odd piece of gravel crunch under my shoe, feeling the weight of my gun in its holster. All those earlier sights and sounds of a neighborhood in early spring faded from my consciousness, until all I could focus on was that utterly still house, and the front door looming ever closer.

We crossed the sidewalk and came to the entrance from different angles, stepping on the grass rather than the paving stones leading up from the street. We reached the door, positioned ourselves to either side of it, our backs to the wall, and paused a moment. Ron's face was glistening with sweat, as I suspected mine was. We exchanged glances, I nodded, and he knocked loudly.

At that moment, instead of the door opening, a snow-white BMW appeared around the bend in the street and pulled up behind the car already parked there. Loud music could be heard pulsing against the tinted, closed windows.

"Jesus Christ," Ron muttered.

The music died with the engine. The driver's door swung open, and Michael Vu, resplendent in a white suit and purple shirt, stepped out into the street. His back still to us, he shook his pants legs loose, slicked back his long hair, and turned to walk around the front of his car. He froze in midstep as he saw us.

Before any of us could react, however, a second car rounded the bend, drawing all of our attention. Blotched with rust, trailing a pale-gray plume of smoke, it stopped abruptly in the middle of the street. Out of it half fell a wild-looking, disheveled Vince Sharkey. One hand reached out to the car hood for support. In the other was a gun.

It was at that moment that the front door opened between us, revealing through its narrow gap a frantic Peter Leung and, behind him, the familiar and malevolent face of Henry Lam.

What followed unfurled like a slow-motion silent movie, where I was so keen on survival that I heard no words of warning, and was only aware of the gunfire as I might have been of a hard rain hitting the roof at night—a distant sound in a dream-like state.

Still facing the street, Ron brought the radio up to his mouth with one hand and cleared his gun of its holster with the other. I threw my weight against the building's front door, reached in to grab Peter Leung by his shirt front, and pulled him past me with all my strength, throwing him into the bushes behind me. Now fully revealed, Lam stood openmouthed, rooted in place with an automatic machine pistol by his side.

Across the lawn, Vince Sharkey brought his gun unsteadily to bear on Michael Vu, and fired a round that starred the white car's windshield. Ron, now down in a crouch, shot once and hit Sharkey in the chest, sending him up onto the hood of his car before he rolled off and landed on his face in the street.

Meanwhile, Lam quickly recovered and brought his snub-nosed machine gun to bear on me as I leaped backward off the stoop and pulled my own gun free. The air between us suddenly burst into a smoky cloud, and I could feel Lam's bullets tugging at my clothes and thudding into the ground around me. Stumbling backward, I fired twice into the middle of the cloud.

For a split second everything stopped. I was on my knees, my gun still bearing on the now-empty doorway. Ron was standing at the foot of the steps, gun in hand but unsure of what to do, and Vu stayed where he had been all along, still looking stunned.

Then the storm broke a second time.

Suddenly framed in the door were two more gunmen, young Asian boys, one with a shotgun, the other a semi-automatic pistol. Both looked utterly terrified.

As from a long, long way off, I heard myself yell, "Freeze—police."

The one nearest me brought the shotgun to bear on my chest. I fired first, sending him flying backward out of sight. The second one aimed at Ron, who was just turning to face him, and unloaded four rounds before Ron responded in kind, hitting him three times in the stomach and bringing him to his knees. Clutching his middle, the young man looked at us with a confused expression, and then toppled forward, landing spread-eagled across the steps.

We stood motionless for a moment, our guns trained on the doorway. I suddenly became aware of sirens, the squeal of tires on the street behind us. I heard Michael Vu being ordered to spread himself flat on the hood of his car.

I glanced at Ron; blood was dripping from his ear and darkening the shoulder of his jacket. "You all right?" I asked, my eyes back on the door.

He opened his mouth to speak, said nothing, and finally just nodded.

I glanced over quickly to where I'd thrown Peter Leung. He was still lying half across the bushes and half against the wall of his home, looking like a discarded rag doll. He was clutching his forearm, and I could see blood oozing from a thigh, where one of Lam's wild shots had caught him.

"How 'bout you?" I asked him.

"My wife . . . "

"We're going in to get her now."

We approached the entrance again, and flattened ourselves to either side of it.

"You ready?" Ron finally croaked, and gestured to the house's dark interior.

I nodded.

"Okay."

We swung inside, low and away from the doorway, cutting to opposite directions. Apart from the motionless figures of the two young Asians, the entrance hall was empty.

On the radio, Ron let everyone know we were inside, and gave orders to secure the area, surround the house, and enter from all possible avenues. As he spoke, I carefully went from one still body to the other, removing weapons and checking for pulses, all with one eye glued to the far doorway. There were no signs of life.

Soon joined by reinforcements, we located Peter Leung's wife in an upstairs bathroom. Her hands were tied behind her back, and she was lying in a puddle of water and vomit in front of the toilet. The two young men had been holding her head under water, trying to find out where she kept her valuables.

After we cleaned her up a little, and got a quick statement, we handed her over to the ambulance crew so she could go with her husband to the hospital.

What followed then was a long, legalistic procedure of precise and demanding form. The house and the street in front of it were cordoned off. Tony Brandt arrived, as did, in quick succession, Alfred Gould—the local assistant medical examiner—State's Attorney Jack Derby, and his investigator, Todd Lefevre. Also, since this mayhem had involved local police officers, a "post-shoot" team from the Vermont State Police was called in to collate the details and run the interviews. Several hours later, the large green truck from Waterbury carrying the state crime-lab people arrived to photograph, measure, and remove for later analysis a small museum's worth of forensic evidence.

Ron, the two patrolmen we'd left at the street's entrance, and I were interviewed several times by different people, as were some of Peter Leung's neighbors. Michael Vu was taken to the police department until his role in the shoot-out could be legally clarified.

At some point, much later, after our stories had been officially recorded and we'd been cleared to speak to one another once more, I searched out Ron Klesczewski. I found him in the living room, sitting on a small hard-back chair, staring out the window.

I pulled up another chair and sat next to him. He made no acknowledgment of my presence. Suddenly exhausted, I let out a sigh. "How're you holding up?"

He turned toward me, but his eyes were unfocused, his mind obviously snagged on the recent past. "Fine."

"Well, I'm not," I said flatly, hoping to break through his blank expression.

My words hung in the air before him. He blinked once slowly and looked at me more attentively. "What?"

"We were almost killed, and we just shot four people to death."

He nodded deliberately, and went back to staring out the window. "Kids," he murmured. "It didn't really sink in till a while ago."

"Dangerous kids," I amended, "who were about to take our heads off."

His face became more animated. "What the hell was that all about? They couldn't've been more than sixteen, seventeen. They would've gotten a slap on the wrist for this—been out in no time. Why come out blazing?"

"They didn't see it that way. You spend your whole life surrounded by corruption and violence and death, you don't end up thinking much about the future. You take what you can when you can."

He was quiet for a while. "So stupid."

"You had no choice. You know that, don't you?"

"Yeah—I guess."

"How's the ear?" I asked.

Unconsciously, his hand went up to his bandaged ear and touched it gently. "Throbs a bit. Amazing luck."

I laughed and spread my arms to show off a borrowed uniform shirt, my own having been taken as evidence. "Six holes in the jacket, one in the shirt. I can't believe he missed me."

He shook his head and held up his hand, its thumb and index finger a fraction of an inch apart. "We came that close, and so fast. It could've been over before we knew what hit us. Get a tip, go on a drive, knock on a door, and—bam. You're dead . . . Were you expecting anything like this?"

HIGHLAND PARK PUBLIC LIBRARY

I shook my head. "We get lulled into a false sense of security in this town. We think all that big-city crime is far away. Did you call your wife, by the way?" I added. "This's been on the radio by now, maybe the TV, too. They're going to make a big deal about it."

"Yeah. She was crying. I told her it would be hours before I could get home. She's pretty upset."

I squeezed his shoulder. "Go home, then. Give her a hug. You'll have to come back to the office for a post-stress debriefing tonight, but that gives you a couple of hours at least. Leave your phone off the hook. We'll page you if we need you before then."

He looked at me doubtfully, but I rose and took his elbow in my hand, forcing him to stand. "Go on. I'll see you later."

He nodded tiredly and walked toward the door.

I stopped him just as he reached the threshold. "Thanks for what you did today. You not only went by the book, with no mistakes, but you probably saved my butt as well."

He gave me a wistful half smile. "Thanks. You, too, Joe."

*   *   *

It was getting dark outside. In an odd replay of what Ron had been going through a short time earlier, I found myself sitting on an upstairs bed in the Leung home, my back against the headboard, my eyes watching the endless flickering of red and blue lights reflecting off the ceiling. I wasn't traumatized by what I'd just gone through but, like Ron, I was experiencing the weight of the day's events, and feeling very, very tired. Despite Hollywood's willful misperception, killing a person wasn't something a cop ever took in stride, especially if your beat involved but a single homicide a year, as it did in Brattleboro.

I was still lost in my thoughts when Tony Brandt's voice softly broke the silence. "Joe? You in here?"

I could see his pale shadow settling into a nearby armchair. "Yeah—kind of debriefing myself."

"Don't you think you ought to be heading back? We're basically done here. The debriefing's in half an hour."

"I will soon." I jerked a thumb I wasn't even sure he could see toward the window. "What's happening out there?"

"'Bout what you'd expect. Phones flying off the wall, politicians scrambling for an inside angle so they'll look informed, reporters swarming like proverbial locusts, cops wondering how the hell the whole thing went down. I've already held one press conference, along with Mitch Gauthier—he's heading the VSP post-shoot team."

"How's he seeing it so far?"

"Right now, he says it's clean. He does think you two were a little casual in your approach, given you thought this might've been an extortion, but that's hindsight, and he knows it. He does credit Ron having the special-reaction team close by. He'll back you up—he won't have any reason not to. And Derby's already issued a preliminary decision clearing you both, pending Gauthier's investigation. So you're back on the job whenever you're ready."

"What did Michael Vu say?"

"That he was stopping by to see his old pal Peter Leung. That he can't believe Brattleboro has joined the ranks of New York City. He claims he had no idea what was going on inside the house, and that he'd never laid eyes on any of the hoods, including Vince Sharkey."

"So he's out?"

"Free and clear. But you know what that means. Our screwing up this little deal cost him plenty in clout. He's going to have to move fast to save face."

I shook my head mournfully. "Christ, if only I hadn't pulled the plug on Sharkey's tail, some of this could've been prevented."

Instead of letting me off the hook, however, Tony slipped in one of his own. "If you hadn't put that bee up Sharkey's nose about Sonny screwing him, you wouldn't have needed the tail in the first place. That was your first mistake."

He was right, of course, and it reinforced how little control we had over this case, and how desperately I had been grasping at straws. With today's events, we were now engaged in the bloodiest investigation in the police department's history, and I still was no clearer on where we were headed than when I'd been staring at Benny Travers's charred remains.

Something was going to have to break soon, or Tony's irritation was going to be the least of my troubles.

Chapter Ten

Gail stirred next to me, and I turned my head to look at her, happy to have her back home, regardless of the reasons. I had tried to call her yesterday, before news of the shooting reached her otherwise, but she'd been unobtainable, and I'd been forced to lay down a paper trail of calming messages instead. Notwithstanding that the gist of those had been to tell her to stay put and not worry, by the time I found her waiting for me after the post-stress debriefing, I was delighted she'd ignored them all.

We didn't talk much during the short drive home. The emotion of our initial embrace had rendered most of that redundant and trite. And, afterward, we immediately went to bed. At first we were content to merely hold one another, knowing the following morning would be ours to enjoy alone. But that had finally proven inadequate. Giving in to a need more demanding and soothing than sleep, we'd made love as long and as passionately as I could ever remember. Only then did we stop fighting exhaustion and give in.

And yet I woke early, the dawn's light not quite washing the skylight overhead. I hadn't been wracked by nightmares, or by misgivings concerning Ron Klesczewski's shaky mental state. It was the persistent frustration of the night before, coupled with the knowledge that, by killing Henry Lam, I'd eliminated one of the few suspects who might have been of use to me.

Gail opened one eye, half veiled by long brown hair, and stretched her arm across my chest. "Yesterday catching up with you?"

"Not the way you mean. The sole effect of yesterday's fireworks will probably be to attract some federal agency who'll swallow the case whole and leave us looking like dumb yokels."

She watched me for a few seconds in silence. "What was it like, being shot at?"

I thought back, pretty sure where she was heading. "A slow-motion blur, mostly. I just remember thinking I better do everything right."

"How 'bout now?"

"I don't know . . . It's over," I said dismissively.

She scowled slightly and sat up straighter.

"How are *you* doing?" I thought to ask, just a bit too late.

"The first radio report said a shooting with three dead and one cop wounded. All the way to Brattleboro I tried to keep calm, but after what happened to you last year, I knew the cop was you. That your luck had run out."

Last year I'd been knifed by a man on the run, and had spent several weeks in a coma. "I tried to reach you."

She gave me an odd glance, and I realized I'd selfishly missed her point. "The whole drive down, I wasn't telling myself that you'd be all right. I only thought about how I'd react to hearing you were dead."

As she finished, I saw a tear cascading down her cheek, wetting the rumpled sheet she'd pulled up to her chin.

Embarrassed, I put my arm around her and drew her against me, kissing the top of her head.

She returned the hug. "It's okay," she murmured. "There's not much anyone can do about it anyway."

The silence that filled the room made a lie of that statement, and I found myself forcing the obvious words into the void. "I could quit. God knows I've put enough time in."

But mercifully, she shook her head. "You can't do that. I don't want you to, either." She craned her neck up and kissed me softly. "Thanks for saying it, though."

I frowned, suddenly unsure to what degree I'd meant it, imagining the media circus I knew was almost upon me. "Sure."

"So, you're worried the feds will take the case away?" she resumed in a stronger voice, as if setting off on a brisk walk.

I took her lead, leaving the fear and concern behind us. "They can only do that if Jack Derby says they can. But I'm worried he'll feel politically exposed enough to try to find a buyer—based on the premise that we don't have the manpower, the resources, or the ability to deal with it."

"Do you?"

I smiled at her bluntness—and the return of a direct, clear-eyed manner I both cherished and needed. "No. But we have the self-interest."

"Meaning what?"

"A few weeks ago, a bank security investigator—an ex-FBI agent, in fact—told me about an employee who'd wired sixteen thousand dollars of the bank's money to a dummy address in another state, just before she blew town. The bank was local, with no branches in the other state, so the investigator had no jurisdiction. But interstate wire fraud is a federal offense—an FBI specialty—so this man called his former employers and tried to sell the case to them. They took down all the information, but they warned him not to expect anything—that it was too small. Not worth the overhead to pursue."

Gail scowled. "That's hardly the same thing. You've got a pile of dead bodies, for crying out loud. They can't ignore that."

"Except that most of those bodies were killed by us. Sensational maybe, but not a federal crime. The federal aspects of this whole mess involve things we haven't been able to prove yet—organized crime, illegal aliens, money laundering, contraband weapons. If we had a longer reach, we could dig where we can't now, in order to make a case. The feds have that reach, but they wouldn't have the vested interest. In fairness to them, they've got enough on their plates without fooling around with a small local problem that may or may not grow bigger. Let's face it, for all the noise this has generated, we don't have much to go on."

Gail straightened up, her expression quizzical. "I don't understand. If that's true, then how could Derby unload the case?"

"Because his problems are more political than legal right now. For him, there is no case—just a huge PR stink bomb. If he can get the US Attorney's office to assign it to an agency outside his jurisdiction—politely saying it's more than us local flatfoots can handle—then he's free and clear, especially since all the victims were either deadbeats or outsiders."

"Even though that agency won't do anything with it?"

"They might in the long run, but only if something else develops that makes it meaningful to them. Otherwise it'll end up on a back burner."

Years ago, when Gail and I first met, she was far readier to use outrage as a means of spurring action. That was no longer true. She was as idealistic as ever, but over two decades as a businesswoman and a local politician, she'd become craftier.

"Sounds like you and Derby need to get together. If he does want to kick the case loose, maybe there's a way you could stay with it—keep everyone happy."

I mulled that over in silence. It was technically possible, but only if an unreasonable number of factors fell into place in the right sequence.

"A sneakier approach," she continued, sensing my skepticism, "would be to locate the kind of evidence that would attract federal attention. It might help you sell yourself as an integral part of the package."

I stared at her in wonder. "I shudder to think what'll happen when you pass the bar."

She smiled.

*   *   *

Ron Klesczewski wasn't in the next morning. Stimulated by my talk with Gail, I'd come into the office early to talk on the phone with Dan Flynn, and had watched Ron's empty desk outside my door throughout our conversation, increasingly concerned about where he might be.

As soon as I hung up, I dialed Harriet Fritter on the intercom. "You hear from Ron this morning?"

She hesitated before answering. "He called in. He said he was taking the day off."

I tried interpreting what she hadn't said. "He okay?"

"He sounded terrible."

I cast back to his state of mind the day before, and to his listless behavior at the post-stress meeting later on. "I'll give him a buzz," I told her, and punched a button for an outside line.

The phone was answered almost immediately by a timid, hesitant, woman's voice.

"Wendy?" I asked, suddenly unsure of who was on the line.

"Yes."

"This is Joe Gunther. Is Ron there?"

There was a brief, telling hesitation before she said, "He's not available right now. I'm sorry."

"Harriet told me he sounded a little rough this morning. How's he doing?"

Her silence made clear I'd unwittingly stepped through an open manhole. "Is everything okay?" I added.

Her voice cracked slightly. "Not really. I don't know what's happening. He won't talk, won't eat, won't sleep. I was so happy he wasn't badly hurt . . . I don't understand."

"Has he called the department counselor?"

She sounded more hopeful. "Yes, this morning. He didn't tell me what they talked about."

"That's a good sign, though. Shows he knows he's in trouble. I am sorry, Wendy. I totally misjudged how hard this hit him—people react so differently. Look, tell him I called, that I totally understand, and I think he's doing the right thing. I'm putting him on administrative leave as of now. That way, he won't have to worry about showing up at the office, and neither of you will have to worry about his paycheck. Okay?"

"Sure . . . I guess so."

"I'll tell the counselor what I've done, just so he knows. Do you think if I dropped by, that would be a good idea?"

"I don't know. Maybe not right away."

I quickly retreated. "Just an idea. If it's better that we all stay away—"

"No, no. I think he should see *you*. But maybe after a couple of days."

"Of course. I'll let you call the shots. If there's anything we can do, though, don't hesitate. And let me know if he gets any worse."

I added a little more forcefully, "And if he stops getting help, I need to know that, too."

"I understand. Thank you, Joe."

"Sure. And call anytime—day or night."

She murmured something unintelligible and the line went dead. I hung up and stared at the phone for a moment, wondering about all the unacknowledged agonies I'd just glimpsed.

*   *   *

I looked directly at Jack Derby. "Are you going to hand this over to the feds?"

He looked from me to Tony Brandt and back. We were all three sitting in Tony's office, and Tony was pretending to dig around inside his pipe bowl with a small scraping tool. "Seems like a reasonable option," Derby admitted slowly, his political sensitivity heightened by the presence of no fewer than three television sound trucks in the parking lot outside. "It smacks of organized crime—that's a Washington hot button right now. I thought the FBI might be interested."

"All right," I countered, "but if you make that call through conventional channels, it'll be to the Bureau's Rutland office—Brattleboro's in their jurisdiction. That means their senior resident agent, a guy named Joshua Bishop, gets the case, which in turn means we never see it again, because Bishop doesn't work with locals. He doesn't trust their security, their integrity, or their ability—he was burned one too many times when he was working in New York."

Derby was slightly confused. "So what's your proposal?"

"We approach the FBI through its Burlington-based supervisor—that's Bishop's boss—using the VSP as a conduit. I talked to Dan Flynn this morning about it, and he's interested in helping out—"

"Why?" Derby suddenly interrupted.

"Because he sees this—like I do—as being bigger than just Brattleboro—that it's a statewide problem in the making and that it needs to be nipped in the bud. Also, he has a selfish interest in seeing VCIN shown in a good light. He still has some old-school superiors with strong reservations about his informational lending library."

"All right," Derby conceded, still probing for where I was heading, intrigued by now despite himself. "But why will the FBI's Burlington supervisor be any better than Joshua Bishop?"

"He came up through the ranks 'far from the flagpole,' as he puts it, in Montana, Wyoming . . . places where he was the only agent for hundreds of square miles. His name is Walter Frazier, and he's spent his whole career working with other agencies, and mostly in rural states. He's perfectly happy to take an overseer's role in a case, trusting the locals to do a professional job. We could put together an FBI-sanctioned task force, largely run by us and the Vermont State Police, working under the US Attorney's office in conjunction with you. That way, we would gain the advantage of having some federal clout, the state's self-interests would be served with a fraction of the effort, and everybody'll come out looking good."

Derby actually laughed. Brandt, his fiddling with the pipe concluded, sighed and stared stonily out the window.

"And you think they'll all buy that?" Derby finally asked.

I smiled back at him. "You know as much as I do that personalities count for a lot in this business—getting the right judge on a case, treating the clerk of court decently, showing other cops you're on their side. What do you think about what I've said—purely from your own perspective?"

"I don't think it's particularly realistic, but it would make for some good politics."

I leaned back in my chair. "People don't think ideas like this are realistic because they don't think they could get them to work themselves. But if you picked your way through the system carefully, you might be surprised. You just admitted you're half won over yourself."

"Well, I'm not," Brandt finally growled, chilling the air. "Five people have died in this town in the last two weeks. We may have an Asian gang trying to take over the streets. Ron Klesczewski is out on indefinite leave; I've got media people jamming the halls like vagrants; and now you want to disappear and play federal task force with the VSP.

"As the one person who has nothing to gain from this scheme, I don't buy it. To me, it means another man lost whose salary I still have to meet. ATF and FBI and all the other alphabet soups have regional offices precisely so they can inherit cases like this from over-worked, understaffed, poorly funded outfits like ours."

He turned his attention to me. "And I don't agree that by working with the feds you'll solve our problems here any quicker. You could do that best by staying put and working from this end while the feds work from theirs—that's the sort of cooperation that'll do us the most good."

He got to his feet and crossed over to the window, propping his elbow on the high cement sill. When he spoke again, his voice had lost some of its edge. "I'm not denying you have real concerns for the town's welfare if this case isn't properly handled. But there may not be a hell of a lot any of us can do about that—that's the reality of the system. We do what we can, and then we let it go, which—I'll admit if you won't—is not something you do well.

"I'm also wondering about the effects of this shooting on you. As far as I know, you haven't reacted to it at all. You shouldn't be here now. You should be at home with Gail, like Ron is with his wife, or spilling those overly controlled guts of yours to a department-paid shrink."

I felt hammered by this. Tony had suddenly diverted the discussion onto a totally different path, reducing my advocacy to some sort of psychological avoidance of reality.

I couldn't find anything to say to him that wouldn't bolster his argument and make me sound defensive, so I stayed silent, trying to sense through my own anger if he might've been right.

Tony removed his glasses and rubbed his eyes. "Look, we all agree on one thing: We probably won't have this case for much longer. Why don't we do it by the numbers—keep working on it for a couple of more days, at least until we get some feedback on the inquiries we've sent? Maybe by then we'll have found something juicy enough to make the FBI really take notice."

"Sounds good to me," Derby quickly answered and rose to his feet.

I got up also, nodding in agreement. Tony, in an effort to make amends, added with feigned hopefulness, "That's probably what'll happen. We're due for a break."

"Right," Derby said from the door. "We'll kick it around later."

I made to follow him out, but Tony stopped me. "Joe."

"What?" I said, not looking back, unsure of what he'd hit me with next.

"You all right on this?" he asked, his voice softened by concern.

"Sure," I answered, my earlier anger sapped by the knowledge that we were both merely twisting in the same stressful breeze.

"I got a call from *Time* magazine an hour ago. They're going to use this in a cover article on violence in rural America. They want a list of people they should talk to."

I turned then and watched him standing by the window, the TV trucks outside as a backdrop.

He crossed over to his desk and sat down heavily. "I know I took a cheap shot at you just then, but I am worried. If we screw this up, it'll be open season on the entire department. With the networks, *Time* magazine, and who-knows-who-else zeroing in, our people'll be made to look like total hicks. I just don't want to feed that."

I crossed the room and sat back down. "They may be better at protecting themselves than you think."

He made a face as if tasting something sour. "Maybe."

He put the fingertips of both hands up to his temples and gave himself a three-second massage, his eyes shut. Then he hunched forward, put his elbows on his desk, and looked up at me. "I'm not dead against you on this. I just don't want to jump the gun. I want it clear to everybody we know what to do and how to do it."

I got up and returned to the door, satisfied that we'd cleared the air.

Tony stopped me for the second time. "Joe."

"Yeah?"

"Things okay with us?"

I leered malevolently at him and tapped the side of my head. "You know me, Tony—'Never Forget. Never Forgive.' Have a nice day."

He shook his head, but at least he was smiling back.

Chapter Eleven

I found Sammie Martens tucked away in her cubicle in the far corner of the detective squad room.

"Everyone else at lunch?"

She looked up at me in surprise. Small, athletic, and occasionally quick to temper, she was to me the most intriguing member of my crew. As experienced as Ron Klesczewski, she was blessed with more boldness, imagination, and perseverance. She could also be a victim of her own determination, however, pursuing a lead to the point of obsession. But she was utterly dedicated and, in her own tough way, caring.

"What are you doing here? Didn't Gail come down last night?" she asked.

"She's still here," I answered vaguely, not interested in repeating the polemics I'd just gone through with Tony Brandt. "I hear you're trying to ID the two shooters that were with Henry Lam."

She scowled at the litter of scribbled notes on her desk. "Yeah, and getting nowhere fast. I can't find anything on them, they don't appear in our new photo album, nobody at the two crash pads in town will admit knowing anything about them, and the car out front was registered to Lam. Willy, Dennis, and J.P. are out showing mug shots to all the restaurants and motels, but until we pin names or DOBs to 'em"—she gestured to the computer terminal across the room—"that thing's going to be pretty useless."

"You've got Lam's name."

That only increased her frustration. "Yeah, right, but the only record I found anywhere on him says he's the lawful owner of a Massachusetts car."

"Any distinguishing marks on the bodies of the other two? Tattoos, maybe?" I asked.

"The youngest-looking one had a tattoo of a panther crawling down his left arm, and the letters 'CTG' inscribed in the web of his hand, between the thumb and index."

"How old do you think he was?"

She shook her head. "I don't know. I suppose he could be in his twenties."

"On the off chance he was underage, put a description out to all juvenile-detention facilities. Maybe you'll get lucky. Also, you could try running those letters by the various antigang task forces, organizations, and whatnot. They might stand for some known group."

"Or his mother's initials," she muttered bitterly.

My mind wandered back to my earlier conversation with Derby and Brandt, and the potential usefulness of any federal violations. "Anything on the weapons they used?"

She shook her head. "Nothing so far. They're not on any hot sheets I've consulted. I still have feelers out, though. It's all pretty early yet . . . plus, any inquiry from Brattleboro, Vermont, pretty much gets hind tit, especially from the feds."

"It would help if these gangs weren't so mobile," I added. "You might want to push the Canadians for something on Lam. When I talked to him during that traffic stop, he implied he lived around a lot of snow. That may have meant Boston, but you never know. What about Vince Sharkey? Have we traced his last movements?"

Her expression brightened. "We found out where *his* gun came from, at least, and there were a couple more at his apartment—all from the Paul's Guns and Ammo heist last year. Willy was working on why Vince went after Vu when he did, but I asked him to help the others on the restaurant-motel detail. He's pretty pissed off about that—just so you're prepared."

"Don't worry about it," I counseled. "What had he dug up till then?"

"That Vince was sniffing glue and blowing dope all last night with some friends, getting weirder as he went. But he talked more about doing you in than Michael Vu." She gave me a suddenly wry expression. "Of course, you have to consider our sources—Christ knows what he really said."

"Interesting that while I yanked Vince's chain about Sonny, he went after Michael Vu. I didn't even mention Vu."

Sammie looked at me, not knowing what to say.

I checked my watch and then added nonchalantly, "You interested in being my second till Ron comes back? He's taking a few days off. Might help you in dealing with Willy."

She didn't try hiding her pleasure. "You bet." She hesitated then, and asked, "Is Ron okay?"

"Between you and me? I don't know. Wendy says he took it pretty hard. It might take some time."

The sudden silence emphasized the unasked questions, and the equally elusive answers. "Has anyone interviewed Peter Leung yet?" I finally asked.

"VSP did, but only about the shooting," she said quietly.

"Okay—if anyone asks, that's where I'll be."

*   *   *

Peter Leung was still in the hospital, the focus of a lot of medical, legal, and media attention. I doubted he'd be in any better state of mind than when I'd seen him last, when a real gun was to his head, but I was hoping he'd remember me as the one who'd pulled him clear and helped save his wife from further harm.

I found him on one of the upper floors, in a private room guarded by a state trooper, but knowing the trooper personally, I was allowed inside with no more ceremony than a nod of the head.

I knew from the medical report that Leung's right femur had been broken by one of the bullets, and his right forearm grazed by another, so it was no surprise to see him trussed up in plaster, with his leg in traction. He gave me a forlorn expression as I entered. His wife was sitting quietly in a far corner of the room.

"Mr. and Mrs. Leung? Joe Gunther—good to see you again. I was wondering if I could ask you a few questions."

"You spoke to the other officer?" Leung asked hopefully, obviously wishing I'd quickly nod and disappear. His wife merely watched me in silence.

"Yes, I did, but he's interested in the shooting. I'm interested in what led up to it." I didn't add that the state-police investigator had found both Leung and his wife incredibly frustrating to interview.

I pulled up a chair and sat next to the bed. "I realize all this makes you uncomfortable, and I will try to respect your privacy as much as possible, but we've got to have some clear answers from you."

He remained silent.

"You were seen removing a large amount of cash from the bank. Did the men in your house threaten to harm your wife if you didn't pay them the money?"

"To kill her."

"Why do you think they picked on you?"

"They thought I keep our money at home. Many Chinese do."

"So they were hoping to rob your house while you were at work?"

"Yes. They called me when they found no safe."

"Does the name Henry Lam sound familiar?"

"No."

"Do you know who the other two men were?"

"I had never seen them before."

"Did any of them refer to one another by name?"

"No."

I turned to his wife. "Mrs. Leung? Did you hear any names mentioned?"

She slowly raised her eyes to her husband, and I realized then that I'd merely increased their anxiety with no counterbalancing reassurances. The fear on her face was as real now as I remembered it being twenty-four hours earlier. *No* was all I was going to hear unless I tried a different approach.

"Let me say something first," I added quickly. "I know a little about what you've both been through, and I know you were threatened with reprisals if you spoke to the police. But things have changed since then—one is that all three of the men who made those threats are now dead. And because of the shooting, everyone knows what happened anyway. The general assumption will be that because the police are involved, the identity of the people who terrorized you will have come from police sources—criminal records, fingerprints, and the like. No one will know that you gave us any information. Do you both understand what I'm saying?"

"We will not be involved?" Peter Leung asked. "We will not appear in court or be mentioned in the newspapers?"

"Not as sources of information, and there's no reason for you ever to appear in court, since there's no case to try. Your wife's probably already told you that the newspapers published your names this morning—but only as victims of a sensational crime. As far as I know, you've refused to speak to them, and you can continue to do so. None of them will ever find out that we've spoken.

"I should warn you about one thing, though," I added, wishing I didn't feel honor bound to do so. "If you do mention other people by name to me—people who are still alive—then that could make you a witness in a legal case we might bring against that person at some future date. I am hoping you'll overcome your fears and be as forthright as possible, but I don't want you to think I'm trying to trick you in any way. Of course, your best defense is to help us catch them. But I won't push you on that."

I saw them exchange glances. Peter Leung then nodded slightly. "We will try to help. This is our new country. We have done well here and we would like to repay our debt. But we come from a country where the police are not our friends, and where to speak to them is to call for your own death."

"I understand that," I answered. "Does this mean you do have some additional information?"

"Yes. The leader was called Henry by the others. He didn't only wish to rob us. He wanted me to use my business to clean his money. The robbery was to show he was serious, and he was angry I had no safe."

I felt a tingle of excitement at the nape of my neck. From the research I'd gleaned from inter-agency intelligence bulletins, I knew that standard Asian home invasions are fast and uncomplicated, and usually conducted by people from far outside the region. It was one of the routine ploys that Asian gangs used to avoid detection—exploiting the loose, and therefore flawed, informational-exchange systems between law-enforcement agencies, counting on the fact that any fingerprints or identifications made at the scene wouldn't find a match elsewhere for months or even years.

The revelation that this attack had been made to stimulate a local money-laundering operation broke that mold. It indicated a long-term interest in a specific area by criminal elements, and introduced the possibility of a conspiracy, which could be used as a selling point to the feds.

I tried to keep the satisfaction out of my voice. "Was Henry the leader, or did you feel someone else might be pulling the strings?"

Leung's voice was definite. "No. They referred to another—a *dai ca*, which means 'big brother.'"

"*How* did they refer to him?" I asked.

He gave me an apologetic look. "I am sorry. I don't speak Vietnamese—just a few words."

That was a disappointment. "They only spoke Vietnamese?"

"No—a little English, too, but not very good. That's how they told me about the money cleaning."

"So when they spoke to each other, you didn't understand anything?"

"Very little."

"Did you catch any names beyond 'Henry'?"

Leung nodded, his mood improved from just a few minutes earlier. "Yes. One was called An, and the other Ut—those are first names."

"Which one had the tattoo?"

"Ut."

"Did anyone refer to Michael Vu, or Sonny? Or anyone else?"

Leung shook his head.

"Did any of them make any phone calls from your house?"

"Yes—the man Henry did, a few minutes before you arrived."

A few minutes before Michael Vu arrived, I thought sourly, knowing the Leungs' phone bill would reflect no local calls.

I let out a sigh, my earlier eagerness tempered. "Is there anything else you can tell me?"

"I regret, no."

"Nothing was said to you other than what you've just told me?"

"Nothing besides the instructions to go to the bank. The man Henry bragged that Brattleboro was going to be a pot of gold."

"Did he elaborate? Brag about other people he'd attacked?"

Leung shook his head sadly. "I am sorry."

I rose to my feet. "Don't be. You've been more help than you know."

*   *   *

The high-school cafeteria was jammed with students, their laughter and noise filling the large room. I stood with my back to a corner and scanned the crowd carefully. I finally spotted Amy Lee sitting at a middle table, talking quietly with another student. She looked better, not as skinny or forlorn. Her expressions were still muted—she played no role in the cheerful cacophony that vibrated off the walls—but the haunted look of a victim was gone.

I didn't want to embarrass or scare her by a direct approach, so I asked a passing student to tell her that I'd be waiting to speak with her in the library down the hallway.

She took several minutes to appear at the door. It was immediately obvious my attempt at diplomacy hadn't worked too well. The haunted look was back.

I got up and came to her, taking her elbow and gently steering her to a table far from where anyone else was sitting. "Hi, Amy. How've you been?"

"Okay." Her voice was a monotone, barely above a murmur.

I pulled out a chair. "Have a seat."

She followed my suggestion robotically, and sat staring at the table-top between us.

"Have things gotten better since you went to Women for Women?"

"A little."

"I thought they might. They're good people. Are you still going?"

"Yes."

"Do your parents know about it yet?"

She looked up at me abruptly, her eyes narrowed. "Are you going to tell them?"

"Not at all. That's a private matter between you and them. I'm just happy you're taking care of yourself."

She didn't answer, and went back to looking at the tabletop.

"Did you hear about the shooting yesterday?" I asked.

"Yes."

"Did you see the newspaper pictures of the four men who were killed?"

She shook her head.

"I think one of them was among the three who attacked you. If it's okay, I'd like to show you a photo of him." I pulled the shot of Henry Lam—the one that had made her hysterical earlier—and cradled it in my palm, awaiting her decision.

It was a calculated risk, which was one reason I'd taken the time to watch her in the cafeteria. I'd wanted to see how she was behaving on her own, away from adult scrutiny, and what I'd seen had been encouraging.

She didn't disappoint me. She slowly nodded, raised her eyes to the photo I laid before her, and murmured yes.

I took the picture back and put it in my pocket. "I'm sorry, Amy. If it's any comfort, this also means you'll never have to worry about him again."

She didn't respond.

"Could you answer a few questions about that night? If you don't want to, that's fine. And if you just want to answer some and not others, that's okay, too. Would that be all right?"

"Okay."

That was the first obstacle cleared. Whether it was the passage of time, the influence of her counseling, or the fact that her parents had given her such little support, Amy Lee no longer seemed so concerned with her father's wish to keep silent, which was another reason I was here, and not trying to talk to him again.

"You told me there were three men that night. Is that correct?"

"Yes."

"Was the man whose photo I just showed you the leader?"

"It was him." Neither her voice nor her posture had changed. It was as if I were talking to a soul hovering just outside the body before me.

"Did you catch his name?"

"Henry," she said without hesitation.

"And the other two?"

"One they called Tri. The other one I don't know—he never got near me."

I let that last statement go, not wishing to cut too close to what we both knew had happened to her. "Did they speak in Vietnamese or Chinese?"

She looked up at me, surprised. "Both, and a little English. They spoke Vietnamese to each other. Henry spoke Chinese to my mother."

"How about to your father?"

"Henry spoke English to him. He seemed proud of that—he bragged that he spoke good English."

"Did he?" I asked, remembering my own encounter with him.

"It was dirty." A tone of contempt had crept into her voice.

"You speak Chinese?"

"Cantonese."

"And Vietnamese?"

She shook her head.

"Did they say anything besides giving you orders? Any references to other places or people or events?"

"No."

I reached into my pocket and extracted a thick wad of pictures— mug shots, surveillance shots—all of which we'd accumulated over the past week. Included among them were the photographs I'd shown John Crocker.

I handed them to Amy like a deck of cards. "Could you give these a look? See if you recognize anyone else."

She solemnly did as I asked, slowly and methodically going through the photos, never pausing throughout. She finally shook her head and laid the deck before me.

"Nobody?" I asked.

She looked me straight in the eye. "No. I'm sorry."

I broke the rules a little then, extracting Michael Vu's and Truong Van Loc's pictures specifically. "How 'bout them?"

Again, she shook her head. "No."

I returned the stack to my pocket. "Not to worry. What did the three men want that night? Money?"

"They took money, but they wanted more. Henry wanted to talk to my dad."

It was an almost imperceptible shift, but I sensed her beginning to relax a bit, as if the realization that she spoke better English than had her attacker endowed her with a hint more pride and self-worth than she'd been feeling just moments before.

"About what?" I asked of her last comment.

"I don't know exactly. Part of their talk happened in another room, and mom was crying a lot, and screaming . . ." She hesitated, as if collecting her courage, before adding matter-of-factly, "They'd already raped me. It was near the end."

I was impressed by her frankness—a good sign that she, if no one else in her family, was dealing with reality. "Did you hear any of what they discussed?"

She took a deep breath and seemed to think a moment. A furrow appeared between her eyes as she looked up at me. "I remember something about credit cards. Does that make sense?"

I smiled and squeezed her hand. "Yes, it does. When you've been out shopping with either one of your parents, have you seen them use credit cards?"

"Sure. Not often, though. My mom always pays cash."

"What card does your dad use?"

"It's a Visa . . . I think."

"Okay—going back to the night of the attack, what did they take from the house? Anything?"

"My dad has a safe in his bedroom. They made him open that up. I think it had a lot of money, and maybe some jewelry."

"Any pieces you could describe?"

"There was a pendant my mom let me see sometimes—gold and jade. It had the Chinese characters for her family name—Ho—engraved in the stone. I'm pretty sure they stole that."

I opened my note pad to a blank page and pushed it over to her. "Can you draw it, along with the name?" I asked.

She took my pen and quickly drew the piece of jewelry, returning the pad with an apologetic smile. "It's not very good, but that's pretty close. The name's right, at least—she taught me how to do that."

"How's she doing, by the way?"

A flicker of irritation crossed her face. "Who knows? She doesn't say anything anymore. She cooks and does the housework and stares out the window and cries a lot."

"And your dad?"

"He's changed, too. When he looks at us, I think he's sad, but sometimes, when he thinks he's alone, he looks angry."

"Do you think everything's going all right at the restaurant?"

Again, she gave me that quick, slightly surprised double look. "I don't think so. He stays later at work than he used to, and he doesn't seem to like it much anymore."

"Sounds like home isn't much fun, either. How're you holding up?"

She shrugged. "I got my friends, and dad never did much with me anyhow." She paused, and then placed her hand against her cheek. Her eyes slowly lost their focus, and she went back to looking at the polished wooden surface between us. "I miss my mom, though."

Chapter Twelve

I sat in my car and watched Sally Javits receiving her dripping-wet wards at the exit of the car-wash tunnel. She'd motioned impatiently to the driver to proceed to a line painted on the asphalt, and then she and several others would launch themselves at the vehicle, thrashing it with towels and chamois cloths with all the enthusiasm of an anger-venting therapy group. Several times, I thought I could see a look of alarm growing on the distant faces of the drivers, just before the buff-'n-shine crew abruptly withdrew, turning their backs contemptuously, to let the car timidly roll away.

This was her latest job, to be held, if she kept to her statistical norm, for a month at the most. It followed a string of similar employments— washing dishes, mopping floors, sloshing coffee at broken-down donut shops. Chances were always fifty-fifty that she'd get bored and leave before getting fired.

Still, she worked, albeit erractically, as did many of her streetwise cohorts, which is what distinguished a town like Brattleboro from the urban battlefields that monopolized the nightly news. We'd been spared the full-time preoccupation with drugs, violence, and general hopelessness that crippled those other places. So far.

I was parked inconspicuously down the street, waiting for Javits's shift to end, and for a private moment in which to draw her attention.

A couple of cars later, a new team sauntered onto the receiving apron, replacing Sally's crew in a ritualized exchange of physical and verbal insults. A few rags flew through the air, a sponge or two was thrown at a ducking head, and then she was walking down the sidewalk after punching out, her square, compact body straining the fabric of her damp uniform T-shirt.

I started up my engine and slowly drove up alongside her as she walked. "Hey, Sally."

She barely glanced at me, her face still flushed from the enjoyment of her boisterous departure. I was happy to see she was in a good mood. "Hey, yourself, Gunther."

"Got time for a chat?"

"'Bout what?"

"I'll buy you dinner."

She stopped and gave me a dubious look. "Where?"

"Your call."

Her face cleared. "Yeah? No shit. How 'bout Toney's?" She pointed to a tiny grocery store on the corner where Elm Street slopes away from Canal to cross a bridge over the Whetstone Brook. The store served grinders from a rear deli counter, the quality of which was famous all over town. A good many of the department's patrol division considered this an altar of affordable *haute cuisine*.

"You got it," I agreed and parked by the curb.

She ordered meatball, and I, despite knowing Gail was making something at home, had a bag of chips and a Coke. After receiving our food, Sally led the way outside and headed back up the street toward the recently opened Little Caesar's. "Wanna dine with a view?" she cracked over her shoulder.

She entered the fast-food restaurant's parking lot, walked to the rear, and plopped herself down on one of the six-foot-long concrete wheel stops marking the lot's boundary, using the bumper of a parked car as a backrest.

"Wicked, huh?" She gestured out ahead of us as I settled down next to her. The ground fell away precipitously at our feet as a fifty-foot embankment went in search of the winding Whetstone Brook far below us. There was a wide field between the foot of the grade and the water's edge, choked with brush and weeds, strewn with trash and garbage, and occasionally clotted with larger items like a stray grocery cart or a gutted sofa. On the distant bank was a holding yard for a lumber company, with metal-roofed sheds and bundled stacks of boards on pallets, and beyond that lay most of lower downtown Brattleboro, climbing, street by parallel street, back up the more gradual opposing slope.

It was the kind of gritty, blue-collar urban view to make a tough kid's spirits soar. I looked out the corner of my eye at her pleased expression, her mouth already smeared with tomato sauce, and couldn't resist a matching smile of my own. "Yeah, wicked."

She took another wolfish bite and spoke through her food. "So, you and Ron almost bought the farm. That why you here?"

She remained, in her fashion, a businesswoman. "Yeah," I answered. "Did you or anyone else know a home invasion was in the works?"

Her chewing slowed. I could sense the caution lights going on in her head. "That's what those people do. It's not the first time it's happened. You guys just walked into it."

"So did Vince."

She stopped chewing altogether and looked at me. "What's that supposed to mean?"

"We figured something was going down—that's why we followed Leung home. How did Vince know where to show up?"

In point of fact, we knew Sharkey had been watching Vu. What bothered me was his timing, which smacked of a double setup. The only catch was that, in order to make it work, the person pulling the strings had to have known about the home invasion.

The sandwich forgotten, she twisted around to face me bodily, wiping her mouth with the back of her hand. Her eyes were narrow with suspicion. "You wanna shit or get off the pot?"

I gave her a scenario I thought she might accept, and maybe even confirm. "Vince was suffocating under Benny, but he didn't have the balls to do anything about it—until Sonny showed up, or at least Michael Vu in Sonny's name. A deal was cut. The Asians would remove Benny if Vince set him up. In exchange, Vince would replace his boss, and then allow Sonny a large hunk of the local action, something Benny had refused to do."

"And you think they planned to off Vince?" Sally reinterpreted. "A double cross?"

"Maybe," I countered, and edged closer to where I wanted to be.

"And maybe not. As things turned out, Vince almost killed Vu. If it hadn't been for us, he might've succeeded, even as high as he was. So if Vince was set up, it means someone was after him and Vu both— or at least didn't care which one got whacked."

Sally turned away, ostensibly to face the view, but I thought in fact to avoid making eye contact. "So what?" she asked rhetorically.

Her studied vagueness was encouraging. "C'mon, you're one of four or five people at most who make things happen in this town."

She snapped back around to glare at me. "What the fuck're you gettin' at? I don't have anything to do with the slopes, and I didn't whack Vince. He was a loser."

I smiled guilelessly at her. "You and I know that. Somebody didn't."

"The fuckin' Chinese," she tried again. "If they set Benny up, why not Vince, too?"

I shook my head. "Using Vu as bait? Doesn't make sense."

There was a prolonged pause as she stared out at her view. Finally, she let out a sigh and chucked the rest of her meal down the embankment, paper wrapped and all. We both watched it tumble and roll, disgorging its crimson contents as it went.

What she said then exposed her confusion. "You're sayin' somebody put Vince up against the chinks, knowing you guys might take 'em both out?"

"I'm saying Benny's death created a vacuum that more than one person wanted to fill. Vince spent the entire night winding himself up and could barely see straight when he pulled that gun on Vu. We talked to the people who got high with him. They don't think the party was Vince's idea—they felt the glue and dope were supplied by someone else, and that Vince was as happy as they were to get it. You got any ideas about that?"

She made a face and spat into the dirt between her tattered sneakers. "You could ask Alfie Brewster. He and Vince didn't get along, and he sure doesn't like what's goin' on."

"You think he could've manipulated Vince into confronting Vu?"

"He's a smart guy, and he's running scared as shit now. After the shoot-out, first thing I heard was Alfie had called in some buddies from Springfield, Mass., to back him up."

"They here now?" I asked, not bothering to hide my surprise. If she was right, Brewster's reaction would fit a man whose plans had backfired. Also, if Vu and Brewster both knew that the latter had tumbled to the home invasion ahead of time, then Vu would now have good cause to go after Brewster.

"Oh, yeah. Alfie's takin' good care of 'em—for as long as he can. His stock is a little low."

His "stock," we both knew, primarily meant girls, most of them very young.

"So what happens when the entertainment runs out?" I asked.

"Who the shit knows? They either leave town or they start throwing their weight around. Alfie's just adding to the problem, if you ask me."

I tried for some specifics. "And what is the problem, from where you stand?"

She shook her head and then looked at me steadily. "You're not going to like it. The other reason Alfie got some troops is that Michael Vu is really ripped over what happened. Losin' his boys like that makes him look bad—there already been a few jokes about it. You might want to check out Lenny Roberts if you don't believe me. He gave Vu some lip, and Vu damn near took his head off."

"Hit him?"

My enthusiasm gave me away. She smiled bitterly. "Forget it. If you want to get Lenny to press for assault 'n battery, you'll have to find him first, and then you'll have to convince him that talking to you isn't the same as a death wish. He was scared shitless, and so are most of the rest of us. Michael Vu isn't fuckin' around anymore."

Her eyes widened suddenly as she thought of something else. "You know, all your bitchin' and moanin' about who's setting up who . . . You were the one who yanked Vince's chain. Got him so pissed off he couldn't see straight. But now that he tried to whack Vu, you're running around planting ideas that somebody else set him up. Scared they're going to figure out you fucked up big time?"

But she missed her target. Instead of hitting what was in fact a guilty soft spot, she brought back what I'd mentioned earlier to Sammie. I hadn't set Vince against Michael Vu. I'd set him against Sonny. So what had made Vince go after Vu?

"Sally," I asked her, "have you ever actually met Sonny?"

She looked away again. "Sure."

Her brevity told me otherwise. The trick was going to be forcing her to admit she was lying without making her look bad. I faked a surprised reaction. "That makes you the only one in town who has— the only one who can pick him out of a mug book, or prove he was in Bratt when this whole thing comes to trial."

"I didn't say I met him face to face," she snarled, her face flushing. "It was on the phone . . . once," she added for safety's sake.

"It's been Vu from then on?"

"Yeah." She hesitated, and then said belligerently, "And from what I hear, you better hope you don't meet Sonny, either."

"What's that mean?"

She stood up, suddenly restless to get away from this conversation. "That means, Joe Gunther, that the best way for a guy like Sonny to take back the juice is to whack a cop."

*   *   *

One of the selling points of the house that Gail and I had bought together was a rear deck with a huge maple tree growing through the middle of it. During the winter, we, or lately I alone, had sat by the sliding-glass door of the living room and watched the snow cluster around the tree in a perfectly flat plane, setting it off so that it looked like a bonsai arrangement with hormone problems, towering overhead, white and crystalline, isolated in its own natural beauty.

I was sitting beneath it now, in the pink afterlife of the setting sun, listening to a soft breeze rustling its new leaves, and keeping out of sight of the two cars parked on the street out front. Both of them contained reporters from out of town. They'd shouted questions at me after I'd parked in the driveway, but Gail's earlier warnings to them had obviously been dire enough to keep them from actually stepping onto the property.

Gail came out with a soda water, and a Coke for me. "You look like you had a rough day." She nodded toward the road. "Were there a lot of them at the Municipal Building?" She stretched out onto the lawn chair next to mine and tilted her head back to enjoy the branches above us.

"They've made the central hallway look like a panhandlers' convention. Every time any of us cuts from one side of the building to the other, we run the gauntlet. Tony's scheduled two update sessions a day, upstairs in the selectmen's room, but it doesn't seem to make any difference."

She reached out and took my hand in hers. "They came by here so often, I finally went to the library to work. What's the mood like at the police department?"

"Not good. You see the paper?"

She nodded. "It's in the kitchen."

"Willy said the only section not covering the shooting is the funnies page. He's not far off. They feel like they're under a microscope, and they don't like the second-guessing that's already started—excessive force, endangering the public, all the rest. There's a rumor that one of the Leung's neighbors is considering a lawsuit because of the stress we put them through. I had a meeting with the squad this afternoon— just to make sure everyone's on track—and you could've cut the air with a knife. Only Dennis was normal . . . Oh, and Ron's on administrative leave. Seems like the shooting totally pulled the rug out from under him."

"Have you talked to him?"

"I tried to—spoke with Wendy instead. Anyway, it means we're a man down." I took a long swig from my Coke. I didn't bother mentioning Sally Javits's last words of warning.

"I take it the case isn't going too well, either?" Gail commented gently.

"I'll give you an example. There may be a crooked credit-card angle tied into the Thomas Lee home invasion, so I called the investigation branches of some of the major card companies and told them I was worried about a possible fraud taking place at the Blue Willow Restaurant in Brattleboro, Vermont. I could almost hear them yawning. They told me—though not in so many words—that certain losses are built into the budget, and that any fraud emanating from a Podunk backwater like ours wouldn't amount to much. They took down the information and thanked me very much, but you know what that means.

"Any other time, we get one dead body, we know pretty much what to do about it. Now we've got five and we're basically nowhere. And on top of that," I concluded, "I'm no longer sure the guy I've been after isn't a figment of somebody else's imagination."

"I've lost you, Joe," Gail said, smiling at my rambling.

"No one's ever set eyes on the mysterious Mr. Sonny. I'm beginning to think Michael Vu made him up."

The phone rang inside the house. Gail moved to answer it, but I got to my feet first. "I thought that damned thing was off the hook."

She gave me a warning look. "Dinner'll be ready in five minutes, okay?"

It was Dennis DeFlorio. "Hi, boss, sorry to call you at home, but I got something I thought you'd like to hear right away. Remember you asked me to look into Michael Vu's background in California, for something beyond his rap sheet?"

I shifted my weight impatiently. I'd received this update right before I'd gone out to meet Sally Javits. "Yes."

"I think I might have found something. It doesn't actually have anything to do with Vu, but Sammie was real excited about it." He paused, as if he'd just given me something I could work with.

"Keep going, Dennis," I encouraged him, used to his style.

"Right, well, after you left this afternoon, I got hold of a cop who'd dealt with Vu. He wasn't real helpful—friendly enough, but kind of busy. I got to talking to him about what had happened here, you know, trading war stories and stuff, and I mentioned Henry Lam. He jumped on the name, said he'd dealt with Lam as a juvie. 'Course, it was a long time ago and, like I said, he was busy, but he told me to talk to a caseworker who'd handled Lam early on, from when he first came to America. He said this caseworker was super involved with the Asians—that since he was retired now and a regular civilian again, he'd probably be free to give you the lowdown on Lam and maybe some of his buddies."

"Up-to-date information?" I asked, my interest caught. Lam's only official appearance in the information network—that of his license registration—had been on the East Coast. This sudden California connection created a potential historical link to both Michael Vu and Truong Van Loc.

"I guess. He hasn't been retired long."

"This is good news, Dennis. Nice job. Did you or Sammie call him?"

There was a predictable pause on the other end. The response, when it came, fit Dennis like a glove. Having started out well, he was unsure of how to proceed. "No . . . Sammie told me to, since she's kind of swamped, and I was about to, but then I figured if this guy is as good as the cop said he was, you'd probably want to talk to him anyway. You know—ask him things I wouldn't think of, maybe."

I smiled at the receiver and shook my head, all traces of my earlier depression washed away. "What's his name?"

"Jason Brown." He gave me the number. "That's a business number. He works full time as a hospice volunteer now."

Gail appeared in the doorway as I was writing it down.

"Dennis," I said, "if Willy's around, put him on, will you?"

Kunkle came on the line a minute later, sounding peevish. "What?" It was more of a statement than a question.

"Relax," I told him. "You'll like this. Find Alfie Brewster. Sally Javits thinks Brewster might've set up both Vu and Sharkey for that shoot-out. Find out if he supplied Vince with the goodies for last night's smoke-'n-dope bash and if he knew about the home invasion ahead of time, okay?"

Predictably, Willy sounded suddenly more cheerful. "Sure."

"But be careful," I warned him. "Sally also told me he's surrounded himself with hired help."

Kunkle merely laughed and hung up.

"No dinner?" Gail asked from the door.

"Maybe. I'd like to see if I can contact this character first, if only to set up an appointment." I checked my watch. "He lives in California— should still be at work." I passed along briefly what Dennis had told me.

"Can I listen in? Sounds interesting."

I hesitated a moment. It wasn't a request she'd ever made in the past, nor was it even remotely within department rules. On the other hand, she and Tony Brandt were my two best sounding boards, and with Tony in his present mood, I wasn't sure how much I could lean on him. Besides, I rationalized, with Gail's ambitions to be a prosecutor, she was almost a part of the family.

"Okay," I said.

She disappeared to turn off the stove while I dialed long distance. By the time she returned, a portable phone in hand, I was waiting for Jason Brown to come on the line.

"Hello?" His voice was deep, quiet, and curiously comforting—the voice of an older man.

"Mr. Brown, my name is Joe Gunther. I'm a lieutenant with the Brattleboro Police Department in Vermont."

"Hello, Lieutenant, what can I do for you?"

I found the lack of usual chitchat about Vermont and its quaint and provincial reputation—or my profession—reassuring.

"I'm on a bit of a fishing expedition, really. Did you ever have dealings with a young Asian calling himself Henry Lam?"

"Yes, I did," came the immediate answer. "What's he been up to?"

It was a fair question—Jason Brown didn't know anything about me. But I also didn't know him—or whether he and Lam had enjoyed a lasting friendship. Telling him right off the bat that I had killed him seemed a little impolitic.

I hedged a bit. "I'm afraid he's dead."

"Ah." Brown's voice trailed off, and I heard the sense of loss in the brief silence. "I thought that might happen."

"You had some trouble with him?" I asked diplomatically.

"Not personally," Brown answered, "but he was more prone to the wrong sort of influence than some of them. He wasn't very old when we met—just nine—but he'd had a terrible time of it, and had already been in trouble a few times. Meeting him was a little like seeing someone just beyond your reach, sinking out of sight underwater."

I could tell from Gail's expression that she was as struck by the image, and the sympathy in Brown's voice, as I was.

"How did he die?" came the inevitable question.

The truth would have been simply, "In a shoot-out with the police," but I took a gamble that a little generosity would serve me well here.

"I'm afraid I had to shoot him. He opened up on me with a machine gun."

The response was unexpected. "Are you all right?"

"Oh, yes. Some of my clothes got slightly shot up, but I'm fine. He was part of a home-invasion team, and my partner and I sort of stumbled into them. We don't know who the other two were—they died, too. We're trying to figure out where they came from, and why they were in our neck of the woods."

"Yes, I don't guess Brattleboro is much like L.A. Tell me something, these other two boys, were they younger than Henry?"

"They certainly looked it—mid-teens, I would guess."

I could almost visualize him nodding at the other end of the line, reflectively taking his time.

I opened my mouth to say something, but Gail shook her head.

She was right. The next thing Brown said was, "Maybe I should tell you what I know about Henry Lam."

I smiled at Gail and merely answered, "Please."

"When I met him years ago, he was already as tough as nails, and God knows he should've been, considering everything he'd been through. He was Vietnamese by birth, but of Chinese heritage, which in Vietnam is a little like being black in the South in the fifties. After the Communist takeover, the fact that his father had been with the South Vietnamese Army made life pretty difficult for the whole family. Henry was only a year old when the US was booted out of there in '74, and his father tried to get by for about six years afterward.

"Around 1980, the whole family—Henry, his parents, and two sisters, one older, one younger—cashed in whatever savings they had and paid some crook for space on a boat heading out. Not surprisingly, things didn't go well. It took me a while to get him to open up—although 'open up' is probably the wrong phrase with him—but I eventually found out what happened.

"The boat was just a small fishing rig—not designed to hold more than maybe ten people at most—and there must've been more than fifty on board. But the plan wasn't to sail too far anyway. The boat owner was in cahoots with local pirates. About a day or two out to sea, he killed the engine, claimed it had broken down, and had them sit there in open water while he faked a repair job. Eventually, the pirates showed up on another, much bigger boat, and worked them over good and proper. Everyone was robbed, virtually all the women were raped, including Henry's mother and older sister, and all the men and really small children—and Henry's father and the other sister—were executed and thrown overboard."

"Jesus," I murmured.

"Right. Hell of a thing for a seven-year-old kid. Anyway, the pirates took who was left with them, sold the women off as prostitutes—Henry never saw his mother and sister again—and were planning to sell the young males as slaves. At that point, things suddenly improved. There was a raid on the place Henry was being held, and the authorities placed him in a refugee holding camp for people hoping to come to the States."

Brown paused a moment. "Is this more than you want to know?"

"No, no," I answered quickly, amazed at my luck. "Go ahead."

"Okay. Well, the camp was the pits—a training school for crooks and perverts, but it also provided one of the most effective networking systems I've ever seen. I mean, not all these camps are as bad as this one was—a lot of it depends on who's running them and which country it's in—but all of them seem to graduate refugees who keep in touch, no matter where they end up. The sense of village unity that most of these folks were born with is transferred onto the larger population of the camp. They become like family to one another. Whether they like each other or not, whether they're crooked or straight, everybody ends up connected for life. Part of it's because many of them spend years in the camps waiting for the chance to finally emigrate, but I also think it's a little like a primer course in ghetto living. The strong ones, the ones with families intact, and especially the older adults, manage to survive. But the kids like Henry are pretty much doomed to end up in what the Chinese call the Dark Root, the underworld. They've got to hang onto someone, after all, and all that's left are the slightly older, equally dispossessed male hoods. They're a tiny minority of the overall population, but because of the social dynamics, they exert an incredible influence that ties into a heritage born of centuries of either foreign domination or dictatorial rule by feudal tyrants.

"In any case, by the time Henry got to California, he was a hardened crook, living off his fellow humans, dedicated to grabbing what he could get, and—although he couldn't have articulated it—living totally without hope, resigned to having his life end violently at a moment's notice."

"How old was he when he reached California?" I asked.

"Nine. I met him less than a year later as part of my job. I was supposed to counsel and evaluate underage offenders, and then file suggestions that might help both them and the state find some common ground. Of course, almost none of the kids gave a damn anyway, and nobody in the bureaucracy either knew what my paperwork was for or had enough money to implement my recommendations. Kids like Henry just kept falling through the cracks, and getting into trouble."

"What kind of trouble?"

"Guns, drugs, gambling. Children are used as runners, lookouts, to hold contraband. The older ones know the judicial system doesn't deal with minors well, so it doesn't much matter if they get caught, since all we do is throw them back. But while Henry never played a direct role in any of the violent stuff, he saw it done often enough that he came to see it as normal behavior."

"We think the group Henry was mixed into here has ties to Montreal."

Brown laughed. "I'll guarantee it, and to New York and Boston and Falls Church and Lowell and Bismarck, North Dakota, for all I know. I'm sorry, Lieutenant. I realize you're trying to do your homework. I talk to the police a lot—or I used to—and the one thing I kept drumming into them is that they should throw out every preconception they have about organized crime when it comes to Asians. These people aren't just mobile—they're fluid, both geographically and in terms of alliances. I was always being asked, 'What about this gang?' or 'What about that leader?' or 'Is this type of tattoo significant?' But those labels will only mislead you. You'll spend all your time trying to put together Cosa Nostra–type organizational charts, and by the time you're done, none of the people you pegged down will be where they were when you started, and few of them will even have the same interrelationships. A leader in one group becomes a soldier in another. Enemies in one town become allies in another. That's what living one day at a time really means.

"It's true that there are established gangs out here—Born to Kill, Ghost Shadows, the Wah Ching, God knows how many others. Some of them have direct ties to the tongs in New York and even to the triads back in Hong Kong or Taiwan, and work almost like branches of a corporate whole. On an organizational level, they make the Mob look pathetic. But underneath that huge, interconnected, well-oiled machine, you've got dozens of nonaligned free lancers, like the people you're probably dealing with."

"I get what you're saying, Mr. Brown," I told him, familiar with much that he'd just told me. "But you said these folks keep in touch, so that no matter where they are, they've always got a place to go. If that's true, then some of the same names must keep cropping up."

"To a certain degree," he agreed cautiously, "although many of them use our difficulty with their names against us, switching them around or changing them entirely. Henry Lam obviously wasn't born with that name, for example, although it appears he kept it to the end. And we're dealing in huge numbers here—while the criminal element is small in proportion to the overall Asian population, that population is still vast—the 'overseas Chinese,' as they call them, are fifty-five-million strong—so we're talking about a criminal element of hundreds of thousands."

"Have you ever heard of Michael Vu?" I asked almost abruptly, hoping to head off a far less pertinent lecture.

"No," came the remarkably short reply.

I thought back to the name Amy Lee had given me. "How 'bout someone named Tri?"

"That's a first name—right up there with 'Bob.'"

That stung—intentionally, I thought. I didn't bother with Ut or An—the two men killed at the Leung house—and sure as hell not Sonny. "Truong Van Loc?"

"No—sorry."

"Edward Diep?"

"Lieutenant," Jason Brown answered, his voice betraying his own thinning patience, "I don't think this is going to get you anywhere. There are just under a million Vietnamese in California alone, not to mention countless Cambodians, Laotians, Chinese, Hmong, and anything else you can think of. You got lucky with Henry Lam. Given all I just told you about their mobility and numbers, I doubt we'll be able to come up with another match."

"One last name," I asked, making even Gail's eyebrows rise at my persistence. "There was a tattoo on the arm of one of the men who died with Lam, and under it were the initials CTG. Does that ring a bell?"

Brown burst out laughing. "My God, Lieutenant. You will make me eat my words, won't you? Yes, it does. Are the initials in the web of the left hand, between the thumb and index?"

"Yes," I answered, smiling with relief, "and the tattoo is of a crawling panther."

"It stands for Chinatown Gang. They operated briefly in the Bay Area, and then were either absorbed by the bigger groups or dispersed. Now that you mention it, in fact, they were sort of like the gang you're involved with—free lancers. They were trying to carve out some territory for themselves—make a name, gain some respect. That's why the tattoo—they had big ambitions to become the next Born to Kill. But if you want to find out what really made them tick, talk to Nicky Tai. He used to run with them. He's straight now—joined an uncle in the restaurant-supplies business. You'll have to deal with him gently, though. He's not a squealer. He left because Chinatown Gang collapsed and he had nowhere to go. Between you and me, he'd run out of gas, but whether he still has a sense of loyalty to that life, or he just knows that talking to cops is an unhealthy pastime, your profession will not be an asset to you."

"All right," I said as I wrote down the phone number and address he gave me.

"One last thing," Brown added, his voice full of good humor. "Just to prove there are such things as miracles. I seem to remember that, as a little kid, Henry Lam used to hang out with Chinatown Gang. He was too young to merit a tattoo, and he moved with other gangs as well, but that's another connection you might be able to use."

I took one last shot, my eagerness overriding good manners. "Do you know if one of the other gangs he hung out with was the Dragon Boys?"

"I believe it was."

I sat back in my chair, for the first time flushed with the feeling that I might be getting somewhere with all this. Michael Vu had been with the Dragon Boys also—back in the old days.

"Thanks for the information, Mr. Brown. You've been a glass of water in the desert."

There was a telling pause at the other end. "Don't make any assumptions, Lieutenant. You'll never really get a handle on all this—no more than any of the rest of us."

Chapter Thirteen

Before she left to return to law school early the next morning, Gail had persuaded me not to call Nicky Tai right off, as I'd been inclined to. She felt that Tai's possible reluctance to talk to a cop should not be too quickly dismissed. Considering the potential value of the information I was seeking, she'd cautioned, a little time spent plotting the right approach might be a wise investment. I unhappily took her point and thus arrived at the office both impatient and hopeful, an attitude that was only somewhat alleviated by the discovery that two of the TV trucks had vanished overnight, and that the building's central hallway was back to its usual abandoned self.

What J.P. Tyler had to tell me as I was finishing the night's "dailies," however—the reports filed by the graveyard shift—improved my attitude immeasurably.

"You got a second?" he asked, poking his head around the edge of my door frame.

"Sure. What's up?"

"I got the blood analysis back from Waterbury. Most of it's definitely a match with Benny—except for what we found on the counter, under that broken glass cabinet door. That belongs to somebody else."

I matched his pleased expression, recalling how dour the entire squad had been only last night. "Which means somebody's running around with a pretty nasty cut."

"And probably stitches," J.P. finished for me.

Nicky Tai was suddenly bumped from first priority. I reached for the phone to call Billy Manierre, speaking to J.P. as I did so. "Round up all the free hands you can and put them onto every doctor, ER, and clinic you can think of. We're looking for a young male Asian with a bad cut, probably on the hand or arm, but maybe the head, who came in the day Benny died or shortly thereafter. I'll tell Billy you're on the way over to raid his manpower. And find Kunkle. I want an update on what he found out about Alfie Brewster."

*   *   *

One hour into our telephone survey, Dennis DeFlorio appeared before my desk.

"Got something?" I asked him.

He looked at me quizzically for a moment, then shook his head. "No, I'm still phoning. I just got a fax from that cop in California. It's nothing much—what they had on Michael Vu and Henry Lam."

"I thought they didn't have anything on Lam, as an adult, I mean."

He looked down at the sheets in his hand. "No felonies. He did some misdemeanors. Most of it's technical junk—date of birth, an address, a description—nothing much."

"Okay. Give it to Sammie. And, Dennis?" I added as he turned to leave, "I found out last night that the tattoo and the CTG initials on the shooter called Ut probably come from California, too. Locate every antigang squad you can out there, especially the ones specializing in Asians, and get them copies of both the tattoo and of Ut's mug shot from his autopsy file. CTG stands for Chinatown Gang. They operated in the Bay Area, so you might try San Francisco, Berkeley, and Oakland first. You seen Willy, by the way?"

"Nope."

A shouted, "Yesss," from the squad room suddenly drew our attention. Sol Stennis, who was working Ron's phone, stood up and announced generally, "Keene, New Hampshire—the Cheshire Medical Center. They treated somebody late on the night of the murder. A deep cut to the back of the right hand—eight stitches. He even said he'd cut it on a broken window."

"When're the stitches due to come out?"

"Tomorrow."

I stepped into the squad room and spoke loudly enough that they could all hear me. "Okay. Contact everyone you've either called or will call and tell them to be on the lookout for a young Asian male wanting those stitches removed—just in case he decides not to go back to Keene. Sol, you go to Keene with the Ident-i-kit and our mug-shot album and either get a description or find a match, along with any paperwork they'll volunteer to hand over. If they hedge at all, get a subpoena. Once you've done that, have J.P. generate copies and have 'em delivered to everyone on the phone list. Stress to these people that all we want is a phone call, though. They are not to do anything beyond what they'd normally do, and they are not to let on that we're interested in this man."

I headed back to my office, and then called out to Sol.

He turned, his phone already in hand. "What's up?"

"This is probably a long shot, but when you're over there, find out if they took any blood samples. If they did, and if they kept them, we can get a subpoena for them, too, and try for a DNA match with what we've got."

Stennis nodded and began dialing. Satisfied I'd done all I could for the moment, I returned to my cubbyhole, closed the door, and dialed the phone number Jason Brown had given me last night.

It was, as he'd mentioned, a restaurant-supplies company, so it took me a few minutes—and a few extra seconds for reflection—to reach Nicky Tai.

Gail had been concerned that if Brown's character sketch of Tai was correct, then the only reason the ex–gang member would speak to me was if he had something to gain. In my little world of Brattleboro snitches, that meant either money or leniency, but as Gail and I both knew, neither applied here. Unfortunately, that's where our brainstorming session had stalled and why Gail had hopefully concluded that a few hours' thought on the matter would probably yield results. I wasn't so sure.

When he got on, Nicky Tai's voice was cautious, almost wary. Clearly he was a man who didn't much enjoy surprises. "Mr. Gunther? How may I help you?"

I dove right in. "It's Lieutenant Gunther, actually, from the Brattleboro Police Department in Vermont. I'm calling on the recommendation of Jason Brown."

The voice didn't soften any. "Oh?"

"I called him last night to ask him something about his past experience with Asian teenagers."

"Uh-huh," Tai said dryly, making me sound blatantly disingenuous for having skirted the word *gangs*, which is what we both knew I was talking about.

"I better get straight to the point here," I hurried on. "We've just had a shooting—a home invasion that went wrong. Three young men tried to extort money from one of our local businessmen—an Asian also—and happened to bump into a couple of our officers. All three were killed in a gunfight."

Unlike Brown, he didn't inquire about the officers or the intended victims.

"Anyway, we're trying to find out who two of those three were."

"And my name came up as someone with past experience who would talk to you."

I paused a moment, wondering how to play this. Tai was well spoken, obviously bright, and apparently not given to snow jobs. I decided to reciprocate in kind. "Not really. Brown said you'd be pretty reluctant—that either you still had some fond feelings for your friends from the old days, or that you knew better than to talk to a cop."

I sensed, however unconsciously, that I'd ruffled his pride. "Well, he's wrong on both counts," he answered sharply, and then added with a hint of face-saving swagger, "although I haven't made a habit of the second."

"I understand that. What I'm after," I continued, "or I think I am, is pretty much ancient history anyhow, so if I ask anything out of line, feel free to let me know. As far as I'm concerned, you're doing me a favor here."

"All right," he said, cautious again, but seeming more in control.

"The only one of the three dead men we've identified was named Henry Lam—that's how we made the connection to Jason Brown, who counseled him after he got to this country. Brown said Lam used to be a runner for Chinatown Gang back when you were a member."

There was a moment's silence on the line. "I remember Lam."

That was the first hurdle, I thought. "What was he like?"

He hesitated again. Despite Tai's denial of Brown's appraisal of him, I sensed the man was in a quandary. Talking to me would have cost him dearly a few short years ago. Not talking to me now would make true the suggestion that he was still too scared.

"Dangerous," he answered in my favor. "He was hard to control. He wanted to be a big man fast."

"I understand he also ran with the Dragon Boys, among others."

"That was done all the time. We all used kids."

"One of the men killed with Lam was called Ut, and had CTG tattooed on his hand. Did you know him?"

His immediate answer was disappointing—and familiar. "Ut's a very common name."

I quickly moved along, not wanting to lose momentum. "All right. The man we think was running all three of them here used to be a Dragon Boy. His name is Michael Vu. Does *that* name ring a bell?"

Another long pause, this one filled with potential. With Michael Vu, I was no longer asking about "ancient history" or dead people, which meant the possible danger to Nicky Tai was no longer to his pride alone. "Why do you ask?"

I shored him up with a real concern of my own. "Two reasons. The obvious one is that I'm trying to file some paperwork and retire this case. The other one is that I don't want the Asian population in general—such as it is here—tainted by something like this. Vermont is mostly white, rural, and lower-middle-class to poor, and racism is always just below the surface. If I can get a fast handle on who's behind this, I might be able to nip a big problem in the bud."

He thought about that for a few moments, weighing my sincerity. I was hoping I'd touched some portion of what had stimulated him to leave the gangs.

"I knew Michael," he finally answered.

"Did he leave Dragon Boys?"

"I heard that. I don't know where he went."

"When was the last time you were aware of his being in California?"

"A few years ago—I don't know exactly. We were not friends. Dragon Boys was one of the reasons Chinatown Gang was destroyed. They saw us as a threat and took out our leadership."

"Killed them?" I was caught off balance, surprised that members of what I thought was a single gang might have once been bloody rivals.

"Yes. There was a shooting at a restaurant in San Francisco. Five of our people died. The police never brought any charges, but everyone knew it was Dragon Boys."

"Did Michael Vu play a role in that?"

"He was a *ma-jai* then," Tai said dismissively, "a street soldier. This was done by higher people."

"So Dragon Boys became a major gang?"

"They got bigger. They absorbed some of our group, and others, too. Taking care of us gave them big face."

Which probably explained what the one named Ut was doing working for Vu. "Did Michael Vu move up the ranks?" I asked.

"For a while. Then Dragon Boys began to fade. Their leadership got in trouble with the cops. People started to leave. There wasn't as much room at the top as there had been. Michael Vu got stuck."

"Sounds like a middle-management crisis," I murmured as an aside.

He actually laughed, if only for a second, but it showed me how far we'd come in just a few minutes. "Yes. I guess someone made him a better offer."

The whole Sonny-as-smoke-screen gambit rose anew in my brain. "Couldn't he have just set up a whole new operation on his own?"

Tai hesitated, and finally compromised. "Not the Michael Vu I knew. People change, of course."

I remembered Heather Dahlin reporting how the Hartford Police had seen Vu meeting with anonymous parties in a motel. Her assumption that he'd been acting under orders apparently matched Tai's reading of Vu's character. "All right, do you have any idea who he might be working for? We're starting to think the people who are giving us problems here got to know each other in the Bay Area."

"That wouldn't surprise me, Lieutenant. When CTG died out, many people went looking for new places to go."

"Could I fly a couple of names by you?" I asked, my voice studiously nonchalant.

"You can try," he said, back to his neutral self.

Not expecting to get much further than I had with Jason Brown, I began with Edward Diep and some of the people we'd seen most frequently in the company of Michael Vu. Nicky Tai showed none of Brown's impatience with the process, but he was also no more helpful.

Until I mentioned Truong Van Loc.

"I knew a Truong On Ha. I think you're talking about his older brother."

I quickly pawed through the papers on my desk and retrieved the report I'd received months earlier on Truong Van Loc, following Marshall Smith's now-famous traffic stop. As I'd remembered, On Ha was in fact the brother who'd been killed in a gang fight. "But you didn't know the elder Truong?"

"No. I only saw him at the funeral. On Ha was one of the victims in that shoot-out I mentioned."

Startled again, I blurted out, "But you said only the CTG leadership was wiped out in that."

"No, no. You misunderstand. Truong On Ha was an innocent bystander—a waiter. He never had anything to do with the gangs."

As in the cartoons of old, I felt a light suddenly snap on above my head. "And the older brother—Van Loc—was he in the gangs?"

"Not ours—or theirs—but I think he had been. But he'd dropped out, like I did." Tai paused a moment, reflecting. "Lieutenant, are you familiar with the concept of karma?"

"What you do now may come back to haunt you later?"

"Crude, but close," Tai conceded. "At the time of the funeral, it was said that Truong On Ha's death was part of his older brother's karma for his past activities."

I did some quick thinking about retired Dragon Boy Michael Vu, the late Mr. Ut of the CTG, and the hard-eyed, upwardly mobile Henry Lam, who as a child used to travel between these old gangs. "Did Van Loc feel his karma played a part in his brother's death?"

"I don't know—it is not something that is asked."

"But did he act on it, as far as you know? Seek revenge?"

"It is not realistic to seek revenge against destiny, Lieutenant."

A mental picture returned to me, drawn a few days earlier by John Crocker, of the driver of the car that had forced him off the road—a face empty of all feeling except cold rage. "Lots of people do, Mr. Tai. They find someone or something to act as a substitute, and then they open up with both barrels."

"I'm sorry. You are right. I can't answer your question. I only saw

Truong Van Loc that one time, and I never heard from him or about him again." There was a noise in the background. Tai quickly muttered, "Just a moment, please," and covered the mouthpiece of his phone for a couple of minutes. When he returned, he said, "I'm sorry, Lieutenant, I must go back to work."

"I understand, and I really appreciate the help you've given me. Could I call you in the future—in a pinch, I mean?"

This was obviously not something he wanted to hear, which made me wonder if his business interruption hadn't been a fabricated convenience. "Perhaps," was all he said.

I therefore pushed my luck a little. "One last question, then. Was Truong Van Loc ever called 'Sonny'?"

"I never heard it if he was. Good-bye, Lieutenant."

I hung up the already dead receiver, pleased despite that final disappointment. Regardless of whether the elder Truong had gone by the name Sonny in California, my instincts told me it fitted him well now, far better than it did Michael Vu. And there was something else: If Sonny and Truong were one and the same man, then I was pretty sure of the seething mechanism that was making him tick.

The big question was: If he was hell-bent on avenging his brother's death, what was he doing in Brattleboro?

Chapter Fourteen

Dan Flynn picked up his phone on the first ring. "VCIN—Lieutenant Flynn."

"It's Joe—who's your Asian crime contact in Montreal?" I asked him.

"Sounds like you're in hot pursuit," he said, laughing.

"Maybe. I'm trying to see if Sonny's actually Truong Van Loc. I want to find out some more about the hit in Montreal a couple of days after we did that traffic stop down here."

I could hear him tapping on the plastic keys of his ever-ready computer. "How 'bout Jean-Paul Lacoste? He ran a seminar on Asian crime last year at Rouse's Point. Big turnout, and everybody gave him high marks. Speaks good English, too, which doesn't hurt. Plus he shares information." He gave me a phone number and an address on Hochelaga Street, which he had to spell out.

"You had any nibbles on the BOL you put out on Truong?" he asked me then.

"No, but I just got off the phone with Customs and the Border Patrol. I asked them to make sure his picture's on top of their pile. You haven't logged any stops or arrests of an Asian male with a bandage on the back of his right hand, have you? We think he might've helped knock off Benny Travers. As soon as we get more details, we're going to circulate a flyer on him, too."

Dan hesitated. "We did have an accident involving two Asians about four days ago. An old lady in Rutland pulled out of a parking space without looking, and the Asians' car wiped out her fender. Everyone was pretty shook up, but that was about it. All the paperwork checked out, the PD didn't issue any tickets, and none of the names they fed me fit any of yours, so I didn't think you'd be interested."

"No, that's fine," I reassured him, although at this point almost anything concerning Asians in Vermont was interesting to me.

"There's been some new activity in Burlington, though," he added. "My contact at the PD there called me a few hours ago—told me there'd been a turf fight between an old gang and some newcomers."

"Any names?"

"No, it was pure intelligence. No complaints or arrests, but the specialty involved was alien smuggling. Maybe Sonny—or Truong, if that's who he is—is grabbing some of the market."

"What was the upshot of the turf fight?"

"Rumor has it the newcomers won. How close are you folks to nailing something down?"

"We're getting there, I hope. Some of the pieces are starting to fit, but I don't think this is a typical gang. If I'm right, Truong Van Loc is more a man with a mission than just a hood on the make. Problem is, the people who work for him *are* hoods. It'd be pretty ironic if their screwups helped nail him."

"What did Brandt say about the task-force idea?" Flynn asked.

"Thumbs down. I think Derby likes the idea, but then he's got nothing to lose. We're already one man short and Brandt's not interested in losing me, so I guess we're out of luck."

"Too bad," Dan murmured, and I could tell from his tone that he meant it. The prospect of officially involving VCIN in a specialized federal task force had obviously been appealing. "Well, keep me posted. By the way, did you fly that photo of Truong by Immigration?"

"No," I answered expectantly. "Why?"

"I just remembered it was one of their customers who said Sonny had arranged his border crossing. If they still have the guy in custody, maybe he could identify Sonny. The INS agent who gave me that is a friend. If you'd like, I can chase it down."

"Christ, yes. I'd appreciate it."

"No problem. I'll let you know what I find out."

"Thanks, Dan," I said, hanging up as Sammie appeared in my doorway.

"Sol's back from Keene."

I rose and followed her across the squad room to the conference area beyond it—a more comfortable setting than my office for any meeting exceeding two people. Stennis was already laying a newly acquired Ident-i-kit portrait on the wide table.

I stood by him, looking down at yet another hard, arrogant young face, a blight on the reputations of a few million other Asians who had shared his troubled past, and yet continued to peacefully strive for their dreams.

"That him?" I asked.

"Yup," Stennis answered, "according to four witnesses. He left an impression, too. He and his buddies scared the hell out of the nurses in the ER." He quickly held up his hand as I opened my mouth— "No, they didn't do anything out of line. And, no, I couldn't get descriptions of the others, except that there were four of them—all males, all young, all Asians. The other three escorted this guy in, and then waited outside in the parking lot."

"Anyone make the car they were in?" Sammie asked.

Stennis shook his head. "No, but I do have some good news." He laid a couple of documents next to the picture. "This is a copy of the patient form he filled out—one of the nurses gave me that, sort of under the table—and this is a copy of the information concerning his blood sample—the cross-matching report, I guess they call it."

"Damn," I muttered, "they did draw blood."

"Yup. Apparently, he'd lost quite a bit. There was a second cut on the wrist—nicked an artery. So, after they sewed him up, they gave him a pint of blood—couldn't do that without identifying what type he already had in his system. If you ask me, the doc who worked on him was suspicious. Not that he'd admit it when I put it to him. Still," he added, his eyes glowing with satisfaction, "he did hand the sample over." With a slight flourish, he pulled a sealed packet from his coat pocket.

"That's his blood?" I asked, understandably startled. "How did you get it?"

Stennis's smile broadened. "Through channels, like you asked. Keene PD applied for the warrant, and a judge issued it, but the whole thing only took two hours—luck of the draw. Everyone was in the right place at the right time."

"That's great." I picked up the patient-information form. "Nguyen Van Hai—he gives the Central Street house as a home address. You've both been taking surveillance pictures over there. His face ring any bells?"

They shook their heads, Stennis adding, "While you were on the phone, I passed it around to some of the others. Drew a blank with them, too."

I stepped away from the table. "All right. Nice job. You might as well get that blood to J.P. so he can send it in for a fast preliminary look—see if we can put Mr. Nguyen with Mr. Truong. Then, if we can actually find either of them, maybe we'll get a lead on the missing third man."

"Any ideas how we *are* going to find them?" Sammie asked skeptically.

I put the patient-information sheet back on the table. "He gave us an address. We might as well shoot for a search warrant and see if we get lucky. Also, now that we have that sketch, and a name to go with it, I think we ought to publish both it and Truong's photo in every newspaper that'll run it, just to see what happens—but not until those stitches are due to be removed. Nguyen may go back to have them out, and I don't want to discourage him. That'll also give us a little time to run checks on him, get the warrant approved by a judge, and maybe figure out if he has any favorite hangouts."

I turned to face Sammie. "We better send copies of that sketch to all the hospitals, clinics, and doctors' offices we just alerted."

She nodded and momentarily left the room to retrieve a folder from her desk. "I got something, too," she said, extracting what I instantly recognized as an autopsy report. "It's Hillstrom's verdict on the John Doe without the tattoo—the one Mr. Leung said was called An."

I opened the report and began scanning its pages—consisting largely of a running commentary on which bullets went where. An was the one Ron had shot several times.

Sammie, clearly impatient, reached over and turned to the page she wanted me to see. "She says he had a bruise running across his chest."

I saw the reference. " 'Consistent with markings resulting from a rapid deceleration against a diagonally mounted, driver's-side vehicle seat belt,' " I quoted. "I'll be goddamned. Dan Flynn was just telling me about a two-car collision in Rutland four days ago that involved Asians." I hunted through Sammie's file and retrieved the portrait taken of An at the morgue. "Sol, find out which officer handled the complaint, fax him a copy of this photograph, and get all the information you can from him—everything on the driver, his passenger, the car . . . the works."

Stennis snatched the picture from my hand and disappeared.

I could tell from Sammie's expression that this was only half her good news. "Remember when Dennis came to you with the stats from California on Vu and Henry Lam, and you sent him to me? Well, I compared them to what I already had. The date of birth on Lam was different, and when I ran the new birthdate through the computer, I got this." She handed me a printout. "Henry Lam's Massachusetts rap sheet as an adult. It didn't click on the name alone earlier because the system is DOB-biased, and I didn't think to challenge it."

"So, the little turkey was operating nearby," I murmured.

"Not only that," she added, again directing me where to read. "But it says here: 'Consult Montreal Urban Community Police for more info.' "

I smiled at her refreshing optimism. "Not bad, Sammie. If An did get sliced interrogating Benny, that gives us two of his killers, as well as two of the three who tried to kill Ron and me. Now we're cooking."

Our self-satisfaction was abruptly interrupted by Harriet's voice, calling for me urgently. She was sitting at her desk, holding the phone out to me as I approached. "It's the hospital ER. There's an Asian male having stitches taken out of his hand right now."

I ignored the phone. "They didn't stall him?"

"They tried to, but one of the visiting doctors overheard them and made a big deal about rendering rapid service."

"Shit. He'll be out of there in no time." I grabbed Sammie by the arm and propelled her toward the door, shouting to Harriet over my shoulder as I followed, "Mobilize what you can find of the SRT, and see if we can't borrow Maxine's van for a take-down team. Also, find out if this guy's alone or with friends, and try to get a description of his car." I paused at the door. "And make sure no patrol units stumble in there by mistake. I don't want to lose control of this. Nobody's to confront until I get to the scene."

Sammie and I ran toward the parking lot to one of the department's two unmarked cars. As Sammie slid in behind the wheel, I paused, noticing two people step out of one of the TV trucks, attracted by our obvious haste.

"Something up?" one of them asked.

"Ran out of donuts," I shouted back. I made a big display of slowly taking my jacket off and draping it over my forearm before I leisurely opened the passenger door and got in, trying to ignore Sammie's revving of the engine.

"Code three?" she asked testily before I'd even shut the door.

"Not on your life—not till we clear the parking lot."

She looked over her shoulder to where I was staring. "Oh, Christ."

"After we hit High Street, you can play all the sirens you want, but only to within a couple of blocks of the hospital. I don't want Nguyen getting nervous."

She did a credible job of starting out slowly, leaving our two specta-tors flatfooted, but once she reached Oak Street, she took off with tires squealing. I pulled the mike from its clip and began orchestrating a coordinated approach, occasionally holding onto the door frame to keep from falling into Sammie's lap.

The setting outside Brattleboro Memorial Hospital's emergency room had several advantages as a take-down spot, assuming we got there early enough to position ourselves.

The ER was tucked away around the east side of the building, its separate, dead-end parking lot perched between the hospital and the top of a steep grassy slope that fell away to Canal Street far below. To the lot's south was the driveway connecting it to the main parking area around the corner; to its west was the ER's ambulance loading dock, sliding glass doors, and the long window of the ER waiting room; and to its north was a short wing of the building, built mostly of windowless brick.

A few blocks from the hospital, Sammie slowed down and killed her lights and siren. I picked up the mobile phone lying on the seat between us and dialed the ER.

"ER—Elizabeth Pace."

That helped. Nurse Pace, although a fairly recent arrival in town, was a friend. "Elizabeth, this is Joe Gunther."

The relief in her voice was palpable. "Joe—thank God. Where are you?"

"About a block away. Is that man still with the doctor?"

"Yes."

"Where—exactly?"

"Room four, a little ways down the hall."

"So there's no way he can hear what you're saying?"

"Yes. I mean, no, he can't. I told the woman at the police department that, as far as I know, he is alone—at least he came in alone. But I don't know what car he's driving."

Sammie pulled into Belmont Street, fronting the hospital.

"That's okay. Is the ER full right now?"

"No. There's a patient in room two, and a couple of people in the waiting room. They just got here."

"Fine. What's this man wearing?"

"A bright-red windbreaker and a dark-blue baseball cap."

"Great, thanks. Now, when he comes out, I don't want you doing anything other than the usual. This is just a man we want to talk with, so I don't want you all worked up. Just do whatever paperwork is necessary, and wish him a nice day, okay?"

"I don't use that expression."

"Give me a break, Elizabeth. Pat him on the ass, if that's what you do, all right?"

She laughed, to my relief. "All right."

"Talk to you later," I said, and disconnected.

Sammie had pulled into the main parking area by this time, and now slowly drove around the gentle curve leading to the ER lot.

I unhooked the radio mike and held it below the window. "M-80 from 0-3. Is the SRT rolling?"

"We're rolling," came the direct response. "We're in Maxine's van, coming up Estey Street. ETA about two minutes. Maxine says she'll kill us if we put holes in this thing."

"How many people do you have?"

"Three."

"Okay—as far as we know, he's alone." I paused to check out the lot while Sammie, having parked, made a big show of pulling a map out and spreading it across the steering wheel. "I don't see anyone in the ER parking area, either on foot or waiting in a vehicle. The subject is supposed to be wearing a bright-red windbreaker and a dark-blue baseball cap."

"10-4. We'll advise when we reach Belmont," came the reply.

The reason for borrowing Maxine's van, instead of grabbing our far more ostentatious emergency-services truck, was that my plan—such as it was—called for surprise and an overwhelming show of force. The anonymity of her vehicle, along with its darkly tinted windows, allowed for both.

"We're coming up Belmont now," came from the speaker under the dash.

I keyed the mike. "10-4. Come partway up the driveway and wait at the curve where you're still out of sight of the ER door. When I give the signal, approach at normal speed, and try to place the subject between the van and the building's north brick wall—that's the best backstop we've got. No rifles, okay? Handguns and shotguns only. I don't want any bullets reaching New Hampshire."

"You got it," Marshall Smith's voice answered, taking advantage of the restricted frequency to both relax on radio protocol and cut the tension a bit.

We sat there a few minutes more, feeling the weight of each second. My brain was working in overdrive, sorting through every scenario I could imagine. I knew from experience almost anything could happen, from Nguyen suddenly tumbling to his exposed position and grabbing Elizabeth as a hostage, to a carful of his buddies arriving to pick him up.

Finally, almost mercifully, we saw the glass doors of the emergency room slide open.

"Get ready," I said on the radio.

A man, his face slightly turned away, stepped out onto the ambulance loading dock and paused there, apparently surveying the distant roof-tops to the east. He was wearing a white shirt and no cap.

"Damn," Sammie murmured, her gun already resting in her lap.

Slowly, as if stringing us along, the man removed a rolled-up bundle from under his arm and shook it out, revealing a bright-red windbreaker, which he slipped on. As his hands came through the sleeves, I could see the flash of a bandage on one of them. He pulled a blue cap from one of his pockets, adjusted it neatly on his head, and began walking toward the wheelchair ramp leading off the dock.

"Here he comes, off the loading dock. Go at a normal speed and pinch him off. Good luck."

Almost immediately, we both became aware of movement behind us. Maxine's van slid silently around the curve of the driveway, entered the small parking lot, and headed straight at Nguyen Van Hai. Sammie pulled the latch back on her door and opened it just a crack.

Nguyen, now crossing the lot, looked up without much curiosity as the dark van gradually approached, running perpendicular to the row of parked cars. Then he slowed, noticing it was not pulling into one of the open slots. From a distance, I could see his expression change—from passivity, to surprise, to downright alarm. He stopped dead in his tracks and quickly glanced around.

"Come on, come on," Sammie muttered under her breath.

Suddenly, the van twisted to the right, presenting a broadside to the man almost right next to it, and, simultaneously, all doors to the vehicle flew open. The van hadn't rolled to a complete stop before three heavily armed men came flying out of it, screaming orders at the top of their lungs. Dressed in black body armor stenciled in gray letters spelling *Police*, they circled Nguyen like nightmarish Dobermans, two of them with their legs planted and their pistols drawn in the classic shooter's stance, the third with his hands free to move in with terrifying speed and take the man down as fast and as hard as he could. In less than five seconds it was over. Nguyen Van Hai lay flat on his face, his wrists handcuffed behind his back.

"Clear," Marshall Smith said into his portable radio, "clear and secure."

Sammie and I got out of our car and walked over to the group. The officer with the handcuffs was carefully searching the suspect. Looking around, I saw a few faces appear at the nearby windows. Behind us, a patrol unit appeared from its hiding place down the street.

"Nice job, folks—picture perfect," I said as I reached them. "Marshall, why don't you and Pierre put him in the unit and escort him back to quarters. I'll be right there."

I jumped up onto the loading dock and headed into the ER. Elizabeth Pace was standing in the middle of the hall, looking anxious. "Is everyone all right?"

"Everyone's fine. I just wanted to thank you and find out how you were."

She gave me a lopsided smile and took my hand in hers, her eyes still glued to the scene outside. I turned slightly and watched with her as the take-down team pulled Nguyen to his feet and piled him into the back of the waiting patrol car. "It was so fast, after all that waiting. What did he do?"

"We have to determine that legally, but it isn't nice. I can tell you that much."

She shook her head slightly. "Thirty years working in Boston, I never saw anything like that. So much for country living."

*   *   *

The police department's interrogation room, complete with the obligatory one-way mirror mounted into the wall, was as miniaturized as the rest of the department, compared to a big-city force. The room itself was six feet by eight, and the observation cubicle was too narrow to hold a chair. The whole thing was tucked into a corner of the detective squad room.

I stood next to Tony Brandt, staring through the smoke-colored glass, watching Willy Kunkle trying to extract some information from our guest. So far, it had been an exercise in futility. Nguyen Van Hai hadn't said a single word since uttering yes to whether he understood his rights.

"Does he speak English?" Tony asked.

"He spoke it fine to the doctor. I called and asked. We're trying to locate a translator, but I doubt it'll make any difference."

"But he is the man we're after, right?"

"Circumstantially, he is. If we're lucky, we'll have the preliminary blood analysis back by tomorrow or the next day. If that works out, then DNA will put his blood and Benny's in the same place at the same time."

"Maybe the same time," Tony amended.

"That's up to the lawyers. According to J.P., it's a fact—the coagulation rates were the same on both samples."

"You search his house yet?"

"I just came from there. J.P. and his crew are still at it, but I don't expect much—mattresses on the floor, piles of clothing, smell of food and unwashed bodies. They were having a hard time telling this guy's junk from everyone else's."

"Any help from the other residents?"

"Minimal."

"I got a call from the governor this morning. Since the media's been speculating about organized Asian crime, he was wondering if we might need some help. I lied. I told him we were right on top of things."

I laughed softly. Twenty-four hours earlier, I thought, and we would've been handing Nguyen Van Hai over to the feds—with Tony's blessing. I slid out of the narrow cubicle to appear at the door to the interrogation room. Willy glanced over his shoulder and gave me a grim smile. "He's all yours."

I took my time getting comfortable in the molded plastic chair, placing it just so at the small table between us. I finally sat back, crossed my legs, and put my hands in my lap—the perfect image, I hoped, of imperturbable permanence. "We were wondering if you'd like to have an interpreter."

Nguyen just looked at me.

"We know you speak English. You were speaking it to the doctor not twenty minutes ago. But we thought we'd make it as convenient as possible. Would you like us to call you a lawyer?"

He remained silent, his eyes watching me closely, utterly without expression.

"I hope you understand that you're not here just for an interview. We know what you've done. We know you tortured Benny Travers, we know you and your two buddies chased him down after he tried to escape, and forced him off the road and killed him. We know one of you shot at him during that chase, and who was driving the car. We even know the gun was a Glock. This is not a situation where we're hoping you'll slip up and say something incriminating."

He didn't speak, he didn't move. I had to watch him closely to even see him breathing.

"You're in serious trouble, whether you talk or not. You can keep quiet through the arraignment, through every conversation with your lawyer, through the trial, and even when they throw the book at you. The end result will be the same—you'll be in jail, where you'll stay for a very long time."

He blinked—once—which made me wonder if that had been the first time his eyes had moved since I'd sat down, or just the first time I'd noticed it. The very question irritated me, and made me realize just who was psyching out whom.

I shifted in my seat lazily, recrossing my legs. "Of course, that's the worse-case scenario. It doesn't have to be that bad. Unlike in the old country, we tend to bargain with our prisoners . . . something," and here I pulled the rap sheet out of my pocket we'd just been wired from NCIC, "I see you already know about."

I paused and reexamined the contents of the sheet—a complete listing of increasingly nasty activity in California, Florida, Massachusetts, and Canada, which was mentioned as his initial port of entry. He was thirty years old, and yet had already spent more than half his life as a gang member. My private frustration was that the pure data of the report gave me no inkling of where he might have hooked up with Truong, Vu, or Henry Lam.

I shook my head and whistled softly. "Boy, the state's attorney's going to want to bury you alive. He's a politician, after all, and putting you away'll be like putting votes into the bank."

All of us had been through practice interrogations before where the fake suspect essentially plays dead. It was a good way for us to examine the various ways of getting under a suspect's skin. But in none of those sessions had I ever received as little feedback as now.

"Still," I kept trying, "they say there's always room to move, and we don't have *all* the answers. For example, we'd like to take a look at the car you drove that day, and I wouldn't mind having a chat with Truong Van Loc. Anything you could give us on him would help your case—perhaps a lot."

I was looking directly into his eyes as I said that name, and saw absolutely nothing. My mind went back over what we'd learned of Benny Travers's death, and of the role the man before me must have played in it. Standing in that kitchen days ago, seeing all that blood, the cut pants, the crimson outline of the fillet knife on the table— used again and again on a man who must've been screaming his lungs out, his head trapped inside a plastic bag—I'd been shaken at the cool savagery of it all, and I'd wondered about the men who'd acted it out. Now, looking at Nguyen Van Hai's silent, unrepentant face, I was left baffled and disappointed—as if I'd just unwrapped a gift box, and found it empty.

I stood up. "Mr. Nguyen, welcome to the judicial process. I'll get out of your way right now. But keep in mind, if you ever get the urge to make things a little easier on yourself, ask for me—the sooner the better."

His eyes didn't even follow me as I left the room.

Chapter Fifteen

"So," Tony Brandt said, taking a seat in my guest chair. "What did you get out of Nguyen?"

"Not a word," I answered truthfully, counting on his good humor to still be intact.

We were in my office for once, and he looked around uncomfortably for somewhere to stretch his inordinately long legs. He seemed chronically incapable of merely sitting in a chair with both feet planted on the ground. "Well, at least we nailed *somebody*. That might be enough to keep the wolves at bay."

"The governor call back?" I asked.

He finally settled for resting his left leg along the top of a stacked row of cardboard file boxes lining the wall. "Closer than that. Having a special-weapons team land on a guy like a brick on a bug—in front of a building full of feeble-hearted patients—aroused some local attention. The newspeople are back on our doorstep, and the only selectman who hasn't called me is out of town on a business trip."

He was smiling when he said it, so I wasn't prompted to defend my actions. "What're you going to do?" I asked instead.

"Not much—stage an unscheduled press conference. I think this latest coup has made Mr. Derby a little more optimistic since our last chat, so he'll probably be joining me in the limelight. Should be a good show, if I can think of something to say."

"Which is why you're here," I finished.

"Just give me the good stuff."

I steepled my fingers in front of my chin, concentrating on how to reduce what I had to headline length. "First, on Benny's murder, I think we can now publicly say it was committed by three Asian males. One of those, Nguyen Van Hai, is now under lock and key; another, Truong Van Loc, has been identified but is still on the loose; and the third is still unknown and at large. We have pictures if you want them. That ought to titillate the crowd."

Brandt shook his head. "They'll want more about the shoot-out with you and Ron. Benny's already old news."

"Okay. We have photos of those three as well. You can expand on Henry Lam a bit—I wrote up a report on his background. You can also milk . . ." I paused to paw through some papers on my desk, "Chu Nam An. He was the shooter Ron nailed. Dan Flynn reported a car crash in Rutland involving Asians, and Hillstrom picked up on a recent seat-belt bruise on Chu's chest. I'm planning on going over to Rutland tomorrow to see what else I can chase down, but it looks good."

"So Chu wasn't alone in the car?" Brandt asked.

"No, he had someone with him—no name given or asked for. Chu's license and registration listed an address in Lowell, Mass., but the Rutland investigating officer also got a local address. Sol asked them to check it out, but the place was empty. Still, I thought I'd poke around a bit. If Chu and some of his pals lived there long enough, maybe the neighbors can tell me something."

Brandt nodded. "Okay. What about the guy with the tattoo?"

"Still checking. First name's Ut, he's got ties to California, but we haven't heard back from the police there yet."

"Your last memo mentioned Truong got his start in California. You really think Truong and Sonny are one and the same?"

I raised my eyebrows equivocally. "It's pure theory right now, but it fits. Dan Flynn's looking into it for me. It sure would explain what's driving him."

"The dead brother?"

"Yeah. But I'm still working on the whys—why here, why now, why this particular approach. If revenge instead of profit is his motive, I have no idea who his target is, and I can't explain why he seems so profit oriented."

"Which brings up the overriding question I'll guarantee I'm going to hear—do we have a gang problem in town?"

I thought about that for a moment. "The short answer is yes, which actually might stimulate people to face it. Besides, the grapevine has it that Alfie Brewster's imported some muscle to watch his back, so if something blows up, your butt'll be covered if you're already on record."

Brandt looked at me closely. "Why'd he do that?"

"I don't know yet. Could be he used the Leung home invasion to set up Sharkey and Vu. That's what Sally Javits thinks, more or less. I've got Willy looking into it, but as usual, he's disappeared . . ."

"Right." He stood up, checking his watch.

"That it?" I asked him.

"Yup. I'm not going to complicate my life right now by mentioning the Canadian connection. The local angle's enough. Besides, I'm due in ten minutes."

I shook my head at this blessedly familiar nonchalance, knowing full well how much he put into protecting the department's image. Years ago, I'd pulled a six-month stint as acting chief, and had hated it so much I'd insisted on a corporate shuffle that made Billy Manierre Tony's next in line.

Tony paused at the narrow doorway to let J.P. Tyler squeeze by, who muttered, "Hi, Chief," with his eyes downcast. Tony was perpetually amused at Tyler's discomfort around anyone with a title, and merely shook his head with a smile before giving me a small departing wave.

"What's up?" I asked J.P., once Tony had left.

"I got a match for the MO used on Benny Travers—a man named Johnny Xi was killed in Vancouver one year after Truong On Ha's death in San Francisco. Xi was the red pole for the Dragon Boys at the time. *Red pole* is the title the Chinese give their head enforcer. It actually applies to triads, but some of the gangs use it, too, for prestige."

Mention of triads made me think back to my conversation with

Jason Brown. The FBI and other agencies were still hedging on whether the Hong Kong and Taiwan-based triads were officially on US soil yet. Part of that may have been due to caution, and part to the constant blurring of distinctions among triads, tongs, and gangs.

"I called San Francisco PD, and they confirmed the ID. They also told me that, at the time, Xi had been their primary suspect as the leader of the team that shot up the restaurant."

I sat back in my chair, pleasantly surprised. "You didn't happen to ask how many other members of that team they'd identified, did you?"

He smiled. "I did, actually." The smile then faded a bit. "But none of them sounded familiar."

"Are they all still alive?" I asked, the question about Truong's motivation still echoing inside my head.

His eyes narrowed in surprise. "Oh," he murmured after a pause, "I see what you mean. I'll find out."

I gestured to him to stay put. "Tell me more about how Johnny Xi died."

"Right. It wasn't an exact carbon copy. He was tied to a door, not taped to a chair; all his clothes were cut off, not just his pants. But the important details match—the bag over the head, the use of the knife . . . and how it was used. Lucky for Travers he got away, even if he did end up dying anyway—Xi was castrated and skinned alive."

"Did the PD find out who did it?"

"No. Benny busting loose actually did us a favor, 'cause that's when this hit team made its mistakes. But there were no mistakes back then. The Vancouver Police couldn't find a thing. There was a lot of blood, but that was all. They made the connection to the San Francisco shooting, but there was nothing they could follow up on. They wrote it off to intergang politics, and dropped the case into the permanent 'open' file."

"The name Truong never came up?" I asked.

"Nope, nor any of the others I ran by them."

*   *   *

Ron Klesczewski lived in Guilford, south of Brattleboro, in a small development of modest, one-story homes, all built by the same contractor some ten years earlier. There were five buildings, placed symmetrically around a large circular drive, forming a layout typical of many crowded suburban sprawls. Except that here it was nestled in the middle of the Vermont woods, like the single lost piece of a jigsaw puzzle dropped from on high.

Wendy Klesczewski, Ron's young wife, opened the door. She stood staring at me, utterly surprised, despite my promise that I'd be by. "Lieutenant . . . I mean, Joe. Hi."

I was a little surprised myself. Wendy was clearly pregnant. "I didn't know you were expecting. That's wonderful."

She self-consciously patted her middle, her smile becoming a little more strained. "Five months along. I miscarried once before, so we didn't want to . . . you know . . ."

"Very smart," I finished for her. "But everything's going all right?"

"Oh, yes—so far, so good."

There was that telltale skip in the conversation, when two uncomfortable people have just run out of small talk. We stared at one another for a couple of seconds before I finally asked, "How's he doin'?"

Her whole face yielded to gravity, her smile collapsing, the corners of her eyes giving in to minute stress lines that tugged toward her temples. The blush of a burgeoning mother was eclipsed by the anxiety of a worried wife. "I don't really know," she admitted, and stood aside to let me enter. "He's in the back."

The *back*, in their parlance, I knew from prior visits, was the one room in the house that defied the tiny neighborhood's forced intimacy. Facing the rear, its one window looked out onto the woods, and a small stretch of lawn reaching out to them.

I found Ron sitting in a recliner, a beer in one hand, staring out that window. I took a seat on the couch beneath it, so he was forced to look at me.

"Hi, Joe," he said softly, a gentle smile on his face. "You want a beer?"

I shook my head. "All set. Thanks."

He gave half a nod and his eyes strayed over my head to the darkening view. There were no lights on in the room, but enough of the day's residue filtered in through the window to let me see his face clearly, and I saw the source of his wife's concern.

For a man of twenty-nine, Ron Klesczewski was looking threadbare and ancient. His face had thinned, his eyes were sunken, his very skin pulled as tight to his skull as that of an old pensioner. He obviously hadn't washed or shaved in days.

I didn't tiptoe around it. "You look awful, Ron."

That brought his eyes back to mine. "I know."

"What's been going on?"

"I can't sleep. I've taken sleeping pills, had half a case of this." He gestured with the beer. "Nothing works. I can tell it's driving Wendy crazy."

"You getting out at all? Seeing people?"

"You mean a shrink?" he asked without hostility.

"I didn't, but aren't you? I thought that'd been set up after the post-stress session."

He flipped his hand feebly. "I am, I am. It's not doing much good, though."

"It's only been three days. Maybe you're expecting too much. You've got to surrender to what's been bugging you—let things come out where you can take a look at them. It takes time."

His brow furrowed. "I know I'm screwed up. That's not the problem."

"The problem's that you can't sleep?" I asked, purposefully incredulous.

His irritation climbed a notch. "That's what I just said. If I could get some rest, I could think this through."

"How 'bout the reverse? Letting it out so you get some rest."

He shook his head angrily, but stayed silent.

"Cops are supposed to be superhuman," I said. "Always calm, courteous, and available when the shit hits the fan. We begin to buy into that. But it makes us feel twice as bad when we stumble and show we're human. We try too hard to live up to the fairy tale—to make the hero image real. But it's not, Ron . . . You really think you can just brush off some kid opening up on you with a semi-automatic? Catch a little sleep and be good as new?"

"You look okay."

"I've been through it before, in the service, as a cop, even when Gail was raped. Even so, it might still hit me like a ton of bricks someday, and at just the wrong time. I'm not an example to follow. It's better if you face it immediately."

His right hand came up and stroked his forehead, less to wipe it, or smooth an errant hair, than perhaps to check that it was still there. His voice, when he spoke, had lost its earlier brittle edge. "I just keep seeing him—his eyes. First when he was shooting at me, and then after I shot him. I keep running it through, again and again, trying to see what really happened. It's driving me nuts. We're about to have a baby, and I'm headed for the funny farm."

"You may look at the world differently after all this settles down. It will always be a watershed event in your life. But whatever happens, you'll survive. I know that much about you."

He rested his head against the back of the chair and closed his eyes for a moment, a long sigh escaping his lips. "God—I hope so."

I rose to my feet and walked toward the door, pausing by his side. "Just keep talking, bringing it out—remember how many people you have in your corner."

He reopened his eyes as I patted his shoulder. "Thanks, Joe."

Wendy met me in the front room, from where I knew she'd been listening, and silently escorted me to the door.

"He'll be fine," I told her quietly. "Try not to worry too much."

Her eyes brimming with tears, she leaned forward and kissed my cheek. "Thank you for coming."

*   *   *

It had been one of my favorite meals—a taboo when Gail was at home—a Velveeta and jam and mayonnaise sandwich, followed by a can of fruit cocktail. The thick, sweet, cloying memory of it lingered in my throat as I roamed the house, like a tourist in a museum.

The downtown apartment I'd lived in for almost twenty years had acquired the patina of an old bear's den—comfortable, shabby, not too pristine, and very familiar.

Not like this house at all.

Lurking behind the furniture, barely covered by the coat of fresh paint and new carpeting, were the shadows and sounds of countless succeeding families, none of whom I'd known, dating back to when the core of the huge place had been built as a farmhouse in the early

1800s. These were not bachelor digs, nor were they truly ours yet. This was still so new to me that I felt like a guest at a dinner party, wandering in search of a bathroom.

But there were a few familiar touchstones—items half lost among Gail's more numerous things—that reminded me of where I'd been born and brought up, and of the small house I'd owned when I'd been married. When Brattleboro was an overgrown village, and the police department had consisted of a small handful of ex-farmers.

Cancer had taken the marriage, and the house, and any hope of a family, and had encouraged me to enter a years-long emotional hibernation. Perhaps a different form of cancer—sometimes malignant, sometimes benign—had also transformed the erstwhile sleepy town of Brattleboro.

Buying this house with Gail had evoked mixed emotions in me, a sense of both moving ahead and traveling back—directions I felt were fraught with dimly perceived peril, and which became highlighted in her absence.

It was a large house, many times remodeled, with blond oak floors, dark beams set against glimmering plaster walls, skylights and double-paned bay windows tastefully spread throughout. The kind of house I'd visited on only a few occasions.

I went from room to room, remembering the two of us placing the furniture, choosing the colors of the paint, my watching how thoughtfully Gail made me feel a part of her decisions. A few of my possessions were logistically but self-consciously present in each one of the rooms. I still had a bachelor pad—two rooms upstairs, filled with my junk, sacrosanct. Gail had told me she'd never enter there uninvited, and had requested the same limitations on her suite down the hall.

I didn't go upstairs, though. Fresh from my visit to the Klesczewskis, I was soaking up the air that we shared, searching for her presence.

*　　*　　*

I lay on the bed much later, the phone in my hand, my eyes staring at a blank window full of night.

"You sound lonely, Joe," Gail said.

"I am—and a little ticked off. I had a good life once, surrounded by my books and my music and my junk food. Life was balanced. I could go for walks, or stay at the office, or go visit you, if you were around. It was pretty good."

"You miss that?" she asked gently.

"No. I wish I did. You ruined everything."

Her laughter filled my head.

Chapter Sixteen

Tony Brandt banged his coffee mug down on the counter with a curse and sucked on a scalded finger, checking his clothing for stains.

"Now you know why people say the stuff's a health hazard," I told him as I poured myself a cup from the officers'-room urn.

"I don't have time to drink it anyway," he muttered, now inspecting his finger. "Just force of habit."

"Got a date?" I asked.

"Yeah." He glanced up at the wall clock. "Early-morning head-bashing session over at the high school. All this talk of gangs has got them worked up, just like we hoped. Shit—I'm running late."

He abandoned his mug on the counter and walked quickly toward his office. I took a side door into the hallway that separated the main part of the department from the detective squad across the way. For the second day in a row, the hall was empty of reporters. The last of the TV trucks had left the night before. As ironies would have it, the press had put us on the back burner just as our momentum was building.

Dennis DeFlorio hailed me from the short flight of steps that led to the Municipal Building's rear double doors and the parking lot beyond. He was carrying a bulging, battered briefcase in one hand, and the ubiquitous donut in the other.

"Joe, where were you last night? I was looking for you."

"I went to visit Ron."

He walked down the hallway to where I was waiting, taking another bite along the way. "I got some good news about the gunman with the tattoo—the one they called Ut. And Dan Flynn called late—said his INS contact confirmed that Sonny and Truong are one and the same. No doubt about it."

Down the hall, near the rear steps, Tony Brandt burst from the department's main entrance. He was wrestling into his jacket, holding a folder in the other hand. "See you later," he called over his shoulder, and promptly fell headlong down the stairs.

Dennis and I broke into a run to see what was left of him.

Brandt was curled up against the double doors, clutching his ankle. The floor was littered with the oversized confetti that had exploded from his folder. "Jesus H. Fucking Christ. I think I broke the goddamn thing."

We clattered down the steps to his side. I gently pried his hands away from his ankle, undid his shoelaces, and removed both the shoe and sock underneath. Dennis, looking a little hapless, began gathering the sheets of paper.

"Can you wiggle your toes?" I asked.

"Hurts like a bitch," he said between clenched teeth, but the toes moved slightly.

I felt around the ankle, which was beginning to feel warm and spongy. There were no hard bulges or any signs of a broken bone. "You may have broken it—but it could just be a bad sprain."

By this time, several people had collected at the top of the small stairwell. "Better call an ambulance," I suggested.

"No. Out of the question," Brandt half yelled.

Everyone stared at him.

"I'll go to the hospital, but in a car. I don't want an ambulance."

"That's crazy. They . . ."

He grabbed my arm with an unmistakable ferocity. "No ambulance. They'll turn this into a goddamn circus. I'm sick of being front-page news. Besides, what the hell can the ambulance do now? Slap some ice on it and make a lot of noise? Just put me in my car."

I glanced out the glass doors at the parking lot and the department's four-wheel-drive Jeep station wagon, generally reserved for the shift patrol lieutenants. "All right. We'll take you in the Jeep. You've got to keep that foot elevated and your car's too cramped."

The crowd thickened measurably, and Tony capitulated. "Fine— whatever. Just get me out of here."

I yelled over my shoulder for someone to call the ER and let them know we were coming, and then I helped Dennis form a chair with our interlocked hands. We lifted Tony up and out the door, carrying him to the waiting Jeep with as much speed and gracefulness as possible.

We'd just gotten him settled into the front, with the seat tilted back and his foot propped up on a folded jacket on the dashboard, when Harriet appeared by my side with a bagful of ice cubes. "There's someone on the phone for you," she added, "from the Montreal Police."

"Damn." I'd forgotten I'd left a message last night for Jean-Paul Lacoste—Dan Flynn's Montreal contact—asking him to call me as soon as he could.

"Go ahead, Joe," Tony told me, "I'm all set."

Dennis was already sliding in behind the steering wheel. "I'll drive. Harriet, could you make sure they meet us with a wheelchair?"

I half smiled at this unusual show of foresight. "All right. I'll also have someone call the school and tell them not to expect you."

"Yeah, right," Tony growled, half to himself. "They'll be impressed how far I'll go to avoid a meeting."

I laughed. "I'll come see you later."

Dennis dropped the key as he was about to put it into the ignition. He was groping around near his feet when I told him, "You can fill me in on what you found out when you get back."

"Right—if I can ever get out of here," he muttered irritably.

I hurried back to the building, glancing over my shoulder at the door just as Dennis shouted, "Found it."

He leaned forward slightly to turn the ignition; Tony's foot was propped up on the dash, looking comically out of place.

What happened next froze me where I stood. A flash of angry red light arrowed up from under the steering wheel, enveloping Dennis's still-passive face in a demonic flame. A sudden and terrifyingly large burst of white smoke then erupted from the Jeep, accompanied by the concussion of a short, deep-throated explosion. Just before it was enveloped in a curling white wreath, I saw Dennis's head snap back, his mouth torn open by the shock of the impact. An instant later, I was pelted by a rain-like shower of debris landing all around me.

My nose stinging with a sulfurous stench, I saw the hulk of the car emerge from the smoke, looking normal below the windowsills, but like a smashed aquarium above—dominated by a menacing white cloud that hung in the air like a nuclear mushroom.

I broke into a run, calling out, slipping on the glistening, still-spinning litter covering the asphalt. A glance at Dennis told me he was dead. Not just the blood, which painted the inside of the car, but the way his head was tilted back—flopped over the headrest.

Tony, on the other hand, was still moving.

I skidded around to the passenger side and tore open the door. Tony lay reclined on his seat, writhing in pain, moaning softly. His clothes were burned and torn, covered with blood; he was littered with chunks of flesh, mostly from Dennis, whom I now saw was missing both legs. Gingerly, I leaned closer to Brandt. "Tony, Tony. Can you talk to me?"

Blood was running from both his ears, which I knew was due to the compression of the blast. His eyes, when he opened them, made me catch my breath. They were bright crimson, red from the inside, as if something had exploded in his brain and his eyes had been made clear windows to the mayhem within.

"Jesus Christ" was all I could say, before reaching out tentatively to see if somehow I could help.

*   *   *

I stood by the window of the ER waiting room, looking out at the parking lot where we'd arrested Nguyen Van Hai the day before, knowing somehow that that event and the reason I was here now were directly connected. Throwing political correctness to the wind, along with some basic civil-rights tenets, I'd ordered Sammie to organize a canvass of every Asian we knew of or could find, even before Tyler had finished roping off the explosion site.

I was having difficulty settling down, accepting that Dennis was dead and Tony badly hurt. I kept having to batten down spasms of anger that burst like firecrackers inside me, and to quell the impulse to lash out at something, or someone. I knew that now, possibly more than at any time in my career, the coolheadedness I preached about to others was going to be crucial—to the department, to the public's perception of it, to the people we were paid to protect, even to the surviving members of Dennis DeFlorio's family.

Furthermore, I knew that although Billy Manierre had automatically become acting chief the moment that blast had gone off, he was in no position to afford me the protection from both press and politicians that Tony routinely had.

Despite the clarity of these insights, however, the whole notion of grinding away on the case as I had been, nibbling at the edges when I knew it would finally extend beyond my jurisdictional reach, was an anathema. In the same way that I wanted to kick a chair or punch a wall to blow off steam, I also wanted to be cast free of having to depend on disinterested, overworked cops, hundreds of miles away, to dig into details that mattered so little to them.

Dr. James Franklin, the hospital's primary general surgeon, stepped into the waiting room and looked around to see if we were alone. Infamous for an irreverent sense of humor that popped up at even the darkest times, he was deadly serious now, perhaps sensing just how far the ripples of this assault were already reaching.

"How's he doing?" I asked.

Franklin joined me at the window and spoke softly. "Better than he should be. It's lucky that bomb wasn't filled with shrapnel. As it is, he still caught several pieces of metal and debris—nothing too serious, though. I gather his seat was completely reclined?"

"Yeah. Pushed and tilted back, both. We wanted to give him as much room as possible to prop the ankle up."

"Right," Franklin said, half to himself. "The ankle. I didn't even look at that. The seat position saved him—took him out of the lateral blast path. With Dennis's seat upright, it shielded him pretty effectively. Jesus, what a mess."

"Is he going to be all right?"

Franklin didn't respond as readily as I would have liked. "Probably. Not that you could tell it looking at him now. He can't speak because of some minor searing of his airway. He's also stone deaf as a result of dual fractured eardrums, and his vision is cloudy. He's got several fractured ribs, a fractured leg, a few burns, the puncture wounds I mentioned from the debris, and a headache to beat the band—all of which will probably heal with time."

"Including the hearing?"

"A little intervention might be called for there. I'm shipping him up to Mary Hitchcock Hospital today or tomorrow so they can check him over. He'll be out of circulation for at least a month, although partly as an outpatient."

"Can I see him?"

"You can look at him, through a window, but he's out like a light. We gave him some meds to make him sleep."

"Did you take a look at Dennis?" I asked after a slight pause.

Franklin's tone became a shade more formal. "The m.e. brought me in for a quick consult, just to help me in my treatment of Tony."

"What did you find?"

Franklin sighed. "I could tell you the old cliché that he didn't feel a thing. That wouldn't be far off the mark. Gould said the metal cap of the pipe bomb hit him like a slug from an elephant gun, right under the xiphoid process, through the diaphragm, and totally bisecting the aorta. There are few better ways to almost instantly kill a man."

"So it was a pipe bomb?"

"Definitely. But like I said, the only shrapnel came from the pipe casing itself and odd pieces of . . ." He hesitated.

"What?" I asked sharply.

"I was going to say *debris* again. But in case you come across it in one of the reports, you ought to know I found bits of Dennis's bone in Tony. That's going to entail some blood work we normally wouldn't do—just in case somebody asks."

"Like an HIV test?"

He made a sour face. "Among others. I know it's not likely, but better safe than . . . well, you know. That *would* be a hell of a note, wouldn't it?" Then he repeated, "God, what a mess. Does this have anything to do with that little show you put on for our patients yesterday?" He motioned with his chin toward the parking lot.

I shook my head. "Who the hell knows?"

*   *   *

Morningside Cemetery occupies the top and eastern slope of a hill overlooking the broad Connecticut River, contoured so that to stand in its middle is to be utterly alone among its hundreds of variously sized gravestones. The curve of the hill masks all other signs of civilization—the town to the west and north, the railroad track and the road paralleling the river below disappear beyond the close horizon. It is an island of utter calm, gazing out at the area's two most prominent features, which the rest of Brattleboro routinely ignores: the river, to which all of downtown turns its back to face Main Street; and Wantastiquet Mountain in neighboring New Hampshire, most often screened from view by buildings, but looming from such a height, and from so nearby, that when it occasionally catches the eye, through an alley or over a low rooftop, it does so like an eminently threatening thundercloud.

Dennis DeFlorio's grave was to enjoy this dramatic, beautiful, neglected view forever.

There were hundreds of people at the burial—most of them in uniform—fanning out in concentric circles from the awning-shaded casket and the decorously camouflaged hole beside it, unhampered by the walls of the small church that had excluded all but a few of them at the service earlier.

The killing of a police officer does that to other men and women who wear badges for a living—stimulates them to convene as they never will for other occasions. They will travel hundreds of miles, from several states away and from Canada, to pay their respects—not so much to a person they never knew, but in homage to an exclusive, lonely, tribal occupation that no one besides them fully understands. Every cop who dies in the line of duty does so alone—in surprise; and, perhaps for that reason, every other cop who can do so attends the interment, if for no other reason than to atone for arriving too late.

Gail was there with me, coming down once more from her studies in South Royalton. As an ex-selectman with an unusually high profile, her presence was noticed by a department that had once perceived her as one of the bosses, and was all the more appreciated given the slant of her politics.

Not that politics came into it here, as it might have in another town, where finding fault or gaining advantage are often knee-jerk reactions to crisis. For a place as culturally diverse as Brattleboro, there was still an intense sense of community, heightened in such times because people felt it slowly eroding away, despite the high pitch of their well-intentioned nostalgia.

Unlike in Boston, or even many of its neighboring communities, this town's civilian population did not take the death of one of its police officers in stride. It was as stunned and bewildered as the tiny group clustered, weeping, by the side of the casket. Dennis's wife, Emily, and his two young children, were like the splash in the center of a sun-dappled pond, where the reflections came not from rippling water, but from the rows upon rows of parade-ground uniforms, from gleaming buttons, belt buckles, and badges stirred in among the dark-clad citizens of the town. The small family's sorrow spread out to the farthest reaches of the crowd, to be absorbed, reproduced, and offered up for public scrutiny by a semicircle of cameramen, photographers, and reporters.

After it was over, after the ritual salute by weapons fire, the folding of the flag, the speaking of words that didn't remotely reflect the man in the casket, the crowd melted away over the monument-studded horizon, and abandoned the cemetery workers to their practical work with shovel and backhoe.

Gail and I went for a walk among the gravestones, some of which dated back two hundred years. We walked without speaking, holding hands, until we found a comfortable-looking marker, wide enough for us to lean against, facing the enormous, silent mountain across the water.

"What are you thinking?" she asked after a while.

"That, of all the cops in the department, Dennis was the one guaranteed to die in his bed—probably from choking on a donut. I was the one who suggested taking the Jeep. Why did he offer to drive? He normally didn't volunteer for anything. I guess he'd gotten into this case—something about it had caught him up—made him enthusiastic . . ."

"Not a bad time to go, if you have to. That's something."

But I shook my head emphatically. "He didn't die at the right time, or for a noble cause. He was butchered. The poor dumb son-of-a-bitch was blown apart by some bastard who didn't give a shit who he killed. Dennis DeFlorio is a monument to somebody's twisted pride—a status symbol, like some fucking tattoo."

I paused to pluck at a few tufts of grass. "Worst part is, I'd been told a cop was being targeted. I just didn't take it seriously."

Then I returned to a sore that had been festering in me for days. "Same thing with Vince Sharkey. Alfie Brewster might've set up that shoot-out, but I was the one who got Vince all worked up. And then I canceled the tail we had on him."

"None of this is your fault, Joe."

I didn't argue with her. "Tony told me the post-shoot investigator thought we'd played a little loose going into that deal. He was right. It wasn't Ron's fault we both almost got killed. I'm his boss. It was mine."

Gail was not cooperating. "You're feeling sorry for yourself. You didn't kill Dennis. And Ron would've been dead, too, if you hadn't been there. Ask yourself instead, 'What do I do now?' The department's in shock, and with Tony out of commission, you're the one they'll be looking to for leadership. You've got to give them something to focus on."

It was then, as if responding to some oddly theatrical cue, that Billy Manierre found us.

He came obliquely, his uniform hat in hand, as if ready to shy off at the slightest notice. His eyes were fixed on Gail, his old-school training sensitive to any hysterical feminine outburst she might spontaneously indulge in.

Instead, she smiled warmly, as most people did on greeting Billy—the living embodiment of the round, friendly, cop-on-the-beat.

"Have a seat." She patted the thick grass next to her.

He predictably demurred, standing awkwardly instead, looking around as if in fear of an ambush.

I got to my feet to make him feel more comfortable. "What's up?"

"I was going back to the station—see to the paperwork and all—but I thought maybe we ought to talk a little before. It'll probably be a nuthouse back there—lot of media back in town, lot of people wanting to bend my ear . . ."

I helped him out. "You'd like an update?"

"If you're up to it. I know this may not be the time or place."

My eyes slid off his face and strayed across the river. Legend had it that once, years ago, there'd been a fire on top of Wantastiquet, and that when firefighters had started climbing its steep, tree-choked slopes, they'd been met and scattered by an avalanche of rattlesnakes, all fleeing downhill in a writhing mass. Apocryphal or not, the story had its own curious appeal to me right now.

"No—that's fine. I can do that," I began, and then, both stimulated by Gail's pep talk and yielding to the smoldering frustration that Dennis's death had finally made unbearable, I added, "I'm about to spring something on you, though. Something I kicked around with Jack Derby and Tony a few days ago. Tony wasn't too keen on it. But I'd like to make a pitch to Walter Frazier that the FBI create a task force—involving me—to take this case over."

Billy's mouth opened slightly in surprise. "Boy, Joe. That's a little out of the blue. I mean, I heard something about it, but . . . What would that mean for us?"

As I spoke, my determination grew, along with an intoxicating sense of relief. "That I'd be reassigned. The department would still pay my salary, and the FBI would pick up the expenses and overtime. That's if Frazier's interested. It would release our manpower to catch up on other work, cut down on the overtime we've been racking up, and allow you to tell the press that the whole mess is out of your hands and that they can serenade the FBI for further details."

"Jesus, Joe. I don't think Tony'll go for this."

"Maybe not, but he's flat on his back with a nose full of tubes. You're the chief now."

His discomfort began to jell into opposition. "I'm acting chief. I can't authorize something like this."

I looked at him closely. "Billy, I talked to a cop in Montreal this morning named Jean-Paul Lacoste. He's their Asian-gang expert up there. He told me the man who got whacked in Montreal right after we stopped that car with Truong and Lam and the other guy last winter worked for a Chinese leader named Da Wang, that he'd been Da Wang's right-hand man in charge of the Montreal-Vermont-Boston illegal-alien pipeline. He was what they call a snakehead—a runner of illegals."

"Okay," Billy said cautiously.

"Dan Flynn says there's been lots of new activity in illegal aliens—that the name 'Sonny' has been cropping up, as a rival snakehead. And using our photo of Truong, Dan's also established that Sonny and Truong are the same person."

"So Truong replaced Da Wang's snakehead?" Billy asked, visibly confused.

I shook my head. "It's more complicated than that. At first, I thought the snakehead had played a role in killing Truong Van Loc's brother, and that he was killed for revenge. But as far as we know, the snakehead had never been to the US. Plus, if that had been Truong's goal, why's he still around? I think Truong is making a grab for Da Wang's business, although I still don't know why."

"Making Brattleboro's troubles part of an international conspiracy," Gail spoke up from near our feet, "which is what would make this attractive to the feds."

"We're not going to be able to solve this case from here, Billy," I pressed him. "And to keep trying is only going to frustrate our own people. But if I go federal and become a liaison to the department, I can keep them involved—give them a sense that Dennis's death is something they're still a part of, if only by proxy.

"Look at what we're holding, otherwise. We already swept the streets for every Asian we could find and got zip. J.P. checked every hardware and sporting-goods store within fifty miles of here for the type of pipe and powder used in that bomb, and found nothing. And that's because it was done by an outside team, just the way Da Wang's snakehead was hit. Sally warned us they were going to take out a cop, and that's exactly what they did. Now it's our choice—we can either keep pissing around, putting names to people we can't locate, or we can confront them on their own turf—and use federal muscle to close them down."

Billy shifted his weight and crossed his arms, staring out across the river. He finally shook his head in exasperation.

"What?" I asked, after he said nothing.

"I was just wishing I hadn't walked over here."

Chapter Seventeen

Walter Frazier looked from me to Dan Flynn. The three of us were sitting in his office in Burlington, several days after Dennis's funeral. "A task force made up of you two?"

"No," I answered. "The state police is the official applicant. That's why we're here and not talking to Bishop in Rutland. Being head of VCIN, Dan wouldn't be in the field. The state police would assign someone, and the two of us would interact with all the appropriate agencies—federal and local—as needed. The number of people involved from other agencies would vary."

"And I'd be running it," he stated, his voice flat.

"Right—or whoever you'd appoint. It would be a Bureau-sanctioned operation,but without the overhead and loss of manpower to you. And if the Bureau pays our tab instead of the department of justice, then I and whoever Dan's bosses assign could be deputized as US Marshals and act as federal officers."

Frazier was beginning to smile. "The US Attorney's office's will smell a rat. They'll wonder why we need a new task force when there're so many around already."

Flynn and I exchanged glances. "In my experience," Dan answered, "there are two types of task forces—the ones where everybody's focused on a specific job, which means they won't want us messing things up, and the ones with virtually open contracts, like the generalized local-federal drug task forces, which can get to be so much like departments unto themselves that we'd end up on the bottom of their *in* tray just like any other new case. The Windham County SA has signed onto this idea, and we flew it by Maggie Lanier—one of the US Attorney's assistants—and she was interested."

Frazier's smile widened. "Which means when you pitch this to the US Attorney himself, he'll already have a letter from Derby, and several in-house memos on his desk from Lanier, all telling him what a good idea it is. What an amazing coincidence." He leaned back in his chair and locked his hands behind his neck. "Assuming I toss this idea upstairs, what's going to make my DC bosses go along with it?"

"Asian organized crime—including money laundering, card fraud, alien smuggling, and murder. Plus, it's international and it'll be good PR with the Canadians."

Dan added, "It's also small, cheap, efficient, and completely under your control, and Joe's already done a lot of the spade work, which was one of the big selling points to Lanier. Not to mention that if it flops, nobody'll probably ever hear about it, while if we hit it big, then everybody shares and you get to look like a benevolent Big Brother."

"Walt," I picked up, feeling more and more like a junk-bond salesman, "we're not asking you to buy into some huge, unwieldy operation that's going to drag on forever. I couldn't afford that person-ally. The only reason I'm here is because my chief is flat on his back in the hospital and I browbeat our second-in-command into letting me make this pitch. But if I'm not back at my desk in pretty short order, somebody else will be."

I leaned forward in my chair. "As that report makes clear"—I pointed at the document on his desk that I'd faxed him a few days earlier—"I think I have a pretty good idea of what's going on. We're after two organizations fighting a turf war in Vermont, both of which have strong ties to, or interest in, Montreal. I've got a growing number of names and faces, one of which is already in jail, and I think, if we can use state and federal muscle, that we can take these people apart. We can go where they go, document what they're up to, and shut at least one of them down, almost like a special-interdiction unit."

Walt looked at Dan. "So how do you fit in? VCIN's role isn't going to be affected by any of this, is it? You'll still be gathering and passing along information like before, right?"

I answered instead. "VCIN's the key to the whole operation. I need the clout, the laws, and the jurisdiction that you can grant me, but I'm going to be working in-state a lot. Dan's still putting his network together, but he already has more contacts statewide than any other agency, including yours. Which means our de facto task force will be as big as VCIN itself—at no additional cost. Through it, I'll not only know what's going on in all the local nooks and crannies that might help us, I'll also know who to contact and who to avoid, including inside the various federal agencies. That knowledge will help streamline things incredibly, allowing us—more or less—to pick and choose who we work with, which will mean cutting down on red tape and on some of the crankier personalities."

The implication was left undefined, but we all three knew the first example of this last advantage was the fact that Dan and I were here, talking with Frazier, instead of butting our heads against his colleague Josh Bishop down in Rutland.

"I do have a selfish interest," Dan admitted. "If this succeeds, VCIN'll come out looking good, something I wouldn't mind my own brass noticing."

Frazier chuckled and shook his head. "God almighty. You two do make it sound fun and easy. You think you can get the US Attorney to give it a provisional nod, conditional on what my bosses decide?"

"We can try, assuming you give it a provisional nod, conditional on what the US Attorney says."

Frazier laughed outright. "What the hell—it might even work. I'll give it a whirl."

*   *   *

Tony Brandt was still in the hospital when I went to visit him— albeit a larger one in Lebanon, New Hampshire—still deaf, still covered with bandages, but at last out of Intensive Care. One of his injuries, however, had been underappreciated early on, and was raising havoc with him now. Somehow, during the explosion, he had inhaled enough superheated air to damage his vocal cords, so he was under doctor's orders not to speak a word.

Those twin disabilities were not slowing him down now, however.

He angrily scribbled on the pad before him and shoved it across his blanket at me. "You SOB," it read. "You know I didn't want you doing that!!!"

I wrote back: "The department needs it, I need it, & the case will benefit. And I'll be coming back and forth. If Billy gets in a jam, he'll know where to find me."

I watched his face as he read that, interpreting the successive waves of anger, frustration, disgust, and, finally, a hint of resignation—the last of which was most eloquent in his choice of words: "Has the FBI signed off on it yet?"

"Not yet," I wrote an answer. "Jack Derby and the US Attorney have—the latter as of this morning—pending FBI approval. But Frazier says he's optimistic. They even called him to DC to make his pitch personally. He says they don't do that unless they're interested."

"What about the selectmen?" he queried next.

That was stickier. No one in town except he and Billy knew what I was up to, and yet the final decision to release me was going to rest with the town manager or, if he was feeling insecure, the board of selectmen. But the fact that Tony had bothered to ask was another sign he was starting to cave in.

"I'll wow 'em somehow," I wrote on the pad, and then stood up.

Tony read those words, and turned slightly to look out the window. He finally let out a sigh. "Don't get yourself killed," he finally printed without enthusiasm, and waved me out the door.

Driving back to Brattleboro, I had to admit his fatalism was not unique. The bombing—and the numbing resurgence in media interest—had cloaked the whole department in a depression. Within the detective squad, or what was left of it, this mood exhibited its variations with each individual. Harriet had become business-like to the point of brusqueness, and J.P. was even more submerged in his swamp of forensic minutia. Sammie had begun virtually living at the office, and Willy still hadn't been seen in days. He had reportedly been spending his time in the streets, working his contacts and chasing down leads, but no one knew if he'd come up with anything—or even if the rumors of his hard work were true. As for Ron, he remained at home, remote, removed, virtually unreachable. My only consolation with him was that he was reportedly still showing up for his regular counseling sessions.

The attentions from the press had followed the norm. White-hot interest surrounding Dennis's death—the parking lot full of logo-decorated cars and trucks for days on end, the hallway clogged with reporters—followed by a gradual dwindling of zeal, until all that was left were the local people we knew by name. Nevertheless, it was here that Brattleboro's uniquely politicized character came most alive. Dennis's death, Tony's maiming, the threat of Asian crime, the fate of wayward youth, and the police department's role in all of them—and more—became fair game for everyone, from the press to the politicians to the unusually large assortment of resident town cranks.

Letters to the editor, call-in shows on the radio, debates on the local cable channel, and a never-ending onslaught of editorials, opinion columns, and feature articles cascaded on the consciences of the department's members to the point of distraction. Initial bafflement or cynical bemusement were slowly burnished into anger, resentment, and defensiveness, heightening a cop's natural sense of isolation to the level of paranoia.

Exacerbating it all was the hard realization that we had made but little progress since the explosion. Just before he'd died, Dennis had mentioned he'd received news about the dead man with the tattoo—the one I'd shot, named Ut. Sammie had spent days going through Dennis's desk and files, trying to put order into a professional lifetime of archival chaos. Eventually, and perhaps inevitably, she'd found a handwritten reference to a contact in California—scribbled on a piece of waxed paper last used to wrap a donut—with the word *Ut*, followed by three exclamations marks.

She'd located the source, and discovered that the tattooed La Luy Ut had been an early member of Chinatown Gang, and had been nicknamed "Louie La" at the time, which had explained why Nicky Tai had drawn a blank on the name Ut. Despite his youthful appearance, La Luy Ut had been almost thirty at his death. His age was an interesting detail—not only had he been a contemporary of Truong Van Loc, Michael Vu, and the late Johnny Xi of Vancouver, he'd also been older than Henry Lam, the reputed head of the three home invaders we'd shot. I'd learned by now how rare it was to have an Asian leader who was younger than his followers. It spoke of a man of ambition, charisma, ruthlessness, and—most interesting to me—connections.

The hope kindled in me that, despite having been remarkably ornery in life, Henry Lam might yet become an ally from the grave. I was beginning to think he might be the string I could follow all the way back to the elusive Truong Van Loc.

That, however, would take research and time, the latter of which was in short supply. We'd lost well over a week recovering from the bombing, and the trail of Dennis's killer was getting colder all the time. The impatience of everyone—inside and outside the department—was approaching a frenzy. In order for my little gambit with Flynn and Frazier to work, it was crucial to *specifically* connect the headline-grabbing bomb attack to the promise of a solution. But since the final approval for my joining a federal task force lay not with the professionals I'd been lobbying—as Tony had so well understood—but our own civilian bosses, I knew I'd need more than a tangled maze of obscure, historical connections before they'd grant me a green light.

It was a predictable irony that, while I might get permission to proceed from the head of the Vermont State Police, the US Attorney's office, the state's attorney's office, my chief, and the Washington office of the FBI, I might still be done in by three out of five beleaguered, anxious, publicity-conscious members of my own board of selectmen.

*   *   *

Sammie's cubicle looked like a war-ravaged foxhole, and she like the sole survivor of some disturbing psychological experiment. The crowded space around her desk was littered with fast-food wrappers, cardboard trays, and Styrofoam cups, and smelled of stale clothes and leftover fries; its occupant was pale, worn, edgy, and needed a shower.

I moved a crusty paper plate from her guest chair and tentatively sat down. "Hi Sam. How're you doin'?"

She gave me a deadpan, humorless glare. "Fine." She'd moved the squad's computer terminal—usually located in Ron's cubicle—onto her desk; its pale-green glow did little for her appearance.

"Can you give me an update?" I asked conversationally, figuring her stamina probably couldn't take any small talk, or her emotions any deviations from the case.

She reached for a legal pad beside the computer. "I better warn you, I haven't been making any friends out among the benevolent fraternity of police departments," she started out. "Just in case you wonder why all your chummy contacts start hanging up on you."

"Been leaning on them a little?"

"That's the way they've been acting." She waved at the glowing screen. "We're hooked up to this piece of shit because we're all supposed to cooperate with each other, right? When somebody calls me and says, 'Hey, I'm up a creek—can you do this or that, ASAP, and call me back?' I do just that. Well, I've been finding that's a one-way street. Everybody and his fucking uncle's been putting me on the back burner."

I shrugged it off. "Pretty natural they take care of their own turf first. Not everybody gives this job what you do, Sammie."

She smiled weakly. "That's a nice way of saying I'm neurotic."

"I'm not complaining." I smiled back. "So what's on your pad?"

She blinked a couple of times to focus. I wondered when she'd slept last. "Let's see. Piddley stuff first: When Chu Nam An had his accident in Rutland, his registration came out of Lowell, Mass., so I asked the PD down there to check out the address. It took 'em forever, but the place was empty. They said it had definitely been a crash pad, and probably been abandoned over a week ago. Landlord knew nothing. All transactions had been in cash. I also asked for Chu's records, but they still haven't sent them on. All I have so far is bare-bones info that shows him being involved in a lot of gang activity—typical Asian-on-Asian MO."

Her voice brightened a notch as she read on, her interest slowly beating back her exhaustion. "The reason I'm pushing so hard for more on Chu is that I finally did get something interesting on Henry Lam. Remember the date-of-birth scam he pulled to cover his Massachusetts history? Turns out he hung out in Lowell a lot—there's a big Asian population there—lot of bad apples. I want to cross-reference Chu and Lam and see if they connect, and if so, with who else. I know in my gut they have a mutual background . . . makes it real frustrating." Her voice tapered off as she flipped the page.

"Here's an interesting one," she resumed. "You'd asked J.P. to check out what happened to the team Johnny Xi led on that restaurant shooting in San Francisco. The PD there was a little faster getting back to us—they have a special Asian-crimes squad—and they said that, as far as they know, most of the team is dead."

"Any common denominators?"

"Half of them got it execution style. It'll take time before the PD can send us the actual names and records."

"How many were involved?"

"Witnesses said seven, all with automatic weapons. They drove up in two cars. I guess that makes nine, with the drivers. Anyhow, seven of them sprayed the place—all hyped up, screaming and yelling—and then they took off. Truong On Ha wasn't the only bystander killed—it was a real massacre. The PD knew right off it was a Dragon Boys hit. Even lined up a few witnesses—that's how they identified the shooters—but the witnesses faded overnight. One was found dead, the others got the message. The cops had to fold their tent."

"But they don't know why most of the team is now dead?"

"Not officially. They had their suspicions, but the whole thing's history now. I tried out all our names on them—Truong, Vu, and the rest—but aside from Johnny Xi and Truong's little brother, none of them connected."

"You said *most* of the team is dead."

She smiled at me. "Right. I noticed that, too. I'm having mug shots, prints, the whole caboodle forwarded to us. The two drivers were never made, I guess because nobody paid attention to them, so that makes five out of the nine who've been killed, and two out of the four survivors that've been identified."

She extended her pad to me, her finger underscoring a couple of scribbled Chinese names.

She sat back and flipped to another page of the pad, resuming her narrative. "I didn't get much else. I tried Henry Lam out on the Canadians. The name did come up on their computers, but all they said was that they'd get back to me. They're pretty close-mouthed, and I got the distinct impression they didn't consider us a high priority."

I resisted telling her of my hopes to improve our prestige considerably. "I take it there's nothing new on the pipe bomb?"

She shook her head. "Worse than that. Michael Vu disappeared, along with most of his soldiers. It's been like finding fish in the middle of a desert. J.P.'s still hoping the bomb fragments might tell us something. I took the liberty of issuing a high-priority be-on-the-lookout on Vu, by the way."

"That's fine."

We both heard the door to the hallway bang open, followed by a man's heavy tread. Willy Kunkle rounded the corner, bearded, wrinkled, dressed in dirty jeans and a work shirt, and making Sammie smell like a rose by comparison.

He leaned against the edge of the soundproof partition and looked down at us, grinning like a contented wolf. "Hey, boys and girls."

"Where you been?" I asked him, none too kindly.

Rather than answering directly, he reached into his breast pocket and held out his one good hand. Cradled in its palm, encrusted with dirt, was a small, delicate, jade-and-gold pendant, attached to a thin gold chain—exactly as Amy Lee had drawn it in my notebook.

"I been poking around," he finally said.

Chapter Eighteen

I gently removed the pendant from Willy's outstretched hand. "Nice work," I murmured, "Where'd you get it?"

"Garage north of Horton Place, right next to a dark-green Trans Am with Quebec plates and a smashed-in front grille."

"Jesus," Sammie muttered.

"I got a unit guarding the place till I get a search warrant," Willy added, his eyes betraying his nonchalance, "so you'll understand if I gotta go."

"Call me when you're ready," I told him. "And take a shower before you meet with the judge."

*   *   *

Horton Place is one leg of a semicircular street that attaches to the east side of Canal Street like one of those large, plastic horseshoe-shaped magnets. The other leg is named Homestead Place. What the back end is called—the part that connects the two legs—is anyone's guess, but it was there that Willy Kunkle led Sammie, J.P., and me about two hours later.

The Horton-Homestead loop has no option other than to double back on itself. It is shoved up against a steep, fifty-foot embankment that looms overhead like a semiforested cliff. Within the confines of the horseshoe are several beaten-up homes and two or three century-old, three-story wooden apartment buildings—all peeling paint and stacked, sagging balconies. Across a weed-choked backyard are two decrepit concrete garages. A squad car, its driver leaning against the fender, was parked in front of one of them.

The structure in question was free-standing, had two solid, old-fashioned pull-down doors on cantilevered hinges, and looked about ready to collapse. It had no windows that I could see.

"'Round here," Willy said, leading the way. He was still unshaven and wearing the same clothes, but he now smelled of too much deodorant.

On the garage's west side was a narrow wooden door. Willy turned the knob, shoved it open, and stepped inside. We paused on the threshold, our eyes adjusting to the darkness. Before us was a single stall with an earthen floor; apart from some tires and a broken armchair, it was empty. There was a second opening, without a door, on the far wall separating this stall from its mate, but there wasn't enough light to see through it. This last fact alone, coupled with the assumption that the Trans Am was parked in the second stall, set off my internal alarm bells.

"Hold it," I ordered, as Willy was about to walk through to the opening. "How did you find this place?"

Willy looked back impatiently. "Last week, when we searched the flophouse Nguyen lived in, I noticed this guy hanging around outside, watching us. One of the residents told me he was called Chui. He was an obvious creep—tight pants, greasy hair, fancy mustache. I didn't have any reason to roust him then, but," and he tapped the side of his head, "I filed him away for posterity. After Dennis got whacked, I went back, staked myself out in one of the alleys across the street, and waited.

"Just like I thought, Michael Vu came and went, giving orders, and then all the boys in the fancy cars took off like rats from a sinking ship. But this guy Chui, he hung loose a while, cleaning up. I followed him around town, saw him visit all the Chinese restaurants, the Asian-run businesses. He was either telling everybody to sit tight, or squeezing them for one last payoff. In any case, he finally came here.

"This," he waved his hand around him, as if showing off a prized piece of real estate, "was a new one on me. It had never figured in any surveillance reports, never come up in any of the dailies. Chui came in early this morning, spent about half an hour inside, and left carrying a big box. I let him go so I could take a look."

I silently swore to myself, having suspected as much. If Willy had trespassed without probable cause, found the pendant and the car, and only then secured the search warrant, every piece of evidence in the place was going to be inadmissible in court. "You entered here?"

There was a stillness while Willy looked from me to the others, catching my drift and calculating what to say. "I had cause. I saw the pendant from the open door and recognized it from the drawing you showed us."

"Oh, boy," Sammie said under her breath.

"You saw the pendant from the door?" I asked, remembering he'd stated that he'd found it "right next" to the car in the search-warrant application.

His confidence grew as he ran his story through his head. He moved closer to the threshold. "Yeah. Stand here. See? The light reaches the middle of the floor, and that's where I saw it. The glimmer caught my eye, and I recognized it."

"From this distance," I stated flatly, my tone of voice indicating what I was thinking.

He crossed over to the spot he'd indicated and dropped the pendant onto the dirt. I'd told him an hour earlier to lock it up as evidence back at the office but, by this point, that was looking like a pretty minor breach of protocol. "You can see it, can't you?"

I did see the gold and the hot shimmer of jade reflecting the sun, enough to match it to what Amy Lee had drawn on my pad, but it had been smeared with dirt then, and wiped off since. Even if Willy had found the pendant so near the door, it would have had to have been ground into the soil not to have been noticed by Chui during his last visit. Besides, early this morning, the sun had been on the far side of the building.

But I consciously gave life to the lie, reacting in slow, burning anger that, after all our hard work and sacrifice, we were having to kowtow to—and cover up—a maverick's careless enthusiasm. "That's your story?"

He took my meaning, eyeing me warily. "On a stack of Bibles."

Sammie sighed next to me.

"It'll probably come to that," I muttered grimly. "Okay, come on out. We better seal it all off and treat it as a crime scene."

Kunkle stared at me incredulously. "For Christ's sake. There's nothing here except the car. I already checked. I've been through the whole place."

I stared at him speechlessly for a moment, amazed at his lack of care—and at my own complicity. "All right," I murmured.

"Having found the pendant—and recognized it," he continued ponderously, "I looked around to see what else there might be in plain view from the same crime." He stepped up to the dividing doorway. "That's when I found the car."

We all trooped into the next stall. Willy crossed to the front door and wrenched it open. Amid the squealing of protesting hinges, the garage was suddenly soaked in bright light. Squinting, we all looked at the dusty, low-slung sports car that John Crocker had so carefully described.

For no apparent reason, I glanced down at my feet, and saw imprinted in the moist dirt—as a ghostly confirmation—the distinct outline of a pendant-shaped object, roughly circled by the impression of a thin chain, right outside the passenger door of the car where it had obviously been stepped on after slipping there unobserved.

I scowled at Willy Kunkle posing by the wide door in his moment of fabricated glory, and discreetly scuffed the dirt with my foot, engulfed in pure rage as I did so. We could have found this legally if he'd just taken note of Chui entering the garage and reported back his suspicions. But he hadn't, and now I'd conspired with him, riding roughshod over deep-seated principles so as not to sacrifice crucial evidence to a fine point of law.

"Did you touch the car at all?" J.P. asked.

"Nope," Willy answered from the door. "I'm not that dumb."

I withheld comment, and listened as J.P. told us what to do.

*   *   *

Two and a half hours later, our backs aching from being scrunched up in awkward positions, our hands hot and sweaty inside latex gloves, we gathered outside the garage's yawning door to examine what we'd found. Tyler had spread a clean tarp out on the ground, and placed our specimens across it like museum exhibits. He was crouching next to them, writing in a logbook, his camera nearby.

As we peeled off the gloves and found places to rest, he ran down the list. "Lots of fingerprints, some partial, some pretty complete. Three sets of blood-stained surgical booties, and three sets of bloody gloves, one of which has been cut, presumably by glass, and which is filled with blood, presumably from the wearer." He looked up at us, a satisfied expression on his face. "With any luck, we'll be able to match that to the blood Sol got from the hospital, and to what we found at the Rivière residence. Along with this rag that was probably used to staunch the flow of blood from his wound, that ought to be enough to convince a jury that Nguyen was at the scene.

"Not to mention this little sweetheart," he continued. He speared a spent bullet cartridge with the blunt end of his pen and poured it into a white evidence envelope. "It came from a Glock. And those," he gestured at a package of plastic trash bags, "which, according to a process I just read about in the *Journal of Forensic Sciences*, we should be able to match to the one they used over Benny's head."

He sat back on his heels, his eyes coming up to meet the shattered car grille directly before him. "And, of course, there's always that. I know I can match it to some of the debris you and Stennis picked up on the Upper Dummerston Road."

"What about these?" Willy asked, pointing with his foot at a small pile of documents.

"They came out of the glove box," Sammie told him. "Owner's manual, map of New England with no marks on it, registration made out to Henry Lam. That's about it, I think."

"A store receipt," J.P. added.

"Let me see that," I said, squatting down next to Tyler.

He extracted it from an envelope with a pair of tweezers, enough so that I could see what was printed on it. There was a short tally of several inexpensive items. More interesting was the convenience-store name printed at the top, along with the date and time of day.

"Montreal," I read. "A week before Benny died. Could you make me a copy of that?"

"Sure." Tyler made a note in his logbook.

I rose to my feet again, satisfied despite the misgivings over how we'd acquired this small treasure. "Nice work, everybody. Maybe some of this will make Nguyen a little more talkative. It'll sure as hell tickle Jack Derby. How soon on the DNA testing for the blood?" I asked J.P.

"Couple of more weeks, give or take. I could lean on them, if you want."

"No, he's not going anywhere. How're you doing on the pipe bomb?"

Tyler shrugged, obviously unhappy. "I sent what I could down to the ATF lab in Washington. I guess you heard we didn't find any local source for the ingredients."

I nodded silently.

"I guess the only thing I have any hope for is a print I found on one of the end caps. The chances of matching a single impression to somebody's record aren't all that great, but we might get lucky."

I turned to Willy. "By the way, what did you find out about Alfie Brewster? Or did you just blow that off?"

Kunkle looked at me carefully, realizing by my tone that he'd stepped over the edge—and had been allowed to survive. "Sorry 'bout that—never got back to you. Not much. My hunch is that while he's not sorry Vince is dead, he had nothing to do with the drug party or home invasion. He is taking full credit for it, of course, bragging to his buddies, but he messed up the few crucial details I quizzed him about."

"So it was either coincidence," said Sammie, "or someone else aimed Vince at Vu."

I shook my head dubiously. "I'm not big on the first choice."

Sammie shrugged. "Too bad they're all dead."

"That doesn't mean some of them can't still talk," I muttered, half to myself.

"Meaning what?"

"Meaning I think I'll go to Rutland for a couple of days—catch up on a little overdue homework."

*   *   *

Rutland is Vermont's second-largest city, which isn't saying much, considering the entire state has just over half a million people. And unlike Brattleboro, even its most dewy-eyed enthusiasts can't claim it hasn't suffered at modern hands. The original downtown section has a strong and handsome turn-of-the-century appeal—a collection of stalwartly elegant old buildings reminiscent of the confident Yankee industrialism that put the town on the map in the first place. But Rutland's fallen on hard times—a mass of railroad tracks slices through the city's center, and a cheap, glitzy, traffic-choked business strip lining Route 7 on the hill east of downtown creates a feeling of disunity. Sticking to Route 7, a traveler could drive the entire north-south axis of town, numbed by its tasteless, endless string of malls, outlets, and fast-food joints, and never know that a few blocks to the west an entirely different city, complete with many old architectural gems, lies ignored.

It was there, nevertheless, at City Hall, on the corner of Washington and Wales, that I met with Detective Sergeant Sandy Rawlings, who'd been assigned as my official liaison. Tall and thin, with the tidy dress and immaculate manners of an overgroomed Boy Scout, he was the kind of person I had a terrible time taking at face value. Our first encounter didn't help. He grabbed my car's door handle just as I was about to open up from inside, and dragged me half out into the parking lot as he pulled it open. I landed, one hand on the door, the other flat on the pavement, staring at his highly polished shoes.

"I take it you're Rawlings," I said, struggling to get up.

"Yes, sir. I am sorry." He made an embarrassed and ineffectual effort to help me.

"Don't worry about it. And call me Joe. I hope you weren't standing around waiting too long."

He either missed or ignored the mild irony. "No. No, Lieutenant. It was a pleasure. Would you like to come upstairs?"

Given the conversation so far, I passed. "Why don't you just take me to where Chu used to live? We can talk on the way."

Things improved on the short trip to the city's west side, literally located beyond the railroad tracks. Having insisted on driving, I inadvertently robbed Rawlings of what he'd no doubt onerously seen as his primary official duty. As a result, after a bit more initial discomfort, he pragmatically opted to relax and enjoy the ride, his strained good manners ceding to something a little more approachable.

He had little to tell me that I didn't already know about Chu Nam An's innocent encounter with the police, and his description of Rutland's Asian population was not unlike our own. Although much smaller in size—"We don't have one," in his words—it was equally diffuse, ebbing and flowing according to its own private mechanisms. Whether it was the city's depressed economic state, or the fact that it didn't lie particularly close to any major interstate, it seemed at best a backwater for Asians—a stopover on the way to somewhere else. Or perhaps, as with Chu, I thought, an off-road holding station for someone with a job to do.

The area Rawlings directed me to—Howe Street—was shoved up against an intersection formed by the railroad tracks and West Street, also known as Business Route 4. It was one block long, worn, nondescript, residential, and abandoned in appearance. Its west side was occupied by a row of weather-beaten wooden homes facing an overgrown field and an empty, gutted, salmon-colored factory building labeled with a barely legible wooden sign announcing the Green Mountain Work Shop. Its serried ranks of shattered windows made clear that, nowadays, its only function was as a target for every rock-wielding kid in the neighborhood. Howe was a carbon copy of the street Heather Dahlin had taken me to in Hartford, and that our own Asians had chosen in Brattleboro. There was a nomadic feeling to all three of them, as if their inhabitants, regardless of race, occupation, or prospects, knew they should only carry the basics, and never completely unpack.

The building he pointed out looked a little worse off than its neighbors—stained, sagging, and covered with old scalloped asbestos shingles, half of which were cracked or missing. The windows were devoid of decorations or shades, and the yard was vacant and neglected.

"Still empty?" I asked, not bothering to kill the engine.

"Yeah. One day they were here. The next they were gone. A few worked at the local restaurants or grocery stores, but they were the exception."

"Nice cars with out-of-state plates every once in a while?"

"Yeah, that's right." He looked at me, a little surprised. "I was the one your office contacted to check this Chu out. According to the neighbors I interviewed, the people who came in the flashier cars were the only ones who caused any nervousness. They usually traveled in pairs or groups, dressed in showy clothes, and had a way of strutting around that made people feel uncomfortable. Our biggest problem here is with Hispanics, so the area's already racially tense—adding a few Asians didn't help. Not that they did anything—they were more like cruising sharks, you know? Swimming around all the other fish. 'Course, we're only talking eight or so people at a time, max."

"And what about the others?" I asked.

"They kept to themselves—maybe fifteen of them at any one time, all living in that one place. We always figured it was part of a pipeline, but that's not our jurisdiction. Like I said, we got bigger problems."

That sounded familiar. I looked up and down the block, and then checked my watch. It was getting near suppertime, and the sky just beginning to fade. "Where's the nearest dive? Bar, dance club, whatever?"

He gave me a quizzical look and jerked his thumb over his shoulder. "A few blocks down west. Why?"

"I was thinking if I drove a fancy car and strutted my stuff, I might want to unwind someplace with the boys."

Rawlings gave me the grin of a man suddenly catching the scent of something interesting—a pure cop's reaction and totally at odds with his tweedy appearance.

"Right," he said slowly and appreciatively, and began giving me directions.

Unfortunately, that first stop came to nothing. The owner of what turned out to be a threadbare, pleasant, neighborhood bar not only didn't recognize the picture of Chu I was carrying with me, he didn't think a single Asian had ever crossed his threshold.

The same held true for the next two places we visited. Rawlings shook his head as we got back into the car. "This could take a while, Lieutenant. If they didn't frequent the local bars, then we've got a shit load to choose from. Rutland has no shortage of gin joints."

"How 'bout karaoke bars?" I asked, suddenly inspired.

"Where you sing along with the music?" he asked dubiously. "Yeah, we got one of those."

We left the west side and went up the hill to the gaudy Route 7 strip, eventually pulling into the parking lot of a building so shoddily built under its camouflage of blinking neon, it looked ready to fall apart. But by this time it was almost eight o'clock, and Mort's, as it was called, was dressed to do some serious, if low-rent, business. Inside, the light was dim and bizarre, supplied mostly by blinking Christmas lights hanging from the ceiling. The music was low and schmoozy. Unfortunately, the magic wasn't working—the place was almost empty. The karaoke fad, it seemed, was on the skids, and I was pretty sure we were about to strike out again.

The bartender greeted us with the traditional, "What'll it be, gents?" as we selected two stools from among the twenty-some available.

Rawlings did his tactful bit with the badge while I groped for the picture inside my jacket. "You ever cater to any Asians?" I asked in the meantime.

The bartender was an amiable-looking bald man with a close-cropped beard, as perfectly suited physically to his job as if he'd come from central casting. He kept wiping a small glass he was holding with a damp rag, just like in the movies. "Sure. They like to do that sing-along crap. Terrible singers. Buy a lot, though."

"How 'bout this guy? Ever see him?"

He looked at the photograph closely, even taking it under a small light suspended over the cash register. "He doesn't look too healthy."

"He's not."

He returned the picture gingerly. "Can't say I have. I'm not too good with faces anyhow. You guys want anything?"

I didn't know later if it was inspiration or dumb luck, but I said yes, and ordered a tonic water with a twist. Rawlings merely shook his head and swiveled around to look at the gloomy room.

The bartender returned moments later with my drink and volunteered, "You know. You might try one of the girls. They spend every night staring into guys' faces, making 'em feel good."

He indicated a corner table, far from the bar, where three shadows were clustered together, hunched over their drinks.

With Rawlings in tow, I walked over to the table, noticing that the closer I got, the more the three women took notice and changed accordingly. Their bodies moved slightly away from the table, the better to be seen, legs were crossed, lips moistened. There was an inaudible comment followed by a shared dirty laugh just before we got within earshot.

My glass still in hand, I smiled down at them. "Hi. Mind if we sit down?"

Two of them were brunettes, the third in blonde disguise. They were all weighted down by an excess of makeup and cheap jewelry, but their enjoyment, perhaps lingering from the joke we hadn't heard, seemed genuine. The blonde indicated the only empty chair at the table, while one of her friends pulled another one over from the next table. "Please do," she said.

"You from out of town?" asked the third. "I know we've never seen you in here before."

"I'm from Brattleboro," I answered, and pointed at Rawlings, "but he's local."

Rawlings smiled tightly and nodded, distinctly uncomfortable, and unsure of my strategy.

"What're your names?"

"I'm Joe. He's Sandy and, to be honest with you, we're both flying under false colors."

The three women quickly exchanged glances. "What's that mean?" one of them asked.

"We're cops. I'm investigating a homicide and Sandy's helping me out here in Rutland—what they call a liaison."

"You got badges?" the older of the two brunettes asked.

"Sure." I whipped my shield out and placed it on the table before them. Rawlings followed suit more slowly. The three of them bent over to read the fine print in the dim light.

"Joe Gunther," read the blonde, her voice warming back up. "You been in the papers?"

"Sure," one of her friends answered. "And on TV. You were the one that got knifed last year—the one that got that rapist."

I signaled to the bartender and ordered another round, "for the ladies." I could feel Rawlings wilting beside me as I fed their curiosity about the case they'd alluded to.

"So now you're working on a homicide?" asked the blonde sometime later. She'd introduced herself as Kim, and her friends as Mona and Candy. "That car bombing?"

"It's connected to it."

Rawlings let out a small sigh. Rule one in law enforcement— among dozens of others—was not to show your cards unless absolutely necessary, especially to civilians. It was, however, one I broke often to great benefit. Since the public had come to see us as tight-mouthed and generally aloof—answering every question with a question—I'd found the best way to win them over quickly was to be just the opposite.

The proof that it worked, at least occasionally, was evidenced by

Kim's understandable delight. "No kidding? That made the national news."

I now reached for Chu's photograph and laid it face up on the table. "Does he look familiar?"

Kim made a face. "Ooh, he looks dead."

"I know him," said Candy, who up to now had been the quietest of the trio. "I went out with him maybe a month ago. He was a creep."

Everyone turned toward her, and she seemed momentarily tongue-tied at her abrupt notoriety.

"Could you tell me about it?" I asked.

"Not that much to tell. A bunch of them came in here one night. Mona and Kim weren't around, and I was feeling lonely. They were throwing lots of money around, and this guy started buying me drinks. It was fun for a while. They sang at the machine—got me to do it, too . . ."

"Candy," Kim burst out, almost in outrage, "you always hated that thing."

"Well," she came back defensively, "I was having fun. Anyway, after a while, he said he had a real nice car, and maybe I'd like to drive around a little. I knew what he was after—I mean, I'm not that dumb—but I thought he was pretty cute, and he talked funny, and the car was beautiful. I should've known it was going to get weird when his two pals came along . . ."

"Candy, you jerk," Kim broke in again.

She didn't argue the point. "Yeah—a drunk jerk, too. It started out okay, though. We did just drive around at first." She gestured to the mug shot. "He found some back roads out of town and really opened that car up. It was fun. But they had a bottle with them and they started showing off, and next thing I know there was a gun being passed around . . ."

"Oh, my God," Mona murmured. "You never told us any of this."

Candy looked down at her lap. "I was embarrassed—maybe a little scared. There were three of them, after all. I know I shouldn't have gone."

"What happened with the gun?" I asked gently.

"I didn't show I was getting nervous. I pretended to be impressed. They even let me hold it once. Then this guy here asked me if I'd ever shot one before. I had shot a twenty-two when I was little—my daddy's gun—so that's what I told him. He laughed and pulled over and fired the stupid thing right out the window. Scared the crap out of me. He tried to get me to shoot it and I wouldn't. That's when things kind of got bad. He put the gun away and made a pass at me, but I wasn't in the mood anymore, and the other two being there put me off, too. It got a little rough, then. They started pawing me, ripping my clothes, trying to get at me . . ."

"Oh, my God," Mona repeated. Kim was rapt, her mouth slightly open.

"I was fighting them off, and doin' all right, since the car was too small for the guys in the back to do much, but then one of them hit me on the back of the head—maybe with the gun, I don't know—and that sort of took the fight out of me. I figured, you know, what the hell? Just lie back, let 'em do it, and that'll be that. What's the fuss?" She added as a face-saving joke, "It's not like I haven't faked it before, right?"

But her eyes were brimming with tears, and Kim wrapped an arm around her.

"It didn't happen, though," she continued. "I guess I ruined it for everybody, 'cause they just threw me out of the car and drove off. So, other than a bump on the head and a ruined blouse, I was okay, except it took me over an hour to walk home. My feet ended up hurting worse than my head."

Mona rubbed her friend's back, repeating that she couldn't believe Candy hadn't shared this with them before.

"Candy," I said, "are you up to answering a few questions about these guys?"

She nodded. "Sure. It actually feels pretty good getting it out."

"Okay—easy ones first. What did this man call himself?"

"Bobby."

I straightened slightly, caught off guard, and repeated inanely, "Bobby?"

"Well," she amended, "he started out with something I didn't understand—something Chinese or whatever—and then when I couldn't get it, he said, 'Just call me Bobby.' And he introduced his friends the same way, as Frankie and Tommy, I think. I'm not positive about that."

"Do you think you could describe either of the other two, including things like scars, tattoos, unusual eye color, anything like that?"

She hesitated, and finally shook her head. "I was pretty far gone when I met them, and all four of us left almost right after. Plus they ended up in the back seat." She grimaced apologetically. "I'm sorry, Joe, all I can say for sure is that they were Oriental and didn't have any beards or mustaches."

"They never said if they were Vietnamese or Chinese or something else?"

"No."

"That's all right. Did they say where they were from? Or what they did for a living? Places they'd been recently? Any kind of chitchat you can recall."

"Bobby did all the talking, I remember. The other two just laughed or said stuff in Chinese or whatever. He said they traveled around a lot, but when I asked what they did, he just said they were traveling businessmen." Her face became suddenly animated, and she leaned forward. "That's how the gun came out. Bobby was talking about business, and how he was going to make a lot of money soon. I was getting scared and pretty drunk, so I don't remember exactly how it all fit together, but there was a definite connection—the gun was going to make him a lot of money."

I couldn't suppress a pleased smile. Just like Henry Lam, Chu Nam An seemed to be playing a bigger role in death than the one that had cost him his life. We still had one missing player in Benny Travers's death, and if Chu was him—and had been paid for his services—that made it murder for hire, which was a federal crime, and yet another tidbit I could use to interest the FBI.

"Okay. Can you remember exactly where you were when Bobby did his target practice? Did he hit anything?"

She broke into a smile. "That's easy. After they threw me out, I remember actually laughing about it. He'd shot at the broad side of a barn."

"Did he hit it?"

"He couldn't miss—that was the joke. We were parked right next to it."

*   *   *

The next morning, I steadied the ladder as J. P. Tyler carved away at a post in the dimness of an old broken-backed barn on the outskirts of Rutland. Sandy Rawlings watched from the side, along with the quizzical owner of the property.

Following Candy's directions the night before, I'd driven Sandy out to the barn to confirm her story and had found that Chu Nam An had done much better than hit the "broad side of a barn." Clearly visible in my headlights, we'd found a tight, ragged cluster of five bullet holes puncturing the old boards.

J.P. pocketed the chisel he'd been using and began descending the ladder. "Aside from the fact that it made for a hell of a lot of digging, you couldn't have asked for a better target." He paused halfway down and pointed to the opposite wall, where the cluster of bullet holes sparkled with the morning sun behind them. "First those boards slowed the bullets down, and then that beam was so rotten, it was like hitting cotton wool."

He continued down and, at the bottom rung, held out his hand. Two slugs were nestled in his palm. "Almost perfect condition. The other three rounds missed the beam and went out the other side."

"Can you tell what they're from?" I asked, sure I already knew.

"A Glock—no two ways about it."

Chapter Nineteen

Walter Frazier's voice was filled with mock incredulity. "I guess this proves how crazy they are at headquarters."

"You're kidding," I burst out, tightening my grip on the phone. "They bit?"

"All the way to the sinker. 'Course, matching the Rutland bullet to the one from Travers's body and faxing the news to DC was a nice piece of work. They loved it, and to be honest, losing one of your own men had a big impact."

I didn't miss the irony of Dennis's newfound stature in death. "So what's next? A background check from the US Marshals?"

"That's pretty much done. I asked them to get it started after you and Dan left my office. A little unorthodox, but I thought it would help you hit the ground running."

"Jesus, Walt, I'm really grateful. I know this only worked because you pushed it."

He laughed at the other end. "Don't kid yourself. They'll be dancing in the streets the day I retire. Anyhow, I thought you'd like to know. I'm generating the appropriate paperwork now, but you better call Dan and find out how their office is going to coordinate things as lead agency. Keep that in mind, by the way—if the state police don't like you for some reason, either now or down the line, they're higher in the pecking order than you are, and I'll have to listen to them. So be nice."

"Does that mean you're running the task force personally?" I asked, reading into his choice of words.

He laughed again. "You think I'd risk putting one my fresh young agents with you? Forget it—I have some loyalty to the flag."

I thanked him again and hung up, finally feeling the white-hot anger born of Dennis's death beginning to cool—if only a little. There were no guarantees this task force would end in success, but at least a failure now wouldn't be for lack of trying. That realization alone bore an element of peace.

*   *   *

The Vermont State Police is headquartered on Route 2, between Montpelier and Burlington, in the village of Waterbury, about a mile from Exit 10 off Interstate 89. The most memorable detail about its location, however, is not that it's part of one of the ugliest, antiquated state-office-building complexes I've ever seen, but that it shares a driveway with the state mental hospital—a geographical coincidence that has forced the VSP to put up with more than their fair share of bad jokes.

Dan Flynn came down to the locked reception area to escort me up to his miniature empire on the second floor—two rooms crammed with computers and filing cabinets, manned by Flynn and a gnomish, silent man named William Shirtsleeve—a statewide phenomenon known to everyone as "Digger."

Digger was nearing retirement, after spending all but the last three years of his adult life as a patrolman. For decades, he'd driven the roads of Vermont, moving among the regional barracks as part of his organization's standard rotation, but never moving up the ranks, never aspiring to, or even accepting, a single desk job. Unmarried, rarely socializing, William Shirtsleeve had lived to do one thing—be a street cop. Wherever he was stationed, he spent every hour he could away from the barracks, visiting people at their homes, dropping in on businesses—legitimate and otherwise—and visiting kids in schools, taking a special interest in the ones who showed the potential of becoming future clients. Without taking notes, or making a display of his intentions, Shirtsleeve slowly began to accumulate what keyboard operators now call data. He began linking names to families to places to events to organizations to trends, constantly soaking up knowledge, until he became a walking encyclopedia of Vermont's less-than-genteel society. For this quiet prowess he was eventually nicknamed Digger, and relied upon by colleagues from around the state to come up with the answers they couldn't discover on their own. When Dan Flynn was given permission to set up VCIN, he had only one man in mind to assist him—the one man he was told would turn him down cold. But Dan had asked anyway, and Digger had said yes without hesitation or explanation. For the past three years, as taciturn as ever, he'd plied his computers with the same dogged zeal he'd once applied to the communities he'd patrolled. Dan's own personal theory was that, knowing his retirement was near, Digger had felt the need to deposit his hard-won knowledge someplace useful, and that VCIN had appeared as if by prophesy. Like some ancient elephant imparting wisdom to later generations, Digger was describing the world as he knew it to the memory chips of Dan Flynn's electronic files.

Knowing all this, however, never helped me in dealing with the man himself, who now—as in the past—responded to my greeting by keeping his eyes firmly glued to the monitor's screen, and muttering, "Uh-huh."

Dan, the exact opposite in all ways, laughed, slapped me on the back, and steered me through to his inner office, a seven-by-nine-foot aggravated closet entirely decorated in Boston Bruins paraphernalia, from stuffed bears to pennants to magnetic hockey pucks to bumper stickers taped to the window.

"Quite the character, huh?" he stated, as always not expecting a response. "Don't know what I'd do without him. Three years into this project, and half our information is still inside his head."

He settled in front of a battered metal desk shoved up under the room's one window, and motioned to a chair wedged in between two tall filing cabinets. His face became suddenly serious. "I'm real sorry about Dennis. And I'm sorry I couldn't make it to the funeral—boss said he couldn't spare me. How's everyone taking it?"

I sat on the edge of my seat, leaning forward to avoid the feeling of being swallowed whole by my two looming metal neighbors. "Not very well. The worst part is, Dennis's death was the one push we needed when it came to getting the go-ahead from the board of selectmen. Billy Manierre made a pitch to the board like a born-again evangelist—I've never seen him so passionate—and Tony weighed in from the hospital with a letter not only saying that I had his blessing, but forecasting the end of the world as they knew it if they didn't go along. I couldn't believe it."

"Lucky they did. A lot of people would've had egg on their faces otherwise."

I sensed something beyond a colorful generalization in this. "You too?"

His seriousness yielded to a smile. "Not me. I'm the knight in shining armor here, helping out a beleaguered colleague. You're the one making my bosses feel queasy—hotdog local cop, hell-bent on becoming a federal officer so he can get revenge."

"And involving the VSP in his schemes?" I finished for him.

He raised his eyebrows sympathetically. "You think they're wrong to be concerned? The death of a colleague can cut pretty deep."

I conceded his point. "No. I'm amazed they went along with it."

He leaned back, his expression amused. "Right—the green and the gold, the stuffy Vermont State Police, the you-guys/us-guys of law enforcement. Surprised you, didn't we? I won't deny we deserved some of that in the old days, but times are changing." He suddenly leaped to his feet and headed for the door. "And as further proof of it, I'm going to introduce you to your partner."

He was gone. I staggered to my feet, hitting a shoulder on one of the cabinets, and swung out after him, catching up as he strode quickly across the hallway to a closed door marked Conference.

He paused there theatrically, and then threw the door open to let me in. Standing in the room, studying a wall map through gold-rimmed glasses, was a tall, sandy-haired, alarmingly skinny man in his mid-thirties. He turned as I entered and gave me a wide, crooked smile. "Hey, Joe—long time."

I laughed and crossed over to shake his hand, the sense of relief like a tonic. "Lester Spinney. I don't believe it."

From the time Dan Flynn had first indicated an interest in joining forces, the question in my mind had always been who they'd team me up with. I'd expressed my concern to Flynn, of course, but he'd reasonably answered that it wasn't his shot to call. Seeing Spinney, however, convinced me that if not Flynn, then someone in the state police had made sure personality conflicts were not going to be blamed if this task force fell apart.

Spinney and I had first met years ago, when I'd been temporarily assigned to the Essex County State's Attorney's office as a special investigator. Ron Potter, the SA, was facing a tough murder case, and had pushed a little hard to make sure his investigator was fully included in what was a state-police case.

Despite the implied lack of trust, no blood had been spilled. With only a couple of exceptions, the state cops had made room for me, and relations had been civil enough. But even the most cooperative among them had taken their gauge of me before fully opening up—except for Lester Spinney. Whether because of his naturally trusting nature or a personality that just happened to perfectly dovetail with mine, Spinney and I had connected from the moment we'd met—a compatibility that, through a bruising, emotionally charged investigation, had only grown. His independence, sense of humor, and spontaneity had formed the perfect link between me and a state organization that in those days had not been famous for any one of those three traits, at least not outside their own ranks.

But inevitably, that's where it had ended. I'd returned to Brattleboro, and he'd continued working for their newly formed Major Crimes Squad—a mobile homicide unit of several specialists who traveled all over the state whenever they were called upon. We had exchanged phone calls a couple of times, he'd dropped by my office once or twice when he'd been in the area, and that had been it. We'd lost touch. The pleasure I felt at seeing him here, therefore, ran deeper than even I would have suspected.

The three of us sat around the small conference table in the middle of the room and caught up, trading war stories and information about mutual acquaintances, with Dan using his own specialized knowledge to fill in the blanks Spinney and I could not. Just as Digger kept Flynn updated on the criminal elements, so the nature of Flynn's job dictated that he know the whereabouts and activities of every trooper within the organization.

Twenty minutes later, however, after we'd either talked up, run down, or reminisced about every mutually known name we could think of, Dan Flynn checked his watch and stood up. "Okay, time to meet the others."

He led us down the hall to a second conference room, this one obviously reserved more for ceremony than for function—with portraits instead of maps on the walls, and a polished wooden table replacing the coffee stained, composite-topped model we'd just left. Seeing who was there to greet us, however, I understood the urge for a little pomp. Seated around the table, chatting among themselves, were Walter Frazier of the FBI, Margaret Lanier from the US Attorney's office, Richard Gibbons, the state's sole US Marshal, and Colonel Jeremy "Skip" McMasters, the uniformed head of the Vermont State Police.

This combination swearing-in and briefing had been arranged several days earlier, after Frazier's bosses had given him the go-ahead, so having everyone here was not a complete surprise. Seeing them rise upon our entrance, however, and touring the table to greet each one, I was struck for the first time by just how big an operation I'd set in motion, and how many people had helped make it happen. Only now did I feel the weight of the cumulative faith they'd all put in me. Remembering also the Brattleboro Board of Selectmen, and Billy Manierre and Tony Brandt and Jack Derby, I realized that if my ambitions proved unsuccessful, I was not going to be the only one disappointed. Of course, that very fact carried its own built-in stimulus—I was obviously also not alone believing the job could get done, or that the effort was worth making. That, as much as the headstone that marked his grave, was a credit to what Dennis DeFlorio had worked for.

The ceremony making Spinney and me Deputy US Marshals was short and only moderately formal; afterward, Walt Frazier, removing his jacket and sitting at the head of the table, took over the meeting.

"If anyone had told me a month ago that I'd be sitting here now, I would've told him he'd lost his mind. So I want to start this thing off by thanking you all for your cunning, your perseverance, and your willingness to take a chance. According to precedent, and maybe even procedure, we shouldn't be here.

"I've come to think that the reasons we are have less to do with blatant self-service—or the lost life of a colleague—and more to do with potential. This case lends itself to cooperation. From what any of us can tell so far, it is relatively contained and involves only a limited cast of characters, but the latter are spread out wide enough, and are mobile enough, to have frustrated any one of us if we'd chosen to act independently."

He leaned back in his chair and crossed his legs. "Technically, I'm running this show, so I wanted—just this once—to bore you with a little philosophy, to give you the pitch I gave to my brass in Washington, so I know we're all on the same wavelength.

"What we're about to do here is an experiment of sorts—a limited, small-scale exercise in mutual aid. I just said this is a small, contained case. I don't actually know that for sure. It's just how it looks now. But if it is, and we deal with it fast and well, people will take notice. There's a lot of paranoia about Asian crime, and I make no bones about being one of the paranoids. Not only do I think this particular criminal element is bigger and badder than anything we've seen before, I also think it has its own built-in booby trap. If Asian criminals are not brought up short at this early stage, not only are they going to make the Cosa Nostra look pathetic by comparison, but they're going to make all Asians look like crooks, and that is a racist by-product that scares the hell out of me.

"These folks are successful because they're fluid, they've got a huge network, they're not burdened by bureaucracy, and yet they respond to a chain of command. They're also loyal to and trusting of one another, *within their individual organizations*, and that's where we hope to have the advantage. Using the broader resources and connections within this room, I think we can beat this particular group at its own game, and maybe set an example that other law-enforcement people can learn from."

He made a small, self-deprecating gesture, and concluded. "Okay— end of speech. Just something I wanted to get out."

I smiled at his style. In short order, Walt Frazier had just rallied the troops, established the theme of our cause, and declared himself our leader, all without becoming either domineering or pompous. And it was on that note that both Gibbons and McMasters took their leave—content to be periodically updated by the regular reports that we all knew were soon to regiment our lives—letting the rest of us get down to nuts and bolts.

Dan Flynn began with the basics. "A couple of housekeeping notes. Since the point of this task force is to be as fast on our feet as the opposition, there is not going to be an official home base. There'll be a central post office instead, and that'll be me, or Digger, if I'm not around. We'll coordinate the flow of information, and my secretary'll make most of the paperwork neat and tidy. If something crops up in the middle of the night, nobody'll be here, since we're basically eight-to-five, but we'll have open computers, phone machines, and a teletype. Digger and I always check them first thing every morning."

He pulled several business cards from his pocket and handed them around the table. "That's got my and Digger's home and pager numbers, just in case the shit hits the fan—not that we'd be able to do much about it till we got back here—but I thought you might like it anyway. The way we're going to handle things from this end is to notify all the departments in VCIN that a special anti-Asian crime task force has been set up, but that it needs all the help it can get. Same rules will apply to them as before—they'll retain their own information through the pointer-card system—but since this is a federal deal, any participants who give up jurisdiction will get a piece of any seized assets, along with official letters of commendation. That ought to encourage participation.

"From our end, we'll keep in constant touch with Lester and Joe, and anyone else you two recommend, so that anything we learn can be acted on immediately."

He paused a moment, as if to shift gears. "From my viewpoint, it'd be nice if all information was routed through here, but I realize you might have to do things differently in a pinch. If so, all I ask is that you let me know as soon as you can."

He was looking directly at Lester Spinney as he said this, a small ghost of resignation in his voice, which told me that Spinney's renegade reputation was still intact.

Spinney smiled, and gave an almost imperceptible nod of the head.

Flynn accepted that response at face value, and yielded the floor.

Next, Margaret "Maggie" Lanier passed out business cards. "The same holds true for me, only you don't have to wait for the shit to hit the fan, or until morning for me to act on your request. If you need a search warrant at 2:00 A.M., either call me at home or on my beeper.

"Now, first off, have either one of you worked on the federal level before?"

Spinney and I exchanged glances. "Nope," I answered for us both. "I've had some training in procedures."

"Me, too," Spinney added, "but not much."

Maggie smiled. "Then you're in for a treat. It's a liberating experience." She pulled her briefcase up onto the table and extracted two thick folders, one for each of us. "These contain some of the basics. We made them up for occasions just like this, where we don't have the time or the leisure to send you to Washington or wherever for the standard crash course. Basically, they're a kind of question-answer primer consisting of the most frequently encountered differences between what you're used to and how we operate.

"You'll find ours is a more proprosecution system, with fewer constraints, more flexibility, and total mobility. If you have any doubts or questions along the way, though, especially given your inexperience—and nobody's available to advise you—just act according to the state rules you're used to. There's no way you can screw up. Vermont is so prodefendant, and your regulations so restrictive, I'm amazed you people put anyone in jail.

"Anyway, if you think you have probable cause at any point, call me and I'll help you write up the warrant application. You can give me the facts over the phone, send them in a fax, or deliver them in person, but whatever method you use, at some point you'll have to appear in the flesh to sign at the bottom. I can't go to a magistrate without that signature."

Spinney looked at her quizzically. "What if I'm sitting on a house in the boonies behind Lunenberg?"

Lanier didn't relent. "Find somebody to do the sitting while you get to me in Burlington. If Walt gives you a federal vehicle, most of them have car phones with scramblers. You can call me on the way, give me what I need to know, and I'll have the application ready and waiting when you arrive." She paused to address his skeptical expression. "The good news is that you can get a warrant at the drop of a hat—probable cause is not what it is at the state level—and in some instances you don't even need a warrant where you did before. Also, you don't have to ambush a judge in the men's room during a break in some trial. I can roust a magistrate just like you can roust me."

"Well," Walt cautioned, "don't get carried away, either."

Maggie shook her head impatiently. "All right, all right. But you're still going to hate going back to the state system after all this is over. I'll guarantee you that. Another big item I should mention: When you want to interview someone who could've told you to take a hike in the old days? Now you can hit them with a subpoena to appear in your office for a deposition. They don't want to do it, they're in contempt and it's off to jail. Same thing with documents. If you think they won't cooperate, you can walk in with a subpoena and seize what you're after. And if push comes to shove, you also have the grand jury, which sits on alternating Thursdays in either Rutland or Burlington. If a witness refuses to talk to you, you can haul them in front of the grand jury and then I'll be the one asking the questions. If they still refuse, the judge can find them in contempt and jail them for the remainder of the term. Since grand juries are convened for up to two years at a time sometimes, that can be a convincing threat."

"Of course," Walter weighed in again, cautioning against Maggie's brisk optimism, "I would tread carefully there. Just because that particular tool is available, doesn't mean it should be overused." I could sense the sweat of his distant masters, and wondered if Maggie Lanier—usually the more conservative, as a prosecuor—was using this opportunity to indulge in a little playful chain-pulling. Politics, I knew, ran hot and heavy among the various federal branches, and you never knew who might be sore about someone else—and who might use you as a convenient, if unwitting, cudgel.

My suspicions were surprisingly addressed by Frazier's very next statement, delivered with obvious discomfort. "Actually, this brings up a point that I don't want to overemphasize—it's a kind of last-ditch loophole, in a way, but I think I ought to get it out in the open, just so you all know . . ."

"An escape clause?" Maggie asked incredulously.

Spinney lifted a single eyebrow and gave me a tired smile.

Walter shifted restlessly in his seat. "That's not its intention . . ."

"Oh, come on, Walter," Maggie interrupted again, drawing out his name, "that's exactly it's intention." She turned to us. "They've written themselves an *out* if this whole thing gets sticky. They've done it before—they've all done it before. In exchange for footing the bill and giving you locals a little extra clout, they reserve the right to either close down or kidnap the case, whichever suits them best."

There was an embarrassed silence. Frazier cleared his throat, caught between the policy makers behind him and the people he'd committed to in this room. It was palpably obvious now why he'd been called down to Washington to fine-tune this deal. I could also tell from his expression that he'd been victimized as much as we.

"There's a snowball's chance in hell it'll be invoked," he said stiffly. "And given that, it's not such a bad deal, considering the risk the Bureau's taking."

"I agree," I said quickly, and was relieved to see Spinney nodding his head next to me. "We knew going in this probably wouldn't fly. That it has—even with a few strings attached—doesn't bother me. I'd be nervous in their shoes, too."

Maggie merely smiled and shook her head. Dan Flynn remained perfectly circumspect. Maggie wrapped up her pitch. "Read through those folders, call me if you have any questions, and now that I've dumped all over Walter, I probably ought to 'fess up that my boss is having kittens, too. He'd appreciate it if you kept in touch."

Spinney looked at me and raised both eyebrows. "Makes you wonder why we don't do this sort of thing more often, doesn't it?"

Chapter Twenty

The border between Vermont and Quebec is one of the few demarcations where a politically drawn line on a map has taken on a distinct and dramatic identity. From forests to farmland, near-wilderness to cluttered civilization, and from rolling countryside to flat plains, the contrasts extend beyond mere differences in language, culture, and architecture—they announce a separateness more pronounced than anywhere else along the American-Canadian boundary.

Part of this is helped by the fact that the vast majority of Canada's population lives along a hundred-mile-wide corridor paralleling the border. Another is that the greatest density of that population is divided between Toronto and Montreal, which is the largest French-speaking city in the world after Paris. Looking at a road map that includes both Quebec and Vermont, one is struck by the disparity between a Canadian crazy quilt of highways, interstates, back roads, and towns, and the vast tracts of uninhabited, road-free timberland to its south.

Smugglers of both people and products, of course, made the same eye-catching and profitable discovery a few hundred years earlier.

Spinney and I were driving north in one of the cars Maggie had mentioned, a bland Caprice, neutral color, regular plates, no radio or air conditioning, but with a state-of-the-art mobile phone with a scrambler, tucked away under the dash. The kind of car that, for all its demure subtlety, could have had *Undercover* stenciled on its sides.

On the seat between us was a blowup of the sales receipt that J. P. Tyler had found in the Trans Am in Brattleboro, marking the date, time, and place of purchase. Slim as it was, this was the nominal reason for the trip—to interview whichever clerk had produced that receipt, maybe get a description of his customers, and scope out the general neighborhood in the hope it might yield something. The futility of such a quest was virtually guaranteed, so the other incentive—less definable but more important—was to finally make the connection between what we had and whatever it was the Montreal police might be willing to share with us.

Despite an hour's worth of travel amid this foreign, crowded environment of villages, silos, gas stations, and a sudden explosion of churches, seeing Montreal finally thrust up into view on the far side of the Champlain Bridge—its massive bulk lording over the flat, vast expanse of the Saint Lawrence River at its feet—was a startling and intimidating surprise. Its shoreline cluttered with piers, breweries, warehouses, and ocean-going tankers, its horizon dominated by the seven-hundred-foot Mt. Royal, itself crowned with a five-story-tall Catholic cross, and with a towering downtown reminiscent of Chicago in between, Montreal presents itself as a huge, muscular, and oddly disjointed metropolis.

"Jesus Christ," Spinney murmured, "this place must keep 'em busy."

I swung left off of Autoroute 10 and caught Notre Dame heading east, the river to my right screened by a drab succession of industrial buildings. I kept my eyes glued to the thick flow of fast-moving traffic, while Spinney rubbernecked beside me with an endless string of awe-struck comments.

"Keep a lookout for something huge," I told him. "Lacoste's office is right near it."

"What's that supposed to mean?"

"He said it looks like the world's biggest harp, anchored to the world's biggest shower cap. It's a leaning tower over six-hundred feet tall." I shoved the map I had draped across my lap toward him and tapped my finger in the vague proximity of where I was headed.

But his eyes were glued to the window again. "Sure is ugly."

I took a quick glance at where he was staring and saw an enormous, thrusting, sharp-pointed object angling up above the low buildings

nearby—so huge and overpowering and out of character with everything around it as to look faintly threatening, like something left over
from an overbudget science-fiction movie. Simulating the harp image,
a row of taut steel cables fanned out from its peak to a bulbous, lumpy,
awkward dome, all of which reminded me of the physical restraints
they strap to straining madmen. I took a left up a side street and
headed toward it.

"What the hell is it?" Spinney asked.

"The '76 Olympic stadium—where the Expos play now. That tower
holds up the roof. Supposedly, it cost 'em a billion dollars, doesn't
work worth a damn, is starting to fall apart, and is still being paid
off. Lacoste was pretty eloquent about it."

I came up to Hochelaga—Montreal's original Indian name,
according to the homework I'd done—and turned right, feeling more
than seeing the looming presence of the tower a mere block farther
north. I then did a U-turn in front of the building we were after—
an unprepossessing, two-story glass-and-steel shoe box with the MUC
symbol outside its front door—the Montreal Urban Community Police
substation Lacoste called home base.

Spinney and I got out, stretched, locked the car, and headed up the
broad cement stairs, to be met at the wide, double glass doors by a
tall, thin, fashionably dressed man with a shiny bald head and a flowing
mustache. "You are Joe Gunther?" he asked, a wide smile spreading
across his face.

I recognized the slightly singsong Gallic accent and the clipped
English. "Jean-Paul Lacoste?"

He spread his arms, the gesture reminding me of some black-and-
white European movie. "It is me. Welcome to Montréal."

I introduced Spinney while Lacoste swept around behind us and
herded us across the sterile entryway to a side door and a set of stairs
leading up. "I saw you from the window," he explained. "The green
license plate. Not too many of them in this city."

We all three climbed to the second floor and a long, low room
strewn with modular desk units and banks of filing cabinets. Most of
the desks had computers, about half of which were being operated by
a varied assortment of men and women in plain clothes. Lining the
walls were a string of fishbowl offices with windows looking onto the
central squad room, and windows facing outside. Bigger, more modern,

more populated, and with more fancy equipment than I'd ever had to play with, it was nevertheless as familiar to me as my own office. The one glaring exception was that everyone was speaking French—not the kind I'd been taught in school, and which my mother had further helped me to conquer with home tutoring, but an oddly guttural, chopped-up version that I couldn't grasp at all.

Lacoste made long-distance introductions as we walked the length of the room, flinging his arm toward one person or another, calling out our names and giving us incomprehensible versions of theirs. Everyone nodded and smiled and went back to work.

Finally, we reached the far end and were ushered into a large, cheerful, well-lit office equipped with three desks, behind one of which was a young man who rose as we entered. "Okay. Voilà. Here we are," beamed Lacoste. "The room of the masterminds—the MUC Intelligence Unit's Anti-Asian Crime Squad." He took a little bow, and the young man smiled nervously.

"This," Lacoste continued, "is Antoine Schmitt, your official liaison. He will guide you to other people inside MUC, or RCMP, or wherever it is you wish—assuming, of course," he added with another broad smile, "you can stand to leave my company."

Schmitt came around from behind his desk, which I realized now was totally bare—merely a place for him to park himself temporarily— and shook hands. His English was just a tad better than my own. "Delighted to meet you. You come highly recommended by some very impressive people. As Jean-Paul just said, if you need anything at all during your visit, don't hesitate to ask. That includes," he added as we all found chairs and settled down, "any privacy you might wish. We understand you'll be working a little on your own now and then, and want you to know that's perfectly fine with us—provided, of course, that you understand your status is no different from any other private citizen. You did, for example, leave your weapons at home?"

We both nodded. Glancing at Spinney's face, I could tell he was less than overwhelmed by Schmitt's upper-class demeanor. I therefore answered for the both of us. "Thank you. Actually, this time we're mostly here for a briefing from Jean-Paul. I'm not even sure we'll be spending the night."

Schmitt looked from one of us to the other, his smile slightly frozen. Lacoste, sensing what I was up to, let him hang. Finally, the younger man rose a little stiffly to his feet, shook hands all around once more, and said, "Very well, then I'll let you get on with it. Jean-Paul knows how to find me if and when the necessity arises."

All three of us waited in silence as Schmitt found the exit and closed the door behind him. Through the room's interior window, we watched him wend his way back through the maze of desks and cabinets.

"He is a good boy," Lacoste said quietly, as the room relaxed. "Does a good job."

He then tilted back his chair and parked an expensively loafered foot in his desk's lower drawer for stability. "So—what is it I can do?"

"You told me on the phone that the snakehead who was killed, maybe by the three men we stopped for a traffic violation, belonged to Da Wang, and that his job had been to ferry illegals through a Vermont-based pipeline. Have you noticed any changes in Da Wang's operations since the snakehead died?"

Lacoste wobbled his head from side to side in an equivocating gesture. "It is hard for us to know. When the snakehead died, there was much movement in Chinatown—many meetings, many young men on the street watching, we think guarding the doors of places where high-level meetings take place. Illegal immigrants are a big business not only because of the money they bring, but also because they are used to carry and receive illegal things."

"Like credit cards and drugs?" Spinney asked.

"Yes, and American dollars for laundering. But these meetings may have been about the shooting only, not damage to Da Wang's business. We cannot know."

He saw Spinney and I exchange puzzled glances, and held up his hand, his broad, ever-ready smile back in place. "Maybe you will let me begin at the beginning? Tell you about Asian crime in Montréal so you understand better what I say?"

"Please," I said.

Lacoste nodded and took a small breath. "Okay. In Montréal, we have maybe one hundred and thirty-five thousand Asians, including thirty-five thousand Chinese. They are the biggest group. The others are Vietnamese—the next biggest group—and then Laotians, Cambodians, Koreans, Japanese, Thais, Bangladeshis, Sri Lankans, and who knows—all in whatever order. About ten thousand new Asians immigrate to Québec every year, although in 1997, when Hong Kong goes back to China, we expect many more.

"In all those thousands, maybe seven hundred are criminals—one-half of one percent—but they are very bad, very cruel, and they affect all the others somehow or the other."

"How are they divided up?" Spinney had pulled out a pad and was taking notes.

"We say five gangs—three Vietnamese, one Chinese, and one Cambodian—but you must be careful. The press, they like to give them names, leaders, tattoos, special clothes, things like that. And cops like to do that, too. We all think of La Cosa Nostra—the Mafia—and we try to make the Asians the same. That is very wrong. These people move, and change loyalties, and sometimes they are working together, and sometimes they are not. Sometimes, the business associations in Chinatown—what you call *tongs* in New York City—are working with the gangs, and sometimes they are only business associations, perfectly legal."

"But there must be some hierarchy," I said.

Lacoste agreed. "Yes, yes, but it is unusual—people like Da Wang, we know he is a boss, but the people who work with him, sometimes they are following his orders, sometimes they are not. This system is thousands of years old. It is part of their life. As long as they are together, it doesn't always matter who is commanding."

"But you have turf wars. Power struggles," argued Spinney.

"Yes. A minority inside the gangs are hungry. They become the bosses, or they die. I was talking about the army—the soldiers. If they are taken care of—if they have money to gamble, and girls, and cars, and a place to sleep."

He held up a finger for emphasis. "Also, Montréal—we think—is different from the other cities. It is a place to be quiet."

"A safe haven," I suggested.

"That is right. Last year, Toronto, who has four times our Asian population, had nine killings. We had none, but we are only five hours away. Sometimes, we think a bad man comes here to hide. Everyone is looking, but here he keeps quiet. He doesn't make trouble. He is given rest. And when he makes trouble again, it is someplace else."

"Can you describe Da Wang's setup?"

"I can tell you what we think. That may be true or not. Some things we know are true. His name is Wang Chien-kuo—his nickname is

Da Wang, or Big Wang. He is forty-three years old. He is from mainland China, not Hong Kong or Taiwan, and it is possible that's why the connections to triads and tongs are less formal here than they are in other places. Da Wang is a restaurant owner, and he is a restaurant supplier, with operations in Boston, New York City, and San Francisco, which is where he started. His restaurants are all in Canada. The biggest ones are in the east—New Brunswick and Nova Scotia—and they can sit six hundred people at once. He has many, many workers, and they move all the time. We think only ten percent are illegal, but they change every week, through the pipeline. Da Wang is very powerful, very rich, because of all this. He is also very private. After a few attempts on his life several years ago—we don't know by who exactly . . . he became very protected with armed guards."

"How do aliens get into this country?" Spinney asked.

"Airplane, mostly, also boat. Coming from Hong Kong, they don't need a visa, because of the old British Empire connection. They only need a passport. Fake passports are big business, and sometimes they go back and forth. Someone enters Canada, sends the passport back home, the name and photograph are changed, and it comes back. RCMP once marked one with a special chemical, and it came back three times.

"Prostitutes come in the same way, often with some man who says he is the brother or cousin. She shows she has employment, so she is allowed to enter. They are usually very young, and usually from Malaysia. The Vietnamese mostly run them.

"It is difficult to stop. We visit the people they tell us about who are the relatives or the employers they will be staying with, and they look good. We know they are probably either criminals or in debt to the gangs, but we can't prove it."

"In debt to them how?" I asked. "Because of what they owe for the trip over here?"

"Yes, that, but the gambling also. Asians love to gamble. They work all day and all night, and they gamble to relax. Da Wang runs some gambling, and some loan sharking so he can control them more. Ten percent a week on the loan. They can't pay it off? Then a favor is owed instead—a lie about being someone's brother, a trip to the US with drugs or money . . . whatever is needed.

"But the violence is not his, not mostly. That is more the Vietnamese, the Cambodians. The follow-home robberies? After a man wins big at gambling? That's mostly Vietnamese. Da Wang is happy enough having loaned him the money and having run the gambling parlor. He doesn't need to rob him, too. He leaves that to the gangs to keep them happy."

"Jesus," Spinney muttered, half into his note pad, "why the hell don't all these people kick his ass?"

Lacoste shrugged. "It is their life. It is karma, to endure. They are happy here. It is much, much better than where they came from, and they are used to the gangs. To be a merchant and to pay three hundred dollars a month is just overhead—they don't even talk about it among themselves, like they don't talk about electricity rates. Sometimes it gets too high. One man paid fifty thousand dollars, total, to all five gangs in one year. That was too much. He complained to us. We arrested one man, then the merchant's home was invaded, his wife was raped, and he was told, 'That's number-one warning.' He came back to us and we caught the men and put them in jail, and that merchant is still in business, but we visit him all the time, to show we are there to help. Still, that is very rare—only about five percent of the crimes are ever told to us. But we are just beginning. This unit was formed in 1989, so we have hopes things will improve. And the more Asians born here and educated here, the better. They know we are not corrupt like the police back on the mainland. So that helps a little, too. In time, the old habits will change, and the people will realize they can, as you say, 'kick their ass.'"

"How does Da Wang get his illegals across the border?" I asked, surprised by the similarities between his situation and the one US law enforcement was facing.

"Little by little, in a car, on foot. It is not like your Mexican border. Here, it is a big holding tank, where money is being made off the illegals while they are waiting to cross. There is no need to ship them in a truck. Safer to let it be a trickle. The backbone of Da Wang's business is not the illegals—they are just a part of the manpower. The money is in the restaurants, because of the money laundering and the credit-card fraud."

"Which is exactly where we think Truong Van Loc is putting the squeeze on Da Wang," Spinney said.

"Why would he care, though?" I asked. "If Da Wang's biggest

restaurants—and the only ones he admits to owning—are all in Canada, what does he care if someone steals a few in Vermont?"

"And Massachusetts, and Connecticut, and New York," added Lacoste. "Vermont is more important than you think. Da Wang's power is in the strength of his face—it is like a reputation, but means much, much more. That is the first thing he must always protect. Also, the credit-card fraud in Canada comes to about fifty million dollars. In the US, it is at least six hundred million. If Da Wang loses the Vermont part of his pipeline, it doesn't interfere with his income too badly, but it shows weakness if he lets it happen. That can threaten all his holdings, and be fatal to him.

"I believe your 'Sonny' is a clever man, hitting Da Wang across the border. It is strategy over greed. In a way, it is like when the lesser army beats the greater one by sending a small force around to the back to trouble the supply line, making the bosses look small. Large armies grow restless when they begin to doubt, and they look to their leaders to put things right."

I laughed. "You're beginning to sound like a fortune cookie."

Lacoste smiled back. "That is okay. I learn a lot from the Asians. The criminals are the worst I know. But the people are wonderful, and have taught me more than I can tell."

"What I hear you saying," I resumed, "is that while you don't know specifically why Da Wang is having all these meetings, you're guessing his organization is definitely under stress."

"Yes, but I would say you should talk to the RCMP about the border smuggling. That is their area, and they might know more."

Spinney looked up from his note taking. "You don't talk to each other?"

Lacoste gazed at us for a long few seconds before nodding gently. "And all of you talk always?"

It was a painful truth we both instantly recognized. "Who do you recommend we contact?" I asked diplomatically.

"Jacques Lucas—Antoine Schmitt will put you in touch. Use my name."

"You probably know Da Wang as well as any outsider," said Spinney. "If you're right about him feeling the squeeze, what do think he'll do about it?"

Lacoste's answer was immediate. "He will do what has been done to him, and he will strike at the source—immediately."

Chapter Twenty-one

Montreal's official Chinatown—the one the tourists photograph—is on rue de la Gauchetière, west of boulevard St-Laurent. It is not very large—a few short blocks of jam-packed restaurants, shops, association headquarters, Mah-Jongg parlors, and apartments, all as covered with colorful posters, signs, and neon advertisements as a newlywed with rice. The street, closed off as a pedestrian walkway, is filled with people, all in movement, and reverberating with the sounds of exotic language and blaring radios. Lacoste parked his unmarked car on St.-Laurent, just beyond the ornate, pagoda-style gateway that arched over the street's entrance, and shoved a few coins into the parking meter that stood guard across the sidewalk, close to the wall.

The three of us entered La Gauchetière, walking abreast, looking as out of place as three gunslingers on an urban movie set—except that only our host was actually armed, with an ankle-holstered .38 he'd strapped on before leaving the office. Despite the fact that I was convinced we had *police* all but stenciled across our backs, Lacoste seemed as upbeat as I imagined he'd be during a stroll in the park. He moved from one side of the street to the other as we walked, pointing out various landmarks—usually those that had featured raids or robberies, or which were hangouts for the local hoods.

"The criminals do not live here. They come here to work—to have meetings, to gamble, to extort the merchants, to run their operations from up there." He swept his arm above us, encompassing the dozens of dark, blank windows that were perched above the street on the upper floors. "It is not a very big Chinatown, but it is like a rabbit's home, filled with tunnels and stairs and rooms you cannot find."

"How many of the merchants are extorted?"

Lacoste shrugged. "Everybody—maybe a couple are not, who are well connected, and that is true not just for this Chinatown, but for the others that the tourists don't know, in Brossard, and Cote des Neiges, and Jean Talon. But the center remains here. See?" He gestured with his chin to a trio of young men in dark-leather clothes, wearing studied malevolent expressions. They were huddled together by a door, smoking cigarettes and murmuring among themselves.

"You know who they belong to?" I asked.

"No, but they probably know me, and they'll be wondering who you are. That will make for some phone calls."

He stopped in front of a worn wooden door with a brass plaque announcing the East Wind Trade Association. "This is where Da Wang does his business. Like to go up?"

Without waiting for an answer, he twisted the knob and pushed his way in. Immediately before us was a dark, narrow, dusty stairway. Climbing two steps at a time, Lacoste swept up to the second floor with the two of us in noisy pursuit. On the hundred-year-old landing, illuminated by a single bare bulb hanging from a wire, were three doors, two of them open to reveal groups of older men clustered around rickety card tables, playing Mah-Jongg. Lacoste waved his badge at them and uttered something incomprehensible. None of them seemed to care. Aside from a couple of sideways glances, no one even looked at us. Lacoste opened the third door, which revealed a large, dark, empty, wooden-floored room. There was the quick shadow of someone outlined in a far door opposite, and then all was still and quiet and bereft of life. As abruptly as he'd entered the place, Lacoste turned on his heel, yelled a cheery *"au 'voir"* to the inattentive players, and led us back down into the street. The three young thugs had disappeared.

"You can see why we are only sometimes successful when we raid. Even with all the doors blocked with men, we find the building empty, when we know it was full ten minutes before."

He looked up at the windows above us, even backing up into the street slightly to get a better view. They were as lifeless as before. "They are watching us now." He shook his head and resumed walking.

"So how do you get your information?" I asked.

"People we arrest. Not because they talk to us, but because they brag. Their machismo is very big, and we use it to help us. Sometimes, if we can make them feel small, they tell us things to make themselves bigger. Sometimes they are lies, but if we get two stories that are the same, then we know we have something. We have tried other methods—wiretapping, intercepting their mail—but they change dialects and write in code. And putting one of our Asian officers undercover would be like killing him. It is not easy."

"What about playing one race off the other?" Spinney asked. "Like the Vietnamese and the Chinese?"

Lacoste gave one of his trademark wide smiles, expanding his mustache to even greater lengths. "Ah—interesting question. Again, it is like with the Sicilians—you guys and us guys—it makes things easier for us policemen." Then he shook his head sorrowfully. "But the Asians are more complex. The Chinese are very conscious of race, it is true—but they also think back to all the generations before. If you have any Chinese blood in you, even hundreds of years ago, then that makes you okay—sort of. Same thing if you marry into their families. Regardless of race, that can be very important."

"So the Vietchin are acceptable?" I was thinking back to previous conversations I'd had on this subject, when I was hoping the race angle might help me identify how the players were aligning themselves.

"To do business with, yes. But that is all. To have Chinese blood does not make you Chinese . . ."

"It just makes you more trustworthy," Spinney finished for him.

"Sometimes," Lacoste agreed, "but they are trying new things. Last year, we had twenty home invasions of Asian homes, but they were done by blacks. We found out the Asians and the blacks were getting to know each other in prison, and starting to work together."

"That ought to make every cop I know properly paranoid," Spinney muttered.

I pulled the enlarged copy of the receipt we'd brought with us out of my jacket pocket and handed it to our host. "Do you know where this store is?"

He read it carefully. "Yes. It is in Brossard, on the south shore.

That is one of our residential Chinatowns, where a lot of the rich people live. Da Wang lives there, too. Do you want to go?"

We returned to the car and he drove us through the center of town, heading toward the Champlain Bridge, giving us biographical tidbits about himself and pointing out the sights as he went. He was a remarkably cheerful man, a lifelong Montrealer, a dedicated believer in a "free" Quebec, a happy father and husband. He spoke of his job as such, discussing its benefits and retirement package, and never once strayed into the routine war stories that all cops and firemen and emergency-medical people seem to think is interesting conversation. Just as I'd been struck by his generosity with the pompous Antoine Schmitt, so now was I impressed by his self-deprecating urbanity. Considering the job we all shared, albeit from different angles, he was the gentleman of the three of us.

In that way, he reflected the city we were touring. As I looked out the window, watching the people and the constantly inconsistent architecture, I was struck not by an outright jaundiced image— like New York's concrete jungle or LA's smog-shrouded sprawl— but rather by a spirit of enterprise and determination, a combination of style and liveliness. Aside from the downtown skyscrapers and the idiosyncratic Mt. Royal, both of which seemed to leap unexpect- edly from the earth, the rest of the city was less demonstrative, more sure of itself, content to be the conglomeration that it was— the Montreal Urban Community, consisting of some thirty-two separate entities, some so distinct unto themselves as to seem hun- dreds of miles apart.

Living in an environment where all the signs were in at least two languages and sometimes totally incomprehensible, where every race and culture seemed to have ample representation, and where two- hundred-and-fifty-year-old buildings shared the same sidewalk with glass-and-steel modern icons, I could understand why this confederacy of two and a half million people yearned to be part of a nation unto itself. Caught between tradition-bound France, which was less than half its size, and a stiff-upper-lip Great Britain, this alienated province had good reason to feel restless.

Brossard, hanging off the south shore of the St. Lawrence River, reflected none of this. As bland as the most boring American suburbia, it was a collection of two-story, residential, pod-like blocks, crisscrossed by shopping mall—decorated boulevards. The only immediately obvious distinction was that several of the malls were filled with Oriental businesses.

Lacoste pulled off Pelletier, the main drag, and drove us by block after block of undistinguished, pleasant homes. "Brossard has about seventy-five thousand people, from sixty-seven different ethnic groups. Ten thousand of those are Asians. Most of the Chinese are from Hong Kong."

That comment reminded me of something he'd mentioned earlier. "Didn't you say Da Wang came from China to San Francisco first?" I asked.

"Yes. That is where he began his business. But some ten years ago he came to Montréal, we think because of the bigger opportunities. Back then, our Chinatown was not much—and Da Wang is a persuasive man."

"You mentioned earlier that there had been several attempts on his life here. Is there any evidence those attempts date back to things he might've done in San Francisco?"

Spinney gave me a quick look, but Lacoste shook his head. "We don't know. It is possible. At the time, it fit that it was a gang problem local to Montréal—a power struggle—but, of course, we have to guess at many of those things."

A few more turns at the wheel put us suddenly in a neighborhood so oddly artificial, it made me think of a Hollywood prop room. But instead of dozens upon dozens of hats or cowboy boots or potted plastic plants, this entire area was filled with brand-new compact mansions, each only slightly different from its neighbor, parked right next to one another like limousines in a car lot. There was no visible room around any of them for lawns, swimming pools, swing sets, or even fences. They were pale pink, gray, white, and made of brick, rock, stone, or wood. Each looked chosen as from a catalog of limited choices, and most of them appeared fresh from the box.

"These are in the three-hundred-thousand to a half-million-dollar range. Some of them are bought sight unseen by people in Hong Kong, just so they have somewhere to move in 1997." Lacoste suddenly stopped the car and backed up. "See that license plate?"

We both looked at a late-model, Japanese luxury sports sedan. There were four 8s on the plate.

"Eight is a lucky number to the Chinese. The owner worked very hard to get a license like that."

"Christ," Spinney mused. "Looks like a trailer park, but with million-dollar trailers."

Lacoste agreed. "They like being close together. That's what makes them strong."

"Is Da Wang's house around here?" I asked.

Lacoste emphatically shook his head. "No, no. A few of these might be owned by triad people, but most belong to rich businessmen still in the old country. People like Da Wang do not live in houses like this. We find that the gangs like cars, sometimes clothes and pretty girls, but they don't care where they live, and they like to live with lots of other people. La Cosa Nostra, they get a big mansion, much land, a fence, guard dogs. Asian criminals mostly do not like that. It would keep them apart from the people they need to survive. Da Wang lives in East Brossard, where there are lots of apartment buildings that look like motels."

We'd left the ritzy neighborhood from Oz and returned to one of the main commercial strips. "There is your place—up there." He pointed to a large gas-station/food-store combination, with flying-buttress roofs over the pumps and a steady stream of traffic filing through. He parked off to the side and we got out and crossed over to the store.

I handed Lacoste the receipt. He discreetly flashed his badge at one of the clerks, who abandoned his customer with a murmured apology and came over to us.

After a quick conversation, the clerk went back behind his counter and picked up a phone. Lacoste explained. "He has to call his boss. We may be lucky today." He pointed to a camera that was mounted over the cash register. "There have been robberies here, so last year they put in those. They keep the tapes for a long time, he says."

"How long?" I asked, even now doubtful we could get that lucky.

Lacoste spread his arms out expansively. "That, we will find out."

Fifteen minutes later, a short, fat, blotchy-faced man arrived, irritable and out of breath. He led us into a small, windowless back room, one wall of which had several closed-circuit television screens mounted near the ceiling. On a counter beneath them was a large console with a touch-pad keyboard mounted on its surface. The man took the receipt from Lacoste, read the time and date, and punched some numbers onto the playback machine. The TV image directly above us suddenly went haywire, streaked by the effects of a tape in fast rewind. About four minutes later, the tape stopped, paused, and then suddenly came to life.

Before us was the same scene as before—the counter, the cash register, the back of a clerk in his smock—but we could tell from the reflections off the distant windows that it was night. We watched as a line of people took their turn in front of the camera.

"There," I suddenly said, both stunned that such a long shot had paid off and unsure of what it meant.

The store owner hit a button and froze the image.

"Who is it?" Spinney asked about the middle-aged man standing alone with his wallet in his hand, a small pile of candy and soda spread out before him.

The image was made doubly odd in that it so closely matched what we had back in Brattleboro—on the tape I'd made of the traffic stop on the interstate. "His name's Edward Diep."

Chapter Twenty-two

Unfortunately, Edward Diep didn't appear in any of Jean-Paul Lacoste's reference files. He cross-checked with RCMP and the Quebec Provincial Police, and even with the American NCIC, as we had done that night so long ago. But now, as then, all we got for our efforts was the record of a Pennsylvania driver's license and an address in Philadelphia.

Using my hard-won new connections as a federal agent, I called Walter Frazier on Lacoste's phone and asked him to have the address checked by someone in the Philadelphia office. I also requested a thorough background search of Wang Chien-kuo, alias Da Wang. In exchange, Walter asked me to stop by his office on our way back through Burlington. He had some new information on Truong Van Loc.

After that, Spinney and I took advantage of our freshly minted alliance with the MUC to introduce Lacoste to our entire rogues gallery, from the largely unlabeled photo album my squad had assembled of Brattleboro's transient Asian population, to the mug shots, fingerprints, and arrest file of Nguyen Van Hai, the only man we had under arrest, who was awaiting trial for the torture-murder of Benny Travers.

Running them all through his own data bank, Lacoste came up with several cross-references. Nguyen, Henry Lam, Chu Nam An. At this early stage, all we could easily locate was some basic information on each man, but it was enough to transform Lacoste from an amiable and generous host into a committed participant. The possibility that we might have handed him something his department could use to its own benefit was enough to guarantee their continuing cooperation, long after Spinney and I had headed back over the border.

We parted company much later that day, with promises to keep in close touch. There, I was not just being polite. I had high hopes that the more he dug, the more connections Lacoste might uncover—connections that might prove crucial to the whole case.

*   *   *

An hour later, we were back among the flat fields of southern Quebec, heading home.

"What do you make of Diep on that video?"

I paused before answering. "When we stopped them on I-91 last winter, none of those three seemed to know each other. I played the what's-your-buddy's-name routine on Truong, and he flunked—called Diep 'Jimmy.' Normally, that would actually make sense. From what I've researched, when a hit is ordered, the contract goes out to a jobber—like a middleman. He calls on his usual people, or others who've been recommended to him, and he names the rate—five thousand, fifteen thousand . . . I read a cop can go for fifty. Once he selects the team he wants—each member of which comes from a different part of the country—the deal's done. The team comes together once, the target's whacked, and the team disperses. They do not trade names or addresses, they keep the small talk to a minimum, and they're only in contact for a few hours."

"Except that this time Truong was contractor, jobber, and hit man rolled into one, so he should've known who everyone was," Spinney concluded.

"Not only that, but Lam and Diep both have links to Montreal, and Truong and Lam originally lived in California . . ."

"And Diep and Lam also lived on the East Coast, and Truong and Lam showed up in Brattleboro to aggravate the hell out of you. In every case, Lam is the common denominator."

"Okay," I agreed. "But if Diep was the newest member, introduced to Truong by Lam, what was he doing in Montreal with Truong, for what we assume was a hit on Da Wang's snakehead? And why was that receipt Diep collected found in a Canadian car that was used to kill Benny Travers?"

Spinney turned both his hands up in resignation. "All right, so the hit team couldn't have been made up of people who didn't know each other."

"Then why didn't Truong know who Diep was when I asked him?"

Spinney didn't answer.

*   *   *

Walt Frazier dimmed the lights and hit a button on his remote. The VCR across the room stirred awake, and the television set above it lit up with a ragged nighttime camera shot of a decrepit one-story bungalow, glistening in the reflected glare of several bright lights. Police in bullet-proof vests scurried back and forth, getting into position. After a moment's telling pause, they rushed the building's front door, the cameraman in hot pursuit. There was no sound track.

"This is a drug raid in Berkeley, California, eighteen years ago," Frazier explained. "The occupants had been ordered to come out. One shot had already been fired from inside."

The first officers at the door swung a two-man metal battering ram against the doorknob, busting it open at the first crack. They then flattened themselves against the outside wall and let the others, assault rifles ready, scramble by them. The cameraman followed and led us through a central hallway, the image jittery, bouncing badly, sweeping to either side as the operator went by open doorways through which officers could be seen fanning out. The camera was moving too fast for me to focus on any of the occupants' faces, but I could clearly see they were all Oriental.

"The cameraman's a cop," Frazier went on. "They were experimenting using videos on raids for training films, and maybe in court. I don't know that it's any improvement. This gives me a headache."

Finally, the lead cops reached the kitchen at the back of the house, joining the team that had entered through the rear. They all stood around a small group of shirtless young men with their arms over their heads, crouching in a corner. The camera lens calmed down enough at this point to pan the group so we could actually see who was being videotaped.

Frazier hit the *pause* button. "Recognize anyone?"

I leaned forward in my chair, squinting. The tape quality wasn't great, and being in *pause* mode didn't help, but in the upturned face of one of these young men, I could clearly recognize the hard-eyed malevolence of Truong Van Loc.

"What was his role in this?" I asked, sitting back.

"Just one of the boys. He was arraigned with the rest of them, treated as a minor, kicked loose in short order. But this wasn't his first arrest. Our office in San Francisco dug up quite a bit on him—the DEA was a big help, too. Interesting story, actually. Truong's an unusual guy. Came out of Vietnam when we closed shop in '75, age around ten or twelve—birthdate's a little vague, along with his family history. He arrived here with a little brother and was absorbed by the Vietnamese community. The brother was taken on by a family named Phan, while Truong got sucked under by the gangs. Difference was, he kept coming back to the brother—visiting him, getting after him on his homework, arranging for private tutors. He paid the Phans for his upkeep, and seemed bent on making sure the kid flew straight."

"So he was in the gangs just to make ends meet?" asked Spinney.

"That's the funny thing," Frazier answered. "He was ambitious—a natural leader. Not that anyone had proof enough to ever make a case. But our intelligence has it that he was organizing smash-and-grabs right off the boat, extorting with the best of them, and hell-bent on climbing the ranks. By the time he was about twenty he was a wealthy man, running a small group of his own.

"Then he quit. Paid off his soldiers so there were no ill feelings, made sure they got relocated with other gangs, and went into the import business."

"Import, as in drugs?" I asked.

"No. Legitimate goods—rugs, fancy foods, yarn, the kind of crap you find in Pier One—hammered-brass spittoons from Burma—junk like that. Customs checked him out, IRS, DEA, Interpol, the Hong Kong Police—you name it. He went straight. But it wasn't like some tear-jerker movie. He was just as ruthless as before. And it's not like he got any closer to his brother, either. If anything, they saw less of each other as time went on. But On Ha kept to the straight and narrow, so I guess Van Loc's efforts paid off."

"Was Van Loc's business a success?"

Frazier gave me another ambivalent expression. "Not particularly. Our sources suspect he probably socked away a pile from his gang activities. He certainly didn't lose money as an importer, but considering the good life he was used to, the switch didn't make much sense."

"I was told," I explained, "that On Ha's death was seen as a reflection of Van Loc's bad karma. Could Truong have gone straight because someone told him he had bad karma? Maybe he felt On Ha was at risk, and he was doing what he could to save him."

Spinney looked doubtful. "I thought Lacoste told us that karma couldn't be changed—if life is shitty, there's nothing you can do about it."

I thought back to a similar comment by Nicky Tai. "I'm just guessing, but if Van Loc was ambitious enough to make it to this country alive and become a kingpin as a snot-nosed teenager—supporting both his brother and the family that was raising him—he might be egotistical enough to think he could change his karma. People try to cheat their gods all the time."

"So he went bonkers because the Chinatown Gang massacre proved him wrong?" Spinney asked.

Frazier killed the video and twisted open the narrow venetian blinds, letting in just enough light not to blind us. "All we know for sure is that he dropped out of sight after the funeral. The business was handed over to an associate, and he disappeared."

The pager on my belt began vibrating soundlessly. I glanced at its miniature display and recognized Dan Flynn's number. Frazier nodded toward his phone, giving me permission to use it.

Spinney was still asking questions. "No credit-card trail? Phone calls?"

Frazier shook his head. "None that we know of. Credit-card use is not a big item with these folks, at least not legitimately. They tend to like cash. My bet is that Truong had a serious nest egg tucked away somewhere."

"And," Spinney added, "if Joe's right about Truong stealing business from Da Wang, he's got a new money source in any case."

*   *   *

Flynn picked up on the first ring.

"What's up?" I asked him.

"How fast can you get to Hartford? Heather Dahlin called. One of her people spotted Michael Vu in White River Junction. He disappeared before they were able to grab him, but he hasn't been spooked. She's put her entire department on the lookout for him, though, along with the Lebanon Police across the river."

I told him we'd be there in under an hour, and explained the situation to the others.

Frazier looked slightly put out. "We haven't really finished here."

"I sure would like the first shot at Vu if they nail him," I countered.

He conceded with a half smile. "All right. I'll stay here and play with my paperwork."

*   *   *

I let Spinney drive. All the ribbing from municipal cops aside, it was true that state troopers—even ones who had been in plain clothes for years—had more experience driving at warp speed on the interstates than any of the rest of us. As if to prove the point, he made the ninety-minute trip from Burlington in half that time.

We found Heather Dahlin standing by her car in White River Junction, near the Route 4 bridge leading into New Hampshire.

"We think he might've gone across," she said, gesturing to the far side of the river with her thumb. "Could be he's rounding up some money."

I introduced Spinney, and she stuck her arm in through the car window across my chest to shake hands. I could tell she was tense and frustrated. "We've had patrols out all over—haven't seen a trace of him since that first sighting."

"What was he doing?"

"He was on foot, entering a building. But by the time they figured out who he was, he'd disappeared."

"But you're pretty sure he didn't spook."

Her brow furrowed a bit more. "Pretty sure. But he's got to know there's a BOL out on him."

The radio in her hand muttered unintelligibly. She lifted it to her mouth and answered. Spinney and I clearly heard what came back. "We might have something on your subject."

I leaned back and opened the rear door for her. "Hop in."

She did so without hesitation, parking both her elbows on the seat back between us. "Cross the bridge, take a right at the light."

Spinney moved the car quickly into traffic and entered New Hampshire. I gestured to Dahlin's radio. "Who's on the other end?"

"Lebanon Police."

Spinney took the right, drove through the village of West Lebanon, and bore right again to take Route 12A into the heart of the most heavily commercialized area along the entire Vermont–New Hampshire border. Almost a mile of plazas, malls, and megastores, this strip of 12A paralleled the Connecticut, crossed the Mascoma River—a small, fast-moving feeder—and went under the east-west bridge of Interstate 89. At the best of times, it was as jammed a spot as any good-sized urban downtown. At the worst, it virtually became gridlock. As we entered from the north, I could see things were about fifty-fifty.

"What's your location?" Dahlin inquired on her radio.

The voice on the other end didn't sound happy. "Below the interstate, east side. Chinese-restaurant parking lot."

Spinney found his way there, having gone beyond the lot, turned left onto the airport road, and then doubled back along a back street. Road planning had not kept up with development.

A Lebanon Police cruiser was discreetly parked between two other cars, its clearly marked tail end facing a music-store window. One of the patrolmen had draped a jacket over the car's roof light, further disguising it. All three of us got out and joined them.

The driver, a tall blond with mild acne, looked disgusted. "We figured we'd wait for you here. Find out what you wanted to do. He went in there"—he gestured to the Chinese restaurant far across the big parking lot—"but we don't know what happened to him then. When he didn't come out after half an hour, we went inside. Nobody. We showed his picture around. They all said they'd never laid eyes on him."

Heather Dahlin kept her voice tightly under control. "You didn't want to call for backup when you first saw him?"

The blond looked uncomfortable. "We weren't even sure it was him. We only caught a glimpse, from across the street."

Her eyes narrowed. "So maybe it wasn't him?"

I moved to defuse things a bit. "Considering he's vanished, it probably was. It sure as hell was *somebody* who didn't want to stick around and chat. Did you check for a back exit?"

The patrolman nodded sadly, and looked over at his partner. "Wayne here did a few minutes after the guy went in—that's why we thought we had him bottled up tight—but I guess he'd already split. He must've cut through the place at a dead run."

Spinney stretched and yawned, seemingly unconcerned that he'd driven at supersonic speed to come to this conclusion. "Well, if he wasn't spooked before, he sure sounds it now."

"Wrap it up?" Dahlin asked of me.

I nodded. "Might as well. A half-hour head start, he could be anywhere." I shook hands with the patrolman. "Thanks, anyway. It was worth a shot."

He merely shook his head, pulled the jacket from off the cruiser's roof light, and got back behind the wheel.

The three of us returned to our car.

"What now?" Dahlin asked as we walked.

I checked my watch. "It's getting late. We might as well bunk down at a motel here, and then head back to Waterbury tomorrow."

Deflated by the anticlimax, no one spoke as Spinney nosed up to the line of traffic and waited for an opening. Heather sat back in her seat, staring out the side window, her radio ignored beside her. Although totally different in style, she reminded me then of Sammie Martens, which made me wonder how things were going back home in Brattleboro.

Spinney was finally waved into line by a courteous driver, and drove up to the red light just south of the interstate overpass.

Reminiscing brought me to Gail, whom I hadn't seen since the funeral. I had been hoping that tonight I could drive down from Waterbury to South Royalton—a short half-hour trip—and spend a little time with her, but that was obviously not to be. I'd call her anyway, even though the phone had become more of an irritant than a remedy to the isolation I was feeling.

Spinney moved forward on the green light, passed under the interstate, and slowed again at another traffic light on the far side. We were just shy of the bridge over the narrow Mascoma River, and stuck between two huge mall complexes, one on either side of us.

I glanced across Spinney, out his open side window, and onto the vast parking lot of the L-shaped Kmart Plaza. There was yet another Oriental restaurant about midway down the row of stores.

Suddenly, I leaned forward in surprise. "There." I pointed toward the distant restaurant, now half blocked by the opposite flow of traffic.

Heather Dahlin sat up as if stung, her face glued to the window. Spinney kept trying to look to where I was pointing and watch for the light simultaneously. "What the hell is it?"

"Go left—into the parking lot. I think I saw him."

"Damn." Not daring to use his siren, in case Michael Vu thought the heat was off, Spinney switched on the blue lights mounted behind the car's grille. Nobody seemed to notice. He inched into the line of traffic, now coming on quickly, jerking the car forward in stages.

"Come on," Dahlin urged from behind. "Where was he, exactly?"

"Going into that restaurant."

Spinney swore and hit the gas, lurching in front of a small red Honda, which slammed on its brakes with a squeal. There was a howl of protest from a horn. Just feet away, I saw its driver contorting her face with a torrent of soundless invective. In a second she was gone, as Spinney sped forward, narrowly missing another collision in the next lane, and finally shot into the entrance of the shopping plaza.

"Stop," I yelled, and opened the door, which was wrenched out of my hand by the sudden arrest of momentum. I leaped out onto the pavement.

"What're you doing?" Spinney shouted at me.

I was thinking of the two cops we'd just left. "Going around back in case you chase him through."

I ran across the end of the long line of shops, and down a paved service road dotted with overflowing dumpsters. To my right, noisy and tumultuous, the Mascoma River hurtled near, far, and near again as it passed through a long, sharp-angled S-curve between trash-strewn, muddy banks.

A hulking eighteen-wheeler appeared at the far end of the road and began trundling toward me, gathering speed, despite the road's narrowness and clutter. I ran faster, hoping to reach the restaurant's back door before the truck cut me off, but I was too late. I was forced to skid to a stop behind one of the dumpsters, and wait until the behemoth went by, my hopes of beating the others to the restaurant defeated.

The outcome was predictable. Just as I began running again, Michael Vu exploded from one of the distant doors. He stopped for a moment in the middle of the road, saw me bearing down from his right, and bolted straight ahead.

Facing him, the Mascoma veered back to within fifteen yards of the rear of the buildings, its current and depth mellowed by the hairpin curves just upstream. At the foot of the gentle bank that Vu was running down, there was an eddy of sorts—a gently swirling radius of calm water, where it looked like someone might take a dip in warmer weather. Beyond it, the water flowed its fastest, pushed away from the far bank by a tree that lay anchored in the sandy mud. Overall, the width of the river was about twenty feet.

Vu didn't hesitate. He reached the edge of the bank at full tilt, and took off in a wild flat dive, landing with explosive force in mid-current. For a moment he floundered, his body twisting and rolling; then he grasped the far reaches of the small tree extending to the middle of the stream. He found his footing on the bottom, which was only some three to four feet deep, and dragged himself to the other bank.

Abreast of him now on the opposite shore, I stopped, my feet in the mud, deafened by the river's tumble. I cleared my revolver, pointed it straight at him, and motioned with my other hand for him to lay down. He hesitated momentarily, suddenly broke into a grin, and began working frantically to pull the tree's embedded trunk free of the mud. He'd realized—as I knew all along—the futility of both my command and my weapon. Vu was wanted, as they say in the movies, "for questioning." And while Hollywood routinely makes that an offense deserving gunplay, we both knew it was not.

Swearing readily now, I started into the water.

As desperate as it had seemed, Vu's flat dive had been the right approach. As soon as I'd waded to the outer edge of the shallow swimming hole, the water's full power grabbed both my feet and pulled them out from under me. I landed on the rock bed, almost losing my gun, and made a wild grab for the tree just as Vu succeeded in freeing it. As both I and the tree were swept away, I saw Vu take to his heels again, across the gravel bank toward a thick stand of saplings.

My ride didn't last long. At the next corner, I managed to catch a rock with the bottom of one foot, right myself, and, pushing awkwardly on the bobbing trunk, stagger to dry land. From there, Vu was no longer visible, but I did see Spinney and Dahlin explode out the restaurant door on the other bank.

I gestured to them to head back toward 12A, while I began running for the trees. It was not easy going—the saplings stood in tight ranks, amid an undergrowth of strangling brush, and halfway through them I had to scramble up a six-foot sheer embankment, reminiscent of some marine-corps training course. On the far side of this thick band of trees, I found myself in a broad, flat field leading up to the paved access road of the town's water-treatment plant. In the distance, almost out of sight behind some storage sheds, was Michael Vu, still going at a dead run.

I shoved the pistol back into my wet holster, and put all my efforts into catching a man who not only was obviously in great physical shape, but who was showing a pathological lack of interest in having a friendly chat.

He was almost back to 12A's ubiquitous line of traffic by the time I reached the access road, and as I watched, he seemed to vanish within it like a stone dropping into a dark well. I ran full tilt, half thinking I might find him spread-eagled and squashed flat by a flood of single-minded commuters. Instead, all I could see was a blur of cars and trucks, and, way off on the other side—moving fast—the diminishing outline of my quarry, about to escape for a second time that day.

Yielding to the same kind of passion I'd observed earlier in Heather Dahlin, and stimulated by a rush of adrenaline, I ran out into the traffic, hearing both her's and Spinney's shouted warnings in the distance behind me.

The effect was bone-jarringly cataclysmic. Horns, squealing rubber, screaming voices, and the deadening crunch of fenders accompanied my broken-field dash across the street. Only once did I have to actually slide across the hood of a car that didn't stop in time, much to the astonishment of its white-haired driver. On the far side, however, Michael Vu was still in sight.

We were now coming abreast of what is called the Powerhouse

Mall, a large, roughly C-shaped plaza expensively built in industrial-revolution style—heavy on red brick and large windows. Vu, steering away from the plaza's trap-like embrace, skirted the parking lot's open north face and ran alongside Glen Road, a narrow street into which it fed, aiming for the far end of the C, and the relative boondocks beyond it.

Knowing I had no chance of catching him, I jogged on, my energy waning, paying no attention to the shouting of the angry motorists behind me.

Partway across the front of the mall's parking lot, however, Vu's luck and mine suddenly changed.

Ahead of us, from farther up Glen Road, came the distant howl of a siren. Vu slowed abruptly, quickly looked back at me, and then cut to his right, directly into the dead end formed by the Powerhouse's three-sided box. Just at that moment, I saw the Lebanon Police cruiser come into view, obviously summoned by Heather Dahlin, hurtling at full speed toward the intersection with Route 12A. Apparently she'd caught them as they were heading east on I-89, and had asked them to take the next exit and double back.

Waving wildly to attract their attention, I began angling to cut Vu off at the mall's central, southern entrance. I briefly saw the blond driver's pale face turn toward me, and then the sounds of his brakes as he fishtailed into the parking lot just a hair too late, sideswiping the high granite curb and blowing a tire. As Michael Vu veered again and vanished into the mall's easternmost entrance, my attention was diverted by a second burst of squealing tires to my back. Expecting Dahlin and Spinney, I saw instead a black sports car with tinted windows swerve to a stop at the parking lot's other entrance, and inexplicably spin around to return to Route 12A at high speed.

Knowing the two patrolmen were now pursuing him on foot, I didn't follow Michael Vu through the entrance he'd chosen, but instead continued toward the south door, in the middle of the mall's C-shape, hoping to hell Dahlin had ordered all the support troops she could locate.

The Powerhouse Mall is two stories tall, elegantly appointed with lots of dark wood and brass, and a long, narrow, lofting central hallway, running east to west, which reaches up to the roof high above. The second floor is restricted to two parallel balconies along this main corridor, meeting at staircases at both ends. Given Vu's speed and the lead he'd gained, it was possible he'd had time to reach the upstairs—or, for that matter, to hide out in any of the mall's dozens of stores.

For the moment I stood motionless, watching, listening, and waiting for the others to catch up. What I wanted was a radio.

Dahlin and Spinney didn't take long to reach me, red-faced and out of breath. With the growing puddle around my feet, the three of us made for quite an attraction, just as I hoped Michael Vu had, bursting through the other entrance.

"Ask the Lebanon boys if anyone saw him," I told her. "Maybe then we can zero in on a general area."

She keyed her radio and passed along my suggestion. Spinney took off for the staircase behind us to block it off. A couple of minutes later, the radio announced, "Someone saw him heading south toward the staircase. Don't know if he took it or stuck to the main hallway."

Dahlin turned to me. "Why don't you join Spinney and work down both sides of the balcony? I'll wait here for the backup. Shouldn't be more'n three or four minutes. The patrolmen can either start working the east wing or stay put by their entrance. Your call. You're running this show."

That was a sensitive technicality that routinely gave feds their resented reputation. I started moving in Spinney's direction, playing down her last comment. "Sounds good. They're already inside—might as well keep 'em coming."

I joined Spinney, climbing two steps at a time, and took the balcony across from his.

The two balconies were about ten feet wide, bordered by a waist-high, ornate railing to the inside, and a string of shops opposite, lined up like a row of fancy New Orleans apartments. I removed my gun from its holster and walked with my hand hidden under my jacket, as if protecting something from the rain—an image my soggy appearance made blatantly ludicrous. I tried to ignore the loud squelching from my shoes.

Each one of the shops had large interior windows, making them comparatively simple to check inside without actually entering. At every door, my badge displayed in my free hand, I inquired of each salesperson if they'd seen a soaking-wet Asian male recently. This process was less nerve-wracking than it could have been, because I was also checking for the same kind of wet footprints I was leaving behind me. It seemed reasonable that where there were no prints, there was also no Michael Vu. Assuming he hadn't taken his shoes off.

Shop by shop, Spinney and I worked our way up the line, keeping track of each other visually, and of Heather Dahlin below.

Until I saw the glimmer of water on the floor.

I was standing opposite a clothing store filled with racks blocking my view of the interior. I stood quietly for a few moments, watching for movements, or reactions from the few shoppers inside. I couldn't see a clerk at the register near the door.

I glanced over my shoulder and saw Spinney looking over at me. I gestured at the store, and then at my feet and the trail I'd left. He nodded and moved up so he was facing the store's front door, albeit across the chasm.

He didn't quite make it. There was a sudden flurry of movement near the counter, and Michael Vu—his long black hair plastered to his face—appeared from a small storage closet just behind the register, his arm wrapped around the neck of a terrified young woman, whose hands gripped his forearm in a struggle for more air. He wrestled her out onto the balcony, staring for a moment at both Spinney and me. In his free hand was a switchblade.

I held my breath. Hostage situations were unpredictable, dangerous, and volatile, and only rarely ended up as happily as on TV.

I showed my gun, as did Spinney. "Let her go, Michael," I said, loudly enough to attract Dahlin's attention from below. In the corner of my eye, I could see her bringing the radio up to her mouth.

"Fuck you," Vu shouted back. "You go away or she dies."

"We're staying put, Michael, and more cops are on the way. Killing her will do nothing for you."

He looked around wildly, as if expecting a marine division to appear out of the blue. "*I* won't be killing her. *You* will."

"Look," I said. "We don't even have a warrant for your arrest. We want to have a talk with you—that's all."

He began shaking, swinging the woman before him like a rag doll. "Oh, sure. Right. A little conversation. That's bullshit, man. You think I'm a dumb fuck?"

Suddenly, he arched his back, lifting the girl's feet off the ground, and shouted, "Well, I'm *not*." He pushed her over the railing and bolted down the length of the balcony.

The girl screamed and grappled at thin air as her body cantilevered over the top of the railing. Only as she was dropping into free-fall did one leg instinctively hook onto the rail and leave her momentarily hanging like a clumsy acrobat. I got to her just as her leg slid free, and snagged her ankle with my left hand. Despite her small size, the sudden weight pulled me to my knees, hammering the railing into my armpit. I gasped in pain, focusing all my strength on not letting her go. I rose slowly to my feet, and began hauling the girl toward me, using her leg like a rope. Moments later, several startled shoppers began helping me pull her to safety.

At the far end of the mall's long corridor, with Spinney close on his heels, Vu reached the bottom of the stairs. Seeing Dahlin sprinting toward him, he whirled around to his left and disappeared under the distant staircase.

Confused about where he'd gone, I too now gave chase, pounding down the stairs, slipping in my wet shoes, and swung around the same corner to discover a glass-door exit, discreetly placed next to the bathrooms. It was just swinging shut after Dahlin's passage.

Outside, to my right, I could see the three of them sprinting toward the Mascoma River, whose waters here ran faster, deeper, and more dangerously than where I'd entered them below the S-curves.

I started after them, my eye on Michael Vu, who was sliding down the bank to the water's edge, just ahead of the others. As he was about to plunge into the rapids and risk a ride toward the Connecticut River, he stopped abruptly and sat down hard. Beyond him, high on the opposite shore, I saw the familiar black shape of the car that had screeched to a stop in the mall's parking lot earlier, now pulling away fast, tires smoking, the sounds of its departure masked by the roar of the water.

By the time I got to the river's edge, both Dahlin and Spinney were on either side of Michael Vu, looking perplexed. Spinney had turned to face the vast parking lot across from us, looking at where the black car had just been.

Dahlin was crouching near Vu, blocking my sight of him. "What the hell happened?" I shouted over the sound of the rapids.

She moved aside, barking orders into her radio, and I saw that Michael Vu wasn't really sitting on the bank—he was lying on it, flat on his back. And decorating his chest—right over his heart—was a large bullet hole.

Chapter Twenty-three

I did make it to Gail's off-campus apartment, long after she'd gone to bed. While my anticipation of our reunion had been altered by Michael Vu's murder, the need for her company was as real as before. Only now, I wanted a place to think, and someone to hear me out.

She took it all in stride. She got back into bed, propped her head up against the pillows, and watched me pace the darkened room as I described the day's events. It was a sign of our friendship that my unannounced arrival, the late hour, and the restless mood I was in were all dismissed without comment.

"Why do you think Vu was killed? And who did it?" she asked after I'd finished.

I paused by the window and looked out onto the silent street below. "The reasonable explanation is that somebody didn't want him talking to us. But since we weren't able to get a unit across the river fast enough to catch that black car, we may never know. Spinney was still running the mop-up when I left, trying to find witnesses. The New Hampshire State Police came in with a forensics team. But I don't think they'll find anything . . . We went back to the two restaurants Vu had visited. In both cases, he'd made a halfhearted attempt to extort some cash. He didn't get much chance to put the screws to them at either place, of course, but I doubt he would've gotten much anyway. Once they heard he was dead, both owners seemed pretty unconcerned—as if they knew he was flying solo and that any threat had died with him."

"So Truong put the word out?"

"Somebody did. Vu didn't do anything for Truong's—or 'Sonny's'— PR in Brattleboro. As far as we can tell, that whole operation's collapsed. Sammie told me this afternoon that things seem pretty much back to normal. It's possible Vu was targeted because of that failure. Our showing up probably just speeded things up a bit. If Vu knew a contract was out on him, cutting a deal with us might've sounded pretty appealing."

"Isn't it a pretty big coincidence that both you and a hit man appeared at the same place at the same time? And how did he know where Vu would run to so he could get off that perfect shot?"

I settled into an armchair opposite the window and propped my feet on the sill before me. "It wasn't necessarily a coincidence. We heard about Vu through our own grapevine, and their's is a hell of a lot more sophisticated. The miracle is we saw him alive at all. That's what makes me think he was being doubly skittish, on the run from both sides. As for the shooter, after he saw us in pursuit, he had to back off; but he knew that Vu would either be caught by us in the mall, or would run for the river. Those were his only two options."

Gail let out a small sigh. "So Truong had him killed."

"Maybe."

She looked up at me quietly for a moment. "You don't think so?"

I gave a half shrug. "He could've done it—he's cold enough for it. But the FBI found out that when he was fresh off the boat, he had a little brother he doted on—paid for his upkeep, his education . . . bent over backwards to make sure he flew straight. All financed with money he got working his way up through the gangs. The kicker is, after he'd built up a grubstake, he went straight, too—started running a legitimate business. A few years ago, the kid was killed as an innocent bystander in a gang shooting."

A long silence filled the air.

"That means he couldn't have killed Vu?" she asked quietly.

"No . . . it means he's a lot more complicated than your run-of-the-mill wise guy. Killing a screwup like Vu is something Vu himself might've done. I'm not so sure about Truong anymore."

*   *   *

The persistent chirp of my pager cut through my dreams like a chainsaw.

Gail's voice was slurred and startled. "What the hell's that? A smoke alarm?"

I kicked off the covers, acutely conscious of the nagging bleating, and of how it might penetrate to the adjoining apartments. Three hours earlier, all talked out, I'd finally yielded to Gail's invitation to join her in bed, and had been enjoying the first deep sleep I'd had in weeks.

"It's Frazier's damn beeper. His way and Flynn's of keeping in touch."

Gail laughed as I tore through my pants, trying to locate my belt in its folds. "How intimate. Compliment them on their timing."

I finally found it, killed the sound, and turned on the light to read its display. "You got a phone?" I asked irritably.

I dialed the number on the pager.

"Where are you?" came Frazier's voice, answering, I was pretty sure, from a mobile phone.

"South Royalton."

"You better get up to Burlington. There's been a shooting. Three dead. A drive-by of a residence by two cars with automatic weapons. They've got one guy in custody. It's an Asian-on-Asian deal. I'm trying to keep the shooter isolated till you get here, but the locals would like the jurisdictional details cleared up fast."

"I'll be there as quick as I can."

*   *   *

I stood beside Frazier and a lieutenant from the Burlington Police, looking through the one-way glass at a young Asian male, pacing like a caged cat from one side of the interrogation room to the other. He had long, expensively cut hair, an assortment of gold jewelry, designer clothes, and was sweating profusely. He might have been seventeen years old, stretching it.

"What do you have on him?" I asked of the lieutenant.

"Name's Vinh Thanh Chau—sixteen. No priors so far. We're still checking."

"I called Montreal," Frazier added. "He's one of a Vietnamese gang that works mostly for Da Wang. He's been nailed for petty theft, pimping, attempted extortion—apparently not very good at his job."

"Ever do time?"

Frazier shook his head. "Too young."

The lieutenant gave the Bureau man—a "feebie" to municipal cops—a sour look for upstaging him, and resumed his narrative. "He was in the second car. It smashed up about half a mile from the shooting—missed a curve. The others got away. We found three automatic weapons in the car, and two handguns."

"A Glock?"

"Nope—Berretta and a Colt—nine millimeter and thirty-eight special."

"He say anything?"

The sour look returned. "I wouldn't know."

I turned and faced him. "Walt tell you about the task force?"

"Yeah."

"Well, it's got more local people on it than not, so we'll make sure the municipal cops aren't left out in the cold. I did want first crack at this guy, but if it looks like you can throw a bigger book at him than we can, he's all yours. We won't make any deals without your agreement, and whatever we learn, you learn. Fair enough?"

The lieutenant didn't answer directly, no doubt knowing my background, and considering me a traitor to local autonomy. "Witness to the crash said he came out of the back seat. Survivors at the scene said that's where a lot of the firepower came from, too. He likes to be called 'Chewy.'"

"Do we know if anyone died from his shots specifically?"

"Hard to tell."

"He been Mirandized?"

"Yeah."

I patted his shoulder as I walked toward the door leading to the interrogation room. "Okay—thanks."

Vinh Thanh Chau stopped his prowling when I crossed the threshold.

He struck a pose, feet apart, hands on his hips, and gave me a look of wilting superiority.

I gazed at him for a moment. "Chewy? That your name?"

"Yeah, man."

"Mine's Gunther. I'm a Deputy US Marshal. Have a seat."

Vinh's eyes narrowed slightly, obviously surprised at the title. I settled into one of the chairs at the room's central table.

The teenager stood uncertainly for a moment, and then strutted over to a chair opposite mine, taking his time.

I waited patiently before telling him, "Guess you got yourself into some trouble. Must be a little scary, boy your age."

His face darkened with anger. "I'm not scared. You grow up fast in the streets. I done stuff you can't even dream about."

"Stuff you won't do again for a long, long time."

He watched me silently, digesting my words.

"You know the difference between a US Marshal and a local cop?"

He lifted his chin slightly. "Sure, I do."

"We enforce federal laws, and we do it with a lot more freedom than the locals. And once we nail somebody, we send him to a federal prison, like Leavenworth."

"I can take that," he said, but I sensed a lack of wind in his sails.

I got to my feet. "Good. Then I guess I can go home. You want to be the butt-fucked toy of some hairy con for the next thirty years, more power to you."

I moved toward the door. Vinh half rose in his seat, his eyes wide with surprise and a twinge of the fear I'd been hoping for. "Wait— that's it?"

I looked over my shoulder. "What do you mean?"

"That's all you're going to ask me?"

"Sure. What did you think?"

"You make a deal. You're supposed to deal."

I turned around completely to face him, my face incredulous. "A deal? For what? You were the triggerman in a fatal drive-by shooting. People saw you do it—we already have their statements. What can a kid like you offer me?"

His voice rose a few notes. "Plenty. I know plenty."

I sighed and looked at my watch. "Chewy, you're a street punk down on his luck. You've grabbed a purse or two, maybe thrown a brick through a window, tried to sell the services of some thirteen-year-old girl. You've got nothing to offer me."

"I work for Da Wang in Montreal. He's like Al Capone—the biggest crook in the city. I know stuff he's done."

I laughed at him. "Chewy—you pulling my chain here?"

He was on his feet now, pleading. "No. I'm not shitting you. I got the goods on him, man."

I leaned forward slightly at the waist and said slowly and distinctly. "He's in Canada, Chewy. I don't give a fuck."

He came around from behind the table, all cool gone by now. "What do you need? I know other stuff, too. I been around. I can be useful."

I made a show of hesitating, as if trying to make up my mind. Finally, I shook my head. "I don't see it. You've never even been in this country before. What could you know that would interest me?"

His eyes grew round with astonishment. "Shit, man—there's *how* I got here. I entered illegally. I can tell you how I did it."

I smiled. "It's an unguarded border, for Christ's sake."

"No. No. It's organized. Da Wang does it all the time. He's got a system for getting lots of people across. The Border Patrol doesn't know anything about it."

I waved my hand dismissively. "They know more than you think. They know Da Wang's been losing his shirt lately to a guy named Sonny—the one who whacked Da Wang's snakehead not long ago."

Vinh was almost quivering with excitement. "But that's why I'm here. Don't you see? We were ordered across the border to mess up Sonny's business. Hit him on his home base—make him lose face big time."

"You were ordered to blow holes in a building in the middle of the night? Why didn't you throw toilet paper on the lawn, too? That would've really pissed him off."

Vinh pounded the table next to him in anger. "No. Shit, man, don't you get it? We fucked up a little is all. This is going to be like a war. We're like soldiers, man."

I shook my head and scratched the back of my neck, reluctantly returning to the table. "I don't know, Chewy. Sounds a little far out. You better take me through it."

*   *   *

Spinney pulled his cardboard cup of hot soup out of the Burlington Police Department's vending machine and sat next to me on the battered, coffee-stained sofa in a corner of the officers' day room. The first paling of dawn was starting to light the windows.

"I hear you got the little turkey to open up. Frazier was impressed."

"Swell," I said, sighing. "Where is Frazier? I was hoping he'd finish that briefing he was giving us."

"He's on the phone." Spinney stared intently into his soup. "You think this is safe to drink?"

"I'm not about to find out. How'd things work out in Lebanon?"

He took a tentative sip and raised his eyebrows. "Pretty good. Lebanon was a wash, as expected. We figured the angle of fire came from the supermarket parking lot across the river—confirms that car you saw."

"Silencer?"

"Not necessarily. The water was noisy enough to cover a cannon. Whoever it was wasn't taking chances on his marksmanship, though. The ME said he used one of those new Rhino jobbies that blow apart on impact. Looked like he'd swallowed a hand grenade. We combed the whole area, canvassed for witnesses . . . they're still at it, more or less, but . . . How 'bout you? What did you learn from your new friend?"

"That Da Wang's declared war. He and his friends were supposed to hit a restaurant downtown, but they got lost and went to Plan B, which was the house. 'Course, Plan B was screwed up, too. They were supposed to kick in the doors and wipe the place out—make a statement no one would forget. My friend, as you call him, blames the lead car— said they lost their nerve and turned it into a drive-by. Da Wang's going to have to improve on his talent."

"What's the scope of this war?"

"That's where this kid fizzled out. I guess they knew enough not to give him the whole picture. He's positive he was one of several teams, but he had no idea what the other targets were. Didn't know who 'Sonny' was, either, although Da Wang's made him their top priority. Nor did he know how much damage Sonny's inflicted, although I guess we can assume things are not going well."

"What about the snakehead angle?"

"That was more interesting. We were right about the alien smuggling—it's a major cash cow, and it's where Truong seems to be doing Da Wang the most harm. Da Wang has a new snakehead, but he's having a tough time getting customers. Word's gotten out the organization ain't what it used to be. The RCMP's been getting tip-offs—presumably from Truong's crew—telling them where the illegals are being assembled prior to crossing. Chewy—the kid's nickname—claims everyone's getting sweaty palms, wondering if Da Wang's losing his touch. Sonny's taken over a lot of the Vermont restaurants, money's started to dry up, and word's gotten back to Da Wang's backers in the old country. Truong has his own contacts there, so now alien and heroin suppliers are either playing both sides or holding off entirely until the dust settles."

"Guess Truong's putting all those import-business contacts to use after all," Spinney mused. "Makes you wonder if we're missing the boat here. Could be all that bad-boy-goes-straight stuff was pure smoke screen."

I silently watched him as he sipped from his cup. It was an uncomfortably plausible point he'd just made, and one to which I was inordinately sensitive. In our line of work, greed, power, and frustration were the most popular criminal stimulants, and they tended to be expressed hot and fast. Ten-year-old, karma-induced revenge rarely came up. What were the chances I was overstating Truong's motive—ennobling a crook whose ambitions were no different than Da Wang's?

I backed away from any hard-set conclusions, biding my time with a short-term truism. "Either way, we get the same mess on our hands."

Walt Frazier suddenly appeared at the doorway, looking worn and tired. Nearing retirement, he probably wished nights like these would be forever banished to his past. In that, he was not alone. Even Spinney, the youngest of us, looked ready for twelve hours of sleep. I doubted any of us would be allowed that luxury.

"We gonna keep Chewy or let the Burlington PD have him?" I asked as Frazier approached.

He pulled a molded-plastic chair over and sat down heavily, stretching out his legs. "That's what I was trying to sort out. Maggie wants to see what we've got first. Nice interview, by the way—too bad it was such shitty news. I suppose we can hope the other hit teams are as brain dead as this one. I wish to hell he could've told us more— be nice to head 'em off, instead of running around picking up the pieces."

"We could do that if we knew what properties Truong controlled," I mused, half to myself.

"Oh—good luck with that one." Spinney finished off his soup with one last gulp.

Suddenly inspired by the challenge, I got up and moved over to a pay phone mounted on the wall. "There might be a way."

I picked up the receiver, dialed Dan Flynn's pager number, and hung up, smiling. "Sweet revenge."

Five minutes later, the phone rang. "Morning, Dan. It's Joe. Walt and Lester and I were shooting the shit up here in Burlington. Thought you might like to put in your two cents."

"Fuck you. What d'you want?" Flynn's voice was barely a mumble.

I laughed, feeling no guilt whatsoever. "A while back, you were telling me how some of the Asian restaurants get their supplies exclusively from outfits in New York or Boston—everything from napkins to noodles to menus."

"Yeah. They don't buy anything locally."

"You said that's what made it difficult to know what was in the delivery truck, or what might be moving from place to place."

"Right."

"What was your source for that? Is there someone we could talk to so we could identify one of these trucks—maybe put a tail on it? We're trying to find a way to pinpoint Truong's properties."

"I heard it at a conference in New York. Someone on the Asian-crime squad down there was talking about it. His name was . . . damn. I don't have my computer handy. Fred something . . . Wilkinson. Fred Wilkinson. Give him a call. He was real friendly."

I thanked him, dialed Information, and eventually worked my way to Wilkinson's office, preparing to leave my name and pager number, along with a brief message. Instead, Wilkinson picked up in person, sounding as tired as I was.

I briefly explained who I was and what we were up to. His response, almost cutting me off in mid-sentence, was, "Ryder, U-Haul, sometimes just a plain step-van. They don't go regularly, they don't follow the same route twice in a row, and most of the time they're clean as a whistle."

"There been any upheavals at your end recently? A change in management at one of the suppliers?"

"Who knows? But I wouldn't waste my time with delivery trucks. Unless you got some inside dope, you'll probably end up busting a shipment of rice."

His disinterest was as palpable as his fatigue. I thanked him for his time, and let him head off to bed—not without some envy.

Spinney read my expression. "No soap?"

"Not really . . ." I scratched my head. "Still . . . there's a restaurant owner in Bratt who was squeezed by Truong's boys. If we can squeeze him in turn, maybe we can get some help about the rest of the pipeline."

Spinney leaped to his feet in mock enthusiasm. "Hot damn. Another drive down the interstate?"

That thought hadn't occurred to me yet. "S'pose so."

Frazier spoke up. "Look, if you two are heading off again, let me at least give you the punch line to my briefing on Truong Van Loc. I think you'll find it useful. The rest I can give later."

We both looked at him expectantly.

"Joe, you were saying that when you stopped his car last winter, you thought none of them knew each other. Turns out that when Truong went legit, he had a small staff—mostly warehouse people to handle the imports. One of them was Henry Lam. Henry disappeared when Truong did. Apparently, they were pretty tight—the San Francisco Police labeled Lam a surrogate son of sorts."

Spinney and I exchanged glances, having guessed at some kind of connection.

"Also, I got the goods on Wang Chien-kuo. Not only was he in San Francisco at the time Truong's little brother got whacked, he was one of the Dragon Boys leaders."

I stared at him, the final large piece falling into place with satisfying logic. "Did he order the hit on Chinatown Gang?"

"He was in a position to. Truong undoubtedly knows more about that than we do. We also found out that of the two known Dragon Boys shooters from San Francisco we thought were still alive, one was found badly decomposed two months ago in a Florida swamp—a confirmed drug killing. It took them till last week to match dental records. The last one hasn't been seen in years—even his own family thinks he's dead by now."

I raised my eyebrows at Spinney. "Profit may be part of what's driving Truong Van Loc, but revenge is starting to look pretty reasonable."

Chapter Twenty-four

Our first stop in Brattleboro was the high school, and Amy Lee. Unfortunately, the hopeful enthusiasm that had fueled another long jaunt down the length of the state was met with sudden and ominous disappointment. According to the school's principal, Amy had stopped coming to classes a week ago. Calls to her home had netted only a succession of excuses, from sickness to a trip to an ailing relative, all of which had suggested a call to us, something the principal had been planning to do the next day.

We assured him we would find out what had happened to her. Personally, however, I was nervous. Given the battle we knew was forming—and some of the techniques we'd already witnessed—the taking of hostages didn't seem too farfetched.

We began by interviewing Amy's friends, comparing the various explanations they'd received concerning her sudden absence. Stimulated by the inconsistencies we found there, we discreetly visited the neighbor who'd blown the whistle on the home invasion earlier, and discovered that Amy had not been seen or heard from for the past week. During that same period, however, strange cars had been stopping by the Lee house for brief visits, most of them sporting Canadian plates.

The Lee house itself, with its shaggy lawn, drawn curtains, and utter lack of life, looked like an abandoned property up for sale.

"Do we interview the other neighbors?" Spinney asked as we sat in my car. "If she was grabbed, maybe one of them saw something."

I shook my head. "I don't want to tip any more people that we're interested." I moved to turn the key in the ignition, and then stopped. "The one we do want to interview is Thomas Lee."

"Thought he told you to pound sand."

"That was before. He might've changed his mind. 'Course, chances are now he has a whole new reason not to be chatty." I picked up the mobile phone, got the number for the Blue Willow Restaurant through Information, and called, asking for Thomas Lee.

"This is Lee," the familiar voice answered eventually, sounding halting and tired.

I disguised my voice by dropping it a few malevolent notes lower. "Henry. We need to talk. About Amy."

There was a pause, and a hint of panic in his response which confirmed our suspicions. "Is she okay? Who is this, please?"

"Depends on you how she is, Henry. You know the Old Guilford Road, out to Fort Dummer?"

"Yes."

"Go there now—take it all the way to the end, and wait." I hung up.

Spinney gave me an admiring smile, something I didn't feel I deserved. "You oughtta be in pictures."

*   *   *

Fort Dummer was Vermont's original white settlement, a blockhouse built in 1724 as a lookout against invaders from the north with designs on the more populated Massachusetts farmland to the south. Named after William Dummer, who with William Brattle and two Bostonians had bought a large chunk of what would become southeastern Vermont, the blockhouse stood as fitting, if symbolic, testimony to the vagaries of human enterprise. Left to stand forgotten in the woods for its first quarter century, the original site was now underwater, after the Vernon Dam drowned it in 1911. Still, sentiment being the historical apologist it can be, misty-eyed citizens eventually established both a monument to Fort Dummer and a small park in its name at the bottom of a dead-end road south of town. It was there that I'd instructed Thomas Lee to meet us.

The Old Guilford Road is long, sparsely populated, has no side roads beyond a certain point, and allowed us a perfect opportunity to see if Lee was being followed. We could also get there faster than he could, which is exactly what we did, parking unobtrusively among other cars in the lot of a converted farmhouse, now home to the Vermont Agricultural Business Education Center.

Ten minutes after our arrival, Thomas Lee drove by, alone, hunched over the steering wheel like an octogenarian trying to see the road.

"Jesus," Spinney muttered, "he doesn't look too healthy."

We waited another quarter hour, during which no other car drove by, and then we pulled out of the lot to join Lee at the park.

"What's our approach?" Spinney asked as we drove the extra half mile along an ever-narrowing road, gradually getting squeezed between a ragged string of occasional modest homes and I-91, which ran like a broad river just to our right and slightly below us.

"Fast and hard. My bet is he's only reacting now to whoever pushes the most."

We passed the open wooden gate and the sign welcoming us to the park. It being early in the season, there was no one manning the small booth astride the dirt road that led to the small parking area beyond. The place was abandoned. Almost.

I spotted Lee's car with its nose against a distant railing, and pulled up quickly on his passenger side, so he could get a clear view of me.

His eyes widened predictably, and he shouted, "You. Get away. Get away. You'll kill her."

He fumbled with his ignition, trying to start the engine so he could drive off. I piled out of our car, crossed over, and slid into his passenger seat. Spinney, more leisurely, came around and got into the back as I put my hand on top of Lee's and switched the motor off again.

He pulled his hand away as if I'd burned him, which in a sense I knew I had. "What are you doing? I don't want to talk to you."

"Then listen instead," I said quietly. "No one's watching us. We made sure of that. I'm no longer working for the Brattleboro Police, Mr. Lee. I'm a federal agent on an FBI task force, and I'm going after the same people who grabbed your daughter."

Lee was breathing fast, almost hyperventilating. His hands were back on the steering wheel, hanging on tight. "They will kill her if I talk to you. That is what they said." His words were choppy, as if torn off and set adrift.

"They don't know we're talking, and it's too late now anyway. If they were watching, she's history. It's not up to you, Mr. Lee. It never has been."

I let those words sink in. Slowly, his breathing calmed, and his hands slid to the bottom of the wheel before finally dropping into his lap. He looked down at them, as if surprised they were there. "Why do you do this?"

"Because it's the only thing *to* do. You're caught between two big rocks, Mr. Lee, and the only way your family can survive is to have at least one of them removed. You don't help us help you, you can pretty much forget about Amy. How's your wife?"

He shook his head. "Not good."

"Amy goes, she goes, too. You know that."

I looked at him, so lost in his woes he barely knew we were there any longer, and I decided to take a gamble. "Mr. Lee, when we first met, your house had been destroyed, your daughter raped, your wife beaten and traumatized, and you had been coerced into using your restaurant to break the law."

His head lifted and he stared at me.

I kept going, encouraged. "Since then, one of the three men who did that has died. The others are feeling the heat. But you're not being squeezed by those people anymore, are you? You're back under the control of Da Wang. Only now, instead of just harboring illegal aliens now and then, or turning a blind eye to the occasional dope deal in the kitchen, you're being turned into a full-fledged crook. They claimed you'd been disloyal. That they didn't trust you anymore. That you'd have to do more for them. And that Amy would be their guarantee of your cooperation. Am I wrong, Mr. Lee?"

He shook his head slightly. "No."

I could hear Spinney audibly releasing his breath, acknowledging the risk I'd just taken. "What makes you think the first bunch won't come back—with a vengeance—and maybe do the same thing with your wife?"

He didn't answer, but took a deep breath and shuddered.

"You know they will, to save face if nothing else. Unless you help us change things, that's the fix you'll be in forever—being kicked back and forth, staying silent for the sake of your family, and watching them all die anyway."

I gave my words time to sink in.

"I do not know what to do," he finally whispered.

"You're worried we'll ask too much—that you'll be exposed and cause Amy's death."

He nodded.

"If you tell us what we need to know, that'll be the end of it. You won't see us again. Nobody'll ever know we made contact."

A small furrow appeared between his eyebrows as he looked at me. "What is it?"

"My guess is that you're pretty much doing what you did before, with a few additions and in bigger numbers—processing aliens, credit-card receipts, laundering money, maybe some drugs . . . Right?"

"Yes."

"And that's what you did for Michael Vu's gang?"

"Yes."

"How was the contraband moved through your place, when you were cooperating with Vu?"

He looked puzzled. "With Vu?"

"Look," I said, delivering my pitch. "I don't want to put your daughter further at risk. Remember I said we need to go after at least one of the rocks you're stuck between? Let's go after the lesser of the two—the one that's not controlling you at the moment. It's a way we can further disguise the fact that we ever had this conversation."

He nodded slowly. "I see."

"So how was it handled?"

"The aliens came and went in cars or small buses, as they do now. All I did, and all I still do, is hold them for a little while."

"And the money laundering? The drugs?"

"A man in a van would come by sometimes—I never knew when—and would pick up receipts and packages. Members of my staff—gang members—did all of that. I was just to run the restaurant. It is a good restaurant . . . an honest restaurant."

"I know that, Mr. Lee—you supplied the cover only. Did this man have a name?"

"I was not told it. I did not want to know."

"How 'bout the van? Was it always the same? A delivery truck, maybe carrying legitimate supplies as well?"

"No—that was the old way, and the way it is now. In between,

Vu used a camping van. Blue . . . and a black top. It had a painting on its side, of the mountains and a setting sun. Very colorful."

"Did you ever see the license plate?"

"No."

"Did you get the impression that its driver made stops all over the state—like a delivery boy?"

"I do not know."

"One last question. When Vu's gang took over Da Wang's territory—right after your home invasion—did you discuss what was happening with any other restaurant owners? Were any other owners forced to join like you?"

"I never discussed it, but I know it happened to others."

"Who?"

"I do not know. They told me it was so—the people who worked for Vu."

"How 'bout your friends in other restaurants? You must keep in touch, compare prices or whatever . . ."

But he was shaking his head. "We never talk about the Dark Root. It is not wise."

I glanced back at Spinney, who tilted his head slightly to one side. We both knew we'd gotten all we could hope to get.

We opened our doors and got out. I leaned back in before slamming mine shut. "Thanks, Mr. Lee. Go back to work and try not to worry. We'll do everything possible to get Amy back."

*   *   *

"That must've filled him with confidence," Spinney said as we retraced our route down the Old Guilford Road.

I was in a sour mood, despite the lead we'd been provided. "Can't do what he won't do for himself."

But Spinney was feeling expansive. "Considering where they come from, and what they've been through, it doesn't surprise me they don't cozy right up to us."

"Lots of people don't cozy up to us. That doesn't mean they roll over and play dead. She's his own daughter, for Christ's sake." I reached South Main Street and drove to the cemetery where Dennis was buried. There I pulled over and dialed Dan Flynn's number on the mobile phone. I understood the source of my rage. Amy Lee was someone who up till now had been spared the exploitation and cruelty we were rallying against, and in short order I'd seen her terrorized, assaulted, humiliated, and now kidnapped. Spinney was right about Thomas Lee—he'd been conditioned to react the way he had. But it wasn't in my nature to stand by and hope for the best.

"Got a hot one," I told Frazier when he got on the line. "Put a statewide BOL out on a blue van, black top, with a setting-sun-behind-the-mountains scene painted on the side—probably out-of-state plates. If we're lucky, that's the runner connecting all or some of Truong's properties."

"No shit."

"Right." I hung up and turned to Spinney, aware of the staggered rows of monuments beyond him—and the one, now along with Amy Lee, that stood as an icon for what was driving me on. "I don't argue with what you're saying, Les. I've just never been where nobody— not the community, not the victims, not the casual observers—will let us in. I know they have their reasons, but I'm on target with this thing, and it makes me nuts they won't let us set things right."

*   *   *

I spent the rest of the day at the Municipal Building, while Spinney went off to touch base with his state-police buddies at their West Brattleboro barracks. I caught up on the local gossip, shuffled the paperwork enough to make it look disturbed, and found out what my squad had been up to. But my heart wasn't in it, and I had a hard time concentrating. Despite the frustration I'd voiced to Spinney earlier, I'd been bitten by Thomas Lee's misery, and wanted desperately to make good my pledge to return his daughter safely. And, somehow, I wanted to prove also that the system I'd worked for my entire adult life was a fundamentally fair and decent thing, despite its many flaws.

Relief came later that night, with the bleating of my pager coming for once as a blessing.

Flynn picked up my return call on the first ring. "We found the van. Outside a motel in Springfield. The driver's checked in, I guess for the night. We got a plain-clothes unit sitting on it. I don't know where he's headed or what he's up to."

"But it is a single Asian male driving it, right?"

"Yup, and with Mass. plates. If I was a betting man, I'd say we just got lucky. I'm not, of course," he added, after a slight pause. "You want us to tag him tomorrow? See where he leads us?"

"Yeah, but I want to use a plane, too—Al Hammond's got one down here. He can stay up for six hours at a time. That way, your boys only need to get close every once in a while. If this character is making the rounds, he's going to be cruising all over the place. I don't want him wondering what all those dark-green Caprices are doing hanging onto his ass."

"Hey—we got sportier models. I like the plane, though. Who do you want where?"

"If Hammond's available, I'll go with him in the air. We could put Spinney in charge of three or four rotating cars, and connect us all with closed-frequency radios."

*   *   *

Al Hammond was a tall and laconic sheriff in the old mold, who knew everyone necessary to ensure his hold on his job, and yet who ran enough of a hands-off operation that his men were embued with the self-reliance that makes for a good department. But Al was no mere paper-shuffler. He'd been a police officer all his life, all over the state, and at one time or another had done business, it seemed, with every other cop in Vermont. He was so unflappable as to appear lethargic at times, a misperception that had cost many a crook or fledgling defense lawyer dearly.

We sat together in the predawn darkness, on the edge of the all-but-empty Springfield airport, in the cockpit of his small Cessna—a single-engine, high-winged four-seater, equipped with long-distance fuel tanks. We had flown here earlier from the grass field in Dummerston, where he normally kept the plane. Not a man much given to idle chatter, he'd been content to sit in silence ever since we'd arrived a half hour earlier, watching the eastern horizon's slow-motion appearance as it was touched by the sun's first glimmerings. That was fine with me. I'd taken advantage of the quiet to catch a long-awaited nap.

"Good morning, sports fans." Spinney's obnoxiously cheery voice came over the portable radio in my lap like some metal-toned jack-in-the-box.

I opened my eyes and brought the radio to my mouth. "You better have more than that."

Al laughed quietly beside me.

"I have a stirring from an early riser."

"Recognize him from any of our mug shots?"

"Yup, but not one of the ones with a name under it. You people took it in Bratt."

That made it pretty likely he was connected to Truong. "What's he up to?"

"Crossed the street for breakfast about fifteen minutes ago. I thought I'd let you sleep in."

"Lester hasn't changed much," Al murmured.

"Al says you're still a pain in the ass."

There was a brief burst of laughter before the radio went dead.

"Nice boy," Al said softly, the white of his hair beginning to gleam in the dawn light.

The radio came to life again five minutes later. "Zulu from Tango One. You might want to start your engines."

Spinney had become official—the serious work was about to begin. We were Zulu—reflecting the aircraft's official handle of N-for-November 4265 Z-for-Zulu—the tail cars were Tango One through Four.

"Where's he headed?" I asked, foregoing the formalities.

"North on Ninety-one."

Al began calmly hitting switches on the equipment-packed console before him. Springfield's airport was a "noncontrolled" facility, meaning there was no control tower, and no personnel to man one. We taxied silently to the foot of the field like the only dancers in a dimly lit ballroom, and Al turned up the engine speed in preparation for takeoff. We both put on sound-deadening headsets, plugged into both the plane's radio and the portable in my lap. The headsets had mouthpieces that hung on wire brackets directly before our lips.

Al keyed the airplane's mike button three times to electronically light up the runway, and announced to any other pilots who might be flying nearby, "Cessna November four-two-six-five Zulu departing Springfield for the northwest." He then turned up the throttle and eased off on the brakes.

Moments later, I called Spinney. "Tango One from Zulu. We're in the air."

"Roger that."

Hammond took the plane up about four thousand feet, cut back on the power, and began lazily floating above the interstate.

"What's your twenty, Tango One?" I asked.

" 'Bout ten miles north of the exit."

Without comment, Al straightened us out, ran along the pale cement ribbon far below for a couple of minutes, and then cut back his speed again. The black roof of the van was as clear as if it had been marked with a bull's-eye.

"Okay, Tango One, you can lay back. We're in visual contact."

"You got it."

*   *   *

The surveillance of the camper van went on for the entire day. In the towns, where traffic was heavier, Al handed it over to Spinney and his rotation of four cars; in the countryside, where any vehicle hanging back would've stuck out, the roles were reversed. Only once, halfway to Burlington, during a two-hour lunch stop by the van driver, did we land to refuel and stretch our legs. And during the whole process, the van did what we'd hoped it would—stopping at Asian-owned restaurants, laundries, nightclubs, and rooming houses in Springfield, Ludlow, Lebanon, Woodstock, West Fairlee, St. Johnsbury, Montpelier, and places in between—slowly but surely working its way toward Burlington. At every stop, Spinney reported to Dan Flynn, who consulted his records and then contacted Walt Frazier, who in turn checked his.

Town after town, the unwitting driver caused the wires and airwaves to hum in his wake. Each business he called on prompted a look into the owner's past criminal history, his financial records, and immigrant status. Name by name, Flynn and Frazier put together family histories, found out how many properties were owned by whom, identified whatever links connected the players, and found out if any of them were on file with the DEA, ATF, the Secret Service, INS, the Border Patrol, Customs, the IRS, Interpol, any state agencies from here to California, the Quebec and Ontario Provincial Police, the Toronto Police and the MUC, the Royal Canadian Mounted Police, and of course the FBI.

My job, however, involved little of that. For hours, I sat high above the state I was born and brought up in, lost in its comforting contours.

Looking down across the spectacularly broken land—the rounded pastures and deep-cut gullies, the streams and lakes and forested mountains—all washed in the verdure that had given the state its name—I felt a return of the inner calm I longed for, and which recent events had so riled.

I took the time to reflect on the losses I'd been refusing to acknowledge, to bury the dead and make a grudging peace with my mistakes. But while that helped to a certain extent, it also allowed me to focus on one of the truly innocent victims of this whole bloody mess. Surrounded by some of the most beautiful landscapes this country has to offer, my mind's eye could only see the troubled face of Amy Lee.

By late afternoon, when the van pulled out of Burlington and headed toward St. Albans, we thought we'd connected all but one of the dots north of Springfield, and that St. Albans would likely be the last stop. There, however, we were in for a surprise.

Spinney was once again in the lead car. "Zulu from Tango One. I don't think he's heading for the barn like we thought. He just cut across the interstate on one-oh-five, toward Enosburg. You boys handle that?"

Our anonymous van driver had proven a gregarious type, staying for long periods at several of his stops, apparently mixing a little chitchat with business. Twice, the surveillance cars had been able to park close enough to observe him through binoculars, eating or drinking with his contacts and obviously enjoying himself. That had also been the case in St. Albans, where he'd had an early supper, and where we'd assumed he would spend the night.

Spinney's question to us, however, was less concerned with a long day running to overtime. All of us were acutely aware of the failing light, and with the adjustments our strategy would have to undergo. It was Al Hammond's call to make.

I looked over at him and raised my eyebrows, causing him to speak for one of the rare times all day. "Night doesn't bother me any."

I waited for more, got nothing, and asked Spinney if he'd copied that direct. I could hear the smile in his response. "I guess if he can do it, so can we."

Route 105 runs along the Vermont-Canadian border, zigzagging from town to town, almost touching the boundary at a couple of points. From Enosburg Falls to East Berkshire to Richford, the gently rolling, sparsely populated land is utterly dominated by the looming presence of Jay Peak to the east, toward which we were flying. In contrast to the soft hills and shallow valleys below, rapidly vanishing into the gloom of the encroaching darkness, Jay stood like a white-topped tidal wave—huge, expansive, vaguely threatening—glowing in the day's sole remaining light.

Similarly, Al and I were still bathed in the soft red glow to our back, reflecting off the curved windshield and casting a pink wash on the map across my lap. And yet we were overflying a world soon to be as opaque as a black hole. Looking up at the orange-and-red-tinted clouds overhead, I suddenly felt vulnerable and alone, cast adrift from the lightness above, and yet abandoned by the very land I'd been receiving comfort from mere moments earlier. It was, I knew, only a metaphorical sensation, stimulated by too much stress and a lack of sleep, but it served as a reminder of what I was facing—and perhaps of my chances of success. Given what had happened to Benny Travers, just for the sake of a little gained turf, or what Dennis DeFlorio and Tony Brandt and Amy Lee had suffered in the name of "keeping face," I began feeling like a tired swimmer in deep water, praying for a foothold.

"Gets you lost in your thoughts, doesn't it?"

I looked up, startled at this intrusion coming over the headphones I'd forgotten I was wearing, and saw Al smiling beside me.

"Prettiest time of the day, as far as I'm concerned—the one time I really do feel like a bird in this thing."

He dipped the plane slightly to my side and pointed across my chest at the now inky-black ground beneath us. "That's him right there—the headlights."

I nodded without comment. Twisting further around in my seat, I could see the lights of Spinney's four-car surveillance team, safely trailing several miles behind. I saw Jay Peak, now quite close and to our right, and played a small pen light across my map, surprised and a little embarrassed at how far we'd traveled while I'd been daydreaming.

"We're coming up on North Troy," Al told me. "Newport's just beyond."

Newport is Vermont's biggest town this close to the border, so isolated from the rest of the state by the comparative emptiness of its surroundings that it's almost become a Canadian extension. This illusion is heightened by Lake Memphremagog, a thirty-two-mile-long body of water that lies almost equally half in Vermont, half in Quebec, and which provides a natural conduit to a well-populated and nearby neighbor.

As we lazily came around the northern shoulder of Jay, now glistening with its summit-top red warning beacons, the pale expanse of the lake came into view, surprisingly long and flat in this mountainous, tree-choked setting. At its base, the scattered lights of Newport lay sprinkled about invitingly. Certainly it was attracting our friend in the van, whose tiny headlights were steadily drawn toward the downtown area.

By now, although we were all in total darkness, there was enough traffic hovering around the town's outskirts to make Spinney's small convoy indistinguishable from any other cars.

"Tango One from Zulu. You better take over."

"I've got him in sight already."

Al put the plane into a gentle bank and slowly circled the lights below, as he had over a half-dozen other towns this long day, waiting to find out if the van was going to make a stop or keep on moving. I suspected the former, since I'd all but convinced myself that this entire part of the trip—straight from St. Albans and with no stops in between—had been to reach a particular goal.

"This is Tango One. He's pulled into a side street and parked next to a jewelry store."

"Can you bracket both ends of the street without showing yourselves?"

"Workin' on it now."

"Is there an airport nearby?" I asked Al.

"Three miles south of here."

We circled a couple of more times. "Zulu from Tango One. He's gone inside. We're in pretty good position here—got all visible exits covered, and a view through the front window. Want us to get closer?"

"Not yet. You have a car available to pick me up at the airport?"

"That's affirmative."

"Okay. That's where I'm headed. Let's just baby-sit this for a while. See what happens."

Hammond straightened us out toward the south and in a matter of minutes was making his approach to land.

"You want me to stick around?" he asked as we taxied toward the parking area.

"Actually, I'd like to ask an even bigger favor. We've been watching this guy play courier all day long, so we know he's carrying something. If he plans to spend the night here, he's going to want to stash the stuff somewhere safe. If that happens, I'd like a warrant so we can take a look."

"Want me to fly someone back to Burlington to meet the US Attorney?"

"If it comes to that, yeah."

Hammond shrugged. "No problem."

One of Spinney's team, detailed from the state police's bureau of criminal investigations, showed up about ten minutes later and drove me back to town. Spinney was in his car, parked inconspicuously at a meter across the street from the Far East Jewelry Store. My driver dropped me off down the block, and I walked the rest of the way, ducking into Spinney's passenger seat as unobtrusively as possible. I noticed as I did so that the dome light had been disconnected.

"What's been happening?" I asked.

Spinney didn't look at me, his eyes fixed on the broad window opposite. "Old-time reunion. These two are chummy."

"What about the van?"

He pointed to a side street to the right of the store. "Down there. About five minutes ago, the two of them—I guess the other one's the owner—came out the side entrance and took in several boxes. Tango Two estimates about four of 'em. They've stayed in the back of the store ever since. The only one I can see from here is the girl at the counter, and she hasn't moved."

He checked his watch. "It's almost eight. I can't tell if they're open, or closed but still have the lights on."

At that point, as if responding on cue, the girl came around from behind the counter, locked the door, and pulled a shade down over it and the large window next to it.

"Damn," Spinney muttered. "Should've kept my mouth shut."

"What'd you think about getting a warrant? Find out what's in the boxes?"

I saw the glimmer of a grin in the dark. "Yeah."

I called Maggie Lanier on the mobile phone, explained our needs, and then flipped a coin with Spinney to decide which one of us was going to sign the application—and thus make the trip back to Burlington. He lost.

I glanced out the window at the night sky. "You'll love it—stars are out."

*   *   *

Nobody left the store that night. Eventually, all but the night-lights were put out on the ground floor, and others came on one floor above. In the few moments before the curtains were drawn upstairs, I could see the corner of what was obviously a front-facing living room. Presumably, the shipment having been secured somewhere safe, the three friends were settling down for a home-cooked meal and a well-earned night's rest. I was looking forward to throwing a wrench into that.

As it turned out, I never got the chance. Some three hours later—shortly before I expected Spinney back—a top-down convertible drove quickly down the main street and slowed suddenly before the store's front window. Half asleep by now, despite the occasional radio chatter we'd been using to keep awake—I was only vaguely aware of what was going on. As if in sluggish slow motion, I focused on the driver, recognized his Asian features, and was bringing the radio up to my mouth when a passenger stood up in the back of the car and aimed something cylindrical at the building. There was a blinding flash as something went shattering through the store's plate glass.

"We got something . . ." was all I got out before the squealing tires of the departing car were overwhelmed by a tremendous explosion. The peaceful scene before me vanished in a stunning roar, rocking the car and sending me flying across the seat, my arm covering my head just as both side windows were blown in, followed by a wave of hot air and the by-now familiar clatter of falling debris.

Chapter Twenty-five

The contrast between endless noise and total darkness was enervating. I kept wishing one would give in to the other.

"Mr. Gunther?"

"Yes?"

"I'm going to take the bandages off, just to see how we're doing, and put in some more drops."

"Be my guest."

The emergency-room doctor—a young woman in her thirties—began peeling the tape that was holding the thick dressing firmly over my eyes. "You have a visitor, by the way."

"Hey, Joe."

I recognized Spinney's voice, its usual levity dulled with concern. "Hey, Les. Did you catch 'em?"

"They blew across the border at Derby Line like a rocket. The Mounties and the provincial police are on it now. Haven't heard back yet. Probably won't, either, if the escape went off as well as the attack."

The doctor murmured, "Okay—here we go," and gently lifted the pads from my eyes. I squinted in pain, even though I could see the lights directly overhead had been turned off, and that the white curtain around my bed did a good job as a filter.

"How's the vision?" she asked me, her face about ten inches from mine.

I blinked several times, trying to focus on her, and finally switched to Spinney's face at the foot of the bed. "I haven't gotten nearsighted, but everything else looks pretty good. They just hurt, and they're sensitive."

She smiled, but stayed put, watching me. "Okay, good. I'm going to shine a light in your eyes, just to make you really uncomfortable, and then I'll put in some more drops. After that, you should be able to get out of here."

She wasn't underrating her fancy pen light—it hurt like hell and made the tears pour down into my ears—but she seemed satisfied by what she saw.

She straightened up, smiled again, and expertly administered some soothing, cool drops. "You're all set. The effects of the flash will pass soon enough, and I seriously doubt you'll have any permanent damage. I'll give you some drops to self-administer, along with instructions and a pair of horrible-looking cardboard sunglasses you can use until you can get some decent ones. I think you'll find you'll need them for a couple of days, though, so don't be heroic, and just put up with the jokes, okay?"

"Yes, ma'am."

She nodded curtly. "You're free to go—you can collect your belongings on the way out. Good luck."

Spinney watched her sweep aside the curtain and disappear into the surrounding hubbub of the rest of the ER. "I always get the old guys with bad breath."

"What's left of the jewelry store?" I asked him, checking my watch. I'd been in the Newport hospital for four hours by now.

"A hole in the ground. The fire chief owns the property till he declares it stone cold, so we still hadn't been allowed in when I left, but those bastards did a job and a half. Maybe they learned from the idiots we caught in Burlington."

I sat up and swung my legs over the side of the gurney, my eyes already adjusted to the semigloom. "I take it nobody survived."

"Nobody and damned near nothing. Based on what you saw, ATF's pretty sure they used a tube-fired rocket. They've got someone heading over to see what they can find in the rubble. It was propane, though, that set the place off like a roman candle. The rocket must've hit the gas tanks on the back side of the building."

I shook my head. "I was half asleep. I only caught a glimpse of the driver—not enough to make an ID. I don't even know what make of car it was . . . A dark four-door convertible is all I remember."

"We got all we need on the car. They caught it on video at the border. The Canadians'll probably find it in a field in a few hours, fresh from somebody's hot sheet. You ready to go?"

I wandered behind him, half blinded, to the counter by the door, picked up my drops and floppy glasses, and finished the paperwork. Outside, it was still dark, and pleasantly cool, so I slipped the glasses into my breast pocket for future use.

I used them at the fire scene, however, surrounded as it was with flashing red, white, and blue electronic strobes, not to mention fire-fighters equipped with powerful, erratically pointed flashlights. "Hole in the ground" turned out to be a highly accurate description of an erstwhile two-story building. Charred black and glistening with water, the rubble filling the cellar barely came up to my waist. Spinney and I and several other members of the surveillance team stood around the spot where we'd been staked out hours earlier, and watched the fire department slowly gather up its tons of equipment from the flooded street.

The fire chief—short, square, and grim—came up to us, still dressed in his dirty bunker coat and helmet. He gave a curious glance at my Halloween spectacles, but addressed Lester Spinney. "I guess it's all yours. I don't suppose you can tell me what it was all about."

It wasn't a question. Spinney shook his head. "Sorry. Thanks for your help."

He looked at us silently for a couple of seconds, shook his head, and left without further comment.

*　　*　　*

It took us twenty-four hours—from the middle of one night to the middle of the next—to sort through the remains of the store. We were helped by not having to determine the cause of the fire—a question that sometimes involves weeks of painstaking reconstruction of the remnants of a building—but we did want to determine the fate of the boxes that had been carried inside just before the blast.

Our methods were a demented cross between an archeological dig and a landfill operation. The cellar hole was surrounded by two back-hoes, several trucks, and a large generator, but it was filled with jumpsuit-dressed forensics types in rubber boots, some of them equipped with tweezers and small bags. Our reward, when it came, however, was delivered by a backhoe. As the blade cleared away one of the few remaining piles in the basement's far corner, a large, sturdy, five-foot-tall metal safe came into view, its blackened, damp surface gleaming in the halogen lights rigged all around the hole. Word went out for a locksmith.

Three hours later, in the privacy of the Border Patrol substation's enclosed garage in nearby Derby, the locksmith turned the safe's handle and began pulling open the door. Spinney stopped it from swinging wide enough to reveal the interior, and thanked the disappointed man with a cheery smile.

The small bunch of us—Frazier had given in to curiosity and had joined us a half-hour earlier—waited until the locksmith had cleared the exit, and then Spinney let us all see what the fire had left behind. It being a modern, fireproof safe, our expectations had been high. What we saw immediately bore us out.

Before us were stacks of money—hundreds of thousands of dollars—as well as banded bundles of credit-card receipts, jewelry, a small pile of gold bar, and several baggies filled with white powder—far more than would have fit into the few cardboard boxes delivered the night before.

Spinney let out a low whistle, and slipped on a pair of latex gloves. "Jesus, Joe. We just made our bosses some serious bucks."

The others laughed at his gleeful expression. I'd forgotten that being "local" officers—and working for a federal task force—both Spinney and I had made our departments eligible to share in any booty recovered during the investigation. An oddly piratical concept, it was a tempting inducement in persuading municipalities to farm their officers out for federal use. Just hearing Spinney's comment, I knew my own previously disparaged involvement here was going to suddenly undergo a drastic facelift.

Ironically, my personal satisfaction in this treasure was mixed. While its cash value would remove a lot of the heat I'd been getting back home, the lack of any documents in the safe meant we had no specific knowledge of how Truong Van Loc was running his small empire.

After inventorying and shifting our findings to the Border-Patrol safe, Frazier, Spinney, and I retired to a small meeting room in another part of the building.

"One thing we have going for us—I hope," Frazier started off, "is that the sheer bulk of that loot indicates most of it was there before last night's delivery."

"Making the jewelry store a bank?" Spinney asked.

"Possibly *the* bank," I added, my enthusiasm suddenly fired by Frazier's comment. "If we're lucky, Truong just took a serious hit to his wallet, and maybe to his whole operation."

Frazier made a deprecating gesture with his hand. "I don't know that I'd go that far. Truong could probably refill that safe in a few months, especially if he squeezed his sources. And we don't know how many other deals he has funding him."

"Don't we?" I asked. The urge was growing inside me to make a few assumptions—always a risk in police work—and to take a few gambles. "His life history's been put under a microscope. Has there been a single indicator recently of any operation besides this one?"

Frazier admitted as much with a silent shake of his head.

"Right, because while Vu and Lam and the others have been allowed to extort and steal what they can, keeping themselves occupied, Truong's goal has been to destabilize Da Wang's business, erode the protective shield around him, and then knock him off. But Truong's monomania has made him vulnerable. He's got one source of revenue, one way of collecting it, and only one bank to put it in."

"Joe—" Frazier began.

"What?" I interrupted. "Have your sources picked up an inkling of something else?"

Again, he conceded the point—unhappily.

"Okay, let's say we've closed the bank," I resumed. "If we ask the local cops to visibly sit on each one of the outlets that supplied the cash, Truong's pipeline'll dry up. And with Da Wang applying pressure from his side, he's going to have to come up with some replacement funds fast."

Frazier pursed his lips, but still remained silent.

"The Vermont pipeline is crucial to Truong," I pressed on. "Illegal aliens seem to be his primary cash commodity, and the pipeline his way of getting them to market. We're guessing his old import-business contacts are busy recruiting in the old country, and that he has a collection of receivers in Boston and/or New York. But if we really have identified most of his Vermont network, and we and Da Wang together manage to even temporarily shut it down, he's going to have to come up with a new way of moving aliens—fast."

Frazier's face was still clouded, so I played my trump. "We've been on the defensive from the start. We got lucky with this bank, so now we need to press him—anticipate him. It doesn't really matter if I'm right or wrong about the specifics of his setup. What matters is if we can somehow force his hand, 'cause, let's face it, if we don't do something soon, we're going to wind up counting dead bodies again."

The allusion to Dennis's ghost did the trick. "How're we going to persuade a half-dozen municipal police forces to sit on Truong's properties for free?" Frazier asked.

"We can ask 'em, for starters," Spinney answered cheerfully, readily accepting the idea. "Then, we can either help them—or embarrass them into helping us. If we use state troopers to do some of the sitting, I bet at least a few of the locals aren't going to want to be frozen out."

"Besides," I added, "we're not talking about a total shutdown here— just a big enough presence to be a deterrent. If Da Wang keeps on the pressure, we won't need a lot of time. Truong's going to have to move fast to survive, and he's going to want to try because he must feel he has Da Wang worried."

Walt finally gave in. "Well, what the hell. You guys work better together than most of us feds do. If you can do it, more power to you. But assuming we shut down Truong's pipeline, what then?"

"Dan Flynn told me a while back," I answered, "that both the Border Patrol and INS had noticed a new operator in the game— that's where the name Sonny cropped up early on. If we coordinate with their intelligence folks, maybe we can pick up a pattern that's specific to Truong's operation, and try to stake it out."

I paused to step back a little. "If any of my theory is right, Truong's most obvious option is to try for a major influx of aliens, either a single large shipment—like in a truck—or a coordinated, broad-based border crossing. The first is quick, cost-efficient, doesn't take many people, and entails one fast drive through Vermont to either Boston or New York. In eight hours, at the most, it's a done deal. But it's dangerous. If it's stopped, he's dead. The second option's safer, but it means more people, more money, and more time. My hunch is he'd shoot for the first, because time and money are two things he's short of."

"Well," Spinney volunteered, "I can coordinate with Dan on squeezing the pipeline. His old-boy system ought to come in handy there."

Frazier looked at me. "I guess the two of us can meet with INS and the Border Patrol and see if we can identify a pattern in Truong's border activities." He shook his head, however, as he said it. "I got to tell you, though, as pie-in-the-sky as this whole deal is, I think finding a pattern is its weakest link. The Border Patrol does the best it can, but it's guarding a friendly boundary, and even they admit that for every crosser they catch, there might be a dozen they miss. How're you going to establish an accurate picture of illegal activity with a ratio like that?"

My mind returned to this expanding case's humble beginnings in Brattleboro, and to the one person we'd been able to put behind bars as a result—the tight-lipped Nguyen Van Hai. "We need an inside source," I answered. "I've got one, but he's going to need some work."

Frazier understood where I was headed. "That, I like better. *I'll* talk to the other feds. You focus on making your man talkative."

*　　*　　*

Nguyen Van Hai was being held in Vermont's maximum-security prison in St. Albans, above Burlington—the Northwest State Correctional Facility—coincidentally located near the Canadian border. But since I had no reason to think that he'd be any more open with me than he had been earlier, I returned to Brattleboro to do some homework first, hoping to discover the right conversational pry bar.

I flew back to Dummerston with Al Hammond, who'd been nice enough—or curious enough—to stick around. I picked up my standard-issue undercover car where it was still parked at what the locals mockingly called Dummerston International, and drove into Brattleboro, relishing the familiarity of my surroundings. Paradoxically, it was only then that the aftereffects of the building blast fully took hold of me, conspiring with and adding to both Frazier's dour outlook and my own previous self-doubts. The closer I got to the office, the less sure I became that any part of the plan I'd outlined in Derby was even remotely attainable.

Seeing Harriet Fritter at her usual post was a help, however, not to mention her maternal reaction at seeing me wearing dark glasses indoors.

She scowled suspiciously. "What have you done to yourself?"

"You hear about that explosion up in Newport?"

Her mouth opened in surprise. "Oh, no."

I pointed at the glasses, which I'd finally replaced with a better-fitting pair of my own from the car. "Slight flash burn. Should be free and clear in another day. Three more Asians were killed, though."

She shook her head mournfully as Sammie turned the corner of one of the room dividers. "I thought I heard your voice. How's the case going?"

The difference in style made me smile. As far as Sammie was concerned, physical danger was part of the job. She wasted little time on nurturing maternal instincts. I followed her back to her cubbyhole at the back of the room and felt her scrutiny as soon as I sat down. In a more private setting, her compassionate side was allowed a bit more rein.

"You look terrible. How bad was it?"

"We were maybe fifteen minutes away from walking into the place with a warrant."

"Ouch." She sat down opposite me, immediately grasping a point even I had been staving off. "You could've bought it with Dennis, too. You starting to wonder about your own mortality?"

I shook my head. "What's bugging me is how this case keeps getting derailed. In my gut I feel we're close, but in fact there's not much to justify it. What I'm looking for now is a way to crack Nguyen Van Hai."

She raised her eyebrows doubtfully, but said nothing.

"Have you come up with anything while I've been gone?"

She looked a little embarrassed. "Not much. To be honest, since you left, we haven't been giving the case top priority. Billy made it clear he didn't want any more time spent on it—said it had cost plenty enough already. I think part of that was so that he could tell the reporters to take a hike—that it was out of our hands. It worked—

I'll give him that." Then her eyes took on a devious gleam. "Still, none of that affected what I could do on my own time."

I smiled, shaking my head at her predictable doggedness. "So what do you have?"

She retrieved a folder from her desk top and opened it, her pleasure immediately tempered. "Not that much, I'm afraid. Old news, mostly. You'd asked for IDs on the hit team that did that restaurant in San Francisco." She handed me a small pile of mug shots, each one stapled to an abbreviated rap sheet. "Those came in yesterday. I was going to send them up to you today, in fact."

I went through the pile slowly, recognizing Johnny Xi, the first— as far as we knew—of Truong's exercises in human carving. There were others—seven altogether, five of them stamped *deceased* across the top. The names meant nothing to me. But the face of the last one in the pile was all too familiar. I'd seen it just a couple of days earlier, on videotape.

I turned it around and showed it to Sammie. "Ring a bell?"

She squinted slightly, and then shrugged. "Maybe," she answered cautiously. "Should it?"

"It's an old shot. It's our pal Edward Diep." I looked at the rap sheet. Diep's name was given as Lo Yu Lung, the same that Sammie had dug up on the phone just before the task force had been launched, but which had meant nothing to either one of us at the time. "We never got anything more on Diep, did we, aside from a Philadelphia address?"

Sammie shook her head. "Nope."

"Can I use your phone?" I reached by her and dialed Frazier's number. "Remember Edward Diep?" I asked him after he answered.

"Not much to remember. According to our Philly office, he's long gone. Nobody seems to know anything about him."

His choice of words caught my attention. "Like he didn't exist?"

There was a pause at the other end. I could hear Frazier rustling papers on his desk. "That's the implication," he finally answered. "Inquiries were made of neighbors and nearby retailers. Nobody pegged on the mug shot. One guy's quoted as saying he would've remembered, " 'cause Asians run pretty thin out there.' "

"Meaning it wasn't an Asian neighborhood?" I asked, my excitement growing.

"I don't know the city. I guess not. Why?"

"Because the one thing we've heard from the start of all this is that Asian crooks especially like to hang together. That's what Dahlin discovered in Hartford, and what Lacoste was driving home in Montreal. Rich or poor, big-time or local, they seek out their own company. If that's true, then why did Diep live so far away?"

"Okay," Walt answered, "I'll bite."

"Because he doesn't exist. And he didn't want to set up a phony address that a quick call to some buddy or relative down the street would prove was bogus."

Having thus stacked the deck, I asked the $64,000 question. "You said earlier that of the two San Francisco shooters still missing, one was definitely dead and the other presumed so. Was the second one named Lo Yu Lung?"

"Yes," came the surprised reply.

"He and Diep are the same person—I've got the proof right in front of me. Which means Truong's right-hand man is one of the people Truong is hell-bent on killing."

"Damn."

"That's why the Philadelphia address makes sense. If you're an Asian and you want to hide from the cops, what kind of address do you hand out? One in Chinatown. But if the people you're trying to confuse are Asians, the reverse logic sets in. Diep—or Lo—was ducking Asians, not us."

"Certainly one particular Asian," Frazier murmured. "All right. Keep in touch."

I hung the phone back up and smiled at Sammie. "Nice work. What else've you got?"

She looked a little startled, and glanced down at her folder, seeing her erstwhile paltry efforts in a whole new light. "I finally heard back from the Lowell PD. Remember I'd been bugging them to give me what they had on Henry Lam and the guy Ron shot—Chu Nam An? I was hoping I could put them in the same place at the same time. It's probably academic by now, but I did come up with a connection, not just between those two, but with Diep as well. All three of them surface at the same address in a door-to-door canvass report the cops did about a year ago, when they were looking for a child-killer."

"Diep must've been wooing Lam to get on Truong's good side later on—using the quote-unquote surrogate son to sneak in under the father's defenses. Sure as hell worked. You're on a roll, Sam."

She read on, "J.P. heard back on that fingerprint he found on the pipe-bomb cap, but we hit a dead end. The print belongs to Greg Binder, who did a short stint for car theft a few years ago, but we can't find a current address. The old one's over a year out of date. It was up in the boonies in Orleans County, and the deputy we asked to check it out said nobody he talked to even remembered the guy. We're still chasing it down, of course, but it doesn't look good." She handed me a sheet of paper. "And there's nothing in his sheet to indicate any connections to Asians, or explosives, or violent behavior, or even Brattleboro."

"I got one idea—a long shot." I reached for the phone again and dialed Dan Flynn.

"Ask Digger something for me," I told him when he got on the line. "See if the name Greg Binder rings a bell."

Sammie watched me, her sallow cheeks regaining some of their color.

Flynn returned. "Says he's known him from the time he was old enough to pry off a hubcap."

"We need to find him. Any ideas?"

There was another long pause before Flynn got on again. "Try his uncle in South Burlington—runs a hardware store called Honest Ed's. Digger says when things got tough for Greg as a kid, that's usually where he headed. Ed Binder's one of your salt-of-the-earth types."

"Thanks, Dan. I'll tell you later what's up." I disconnected, dialed Information, and got the number for Honest Ed's.

"Is Greg Binder there?" I asked the voice on the other end.

"Sorry. You just missed him—went out on a delivery. Take a message?"

"No, thanks—I'll call back." I hung up and sat back in my chair.

"You're shitting me," Sammie stared at me.

I laughed. "When you mentioned Orleans County, I remembered that Bill Shirtsleeve—that's Digger—used to work the outpost out there a few years back. Pure luck."

She was shaking her head—smiling. "You going to check out Mr. Binder?"

I looked at my watch and saw, almost regretfully, that I had time to do just that. I had been looking forward to visiting Ron, and Tony as well, who I'd heard had been shipped back to a regular room at Brattleboro Memorial. But since the bombing in Newport, a new sense of urgency had arisen; if I hoped to deploy the preemptive moves against Truong that Walt Frazier was trusting me to make, I was going to have to move fast. We had to end this soon, and considering the price already paid, we had to be successful.

Chapter Twenty-six

Honest Ed's Tool & Pipe looked as odd as it sounded. Set back from the road, hemmed in on both sides by a crush of prefabricated retail outlets, Ed's appeared as either the cause of it all—the first and oldest roadside store along what had become an endless commercial strip—or a theatrically overdone attempt to go back in time to the "good-old days." It was a wooden building with white peeling walls and enormous, dusty, plate-glass windows, crammed with junk either needing replacement, or at least a good cleaning. Over the front door— each letter highlighted by a trail of neon tubing as garish in color as the latest tricolor toothpaste—was a huge sign advertising Ed's name. It was a helpful if unattractive addition, given that, without it, Ed's might have been mistaken for anything from a closed pawn shop to a holding station for rejected tag-sale items.

It was true, however, that despite its antiquity and its almost militant anti-asceticism, Ed's did fit in. Route 7, south of Burlington—the same Route 7 that blemished Rutland farther down the road—was one of South Burlington's major arteries, and yet another perfect example of a "miracle mile" run amok.

I pulled into the potholed parking lot, reached back in for my ever-expanding mug-shot book, and headed for Ed's front door.

Considering the cluttered windows, I was surprised by the spaciousness inside. The broad, bare wooden floors were free of the piles of junk I'd expected, and the long counter facing me was surmounted by colorful advertising posters. Parked along its polished surface were small clusters of displayed drill bits and screwdriver assortments, and behind it were endless racks of gleaming, heavy-duty tools, many of a size suitable for your average offshore oil rig. In the distance, vanishing into the gloom, were row upon row of stacked metal pipes.

A pot-bellied, red-faced, white-haired man stood near the register looking at me, his hands flat on the counter like a bartender between clients. "Help you?"

"Yeah—is Greg Binder here?"

There was a moment's hesitation, the eyes as cool as the smile beneath it was friendly. "Sure. He done something wrong?"

"You Ed Binder?"

"Yup. Who're you?"

I showed him my identification. "United States Deputy Marshal. I'd like to ask him some questions."

A look of weariness crossed his face. "Oh, boy. What's he done now?"

"That's why I want to talk to him."

He nodded slightly and chewed his bottom lip briefly. "Okay."

He turned around and bellowed toward the back of the building, his voice reverberating among the metal racks. "Greg."

There was the bang of a door, the sound of something heavy being dropped on the floor, and the scuffing sound of sneakers shuffling their way toward us. From out of the darkness came a short, skinny man in his early twenties, disheveled and acne-scarred. As soon as he saw me—and his uncle's expression—he stopped in his tracks.

"What's wrong?"

"Good question," Ed Binder answered. "This man's a Deputy US Marshal. Wants to talk to you."

Greg's eyes shifted from one of us to the other. "What about?"

I removed the pipe cap I'd retrieved from Tyler, still in its white, clearly marked evidence envelope, and dumped it out onto the counter. "You sell this item here?"

Ed leaned forward slightly, not touching it. "We sell things like it—same manufacturer."

"A lot of them?"

"Depends. If it's a job order, yeah. We could sell dozens of 'em at a shot. We don't move many as a single item, though. We mostly supply contractors."

"Why're you asking?" Greg wanted to know, still lingering a few feet back among the aisles.

I decided to show my cards, relying on what I'd heard from Digger about the relationship between the two men before me. "This cap was attached to a pipe bomb that killed a Brattleboro police officer."

Ed grew very still. Greg's eyes widened with fear. "Holy shit. I heard about that. What's that got to do with me? I don't know nothin' about it."

"Your thumbprint's on it."

Greg straightened as if hit with electricity. Both his hands flew up in front of his chest. "Oh, fuck. Uncle Ed, I swear to God, I don't know what's goin' on. I only been to Brattleboro a couple of times— years ago. I wouldn't do this—nothin' like this."

"Slow down, Greg," his uncle cautioned, his eyes on me hard now. "Nobody's said anything yet."

I made that my cue to switch tacks, and laid the mug book, closed, upon the counter. "If I were to buy a pipe cap, maybe two, how would I go about it? Are you the only one who works the counter, Ed?"

The older man shook his head. "It's luck of the draw. Could be either one of us, or my wife—she's the bookkeeper."

"And any of you could fill the order? Locate it in the stock and bring it out?"

"Right."

"Within the last few weeks—could even be the last few months— do you remember selling a pipe cap to any Asians?"

Greg's face flooded with relief. "Yeah. It was like two days before that bomb, more or less. I remember him because he made me do a custom cut—said he only wanted a foot of pipe. I told him we didn't sell that short—even told him where he might go to get a piece. But he didn't want to. Told me he'd buy the shortest length we sold, pay extra to have it cut, and then give us back what was left. He was in a hurry."

"So you did it?"

"Sure. I had nothin' else going—things were slow, and I thought Uncle Ed would be okay over it. I mean, hell, it was almost like selling it and getting it back at the same time. A foot's not much to take off a piece of stock."

"What else did he buy?" I asked.

"Just the two caps and the piece of pipe. And he asked me where the nearest Radio Shack was."

"Where is it?"

" 'Bout a half mile that way." He pointed to his left. "On the other side of the street."

"He paid cash?"

"Yup."

Ed shook his head disgustedly. "My God, Greg. Didn't all that sound a little suspicious?"

His nephew stared at him wide-eyed. "What do I know about bombs?"

"Was he alone?" I interrupted.

"Yup. I saw him drive up. One of those new Mustangs—bright red."

"You get the license plate?"

Greg Binder shook his head.

"All right." I spun the mug book around and opened it to its first page. "I want you to look at these photographs. Take your time. Tell me if you see the man you waited on."

Greg stepped up to the counter and began leafing through the pages. He stopped on the third one. "That's him."

"No doubts in your mind? It's not a great shot."

He actually grinned at that, his sense of relief complete. "Damn— it's just like in the movies. I'd swear to it in a court of law."

"Cut the crap, Greg," Ed muttered to him.

The young man grew agitated again. "I do swear, Uncle Ed. That's definitely the guy. I'm not shittin' you—honest."

I closed the book. "You still have that shortened length of pipe?"

Ed Binder shook his head. "No, Greg told me about it. I put it with the odd sizes and sold it as part of a lot. It's probably mixed in with somebody's plumbing by now."

I thanked them both and took my leave, heading for the Radio Shack Greg had mentioned, wondering what Edward Diep had been up to, all by himself, buying parts for a bomb.

*   *   *

An hour later I was in Walt Frazier's office. "Radio Shack remembered him, too, and had a sales slip to boot—listed him as 'John Sing, Main Street, Burlington.' He bought wire, some alligator clips, and a nine-volt battery. The sales clerk had no more trouble than Greg Binder did in picking him out of the book."

"Okay." Walt was taking the cautious route, waiting for me to make my case.

"The more we find out about Diep, the more of an independent operator he becomes, working all sides of the game. It got me thinking, how that would go down with his pals—at least the ones affiliated with Truong. I called the St. Albans prison to find out how Nguyen's been doing. Turns out, ever since that explosion in Newport, he's gotten several phone calls. I talked to the guard who sees him most, and he says he's more fidgety—blows his cool with the other inmates. The way I saw him in Bratt, he was an icicle."

"So what d'you think's going on?"

"If we're right, he's losing confidence. He felt he was on the fast track, guaranteed to beat Da Wang. Now, he's not so sure. Truong's stash goes up in smoke, the pipeline is shut down thanks to Spinney and the VSP, and we're breathing down everybody's neck. All of a sudden, Da Wang's looking stronger, and Nguyen's looking to make a deal."

"You hope."

I laughed. "Maybe that part's wishful thinking, but he's feeling the heat. I'd like to have another crack at him. He's the only bird we have in hand, he was high enough in the ranks to be in on a killing with the boss himself, and from the phone calls he's been getting, he's obviously still connected. If we can persuade him that things are just about over for him, he might trade for a lighter load. Most of these guys won't talk because they're scared—their families are vulnerable, or they're worried about their own hides. But if the threat is removed, everything changes."

Frazier mulled it over for a few seconds, and then reached for the phone. "Okay, I'll round up the appropriate troops. Let's see what happens."

*   *   *

The process was a legal minuet—a series of small, regimented steps in which all parties were consulted with unctuous propriety.

First to convene was the investigative team—Dan, Lester, Walt, and myself—to make sure a deal with Nguyen was in the best interests of the case. That was done in a conference call, since both Walt and I already knew what the vote would be. Spinney had laughed outright, and claimed that our biggest problem would be not showing Nguyen how desperate we were.

Next in line were Maggie Lanier and Jack Derby. It was the Windham County State's Attorney, after all, who had jurisdiction over Nguyen Van Hai. Murder alone is not a federal crime, and although murder for hire is, and some talk had been made about adjusting the charges, Derby still held the strongest hand. But just as he'd had no reservations about the creation of the task force, he also had no problem about greasing Nguyen's palm. The victim's reputation had something to do with this, of course—Benny Travers had died largely unmourned. Cutting his killer some slack probably wouldn't cost Derby a single vote.

Then it was Paul Doubleday's turn—Nguyen's court-appointed lawyer. He returned Lanier's call within the hour, since he'd been pestering Derby about a deal from the start. The conversation, on which Walt and I eavesdropped, reflected how intricately delicate, formal, and finally competitive the minuet could get. Lanier had to act bored and overworked, claiming Derby had run for cover, dumping the case in her lap. The evidence against Nguyen, she stressed, was so overwhelming that his conviction was a foregone conclusion. She was only calling Doubleday for purely practical reasons. Travers, after all, had been a scumball—not worthy of the taxpayers' money—and a quick, cheap deal seemed the best of moral high grounds. How about twenty years in a federal pen, with no parole, instead of life?

Doubleday worked up a gasp, as if his client was the innocent victim of a monstrous frame. Are you kidding? That's not a deal. Considering the circumstantial evidence, you're running the risk of losing everything if you go to trial. Don't try to buy something with nothing.

There followed a heated discussion about how circumstantial it was to find Nguyen's blood mixed in with that of the man he was accused of killing, but common-sense logic, as always, played little part in it. Doubleday finally said he'd carry an offer to his client of fifteen years, with parole.

The response came the next day. Frazier paged me, and told me when I called him back, "Nguyen says no deal."

That, I'd expected. "Did Doubleday seem interested in talking more?"

"Definitely." Frazier then chuckled, "Though not in so few words."

"Set up a meeting with him and his client, ASAP. I want to try something."

*   *   *

The minuet's final movements were conducted back at the St. Albans Correctional Facility, three miles northwest of town—a prison that would have looked like a modern boys prep school, complete with white-trimmed red brick, if it hadn't been for the double rows of razor wire hemming it in. Myself, Nguyen, Doubleday, and Frazier, representing both the Bureau and Lanier's office, were all sitting together in a plain, square room with four chairs, one table, and a closed door.

"In the interests of reality, Mr. Nguyen," I began, "I should start by pointing out that, despite your lawyer's reassurances, there is a strong likelihood that you will be found guilty and sentenced to life in prison, and that you will serve out your term in a facility like Rahway, or Attica, or Leavenworth. Those are among the worst this government has to offer, and I will make sure you end up at one of them."

"If this is what you brought us all together to discuss, Mr. Gunther . . ." Doubleday started in, but I interrupted with, "No, it is not. I just wanted that made clear before we began talking."

"Things better improve fast, or the talking just stopped."

I looked directly at Nguyen, who had not said a word, but whose expression was much less remote than the first time we'd met. While he was still playing the same aloof role, I knew we had his interest this time—he was clearly less sure of his ground. "You are aware, I know, that your boss's assets just recently went up in smoke. Mr.

Doubleday's presence here is one indication of that. He is from the public defender's office, and is not the hired help your organization once might've been able to afford."

"Let's get to the point, Gunther. You're wasting my time, regardless of how little it costs." Doubleday was irritated, but he was also carefully trying to stall my momentum, and thus any impression I might make on his client. Nguyen, however, was a cut above the kind of knuckle-dragger Doubleday was used to, and remained totally focused on me.

"But money," I continued, "is a funny thing, considering all its ups and downs. Even with the lid we've clamped on your network—another news item I'm sure you've heard about—you're probably thinking, 'Hey, it's a temporary setback. The boss'll find an alternate route, he'll set up a big deal, he'll do something to get back on his feet and get the cash flowing.'"

I leaned forward slightly, boring in. "Problem is, that's not really good news, is it? 'Cause if the organization stays afloat, it can hurt you if you cut a deal at their expense. So what're you supposed to do? Stay quiet and do hard time? Or help shut them down and run the risk they'll seek revenge? Tough choice.

"You could tilt the odds by telling us what they have over you, of course—which family members might suffer or die if you talk. But you know what the police are like. They're all on the dole—just crooks in uniform. We tell you we're different, but what proof do you have? No. The only way out for you is to know for sure that the people who control you are out of the game."

I sat back now and looked at him quietly for a couple of seconds. Even Doubleday—I could tell from his silence—was wondering where this unorthodox approach was leading.

"I've got the solution for you, by the way, although it's a little different from what you're expecting. It's certainly different from anything your lawyer might have come up with. See, I happen to know that your organization has a bigger problem than your being in jail, or our shutting them down, or even than Da Wang trying to kill them. All those are things people expect in this business—it's tough, and there are losses. What may come as a surprise is that you're about to be blown out of the water from the inside. You have a time bomb in your midst—a traitor whose sole interest is to eliminate Truong Van Loc, and ingratiate himself with Da Wang at the same time."

I paused again, my eyes never leaving Nguyen's. "So now you're thinking, 'Okay, let's say he's right—just for the sake of argument. If Truong is knocked off and the organization dissolved, I can still make a deal—maybe identify the guy who killed Travers with me and Truong—and get a lighter sentence. All I have to do is sit and wait.'"

I leaned forward again. "But there's a problem with that. I want your help now, not later. I want Truong before he gets whacked. And I won't forget that you didn't play ball when I asked. And, you know? to be honest, Benny Travers was a pretty scummy guy to begin with, so I'm not that interested in nailing that third man, just to make your life easier. All of which makes this a one-time offer."

I got to my feet and walked to the far wall, the three of them following me with their eyes. There, I turned and leaned back against the wall, tapping the side of my head with one finger. "Okay, but talk is just that, right? How can I prove there's a traitor?"

I began pacing slowly back and forth in front of Nguyen. "Go back in time. Think about the movers and shakers of Truong's organization. Think of what you've been told about Truong's motives. Remember his little brother? The shooting in San Francisco? The end of the Chinatown Gang at the hands of the Dragon Boys? Truong On Ha was the apple of his brother's eye, and he was destroyed in a fight between two gangs—the very kind of life Van Loc had hoped On Ha would never be a part of.

"Truong vowed vengeance, but it was a family matter—a personal problem. And that's how it stayed for several years, as Truong and Lam went after the hit team, one by one. But then came a problem. After knocking off all the underlings he could find, Truong set his sights on the man who had set them in motion in the first place. He went after Wang Chien-kuo.

"But Wang was now a big-time leader, isolated in the cocoon of a well-armed gang, untouchable, especially since a few earlier attempted hits had made him almost reclusive.

"So Truong had to increase the heat, turn a personal vendetta into a financial enterprise—a hit not just on the man but his entire organization."

I stopped in front of him. "Think back, Nguyen, before all that let's-go-for-the-money talk. Remember how it all began."

I opened the folder I'd brought with me and extracted one of the mug shots Sammie had received from California. I slapped it face-up on the table before Nguyen Van Hai, like a playing card. "Johnny Xi was the first Dragon Boy killed, in Vancouver—tied to a door and skinned alive. A killing so brutal it was guaranteed to make the rounds—to put fear into a select few, and give Truong a reputation he could put to good use."

One by one, I pulled out the four shots with *deceased* stamped across them, and slapped them down next to Xi, announcing each one's name as I went. "Each one was hunted down, each one killed for what he'd done. There'd been nine of them altogether, four of whom were never found. But two of them had been drivers, and hadn't actually taken part in the shooting. And one was found dead in Florida just recently. I don't know who killed him." I laid a sixth photograph at the end of the row.

"But one got away. He moved, he changed his name, he severed all contact with his former life—with one large exception, which I'll mention in a minute. And then he did something really clever. He hid in the one place where no one would think of looking for him. Remember the name, Lo Yu Lung? Truong must have mentioned it a thousand times, like anyone does who's nursing an obsession. Ever see a picture of him—the last of Johnny Xi's shooters—the one that got away?"

I slapped Edward Diep's picture down in front of Nguyen.

Considering that when we'd first met, I'd had a difficult time telling if he was breathing, Nguyen's reaction was downright explosive. After an audible intake of breath, he looked up at me with his eyes narrowed suspiciously. "Bullshit."

I laughed with real pleasure, convinced I'd just kicked free the one logjam separating me from Truong Van Loc. I placed both hands flat on the table and put my face a foot from Nguyen's. "Think about it. I can tell you what we've got—how we figured it out, digging and scratching. But you were there."

I tapped Diep's picture with my finger. "Knowing who he really is, go back in your mind, ask yourself why he did things the way he did, why he was at one place when he might've been at another, what he said about himself and his past. Run it through your mind, and then tell me I'm wrong."

I straightened up, tapped Walt on the shoulder, and moved toward the door. I then took my biggest gamble. I turned and added, "While you're at it, ask yourself who planted that car bomb in Brattleboro—the one that stimulated the creation of a federal task force and spelled the death sentence for your whole organization. We've got two witnesses who sold him the parts."

I got the satisfaction of a half-opened mouth and a stare of disbelief. "We'll let you talk to your lawyer alone, Nguyen—for a few minutes. Truong Van Loc is as good as gone. Either we'll get him, or Lo Yu Lung will, right between the shoulder blades. But if Lo beats us to him, you'll be on your own. Time's running out. We'll be outside."

But Nguyen raised his hand to stop us. "This is just to see if I will deal with you?" His English was clear, precise, and carefully spoken.

"For openers, yeah."

"And you are able to get people out of Hong Kong and into this country?"

"How many?" I asked, realizing, as I'd hoped, that even this emotionless killer had a weak spot—something both Truong and I had found a way to exploit.

"Members of my family—five."

Frazier spoke for the first time. "If we can find them, we can get them out."

Nguyen nodded. "I will deal." Beside him, ignored, Doubleday nodded his agreement.

Walt and I sat back down. "We want more than just bits and pieces. We want a breakdown of the organization—who runs it, who's in it, how it's operated—and we want to know all the watering holes, from the Far East to New York and Boston, including every way station in between.

"But," I added with emphasis, "since we know you could feed us a lot of crap we wouldn't be able to check out, we also want a good-faith offering up front. Our sources have it that Truong's going to try to recoup his losses by making a big run across the border, bypassing the pipeline altogether. We need to know how he might do that—what routes he favors, what contacts are left that he still can rely on, and what technique he'll use. If you give us that—along with the other intelligence I mentioned—and it pans out, we'll honor whatever deal we agree to."

"You're not tying this to Truong's capture, are you?" Doubleday quickly demanded.

"No. But the information he gives us had better be useful. We don't want to be standing around in one place and have Truong take a route we knew nothing about."

The lawyer looked at his client. "Can you do that? Can you be that precise?"

The answer was fast and unequivocal. "Yes."

I glanced at Frazier, trying to hide the surge of relief that one word had stimulated.

Walter, the complete poker player, merely nodded. "All right. Let's do business."

Chapter Twenty-seven

"What kind of deal did you cut?" Spinney asked, as we drove toward Swanton, Vermont, the sector headquarters of the US Border Patrol.

"He does ten years in a minimum-security can, and we import five of his relatives from a Hong Kong refugee camp, where they've been available to Truong if Nguyen ever screwed up. In exchange, we get all the dope on the 'Sonny' organization and, more to the point, a description of his border-crossing operation, with names, places, and favorite routines."

Spinney shook his head. "Christ. That's pretty good, considering how talkative he used to be."

"I think Diep was a big shock—better than I'd hoped. He was brought in by Henry Lam, just as we thought. Diep had wooed the socks off him after meeting him and Chu in Lowell, so Truong went along with the recommendation. The night Marshall Smith stopped that car was the first time Truong and Diep had set eyes on each other—they hadn't even exchanged real names. Despite Lam being the matchmaker, they were still playing footsy, protecting their identities until they got to know each other better, presumably by killing Da Wang's red pole in Montreal. I guess you could call it an initiation of sorts. 'Course, Diep knew perfectly well who Truong was."

I let out a short laugh of admiration. "When I talked to him that night, he seemed totally innocuous—all sweat and rolling eyes. The other two scared the hell out of me, but I figured Diep was way out of his element—And it turns out Diep is the missing third man in Benny's murder—that's what really pissed Nguyen off."

"Yeah," Spinney said softly, "I guess killing someone together is kind of a bonding experience." He paused, and then added, "I'm still surprised he agreed to talk."

"There's more," I added. "I took a calculated risk that the car bomb had been a disaster for them, and that they'd assumed Da Wang had done it to pull the rug out from under them. Fingering Diep for it did the trick—Nguyen realized then we really were his only chance. Oh, and by the way, he gave us our second confirmation that Sonny and Truong are the same man."

Spinney stared ahead at the road. "You think Diep—or Lo—is working for Da Wang?"

"That's what I told Nguyen. He certainly used to, and we know he's been to Montreal more than once. It would've been good insurance. No matter who won, Diep would've been on the winning side. Talk about killing two birds with one stone.

"Nguyen got downright chatty after the deal was done," I went on, "and admitted that they'd been pretty upset by the home-invasion fiasco at the Leung residence. Turns out that was Diep's idea, not Vu's, but that Vu ran with it, being both dumb and greedy. Nguyen said flat out he never thought Vu had any brains. Diep probably set it up so it would fail, and made sure a hyped-up Vince Sharkey would appear at just the right moment to screw things up. Nguyen now thinks the plan was for Vince to kill at least Vu and maybe Henry Lam—either of which which would have increased Diep's importance to Truong—before getting killed in the process. The fact that we showed up was pure providence."

"Did Diep get closer to Truong?"

"Nguyen says he's now second-in-command. That's another reason he spilled the beans."

"So Diep was the one who popped Vu in West Lebanon," Spinney said matter-of-factly.

"It fits. Vu was feeling the heat. He was capable of shooting his mouth off to us or Truong. He might've even tumbled to something specific about Diep—that would explain why he was so paranoid that day, trying to raise cash instead of returning to Truong like you'd expect. Diep probably heard Vu was in White River through his own grapevine, and was stalking him same time we were."

"Man," Spinney laughed in disbelief, "these folks are cutthroat."

"I said something like that about Truong to Nguyen, but he says Truong is an 'honorable man,' that he's out to right the wrongs that were done to his family. He gets high marks as a leader—got a few of his people off drugs, always made sure their needs were taken care of, held them responsible for their own families in the old country."

"If Truong's such a saint," Spinney came back, "why does Nguyen feel his family might be toast if he talks?"

I shrugged. "I think that's more of a cultural reaction. From what I was told, Truong never made any threats. Nguyen just knows that's a traditional way of doing business—you do the boss dirt, he makes the penalty up close and personal. Besides, Nguyen did confirm that Truong iced all those people, from Johnny Xi onward. That kind of behavior lends itself to some serious loyalty.

"Speaking of which," I continued, "it turns out we were right about the bank. That was Truong's one pile, and he's feeling the pinch without it. Nguyen agrees with us that Truong's two best options now are to fold or try a massive border crossing. 'Course, he also said Truong was capable of anything—that vengeance is all he lives for—so who knows?"

The conversation ended there, the victim of a mutual need for reflection.

I made no pretense of understanding the rules of conduct that seemed to drive the dreaded Dark Root. I could see how it had come about, however, and why it was still so successful many generations later. Our own crooks and their spurts of chaotic, bloodthirsty mayhem were a reasonable reflection of our often careless, spontaneous society. Why shouldn't the same be true for the Asians, rightly famous for their hard work, determination, family loyalty, and ambition?

*   *   *

The Border Patrol's sector headquarters are located in a solid brick building just south of Swanton center. Self-effacing physically, it is in fact the vessel of an impressively complex and well-managed communications center, linking it within the sector to substations stretching from New York State to Maine. Involved are almost a hundred and fifty highly sensitive infrared monitors, magnetic detectors, seismic sensors, and discreetly placed, low-light television cameras, all of which are strung strategically along the border, some so well camouflaged that they are literally invisible. In addition, several computer consoles, fax machines, and high-security, scrambled radio frequencies keep the center in touch with a coterie of other agencies with an ease I knew Dan Flynn would envy.

The building was also the home of the sector's intelligence unit, as well as a relatively new brainchild called the Canadian Border Intelligence Center, or CBIC for short, which was the primary reason Spinney and I had made the trip.

CBIC had been created as a sort of informational lending library, along the same lines as Dan Flynn's VCIN. But where Dan had to watch out for a small army of potentially fractious personalities—all worried that the other cop's department might try to steal his case by using the system—CBIC was significantly less encumbered. More than a clearinghouse for information, it was an actual depository, where statistics gathered from both the US and Canada could be crunched to form a better picture of who was moving what, or whom, across the border, and where.

Walt Frazier had preceded us to CBIC to see if the Sonny network had begun to leave any kind of recognizable—and predictable—fingerprint.

Spinney and I were logged in at the security window in the lobby, met by an escort on the other side of an electronically operated door, and led through the building to the CBIC office. On the way, we took a shortcut through the windowless dispatch center—the heart of all those various monitors and communications devices. Sitting at a semicircular console looking exactly like some space-age movie set, were two men on rubber-wheeled chairs, sliding back and forth with effortless, practiced ease, talking on radios, answering phones, entering data into computers, all in the eerie glow of some fifteen television monitors that were perched along the top of the console like silent witnesses to the world outside, mundanely observing roads, fields, and bridges, some of which were scores of miles away.

I was suitably impressed, all the more so when I realized that this northern border was by far the lesser of the two this agency was sworn to protect. In rough numbers, for every two illegal crossers each Border Patrol officer caught coming over from Canada, four to six hundred were collected by their southern-based colleagues.

We ended up in a room with a table covered in maps and charts, surrounded by six people: Walt Frazier; Judy Avery, the Border Patrol's "Intel" officer and CBIC liaison; Bob Carter, the Border Patrol sector's agent-in-charge; Abe Gross, one of the two INS investigators assigned to Vermont; Andy Marcotti, from US Customs; and Steve Moore, who headed up the Vermont State Police barracks in Derby. Since INS was interested in bodies, Customs in inanimate objects, and the Border Patrol in catching both as they slid in between ports of entry, these three particular agencies interacted on a routine basis, as did the state police when any one of them needed assistance. It was a congenial group, long past caring politically who worked for whom.

Carter, as host, rose when we entered and shook hands with both of us. "Gentlemen, come on in. Walt's been stealing your thunder a bit with a sneak preview, but you'll be glad to know we haven't decided everything without you."

The slightly forced laughter that generated told me how close it could cut to the truth. One egomaniac with clout in a group like this would be like the proverbial rolling grenade, sending all parties running for separate shelters.

"We've got one late arrival to go," Carter continued. "Jacques Lucas is coming down from the Royal Canadian Mounted Police. Should be about another fifteen minutes. But we can get things started. Have a seat."

I was pleased to hear Lucas's name. He'd been recommended earlier by Lacoste in Montreal as someone with Frazier's degree of generosity in interagency cooperation. Given the vastness of the RCMP—they were the Canadian equivalent of the DEA, FBI, Secret Service, Border

Patrol, ATF, and most everything else, all rolled into one—a helpful, willing contact would be nice to have. Of course, the size of their organization tended to make the Mounties about as fast and flexible as a supertanker in mid-river, but it also endowed them with quasi-supernatural powers—and computers to match.

Judy Avery, still bearing the stylistic rigidity of a military background, began by curtly nodding in my direction when we'd all sat back down after formal introductions. "Nice job on your interrogation. From what Walter's been telling us, your source sounds pretty reliable. We checked out what he told you of past crossings and found several corroborations with our own data." She pulled a map out from under the other paperwork strewn across the table, and laid it open. "Within the last month, here, west of Richford, and here, not far from the railroad tracks west of North Troy, we picked up probes from what we thought might be the Sonny network, and which your efforts have just confirmed. Those were individual crossings, probably made to test our reaction."

"We know they've been successful elsewhere, though," picked up Abe Gross, from INS, "because we talked to a couple of newcomers twelve days ago, and they were *not* professional crossers."

"Right," added Carter. "One of our agents took 'em near Highgate Springs, just north of here. They came in skirting the water, along a footpath where we had a mobile sensor just a few weeks before. It was dumb luck we caught 'em. One of our units drove up before their ride did, on routine patrol."

"You got no information on who was supposed to pick them up?" I asked.

Gross answered for him, "They didn't know. They'd been told where to go, and to wait for a ride—"

"Which we provided them," Carter added, to general laughter again.

Judy Avery pointed to her map. "That's another confirmation by your source, of course, since he mentioned Route One Thirty-three, too. But apart from one other crosser who was caught wading along Mud Creek, just east of Province Hill Road, who did trigger one of our monitors, those were the only entries we knew about. These other spots you've identified are news to us, and some of them are located right where we have sensors."

"Infrared units," Carter mused, "which means if you know where they are, you can step around to their back."

I had gotten to my feet by now, to gain a better perspective on the map. "Can we back up a little? I see a lot of roads that cross the border. Where exactly are the points of entry, and how're the Border Patrol units deployed?"

Avery was across the round table from me, and guided me from her seat, even though the map was upside down to her. "Here we are at sector headquarters, just below Swanton. Our substations in Vermont are east of Swanton on Route Seventy-eight, and in Richford, Derby, and Beecher Falls, right next to New Hampshire."

Andy Marcotti of Customs, looking slightly bored, was sitting next to her. He suddenly joined in, adding, "We've got twelve ports of entry altogether. Most of them aren't manned twenty-four hours, though. They're just little outposts—one-person operations that handle the odd car or pickup now and then. If there're any immigration problems, they'll either call for help or direct the vehicle to the nearest large port where INS has people working alongside ours, usually High-gate Springs or Derby Line, near Newport—those're the two flagship ports."

Steve Moore, the Vermont State Trooper, added, in direct answer to my implied question, "Which means that a lot of those roads you mentioned are just there, open for grabs."

"Well," Carter protested gently, "not exactly. Most of them have barriers across them, or will have soon."

Moore laughed. "Right, and the others have little signs telling you to go to the nearest port and report in."

"Those are monitored, though," Avery explained, unamused, "for the most part with cameras, so if the crosser doesn't show up at the nearest port, we know who to go after."

There was a telling pause, during which a small element of embarrassment in the air told me that everyone had perhaps overstated their case just a little.

Avery, whose intelligence job allowed her the broadest overall view of reality, confirmed that impression. "It's got its holes, and where we've tried to plug them, things aren't always perfect. But our figures tell us our apprehension rate's pretty high." Here, she finally yielded to a self-deprecating smile. "But like they say—there are white lies, damn lies, and statistics."

There was a knock on the door, and a small, gentle-looking, rather dapper man, wearing a suit and a mustache, was ushered in, looking more like a lost European tourist than one of the Mounties of lore. Carter stood up and waved him over. "Jacques—glad you could make it. You know everyone here, right? These two are Joe Gunther and Lester Spinney. They basically got this whole ball rolling in the first place."

Jacques Lucas shook our hands, smiling softly, and murmured in a thick French accent, "I have spoken with Lacoste. You are to be congratulated."

I smiled in return, my mind abruptly reaching back to when I'd been a boy, visiting my Uncle Buster in Vermont's so-called Northeast Kingdom. The subject of Mounties had come up, as it did with a lot of boys near the border in those days, and my uncle had reacted impulsively as usual, piling me, my brother, and a cousin into his truck, and taking us across the border to the nearest RCMP outpost he knew of. We'd marched across the threshold with bated breath, fully expecting a room filled with scarlet-clad, blond-haired young gods, all standing at least six and a half feet tall, and were met instead by a single, older, slightly rotund corporal, sitting at a desk, dressed in a uniform about as colorful as a tree trunk. He'd been very kind, and had showed us recruiting posters of the ideal we'd come to meet— had even pulled out his dress uniform, hanging in a closet—but we'd never recovered, and it wasn't until I was a cop myself when a variation of the same awe I'd once felt for them returned with the realization of just how huge and powerful their organization was.

As a result, despite his demure appearance, I shook Jacques Lucas's hand with respect. I also responded to his praise. "I'm not sure compliments are in order. We may be zeroing in on a whole lot of nothing."

Lucas waved away my pessimism and settled into the last chair at the table, nodding and smiling at the others in a generalized greeting. "I would like to say to all of you that I wear today two hats. The Quebec Provincial Police know that I am here, and I am expected to report back to them also."

Avery was back at her map, brusquely efficient once more. "We were just discussing the points of entry the Sonny network has supposedly targeted. It is pretty obvious to me, at least, that more has gone into the choosing of these spots than just running a few people across and seeing if they get caught. As Bob just pointed out, some of the infrared sensors are being bypassed surgically, which indicates a precise knowledge of their location and orientation. And judging alone by the small number of people we've caught, we know that information wasn't obtained by blind luck. That implies help from local residents, perhaps on both sides of the border."

Bob Carter spoke up again, since it was mostly his troops who maintained relations with the people whose properties straddled or abutted the boundary. "We looked into that as soon as we heard about this network. Comparing that list with the geographic points your Nguyen Van Hai gave us, we did come up with a few that match." He stabbed the map with a blunt finger at three points.

"I don't think Truong'll use those," I said softly. "He'd have to assume that any contact he'd heard about and used through the Asian old-boy system would be known to Da Wang or his confederates and open to attack if things got hot. It makes sense that he would've kept a private route or two up his sleeve."

Judy Avery immediately seized on the idea. "How would he develop them?"

"I don't know," I answered. "The safest approach would be to find someone who lives on the border, but who's never been involved in Asian smuggling before—or maybe any smuggling at all—and who could be bought."

Carter, ever gregarious, laughed. "Hell—sounds like me."

Marcotti, of Customs, whose presence here was obviously a polite formality, let out a gentle sigh. "Let's look at the 'when' for a minute."

Steve Moore spoke up immediately. "The Grateful Dead concert."

Heads nodded all around the table. Carter agreed. "It's already giving us fits. We don't know if there'll be sixty thousand attending that thing, or a hundred and sixty. As it is, we've canceled all leaves, stolen people from other substations, and coordinated with every law-enforcement agency north of Burlington, including you folks." He nodded at VSP Lieutenant Steve Moore.

With everything else I'd had to focus on, a Grateful Dead concert rang only a vague bell. "When is this, and where?"

Surprisingly, I thought, it was Jacques Lucas who answered. "In two days. We and the QPP have also gathered as many men as we can. It will take place in Swanton."

"At the fairgrounds, east of town," Carter added. "Right next to our substation there. In fact, we're telling the whole Swanton crew to bunk in for a couple of days, 'cause getting back and forth by car's going to be a joke."

There was a moment's silence as we all considered the obvious— the concert was a custom-made opportunity for Truong to make his move.

"Yeah," Spinney asked, "but does he melt into the crowd, or cross over as far away from the action as he can, where we got one cruiser covering twenty miles?"

Almost simultaneously, several voices answered for one choice or the other. Avery straightened from studying the map and looked around. "Guess we've got a problem."

I leaned toward Spinney and whispered in his ear, "Hold the fort— I want to give Dan a call."

He nodded, and I slipped out to find a phone.

Dan Flynn answered, as usual, halfway through the first ring, "VCIN—Flynn."

"It's Joe. Can you put Digger on the other line?"

"Shirtsleeve." Digger's voice had all the enthusiasm of a bored morgue attendant.

"I think Truong's going to bypass everything Nguyen gave us. He knows damn well we'll make an offer, and he knows what Nguyen's got to trade. Who do you have in your system up here who's really wired to the locals—goes to church with 'em, maybe busts their kids when they get drunk, remembers birthdays? Somebody who's as local as they are."

I could hear Flynn start to type in the background, but Digger merely growled, "Richard Boucher—Border Patrol. Works out of Derby."

"He's tied into the locals, including the ones living on the border?"

Digger sounded disgusted. "That's what you wanted, right?" The line clicked as he hung up his extension.

Dan laughed a little nervously, no longer typing. "Well, I guess there you have it."

It being near the end of his shift, Richard Boucher was still at the Derby substation. I explained who I was, what I was up to, and why I was calling. He'd already heard the first two pieces of information—no surprise considering that we'd used his substation to store the contents of Truong's fire-blackened safe.

His voice was low, slow, and oddly comforting. He picked up immediately on the kind of person I was after. "Someone we've never thought twice about—maybe the average honest citizen who's suddenly in a financial jam, and has something Truong could buy."

There was a thoughtful pause. "There's Eugene Blood. He lives alone with his sister, and she's dying of Alzheimer's. He's had to mortgage his farm to pay the doctor bills. He's got a hundred acres east of Derby Line, and the boundary cuts right through the middle of 'em."

"What made you think of him?"

"I don't know how much you know about me, but I was born up here and I've lived here all my life, except for the first few years as a patrolman on the southern border. So I've known the Bloods since I was little, and I'd never seen Gene so low as these last months. It got so I dropped by their place almost every time I went on patrol, just to give a little support. About three days back, Gene seemed a whole lot happier. But when I asked him why, all he said was that he'd sold some equipment and come into a little money. He wouldn't go into details, and tried to get away from the subject as quick as he could. I hate to say it about an old friend like that, but what you just asked me fits him pretty well."

"He have the personality for it?"

Boucher laughed softly. "He did in the old Prohibition days—at least according to the stories he tells. Plus, he wouldn't have to do much—just tell whoever it is where our sensors are planted and keep quiet. That alone could be worth a lot."

I made a mental note to ask Maggie Lanier for a search warrant of Blood's bank records, to see how much that sudden windfall amounted to. "I take it you don't swallow the equipment-sales angle."

"He could get maybe ten cents on the dollar for the junk he calls equipment. He sold all the good stuff a long time ago—this thing's been draggin' on forever. He doesn't have anything else."

"I'm assuming your knowledge of the locals only covers the area around Derby. Are there others like you in other substations that keep close tabs?"

"I'm the only native Vermonter, if that's what you mean, but there're other guys who spend a lot of time drinking coffee on these people's porches. You want me to call around?"

"I'd appreciate it. I want to see if there're any other Gene Bloods out there." I gave him my pager number. He said he'd get back to me in a couple of hours.

I returned to the conference to find everyone standing around the maps, talking fervently and taking notes. Lester stepped away from them and spoke to me quietly by the door. "This is about to break up. Nobody's too happy with just letting us take fifty men and staking 'em wherever we want, so a few compromises've been made. The largest concentration is going to be around the concert site—Lucas and his boys on one side, Carter and his on the other. A smaller staging area will be Derby, near Newport, just in case something pops up to the east, and then there'll be a third unit here, monitoring things in the communications center, with a helicopter on standby for quick transport. A few patrol cars—VSP, sheriff's men, Border Patrol, you name it—will be positioned along the boundary in between on regular shifts, advised on what it is we're looking for. All this'll happen ASAP. I told them I'd stay with the mobile unit here, since this is the eyes and ears, but I didn't commit you one way or the other. What did you get out of Flynn?"

"A line on a farmer named Eugene Blood. He's been clean as a whistle up to now, but he's got a barrelfull of medical bills, and I just talked to a Border Patrol agent named Boucher who thinks he may've come into a lot of money in the last few days. He's got a hundred acres on both sides of the boundary. Boucher's calling around to the other substations to find out if there might be other people that fit the same bill. He's supposed to get back to me today."

Spinney raised his eyebrows. "But you're putting your money on Blood?"

"So far I am. I was impressed his was the one name Boucher came up with right off the bat, but I'll know better in a couple of hours. I'd like to put some mobile sensors on his property in any case—ones he won't know about. I wouldn't mind getting a peek at his bank records, either, assuming Lanier thinks there's enough for a warrant."

"I can take a shot at that," Spinney said quickly, and then smiled a little self-consciously. "I kind of like working with Maggie."

I smiled back and gave him Richard Boucher's name and number for help on filling in the details of the affidavit.

*   *   *

As motel rooms went, it had seen its better days, as had the bed I was sprawled across. It was generally dark and dingy, decorated in hues to mask the more flagrant stains and signs of wear. I had the television on with the sound off, a paper plate of Cheez-Whiz and crackers and a pickle balanced on my chest, and I was watching a small cluster of cowboys hiding behind boulders, high on a hill overlooking an Indian campfire. The requisite blond, busty, perfectly made-up frontier woman, one shoulder of her dress attractively torn, was lashed near a fire to what looked like a utility pole planted in the desert by a forgetful service truck.

"You don't think this is going to work?" Gail asked on the other end of the phone line.

"Oh, I don't know," I said, sighing. "If it doesn't, it won't be for lack of planning or cooperation. It's been a textbook case of how the system's supposed to work."

"So why're you in the dumps?"

I didn't answer for a moment, watching the cowboys split up. The hero pulled his hat farther down on his forehead. "Things have come up that make Truong a little less the monster I thought he was. He's no pacifist, but he probably didn't have anything to do with Dennis's death, or the shoot-out Ron and I were in. And he didn't grab Amy Lee, either—that was Da Wang's doing."

"But he did kill Benny Travers?"

"As far as we know." I tried to get a better handle on what was bothering me. "It's not that he's not guilty. It's just that, usually, the further we dig into a case, the more dirt we get. That's been true here, too, of course, but it's a little different. I mean, I realize everyone always has a reason for knocking the other person off. People get pushed to that fine line, and then they rationalize crossing it. Truong's no different, and considering he's been after his brother's killers for years now—and carving them to death, one by one—you can't say he's the victim of any sudden impulse. But look where he came from, the models he had to follow, and the effort he made to defy them all. That was no slouch."

"You don't feel sorry for him, do you?" Gail asked in the pause that followed.

The hero cowboy cut the ropes tying the Indians' horses in place, and he and his buddies quietly slipped onto the backs of a few of them, preparing to start a stampede. The supposedly wild, prairie mustangs looked as wired as a bunch of overfed cows.

"Not exactly, but I do feel sorry. I can't put my finger on it. Somehow, there's a sense of betrayal and disappointment that keeps pulling at me. I don't know if it's Truong losing his brother, and then being stabbed in the back by his own lieutenant, or the constant sight of people hell-bent on grabbing the American Dream, being screwed by their own countrymen, and then somehow taking it in stride. Could be I've been drawing parallels between Truong's brother and my avenging Dennis, even though I know it's not the same. Maybe I'm getting old enough that all the blacks and whites are fading into grays. We're getting ready to begin the biggest operation I've ever been a part of, and I don't think any one of us knows a damn thing about the people we're about to close down. If it works, we'll slap ourselves on the back, and everybody'll file reports bragging about how well things worked—I'll even be handing the selectmen a bundle of confiscated cash they won't believe—but none of it'll have the slightest effect on the root cause of the problem.

"Not only that, but I don't know if any of this will help find Amy Lee. Maybe that's what's really getting to me. After all the rest of this is history, she may still be out there, like some tossed-away pawn— the one person who should've had nothing to worry about."

"You can only do what you can, Joe." It was a platitude—but a truthful one nevertheless.

The hero, in the lead, charged his mustangs across the campground, scattering the Indians. He flew off his now wild-eyed steed, slashed the ropes holding the young lovely to the pole, and swept her up in his arms, oblivious to the peril of being flattened by the horses behind him, or stuck by an arrow from one of the suddenly displaced two hundred Indians.

They kissed and faced the camera, smiling. Neat and tidy—no questions left hanging.

Chapter Twenty-eight

It was pitch black, drizzling, and a thick ground fog had settled into the low spots. Gene Blood's farm lay like a dark, misty blanket across the high undulations east of Lake Memphremagog, the rough edges of its streams and shallow ravines—even of the boulders lining its fields—smoothed and contoured by years of northern ice and snow and bone-cracking wind, making it all at once beautiful, soothing, and utterly hostile.

It was as quiet as a graveyard.

I was crouched in the lee of a small outcropping of rocks, high on a field that fell away to a row of trees marking the boundary with Canada. The fog had piled up against the base of the woods, so even with the pair of night-vision binoculars I'd been issued, all I could see at the bottom of the field was a slowly shifting, impenetrable haze, which in the artificial green glow of the binoculars, looked like a slow-motion surf, rubbing up against a dark and mysterious forest, full of promise and threat.

I ran a finger between my neck and the tight throat-mike fitted just to the side of my vocal cords. It was about as comfortable as those cheap, elastic bow ties waiters are forced to wear, but it enabled me to talk on the radio in a barely audible murmur and still be clearly understood at the other end. Strapped to my right ear, also with constricting bands that ran around my head, was a single large, padded headphone. A receiver on my belt allowed me to change frequencies between the small group of people hidden along Gene Blood's farm, the Border Patrol dispatcher in Swanton, and Lester Spinney, who was standing by the helicopter we'd been lent by the New York State National Guard.

I made sure I was on the local channel. "This is Alpha One with a wake-up call. How's everyone doin'?"

One by one, the six people I had assigned to me checked in, all with nothing to report. The last was Richard Boucher, the Border Patrolman who'd put me onto Gene Blood in the first place. We'd met shortly after that first phone conversation. I'd liked him instantly, and had gone to some pains to make sure he was made my on-ground liaison to his superiors.

"I had a doe trigger one of the infrareds about half an hour ago, but that's it so far."

"10-4." I took my finger off the *send* button and sighed. We'd been out here for four nights running. The concert in Highgate had come and gone, along with the almost fever-pitch tension that had accompanied it. Forty-eight hours earlier, a wandering doe would have triggered an instant recon patrol and brought everyone on the team to the edge of their seats. This time, I was sure, Boucher had merely waited for the animal to clear the woods and had checked it out with his binoculars. We were, after all, only some five hours shy of dawn—and of bringing this entire operation to a close.

There had been some bright spots, especially far west of us, above Highgate, where quite a few people had been rounded up crossing the border to see the concert. Those "hits" had apparently justified our putting the majority of our manpower there, despite my personal opinion that Truong would opt for a place of calm over chaos. That's why he'd chosen to undermine Da Wang from Vermont in the first place, instead of fighting him directly on his own Montreal turf— and why he'd taken so long to reach this point in his plans, after years of tracking down and eliminating the lesser players, slowly nibbling away at a nemesis who'd been watching him get closer for years.

I couldn't complain, though. The committee running this coordinated operation—nominally under Frazier's guidance—had listened to all viewpoints, and mine had been catered to with my squad of six now-very-bored people. They'd even gone beyond that. Boucher had found a couple of others like Blood—people living on the border with no past smuggling histories, but who were on the financial ropes and vulnerable to persuasion—and the committee had placed small squads on their properties, too.

So now I was trying to come to grips with the fact that despite my instincts—and my further belief that, of all the candidates, Blood was the best—I'd still been wrong. Either Truong did have enough money elsewhere to keep himself going, or he had other means to restock his coffers. It was possible he'd undermined more than one of Da Wang's pipelines, that despite Nguyen's denials and all the other intelligence we'd gathered on him, he'd still managed to keep some part of his business from all of us. But I still didn't believe it, even when confronted by the obvious.

A small tone went off in my ear, indicating someone wanted me on channel two—the frequency of the Swanton headquarters dispatcher.

"Alpha One from 6-40," came the flat, disinterested voice, "We got a hit on Whiskey-Three. 2-53 investigating."

I switched my radio over and murmured an acknowledgment. I wasn't as attuned as the Border Patrol was to the names and locations of all their dozens of monitors—I relied on Richard for that. I switched back to channel one in time to hear his low, calm voice say, "Memphremagog, eastern bank."

"10-4." I shifted my weight to get more circulation to my left leg. Normally, sensor hits were recorded by the dispatcher, and either checked remotely by camera or by a notified patrol unit. Given this particular detail, however, and the fact that none of us knew for sure where Truong might try to cross, all of us were being told of every "hit," regardless of where it was located. Only the small mobile sensors, like the several Richard was monitoring, bypassed this system, since their broadcast strength wasn't enough to reach the Swanton receiver.

Of the three types of sensors, the infrareds gave off the most alerts, since they were designed to capture anything that broke their invisible beams, including animals, falling branches, and even occasional tricks of light. The seismic units, triggered by the vibrations of passing vehicles, and the magnetics, which could pick up the metal shoelace holes on a single pair of boots, were custom-made for this kind of surveillance. But the infrareds were the cheapest, the lightest, and the easiest units to install, and as such accounted for the majority out here. I therefore assumed the sensor by the lake was one of them, and that its object of interest was either a floating log or two lovers in a canoe with a fetish for frostbite.

The tone went off again in my ear. This time, the dispatcher sounded a little more interested. "6-40 to all units. Whiskey-Eighteen just went dead. 6-40 to 2-53."

2-53 was the Derby-based car that had gone out to investigate the first hit. "6-40. This is 2-53. I'm on City Farm Road now, heading north. I'll take a look from Allen Hill."

I stayed on the main frequency, eavesdropping. I remembered Allen Hill from the guided tour of the landscape Boucher had given me five days earlier. From the top of it, the lake had spread out below like a vast black oil slick, curving around the tree-spiked humps of the islands and peninsulas with a menacing invasiveness. It was easy to imagine the lone patroller now, sitting in the warmth of his vehicle, adjusting his night-vision goggles to fit against high-power binoculars, steadying his elbows on the steering wheel.

"6-40, this is 2-53. We have multiple craft on the water, northeast of Black Island. Looks like they're heading toward the Holbrook Bay area, moving fast."

The Swanton dispatcher slipped into his Chuck Yeager, calm-in-any-storm voice. "10-4, 2-53. Advise you stay put for further incursions while we tend to mop-up." He followed with an alphabet soup of call letters, directing multiple units—both vehicles and boats—to converge on the scene.

He was interrupted by 2-53 again: "6-40, you better step up the response. Now I've got more Charlies heading south, maybe to Indian Point. They're spreading out to hit the shore on a broad base. We're going to need everybody we can get."

Swanton Dispatch reacted accordingly. Unit by unit, he read off numbers, including Spinney's helicopter crew. Like heavy footfalls coming along a corridor, I could hear him getting closer to me and my small, suddenly alert band.

"Alpha One," he finally said. "2-57 is to follow the Johns River SOP. Your command has been terminated."

2-57 was Richard Boucher, and he was being ordered to take over from me and abandon the Blood farm. In the pause that should have been filled with my own curt and acquiescent "10-4, Alph One command terminated," I heard the double tone of our own frequency go off in my ear—Boucher wondering why I was hesitating, and impatient to get going.

I switched channels. "Go ahead."

"Joe," he said, without all the formalities, "you hear that last request?"

"Yeah. I'm thinking. Anything going off on your monitors?"

"Negative. The action's on the lake."

"It is right now—out in the open where everyone can see it."

Swanton signaled to me to answer. I went back to their frequency and told them to wait. When I returned, Richard asked, "What're you saying? You still think he'll hit here?" His voice was incredulous, and a touch irritated.

"This could be his last shot. He laid the ground, did his homework, took his time. I have a hard time believing it all boils down to a bunch of boats flying across open water in clear weather, especially since he must know we're on high alert."

This time it was Boucher who hesitated. "They're still going to need troops along the eastern shore."

"Fine. How many will it take?"

"I'm running the sensors," he said. "How 'bout you, me, and Steve stay put, and I cut the other three loose?"

I knew what that decision was costing him. The northern border was normally quiet enough to be considered by some a retirement post. To be on duty and miss an event like this cut deep. "Thanks, Richard. I appreciate it."

I let him do the honors of breaking the news to 6-40. In true military style, they took it without comment, saving their wrath for when it could be dished out face to face, by the man with the most brass on his shoulders.

I stayed on the general frequency, as I knew Boucher and Steve were doing from their hiding spots. Tucked away among my little pile of rocks, I could hear all hell breaking loose, as VSP, Newport Police, and sheriff's units were called in for backup, visualizing from experience what was taking place. Five minutes later, adding to the unreality, I heard the distant thudding of Spinney's helicopter through the ear that wasn't covered by the headphone, some six miles to the west.

As the minutes dragged on, I began wondering if the antici-pated dressing down I'd be getting later wouldn't be richly deserved.

The small double tone went off. I switched over.

"Joe, I got a hit, about halfway between us," Boucher reported.

"Okay. Hang on."

The trick to mobile sensors was to place them strategically, far enough apart to give the listener not only a sense of which direction the object was moving in, but also at what speed. Richard and I were waiting for the second hit.

"Got it," he said moments later. "He's heading toward you, and he's on wheels, moving fast." Then he added quickly, "I got another one on the first sensor—something big."

I aimed my binoculars to the left, and then made a calculated gamble. "Drop everything and head back to your pickup, Richard. If he is mobile and I miss him, we'll be shit out of luck without a vehicle. Steve, you find out what triggered that second hit, and call for reinforcements. I think this is it."

"What if this is another diversion? Or a midnight joyrider?"

"Just do it. We don't have much left to lose."

I heard something in the distance and tore the headphone off my ear to listen. It was the high-pitched whine of a small engine. I disconnected the radio from all its covert paraphernalia, the need for silence over, and told Richard, "I hear it coming. Sounds like an ATV."

Boucher was breathing hard, running for his pickup. "10-4. I'll be headin' your way in a sec."

The fog bank by the trees told me nothing. As before, it lay there, trapped, opaque as green phosphorescence through the low-light binoculars, disguising the source of the approaching engine's growing howl. I was frustrated by the binoculars. Richard and a few of the others had been issued sophisticated night-vision goggles from the Border Patrol's limited supply, which not only could be conveniently strapped onto one's head, but could also be left in place while shooting a gun. If it came to that, I knew I wouldn't do much with a pair of binoculars in one hand and a pistol in the other.

At last, much closer than I expected, the fog gave up its malevolent gift. The dark, squatty form of a four-wheel all-terrain vehicle, towing a small trailer, burst from the bank like a shark clearing water, and came charging right at me, its lights extinguished.

I exchanged the binoculars for a powerful flashlight, stood clear of the rocks, steadied my gun hand on top of the hand holding the light, and switched it on. "Police—stop."

But we were too close. It had happened too fast. There was no room left for either one of us to choose a peaceful option. The driver was also wearing night goggles, and the glare from my light totally blinded him for an instant, making him instinctively tear them off and throw them aside. He swerved at me, only barely in control of his machine. Just before diving out of the way, I saw the dazed face of Truong Van Loc.

I ended up against one of the rocks, momentarily stunned, the stench of the ATV's exhaust in my nostrils. He hadn't missed me by much. I dug my radio from the holster on my belt. "Richard— it's him. He got by me. He's heading for the road."

I scrambled to my feet and began running, my flashlight now lost, but my gun still in my hand. The road was a couple of hundred feet away, and Truong, now minus his goggles, had switched on his headlights. But I knew we were too late. Richard hadn't been able to get to his pickup quickly enough. Even now, almost reaching the road and seeing Truong picking up speed in the opposite direction, I could barely see Richard's lights coming over the rise far to my right.

Breathing hard, I staggered into the road and waved at the pickup to stop. He slowed down enough for me to pile into the passenger seat, and then poured the speed back on.

"He's right ahead of us—four-wheel ATV with a trailer—using lights."

Over the radio, we heard Steve reporting that he'd secured a large truck, minus the driver, and that he'd contained its human cargo by locking the back door.

Driving with one hand, the countryside ripping by in a frightening blur, Boucher unhooked his radio mike and relayed our situation to Dispatch in a calm, measured tone. "There is one thing going for us," he said after he'd signed off. "Unless he really knows this part of the woods, he's going to have to double back to keep on any kind of decent road. They all crap out about three-four miles east of here."

I remembered that from studying the map earlier. Somewhere near where Orleans County ended and Essex began, the dozen or so marked roads all either dead-ended or looped back around to the west. But there were a lot of them, mostly interconnected, and unless we could seal them off quickly, Truong still stood a good chance of escaping, especially if he put his cross-country vehicle to its intended use.

"There he is," Boucher murmured, almost to himself.

Ahead of us, around a curve in the road, a quick, jittery glow flickered briefly across the treetops. I hung on as Richard approached the bend without letting up on the accelerator.

Tires squealing, odds and ends shifting noisily around inside the cab, we took the corner almost on two wheels. Straightening out, we found the road ahead—straight, broad, and flat—totally empty.

Richard slammed his hand against the steering wheel, coming to a stop. "Damn. The son-of-a-bitch. I should've known it."

He threw the truck into reverse, turned us around, and sped back to a small gap in the woods I hadn't noticed on the inside of the curve. Again, he grabbed the radio and gave a short update. Then he positioned us so our lights shined directly into the trees.

I looked dubiously at the narrow gap, which in the shadows looked about big enough for a bicycle. "You sure?"

"I know every deer path in this county. He's down there, all right, playing hide and seek."

"So we wait?" I asked.

A slow smile spread across his face as he shook his head. "Too many options in there. He could come out at a half-dozen places, cross another road, and keep on going. We're going to have to force his hand." He put the truck into four-wheel drive.

"In this?" I asked incredulously.

He laughed. "You never been jeepin' before?"

The truck leaped from the road into the brush with a tremendous crash. Branches flew by the windshield as if caught in a tornado, and I could hear the truck's undercarriage squealing and groaning with the strain. I held onto the dash with both hands, wondering how I could have been so wrong in gauging Boucher's character.

After the initial onslaught, the branches faded back a bit, allowing us some vision, and up ahead, exactly on cue, another pair of headlights suddenly came to life.

"I got you, you bastard," Richard shouted gleefully, and put on more speed.

As he did so, two sharp muzzle flashes punctured the darkness. Our windshield cracked like a snapped bone and we were sprinkled with tiny shards of glass. Boucher's face, glowing green in the dash lights, merely hardened in silence.

The chase became a slow-motion cataclysm of violent sound, motion, and half-perceived disasters. Adrenaline-pumping images of grazed boulders, hip-checked trees, branches further smashing the windshield, and an occasional view of the vehicle just ahead, its driver hunched over the handlebars, crowded in on me in chaotic order. The maelstrom of jumbled impressions was so confusing, so immediate, and so life threatening, I actually found myself wondering if any of it was real.

And then abruptly it stopped. Boucher screamed, "Shit," and slammed on the brakes. Ahead of us—almost under us—was Truong's trailer, twisted, broken, completely blocking our way. Beyond it, receding rapidly, we could clearly see the fading lights of the ATV.

Once again, Richard grabbed the radio. This time, however, I reached out and took it from him.

"4-60 from Alpha One. Where's the chopper now?"

"Near the intersections of Holland, Morgan, and Selby Roads."

I glanced at Boucher.

"That's just ahead. If we can move that trailer, I can get you there in five minutes. We almost had him," he added as an angry afterthought.

"Can you land there?" I asked the helicopter.

"10-4. What about the ATV?"

"Have you inventoried the truck yet?" I asked instead, knowing the noise of our cross-country pursuit had drowned out anything that might have come in over the radio.

"10-4. One hundred and twenty illegals."

"Then I recommend you track the ATV, but do not apprehend. Watch for it to go back the way it came—back into Canada."

Boucher and I swung out of the truck. "Boy—they aren't going to like that," he said. "What're you up to?"

We both grabbed a corner of the trailer, noticing the tow bar had been destroyed, and pushed it farther into the brush. "Open it for a quick look," I said instead of answering him.

He slipped the catch from the top of the trailer and threw back the door. Inside, lit by our headlights, was a trashed jumble of suitcases, cloth bags, and bundled clothing.

"The truck was the mother lode," I explained with relief. "The armada on the lake was just to draw our attention."

We returned to the truck, and Richard drove us rapidly to the road a few hundred yards farther on. He took a hard right and accelerated to where we could already see the helicopter landing lights searching out a good place to settle down. The truck didn't sound too healthy, despite the smooth road.

We reached the crossroads simultaneously. I ran, doubled over, just as the helicopter touched down, opened its waist door, and jumped inside, surprised as I did so to see not just Spinney, but Lucas and Frazier as well.

"Have you located him?" I shouted as the rotors revved up and we pulled away from the earth. Spinney handed me a pair of headphones similar to the ones Al Hammond had used in his airplane.

Frazier answered my question. "Yes. We have him on a loose tail, and he is heading back for the border, but I'm not sure I'm real happy with this. What the hell're you doing? I thought we wanted to nail this guy."

"Without the truck, he's probably out a half-million dollars or more. I think he took his last gamble—like we thought he would—and he blew it. His only option now is to go after Da Wang directly, except that with the protection Da Wang's got, Truong's going to need Diep and anyone else he can round up to pull it off. If we really want to put an end to this, we need him to lead us to the others."

Lucas put his hand on my shoulder. "You will have a stronger case if you stop him in this country. With all due respect, your laws are tougher than ours when it comes to people like this."

"But the evidence against him is still here. Can't we extradite him?" I asked Frazier.

"I don't have a problem with that, but we've got him now. Why risk losing him just because he may or may not lead us to Diep? And what if it goes wrong? This could lead to a bloodbath."

"Because we're always grabbing what we can, and letting the rest get away," I shouted back, since even with our headphones on, the helicopter put out a terrific noise. "They expect that—they count on it. Why do you think he threw us all those poor bastards on the lake? Were any of them carrying contraband?"

"We're still rounding them up, but, so far, none of them are even illegals—they're all Canadian landed immigrants. The ones we've caught are claiming they had full intentions of declaring entry at the port."

I shook my head in amazement at the depth of Truong's planning. "Let's take the gamble and do it right. We've done pretty well so far. We already shut him down. Taking him now and letting the others walk would be a total waste. He's the best chance we've got to round up the rest of them—maybe even Da Wang." And Amy Lee, I thought privately.

I looked at them all in the dim red glow from the bulkhead light. All of us were trained as rookies to do as Frazier had suggested—to be content with a clean bust as soon as you can get it. Conversely, we were by now all veteran officers, and we knew that carefully considered gambles were also a part of the business; that without undercover operations, stings, snitches, prolonged surveillance tactics, and the taking of risks, none of us could have made some of our bigger cases stick. It also didn't hurt that my credibility was pretty good at the moment.

Frazier finally turned to Lucas. "Jacques, this is as much your call as ours. We're going into your jurisdiction."

Lucas nodded and moved toward the cockpit. He had the co-pilot key in a special radio frequency, and then plugged his headset directly into the dash, taking him out of our communications loop.

I turned to Spinney. "Assuming he says yes, think we could fake a good pursuit, just so Truong doesn't catch on?"

Spinney grinned and switched over to the VSP radio.

Five long, tense minutes later, when any decision was getting close to being too late, Lucas returned to us. "Okay."

Spinney immediately set his plan in motion, orders were given to the pilot, and the four of us moved to the windows to see what would happen.

Far below, isolated by the blackness of the empty land all around them, we could clearly see two sets of light—one small and jerky, the ATV charging cross-country—the other, farther off but closing rapidly, sparkling like some runaway Christmas ornament—the unit Spinney had set after Truong. I watched with growing concern as the two drew ever closer, wondering if the trooper understood that the ATV was supposed to escape.

Suddenly, and with some relief, I saw the cruiser's lights swerve violently and then come to an abrupt stop. Spinney burst out laughing: " 'Attaboy—right into the ditch." He hit the *send* button on his radio. "You all right down there?"

"You sure my butt's covered on this?" was the reply.

Spinney laughed again as we all watched the smaller light flicker down the field where I'd first met it, and work its way back into the woods.

The smiles slowly died on all our faces. I looked over to Lucas, the memory still painfully sharp of how I'd set Vince Sharkey against Michael Vu. "Guess I stuck it to us now."

He kept his eyes glued to the window, as if trying to memorize the details below. "I am hoping not," he finally muttered, and turned away toward the cockpit.

Chapter Twenty-nine

Twenty minutes later, we switched helicopters in a field north of the border, the landing zone marked off by a wide circle of police cars, all with their headlights pointing toward the center. Spinney, Frazier, and I left our unloaded weapons on the National Guard unit, and with them our authority. As we ran, crouching, from one thundering aircraft to the other, we became mere privileged observers, as vulnerable as our case to whatever vagaries the Canadian officials might decree. It was at that moment that my adrenaline for the chase—which at its height was no doubt as powerful as Truong's—underwent a sudden and sobering nose dive. I began fervently hoping that Lucas was all I'd privately made him out to be.

Certainly the influence of the Mounties seemed to live up to their reputation. Between the time we'd decided to let Truong return to Canada, and when we took off again in an official RCMP chopper, the quiet, diminutive Lucas had coordinated an impressively large operation.

As the helicopter gained altitude, Lucas informed us. "Truong abandoned the ATV outside of Rock Island about five minutes after we saw him cross the border. He was followed on foot into town, where he picked up a delivery van not far from the Customs building. He then took Autoroute Fifty-five North toward Sherbrooke. We are expecting that he will take Autoroute Ten West into Montréal. The van is white, with the name of a Chinese catering service in Montréal on its side. It has not been reported missing or stolen, so we are assuming it is being used with permission. We will be tracking his progress most of the way in this," he patted the wall of the helicopter, "with the aid of several ground units."

The junction of Autoroutes 10 and 55 appeared in the darkness below us as the confluence of two sporadically dotted lines—each line being an irregular stream of vehicles. Given the hour, there wasn't much to see.

Lucas pointed to one set of lights in particular "That's him. All we have to do is now keep our eyes on him until we approach Montréal."

An hour later, the traffic just outside Montreal thickened enough to make our vantage point unreliable. We handed the surveillance back to the ground units, and landed among a cluster of railroad tracks, just east of downtown, on the river's north shore. There, Lucas led the three of us to an unmarked van.

Once underway, he gave us another update. "He's been followed to the Chinatown area—rue de la Gauchetière. He's in his vehicle, parked on St-Laurent."

"Just sitting there?" Spinney repeated, grabbing the seat ahead of him as the van took a fast corner. "Isn't that where Da Wang hangs out?"

Lucas agreed. "Yes. That is the problem. You know Jean-Paul Lacoste, correct? He is going there with his team. There is much activity apparently. We are thinking the affair at the border has caused the need for a meeting, but Truong's presence worries us."

I felt a sudden coldness settle in my chest, sensing at last the potential carnage I'd set in motion—the very bloodbath Frazier had cautioned against, and that Nguyen had said Truong was capable of creating. I realized then the significance of those two shots Truong had fired at Boucher and me. They'd been the mile markers of a man whose despair had hit bottom, whose last option was to offer himself up in the name of his cause. Just as my argument in the helicopter had reflected my own obsession, and had been used to browbeat others into an enthusiasm they weren't sure they shared, so Truong had now dispensed with the niceties of any carefully thought-out plan, and had yielded at last to the despair and pure rage that had launched his vendetta at the edge of his brother's open grave.

I gave in to a moment of self-doubt and guilt. "Let's grab him now. Get it over with before we lose control."

There was a moment's startled pause at my abrupt turnaround. Spinney murmured, "Little late for that," as Lucas shook his head. "We do not have enough men in place yet. Besides, I think it would be premature."

Suddenly distracted by a message on his radio, Lucas spoke rapidly to the driver. The van's hidden siren burst to life, and the red and blue lights behind the grille pulsated off the dark buildings nearby, as other traffic made way for us.

Lucas explained, his arm thrown over the back of his seat. "He was seen leaving the van with a small bag, heading up La Gauchetière. He entered Da Wang's building, and now there are reports of multiple gunshots. All our surveillance units are changing to tactical mode, but our special-support teams are still not there. It is all happening too fast."

We squealed around a corner I recognized from our last visit, one block shy of the Chinatown Holiday Inn, and came to a shuddering stop opposite the rue de la Gauchetière's ornate Oriental gateway. All around us, emergency lights from dozens of haphazardly parked and rapidly converging vehicles shimmered in the night sky.

We followed Lucas up the street at a run. Ahead, we could hear the sharp, staccato beat of automatic gunfire.

At the end of the block, we came to a group of plain-clothes officers, Lacoste's tall, thin form prominent among them.

Spinney pointed to the East Wind Trade Association building we'd visited earlier, another half block farther on. On the sidewalk opposite, we could see three lifeless bodies. Beyond it, under a safely distant streetlight, stood another group of officers, among whom I recognized Antoine Schmitt, the MUC liaison officer we'd met during our first trip to the city.

In just the few minutes we'd been waiting, the entire neighborhood had filled with cops—plain-clothes, uniformed, and combat-ready. Things were obviously quickly getting organized, and we were obviously not to be a part of it.

A young woman split away from the group Lacoste and Lucas were in, and approached us with an apologetic smile. "I am sorry, gentlemen. Monsieur Lucas has asked me if you would be so kind as to return to the car? He does not want you hurt in this situation."

Frazier, as our senior representative, acknowledged the message, thanked the young woman, and led the way back. As we reached the first corner, however, I glanced over my shoulder, and saw Schmitt and his group still loitering where they had been. Unable to envision sitting out this drama's conclusion, I yielded to my growing anxiety and cut away unobserved, intent on circling the block and coming up behind our erstwhile liaison. I didn't know why Schmitt was here, but I was hoping that, given his diplomatic assignment, he might be more amenable to my being closer to the action.

Frazier and Spinney, distracted by the activity at the staging area just ahead of them, didn't notice my departure. It was just as well—running around in flagrant disregard of an order by the RCMP didn't strike me as something Frazier in particular would condone, especially since my last decision had been the direct cause of this mess.

The street I took, a block shy of St-Laurent, led to a broad avenue named Viger, where I turned right again. As I approached the Holiday Inn, with its distinctive pagoda roof, I noticed that across the street—and connected to my side by an enclosed overhead walkway—was a Metro stop, housed within a long, low, ugly concrete office building. There was very little traffic and no sign whatsoever of the drama unfolding just one block to the north.

I did a slow jog along Viger, past the hotel, and turned up a short dead-end street that led back to La Gauchetière, my eyes on the reflected glow of the revolving lights. About halfway up the empty street, however, something made me stop—a slight noise, a sense of movement. I wasn't sure. Instinctively, I slid into a doorway and looked back at a narrow alleyway I'd just passed. Emerging from it, and walking quickly away toward Viger and the Metro station on its far side, was the dim silhouette of a thin, quick-moving, energetic man.

From the back, it looked just like Truong Van Loc.

I whirled around, but there was no one to call to at the end of the street. I could still hear sporadic gunfire from deep inside the block of buildings next to me, presumably from the police assault. I faced

Viger again. The man I'd seen was halfway across the street already, his goal now utterly clear—along with my responsibility. Ruing my decision not to have enlisted at least Spinney in my impulsive side trip, I ran across a small plaza that led to the enclosed overhead bridge I'd seen earlier, and headed for the Metro station by the high road, thereby avoiding the chance that Truong might see me.

Not that I was all that confident I was following Truong. The continuing gunfire threw me off, not to mention that this man had appeared out of nowhere, and at a considerable distance from the action.

My route led me to a broad set of stairs leading down to a large, empty lobby, to the left of which were the doors to the Place d'Armes Metro Station. I waited a moment while "Truong" negotiated his way through the electronic turnstile and disappeared down the right staircase, under an orange sign reading Henri Bourassa.

I then pushed through the station's double doors and ran up to the attendant in his booth. Beneath my feet, I could feel the slight trembling of an arriving train. Fearing it might be the one Truong was waiting for, I silently thrust a five-dollar bill at the man behind the glass, rather than trying to get him to call the police on my behalf, on the dubious strength of an American badge and a weird story about chasing Asian gangsters. He gave me several paper tickets.

I quickly went to the turnstile, fed it one of the tickets, and bolted through the gate and down the same stairs Truong had taken just a few moments earlier.

It had been his train pulling in, and as I reached the bottom step, I could hear a series of warning beeps going off overhead, telling me the doors were about to close. Choosing the risk that he might see me over the certainty that I'd lose him otherwise, I ran to slip in between the doors just before they hissed shut.

I was alone in the car.

I tried to orient myself in relation to the city above. We were heading east, and according to the Metro map mounted on the car's wall, we were on the Orange Line, or the Cote Vertu/Henri Bourassa Line. Our next stop would be Champs Mars. Even as I figured that out, I could feel the train's momentum ebbing, and an incomprehensible announcement in French came over the loudspeakers. I moved across the aisle and crouched next to the sliding door. As I waited, I pulled my Swiss Army knife from my pocket and unfolded one of its blades, hoping to hell no one would be standing on the platform with plans of using this particular door.

The train entered a brightly lit, totally empty station, and came to a gradual, smooth stop. The doors slid open, and I immediately poked the end of the blade out past the threshold, using its shiny surface as a mirror to watch the platform ahead of me, while I flattened my head against the car's interior wall to obliquely watch the area to the rear of the train. No one appeared on the platform. A minute later the doors closed, and we pulled out again.

The next station was Berri-UQAM, a junction of three separate lines, heading off in different directions—and a perfect place for things to get complicated.

As we pulled in, seeing that a few predawn commuters were sprinkled along the platform, I changed tactics slightly. I stood by the door and, when it opened, I ducked my head out a couple of times as people brushed by me. As the warning beeps sounded, I saw Truong exit from two cars up and cut across the platform into a wide, arched hallway. I slipped free of the train just before the doors closed and flattened myself against the station wall. Risking a quick glance around the corner, I saw Truong's back receding down a flight of stairs to the right.

As he disappeared from view, I moved cautiously to the top of the stairs, and then waited until he'd vanished along a lower-level passageway. About halfway down the stairs after him, suddenly troubled by the sounds of my shoes, I took them off, shoving them into my jacket pockets.

Truong continued on through an intersection with another pedestrian walkway, and committed himself to a passage marked Longueuil. From my earlier reading of the Metro map, I remembered Longueuil as being on the south shore of the Saint Lawrence, a neighboring district of Brossard where, days earlier, Lacoste had shown Spinney and me the residential highlights of the Asian community. I began to imagine where Truong might be heading.

I followed him down yet another set of stairs, this one ending in a rough cement, low-ceilinged, gray station, a dingy imitation of its bright vaulted counterpart two flights up.

There I found myself in a bit of a squeeze. I could see Truong—

whom I identified with certainty now—standing nervously by the edge of the platform, but I was worried that another prospective passenger might come up behind me and wonder why I was lurking in the entrance tunnel.

Predictably, I immediately heard footsteps clattering on the cement steps behind me. As an older man came into view, I crouched down and innocently began tying the laces to the shoes I'd just put back on. He walked by me without a glance.

Truong studied the man carefully, and then abandoned his exposed position by the platform's edge, opting for the safety of a bench located in one of the alcoves lining the concrete wall. This gave me a sudden double advantage—I could vacate the exposed passageway, and secret myself instead in another of the alcoves, far from Truong's.

As I moved, I noticed a bright-red sign along the station's wall, labeled S.O.S. It was suspended over a red phone and a small fire extinguisher, both mounted inside a cabinet. I hoped our final destination would have an equally visible phone I could use to call the police—and that I'd have the opportunity to do so.

Another clean, quiet, rubber-wheeled blue train rushed into the station. Truong crossed the platform, getting on near the front. I boarded last, watching that Truong didn't reverse himself at the last second. He didn't.

According to the map, there were only two remaining stops ahead—Ile-Ste-Hélène, and the terminus, Longueuil. Ile-Ste-Hélène was one of the two islands in the middle of the St. Lawrence that had been used in the Expo '67 fair, almost thirty years earlier. The whole of Ile Notre-Dame just beyond it, I remembered, had been created especially for the event, and now was home to the city's highly lucrative casino—which made me wonder if that might be Truong's destination.

Truong got off at Ile-Ste-Hélène, and quickly vanished into the exit tunnel.

Swearing at his sudden speed, I ran for the red S.O.S. phone and hurriedly told the operator, "This is a police emergency. Please contact Jean-Pierre Lacoste of the MUC or Jacques Lucas of the RCMP and tell them that Truong, the man they're after, just got off the Metro at Ile-Ste-Hélène. Tell them that Joe Gunther is in pursuit and needs help fast. Got it?"

"This is who?" came the startled reply.

"Shit," I muttered, hanging up and taking the steps two at a time, worried now that even if they did get the message, I wouldn't be able to tell them what direction Truong had taken.

I slowed at the top of the stairs—on the chance he might be waiting in the lobby—but the place was empty. I ran to the bank of glass doors and out to a large, empty parking lot, blinking to adjust to the darkness, now just tinged with gray on the eastern horizon.

My environment was a startling transformation from where I'd disappeared underground just twenty-five minutes earlier. I was standing in the midst of a strange other world, highlighted by exotic and contrasting icons—a dark and gloomy forest to my back, just beyond an old, monastery-style building on the edge of a huge, empty, soiled swimming pool; the looming, twenty-story-tall Buckminster Fuller geodesic dome, glowing like a skinless golf ball with indirect interior lighting; and beyond it, in the far distance, the Montreal Casino on the other island—the old '67 French Pavilion—ablaze with light, looking like some oversized geometric mobile that had been cut loose and dropped to the earth in a heap. In the darkness, the whole area seemed like a dumping ground for Montreal's rejected monuments.

Most impressive, however, was that it was all utterly abandoned. I heard no sounds, saw no signs of life—and could see no trace of Truong.

I moved away from the Metro building, toward the huge dome, and came to a junction of pedestrian footpaths. There I heard the smallest scrape of a foot against pavement, far to the left, in the gloom skirting the edge of the monastery by the swimming pool. Again, I pulled off my shoes and began jogging in the same direction.

Beyond the building, the darkness became near absolute. Before me was a low, wooded hill, part of a park crisscrossed with paved walkways, its details discernible only against the distant, feeble glow of the city across the wide river—the flashing Molson sign, the string of lights outlining the Jacques Cartier bridge. The slight sound that had lured me here slowly lost its serendipity, and began to feel more like part of an elaborate trap. I stood absolutely still, a rabbit caught in a pair of metaphorical headlights, wondering from which direction an attack might come.

Until I heard the sound again.

It came from up ahead, across the narrow road that went by the monastery's front entrance, deeper in the park. Running silently toward the sound, I gave chase.

I found him about halfway up the opposite hill, among the trees, walking quickly and purposefully, intent on his enigmatic goal. Following by several hundred feet, just barely keeping his shadow in view, I wracked my memory for the details of this island, which I'd last visited in 1967 during the fair. The woods, I knew, eventually yielded to the Cartier bridge, an old British-built fort, and an enormous amusement park that occupied the entire northern tip of the island. There were also several parking areas, and it was toward one of those, I began thinking, that we must be headed—a perfect meeting place—out of the way, and with instant access to a major road out of town.

I caught sight of a strange light from the top of the hill, flickering as it filtered through the leaves of the tightly clustered trees. Truong reached a fork in the path, and without hesitation headed directly for the light. I continued following, wishing for the sounds of sirens—some sign that my message had been passed along and coherently delivered.

Gradually, separating itself from the darkness of the enveloping woods, there loomed a larger, thicker, more statuesque shadow—that of a heavy stone tower marking the crown of the hill. The light we'd both been following shimmered from its top, giving the grassy, treeless area at its base some faint distinction, which was further aided by the increasing glow from the east. I hung back more, worried about being spotted.

Truong continued undaunted, leaving the trees and approaching the final, steep climb to the tower itself. I peered ahead, wondering what he knew that I didn't, and saw a second shadow separate itself from the darkness of the tower's mass. It was then, more instinctively than from anything I could discern of that second shadow's intent, that I knew the other man to be Lo Yu Lung—Edward Diep—whose only option now, I was convinced—with the sudden and chaotic turn of events Truong had just precipitated in Chinatown—was to complete the destruction he'd begun so many years ago in that San Francisco restaurant.

The inevitability of what was about to happen welled up inside me with the white heat of frustrated certainty. Truong himself was about to be put down like an overly trusting dog by Dennis DeFlorio's killer, who would then escape into the night while I impotently stood by.

Without thought or plan, I shouted at the top of my voice, "Stop."

The effect was instantaneous. Truong dove off the trail, back into the woods, and Diep vanished as if by magic, reabsorbed by the tower's shadow. I took cover as fast as I could behind the nearest tree trunk, knowing clearly but too late that I was the only one without a gun, and that the other two still believed themselves to be allies.

"Truong," I shouted again, seizing my only weapon, "this is Joe Gunther, from the Brattleboro Police Department. Give yourself up to the Canadian authorities. We know about your brother, about how you went after his killers. We know you kept Da Wang for last. I was in the truck that chased you through the woods a couple of hours ago. I followed you from Chinatown just now. You've been under surveillance for a long time. You've got nothing left. You'll die tonight if you don't give up."

My words floated off into the air, replaced by the anonymous hum of the glimmering metropolis across the water.

"Did you ever wonder how Edward Diep found you, or where he came from?" I started again. "You took Henry Lam's word for it that he was okay. And because Henry trusted him, you trusted him. But Diep was playing you all against each other. He was the one who planted the car bomb that killed that police officer. He was the one who undermined your whole operation in Brattleboro. You know why?"

Again, I could hear only silence, and I began to fear that while I was shouting to the trees, one or both of these men was busy moving around to my back. I paused to reposition myself about forty feet away.

"Whatever happened to Lo Yu Lung?" I yelled out. "Didn't you wonder why you couldn't find him?" A muzzle flash and an explosion lit up the night about halfway down from the tower. The bullet smacked into a tree nearby.

I shifted position again. "He's getting nervous, Truong. Trying to shut me up."

Two more shots were fired, still comfortably off target, "Lo and Diep are the same man. I've got proof. He killed Michael Vu so Vu couldn't tell you. He told Da Wang where you kept your bank in Newport. Your pal Nguyen knows all this. He knew you were doomed—that you'd been stabbed in the back a long time ago. You just didn't know it."

I moved again, hoping I'd said enough, knowing that all this shouting might well be suicidal.

The next shot, when it came, was farther off, directed at someone else. For once, it was Diep who'd had the rug pulled out from under him, and who was scrambling for cover. That last shot, coming from near the tower, revealed his new priorities. Of the three options open to him now—escape, killing me, and killing Truong—only the last held out the hope that he might survive. Left alive, Truong would be a persistent threat, even if he spent a few years in prison.

Ignored for the moment, I circled around the peak of the hill and came up behind the tower, pausing briefly to put my shoes back on. The sky was paling steadily now, and the woods below beginning to gain definition. The cat and mouse were running out of time.

Nevertheless, I didn't actually see what happened next. There were several flashes from opposing gunfire, and suddenly a yell. Only then did I catch some movement—the flickering of a shadow on a path leading downhill, in the direction of the glowing geodesic dome beyond the woods. The echoing of footsteps on the pavement told me of a chase. In the distance, hopelessly far off, I could finally hear sirens wailing.

Cautiously, I brought up the rear, jogging along the footpath I was pretty sure they'd taken. As I cleared the woods and came into the parking lot of the fancy restaurant near the dome, I saw both of them ahead of me, Truong leading, limping, running incongruously toward the erstwhile American Pavilion.

The dome had burned several years ago, the fire gutting its contents and removing its plastic skin. Gradually being rebuilt, it had been left open to the elements, its latticework of interlocking tetra- and octahedrons a visual wonder and a magnet for pigeons. An odd, space-age structure had been erected within its cocoon—an upended, ten-story-tall concrete, steel, and glass box, almost like a diving tower, with various appendages sticking out from its sides—observation booths, staircases, balconies—the most prominent of which was a long, wide platform, free floating on thin pillars, hovering some seventy feet above the ground like an enormous diving board.

As I watched, Truong leaped through the dome's dizzying latticework and staggered up a metal staircase that led—switchback on switchback—up to that celestial platform. He paused at several points to fire in Diep's direction to keep him sufficiently at bay. Only when he was near the top did he wait too long. Diep took advantage of that one extra split second to step clear of his barricade and squeeze off a lucky shot that caught Truong in the back.

Truong staggered on, finally gaining the protection of the wing-like concrete projection.

As I watched from the shelter of an empty information booth at the edge of the parking lot, Diep moved out into the open, looking back at me, trying to gauge how best to get at Truong, as cognizant as I was of the approaching sirens. But his nemesis had chosen well. As odd at it had seemed at first, the platform was an ideal defensive position, especially for a man no longer seeking to escape. Utterly protected, approachable from one highly exposed avenue only, it forced Diep to either commit or abandon.

Perhaps responding at last to his own sense of fatalism, Diep committed. Turning his back on the reality around him, he began climbing the staircase.

I ran to the south side of the dome, where the platform jutted out without seeming function or purpose. Stepping through the veil of interlocking steel triangles, craning my neck to look up, I could only see the lip of the concrete slab and, in the distance, to its rear, the small figure of Diep, climbing.

Like a spectator at a movie in which I could not affect the outcome, I watched, and waited for the inevitable.

There was a movement above me, at the railing on the platform's edge, as far from the stairs as possible. A hand gripped one of the tubular cross pieces, and I saw Truong pull himself with grim deliberation to a sitting position, and wedge himself against one of the uprights. Instinctively, I knew he must be mortally hurt. *Let Diep come on*, his long crawl along the platform's length said.

But I was wrong, yet again. From high on his perch, with Diep cautiously advancing, Truong turned away and looked down at me, his gun in his hand.

Curiously, I felt no danger. I looked up at him, as if responding to some incomprehensible communication, and I spread my empty hands wide, indicating I had no weapon.

I thought I saw him smile then; he gestured with the gun, as if offering it. Although I made no response, he dropped it to me anyway. It landed in the gravel near my feet with a crunch. Reacting by reflex, I walked over and picked it up, popped out the clip, and saw it still had several rounds.

I looked back up at him, noticing that Diep was no longer visible on the staircase. He had obviously made it to the platform. Only now did I understand. Take out this man in my name, Truong had implied, in my brother's name, perhaps in your fellow slain officer's name. Kill the man who would kill me, for I no longer have the strength.

I stared up at him in wonder. He was right, of course. With his gun, now I had the advantage over Diep, who was cornered. But he was also wrong. While our roles might have appeared similar, our motivations couldn't be. I didn't share the passion, the beliefs, the cultural obligations that had brought him to this place. I wasn't even sure I understood them—not as he did.

Looking up at him, our eyes locked, the air around us now vibrating with sirens coming from all angles, I shook my head, and dropped the gun.

There was a moment's pause, before he turned away resignedly. Seconds later, several shots rang out, Truong's body spasmed briefly, and one arm slipped out between the railing, dangling lifelessly in the air, its hand open.

I turned at the sound of cars squealing to a stop behind me, and saw both uniformed and plainclothes officers spreading out in tactical positions, making me doubly glad I'd dropped Truong's weapon. I recognized Lacoste among them, and then saw Frazier, Spinney, and Lucas all stepping out of their van.

Following their gaze, I looked back to the edge of the huge, floating platform. Standing next to Truong's dead body, Lo placed both his hands on the railing's top rung, still holding his gun. He looked down at the impressive display of vehicles and police officers fanned out below him.

I heard Lacoste's distinctive voice, slightly blurred by a loudspeaker, demanding Lo's surrender. But predictably, almost anticlimatically, Lo exploited his other option, bringing this cataclysm to an end. He raised his gun, took aim at the crowd beneath him, and died in a last angry outburst of bullets.

Chapter Thirty

Gail pulled over to the curb and cut the engine. "He wanted to meet you here?" I looked past her at the gentle curve of Morningside Cemetery, the ragged rows of individual and sometimes idiosyncratic monuments, the hulking, dormant mass of Mount Wantastiquet beyond. The air was tinted with the perfume of spring in full flower. "I called Megan Goss about him yesterday, after he asked me here. I wanted to run his symptoms by her to see what she thought. She said it sounded like he was in mourning—for a loss of innocence, maybe, compounded by what had happened to Dennis, and exacerbated by having a new baby on the way. Her guess was he wants to tell me he's quitting the department. I guess a cemetery's as good a place as any to do that."

Gail studied my face for a moment, and then reached across and squeezed my hand. "He's not the only one in mourning, is he?"

I smiled slightly. "I suppose not. I hadn't allowed any time for it till now." I paused, and then added, "I'd hate to lose Ron as well."

Gail released my hand. "You better find out what he wants."

I leaned over and kissed her on the cheek.

* * *

I found Ron Klesczewski crouching at the foot of Dennis's grave, staring distractedly at the broad river far below. I sat down next to him, using a neighboring stone as a backrest. "Hey, there."

He didn't turn his head. "Hi, Joe."

"Guess you heard we closed the case, shut down the task force. We found Amy Lee, too—scared, but all in one piece."

"I saw it in the paper," he answered tonelessly.

I didn't know what else to say, and despite my gloomy prognostication to Gail, I had no idea how this was going to end. The last thing I wanted was to precipitate a gesture he hadn't been intending.

Groping for something benign in the silence, I finally said, "Willy put a donut in the coffin."

Ron slowly turned away from the view and stared at me. "What did you say?"

"Willy said he put a donut into the casket when no one was looking at the funeral home, tucked just out of sight under the bottom lid panel. He thought Dennis would appreciate it."

Ron shook his head, puzzled. "I thought Kunkle hated Dennis."

"Dennis was a cop. Willy never dumped on him about that."

Ron's anguished face cracked a smile. "A donut? Jesus Christ."

"Honey glazed—right on his chest, where he could reach it. And a napkin."

Laughing now, Ron sat down against the stone next to me, and stretched his legs out before him.

Seizing the moment, or maybe just wanting to get it over, I asked him, "You gonna quit the department?"

The laughter stopped, but the smile lingered encouragingly. He shook his head, his eyes fixed before him. "I was going to this morning. Even told Wendy."

"What did she say?" I asked in the silence that followed.

He looked up at me. "Not to do it. She said she'd never seen me happier than the day I made detective. That it wasn't something to give up just because I was in the dumps." He rubbed his forehead. "That surprised me. She was one of the reasons I was thinking of quitting—Wendy and the baby."

"Not bad reasons," I murmured, thinking of Gail.

He sighed. There was still something unaddressed—some issue we'd stepped over that I hadn't noticed.

"What is it?"

"I feel guilty." His words were barely audible above the soft breeze from the river.

"Because you lived to worry that you almost got killed? You gotta see the irony in that."

He smiled again, but I knew I hadn't quite hit it. I had picked Ron as my Number Two a few years ago, over Brandt's reservations, and I'd worked hard to make him feel comfortable in the role—perhaps too hard. I thought back to Truong Van Loc, and his relationship to his brother, on whom he'd pegged so much. I realized I too had been selfish, albeit a little less dramatically. Ron's anxiety was as much my fault as a result of his own insecurities. I hadn't paid attention to the price he'd been paying for a decision all my own.

"I'd be happy to switch things around a little, if you'd like—take you off as my second," I told him.

He turned to me, surprised—and I thought a little relieved. "You sure that would be okay?"

"You've got a lot on your mind, especially with the baby due. Good time to step back a bit—not be so wrapped up in the job. Maybe Sammie'd be interested. You think she'd take it?"

He laughed. "In a heartbeat."

I got up and walked to where the hillside fell off sharply to the railroad tracks and the near shore of the river, a hundred feet below. That was it, then. Life would resume for us all again, if in modified form.

At least almost—for there was loss lingering still, and a few things left I had to set right.

*   *   *

The Lee residence looked much as it had the last time I'd seen it— abandoned, neglected, in mourning, sitting among its tidy neighbors like a scream in the night no one wanted to acknowledge.

Amy Lee sat next to me, tired and wan, her face reflecting the ethereal glow from the dashboard's instrument lights. Unmolested and in good health, she'd been found in Da Wang's stronghold in Montreal by Lacoste and his people. It had taken time for them to confirm her identity, and for me to get to her and vouch for her. The paperwork to bring her back had prolonged things further, forcing me to precede her back to Brattleboro. An INS agent had finally picked her up at the border and driven her here in his car, rather than having her ride a bus, as was standard.

I'd intercepted her at that point, not wanting some anonymous federal employee delivering her home. My motives were also self-serving, of course. Having visited both Tony in the hospital, where he was fully recovering, and Dennis's family at their home, I was engaging in a quest of sorts, taking an inventory of my world, making sure that what was left of it was secure and in place and on the road to recovery—reestablishing that the differences between me and Truong Van Loc were as broad as I'd once imagined them.

Amy looked over at the still house, its few lights barely glimmering from behind tightly drawn curtains.

"You okay?" I asked her, anxious that this reunion, of all things, should go right, and that this young voyager between cultures—a victim and a beneficiary of both—should recover. For all our sakes.

"I think so," she murmured.

The door to the house opened, spilling light onto the shaggy lawn, and the outlines of two small, slightly bent people reached toward us. Amy, hesitant no longer, bolted from the car and ran to them, her own shadow melting into theirs. Slowly, as a group, weakened by exhaustion, happiness, and jittery relief, the three of them slumped to their knees in the grass, their arms intertwined, their heads buried in each others' hair.

I stood by the car, smiling inanely in the darkness, rewarded at last by some palpable measure of success. All the misery and loss that had led to this one, small embrace was by no means a total redemption, but what I was seeing at least gave it some meaning.

I was getting ready to leave when Thomas Lee's pale, oval face turned to look at me. He slowly disentangled himself, and came over.

For a split second, I was appehensive. The police had meant nothing but trouble for this man, whether here or in the country of his birth, and despite the joy of his daughter's return, I was braced for the worst.

He stopped short of me, his expression shaded and hard to read. Then abruptly he stuck out his hand. In the dim light, I could just see the glimmering of tears on his cheeks. "Thank you, Mr. Gunther, for keeping your word."

The handshake was warm, and firm, and brought with it the measure of peace I was seeking. "Thank you, Mr. Lee."